REBECCA CHIANESE

MERCY

Mercy

ISBN: 978-0-692-85749-6
Editor: Elizabeth Van Hoose
Cover and Interior Design: Mallory Rock
Proofreader: Mallory Rock

Mercy is a work of fiction. Names, characters, places and incidents are products of the author's imagination, or the author has used them fictitiously.

Where are you going and what do you wish?
– Eugene Field
"Wynken, Blynken, and Nod"

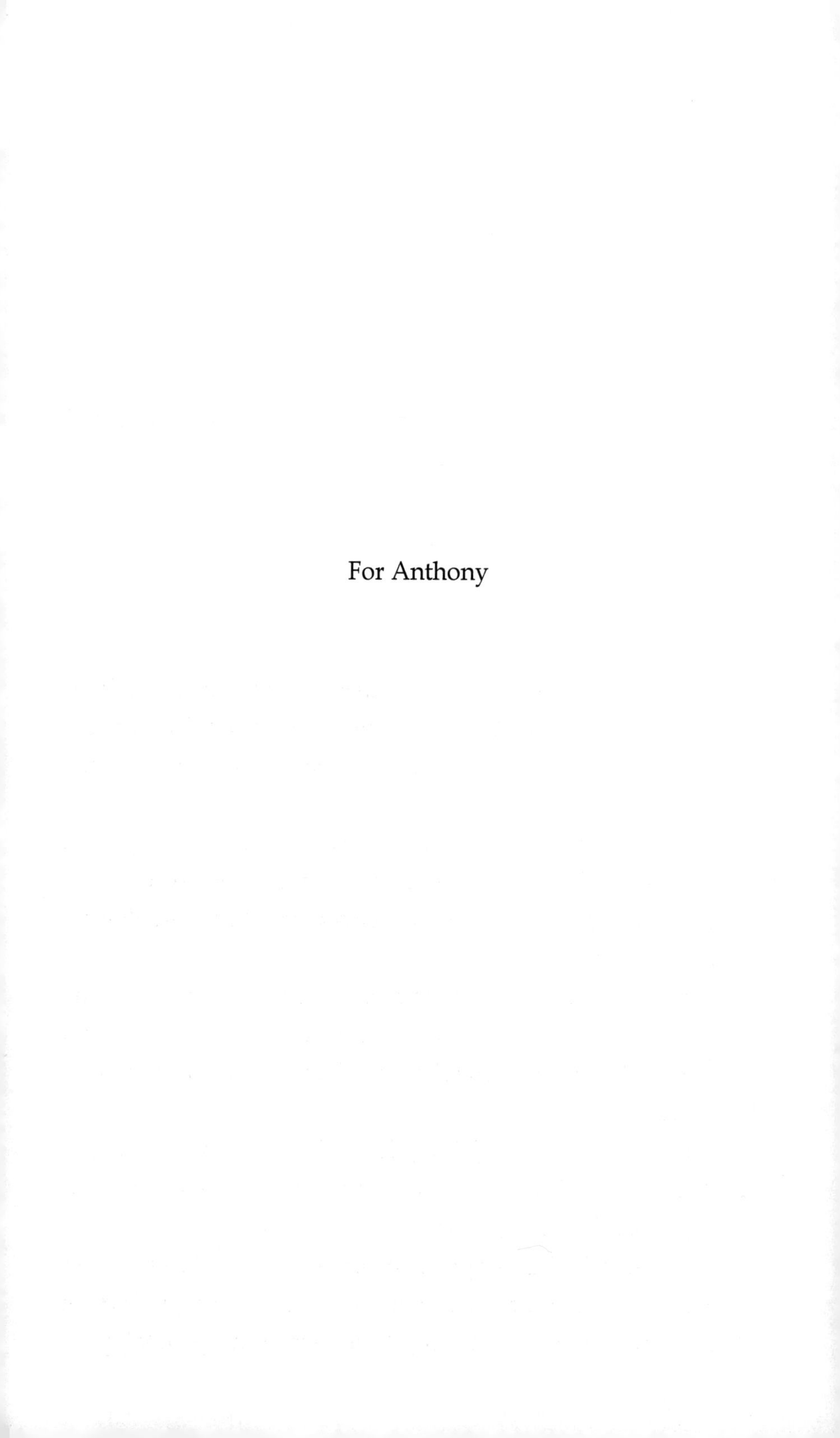

For Anthony

CHAPTER ONE

"All journeys have secret destinations of which the traveler is unaware."
– Martin Buber

Coming across a sobbing woman in an SUV in the parking lot of the Stop & Shop on a rainy fall day would probably make anyone pause. There was a man outside the car, looking in at me.

He bent down quickly and suddenly we were eye to eye, the water and glass between us. "Are you all right?" he asked.

I nodded, trying to control my heaving chest and shoulders.

"Do you need help?"

I shook my head and tried to mouth words of common courtesy. My face contorted and the sobs took over again. Impolite, ugly, I waved him away. The shadow of his body lifted, and I was alone again.

It was the anniversary of Johnny Cash's death, and I was having an irrational response. On the short ride between my house and the parking lot, the radio host had played two of his songs and aired a snippet of an interview with his daughter, Roseanne Cash. The incessant rain led me to stay in the car and listen to two more of his songs. And the last one, 'Sunday Morning Coming Down', had been my undoing.

Determined to end the cry-fest after the embarrassing moment with the worried man, I turned off the radio with an aggressive poke to the button, slid some gloss on my lips, hid behind sunglasses (despite the torrential downpour), and forced myself out of the car and into the rain.

Turning up the thin collar of my jacket, which was inadequate against the weather, I attempted an awkward dash through the parking lot. Chilled raindrops slid between my shoulder blades just as I hit the bright, cold interior of the store.

Grocery shopping had once been my favorite chore. All those years while the kids were growing up, I'd been grateful to be able to afford whatever we wanted, stacking the cart until the precariousness of the groceries forced me to stop. I was soothed by the rhythm of loading and unloading and the therapeutic challenge of fitting everything into the expansive kitchen cabinets. My children would never be hungry or haunted by deprivation. They would never teased by other people's children because they wore hand-me-downs, cheap sneakers, or the wrong clothes. I was giving them a different life; the one I'd wanted as a child.

Now I shopped like a divorced empty nester. I'd officially changed my name back to my maiden name. I was Carly Manning again, after 27 years of being Carly Lowell. Changing back to my father's name felt hypocritical; our relationship wasn't much better than the one I had with my ex. Yet my mother still had his name, even after 44 years of being divorced from him. I'd turned forty-nine years old a couple of weeks ago and our daughter Dani was a college graduate, our son Dylan a college freshman.

My job was done. I'd launched them into the world. It was time for Act 2. I'd planned to paint seriously again; to take a full-time job that interested me instead of the part-time ones that allowed me to meet the bus or attend sporting events. Yet, it took every bit of strength I had just to get to the grocery store.

Maneuvering the shopping cart past neatly piled boxes of cookies, cakes, and snacks that no longer held my children's interest, I peeled the soggy shopping list from my jacket pocket. Cat food. Laundry detergent. Tea bags. Stuff I could no longer ignore. Food shopping was easy to put off, but necessities....

From time to time during my children's high school years, when I was driving frantically from soccer game to band practice to dance class to basketball, I'd imagine these years: The dinners I'd prepare for Scott and myself. All his favorites, some of mine as well, fresh fish regularly, several vegetable dishes, foods the kids wouldn't eat.

The one thing I'd never imagined, although I probably should have, for so many reasons, was being divorced.

My eyes wandered over the fresh vegetables. Scott hates Brussels sprouts and I love them. Spaghetti squash rolled around in my cart; he hates that, too. I wasn't fond of it either, but I tossed it in anyway. Fuck him.

Just last week my mother had warned me about the perils of this way of thinking. "Carly," she'd said to me, "you need to decide who you want to be: one of those bitter, vituperative women who live to spite her ex—or a strong, independent female." I'd preemptively thanked her before she could launch into the full lyrics of Beyonce's song, which she'd been doing ever since I'd told her about the split. But it was too late. She was bellowing: *"All the women who are independent, throw your hands up at me."*

"Mom, I don't want to be Bitter Vituperative Woman."

"All the honeys makin' money—"

"Gotta go!" I told her. "Someone's at the door."

Yet, I knew enough to listen to her. When my dad went on tour with his band, he left for good. Unlike Johnny Cash, he never sent money back, and the courtrooms in Brooklyn during the 60s and 70s were not a friendly place for abandoned mothers. The term "dead-beat dad" wasn't part of the lexicon yet and the shame was the mother's and the child's to bear when a father left them behind.

I didn't want to be Bitter Vituperative Woman, I assured myself. I just wanted to eat the things I'd never prepared during twenty-seven years of marriage.

Turning the corner to avoid the baking and cereal aisle where land mines of kid memories were buried, I headed for the divorced-empty-nester food. Yogurt.

That's when I saw him. I put my head down and hoped the ridiculous sunglasses would shield me. No such luck.

"Hey, there." He reached a hand out, as if to steady me. "Hey?"

I stopped in spite of myself.

His hand touched the wet denim of my jacket.

He smiled at me. "Sorry about before—didn't mean to intrude." Devastating smile.

I stared at him through my smudged glasses. *Say something,* I thought. *Something to counter the visual evidence that you are a complete lunatic.* "Johnny Cash died."

He grinned. More devastation. "You're a fan?"

I shrugged. "My father is."

"And you?"

"I don't know. I guess."

"You were pretty upset."

"Yeah, well." I shoved my sunglasses on top of my head and felt the limp strands of wet hair smack my cheek. "They've been playing his songs on the radio. Never realized how sad they were."

"'Folsom Prison'?"

"Yeah. And 'Sunday Morning Coming Down.'"

He grinned again. "Sounds like you're a fan."

I smiled back. "A reluctant one, I guess."

"How come?"

"I grew up listening to him because my dad was a fan, but I never was."

"Who did you like?"

"Anything Motown. Jackson Five."

"But not Johnny Cash."

I shrugged. "Not then."

"But now you like his songs?"

"Yes."

We stared at each other for a while. I didn't add the part about my father being a Grammy-winning crossover country singer and my jumbled association of his music with Cash's. Yet, I wanted to, which surprised me. I rarely talk about my dad---and I have never in my life had the urge to blurt about his musical career to a stranger.

"Anyway, thanks for checking on me." His feet seemed precariously close to the wheels of my shopping cart, so I backed up, but he didn't move. I gave an awkward finger wave as I struggled to maneuver the cart with one hand. "So, um, see you."

He smiled. "Hope so."

Was he for real? I checked his ring finger.

He caught me, wiggled it, and laughed. "Divorced."

I glared at him. "Yeah? How long?"

He grinned again. "Longer than you."

"Rude."

"True, though."

"How do you know?"

He gave me a pitying glance. "You were sobbing in the car because Johnny Cash died."

My eyes narrowed. "Something your ex used to do?"

"Doubtful."

"Something you used to do?"

"Never."

"So?"

"It was the way I felt. For about three years."

"I won't survive if I feel this way for another two years!"

He laughed. "You'll survive. You have no choice." He slid a card from his wallet and handed it to me. "Here's my number. Call if you ever want to talk."

"What are you, a therapist?"

"No."

"Rebound guy?"

He looked horrified. "Hope not."

I narrowed my eyes again. "AA?"

He laughed harder. "No. Just a friend."

Then he walked away. That's when I realized he didn't have a cart. And I felt the goosebumps rise along my arms.

"Creepy stalker guy?" I whispered.

He must have heard me because he laughed again, but he kept walking.

CHAPTER TWO

"But we both know what memories can bring, they bring diamonds and rust."
– Joan Baez

That night I dreamt of fire. My dad was standing in the middle of it, begging me to help him. The world around him was the pale-milk color of a winter sky. He was wearing prison grey and begging me to come in and get him. The only color in the dream was the violent red of the flames circling him, taunting me. I reached out to him, impervious to the heat. I realized my dad was no bigger than a child because he was eye level to me, and I was six years old.

I woke up slick with sweat. The covers twisted between my legs, my throat raw. Disentangling myself, I stumbled to the bathroom, gulped water from the tap, held the inside of my wrists under the cool flow until I shivered, looked in the mirror, and realized I was crying.

I didn't even know why I was crying anymore. An image of my son floated before me. I'd kissed him goodbye when I'd dropped him at his dorm and pulled back from the strange new stubble on his cheek. Only a short time before his cheeks had been smooth as a child's.

Overwhelmed by what I knew was an irrational sadness, I tried to remember the last time I'd kissed him, but I couldn't. It was like everything else about raising children. I always remembered their firsts: teeth, steps, words but never their lasts. The last time I carried him before I knew my back would go out. The last time he sat in my lap. The last story I read aloud. The last time I kissed a little boy's cheeks.

I splashed cold water on my face, realized there were no clean hand towels, and decided to do laundry. My cat Bridey, excited by the middle of the night wake-fest, showed her approval by jumping in front of me and stalking down the stairs. I followed carefully, carrying a basket of towels and underwear.

Placing my underwear and bras into the mesh lingerie bag, I realized how frayed and discolored and unattractive they were. I rationalized that no one would see them anyway. I tried to cheer myself up by pouring a generous capful of expensive lavender "lingerie wash" left over from the heyday of being somebody's wife.

Bridey jumped onto the laundry room shelf and gave me her "what next" stare. I addressed her: "Would it be really bad to hit the booze?"

Bridey definitely disapproved.

"Cough medicine with codeine?"

She blinked and turned from me in disgust. I left the comfort of the well-organized laundry room and went upstairs to face the loneliness of the house. Center Hall Colonial. The home of a little girl's dreams.

I settled for chamomile tea. While the water was boiling, I took a perfunctory tour around the first floor. Just last week, the square white gaps on the walls that were left when Scott took his share of the paintings (corny oils of hunting scenes) had finally been replaced with colorful abstractions of mood and emotion. These were paintings done by three of my college friends; wedding presents that had been relegated to the sunroom for a quarter-century.

The bookshelves had been partially emptied when he moved out, but they were filled to the brim again. Photographs lined the shelves. Dylan in every sports uniform imaginable from infancy on. Danielle at each stage of her life, from the smiling, grey-eyed, chubby-cheeked baby to the beautiful, sleek-haired woman clad in outfits that no one except runway models should ever wear, but which somehow she looked at home in.

The teakettle whistled, but I found myself unable to move from the center hall. A month earlier, in mid-August, I'd stood right here in a ratty old T-shirt and a pair of cut-off jean shorts that had grown baggy. I'd looked down at my dusty end-of-summer feet, cut and calloused from months of walking on gritty sand and the stony bottom of the Hudson River bed. The faded polish on my toenails was chipped to scabs.

Aware of my defensive posture, arms wrapped around my waist, shoulders slung forward, I had tried to feel something. Remorse, humiliation, shame. Jealousy, anger, hatred, rage. Love.

I'd certainly run the gamut of emotions, and I couldn't quite believe they'd finished their course. Was I really so unresponsive and frigid that on the day my husband officially moved out, I couldn't feel anything? Had he been right about me all along? Was I so cold and unloving that I was unworthy of love and affection in return?

The last of the boxes were being removed by burly men in beige jumpsuits. *They must be used to this,* I thought. Carting people's lives around and apart. Reducing experience and memory to the task of lifting, packing, and fitting. They seemed uninterested in the tiny drama playing out before them.

I amused myself by imagining the variety of scenes I could treat them to. Crying. Throwing myself on Scott's ankles, wrapping my body around his tanned, golden-fuzzed shins, and having him drag me about the house like a scene from an ancient silent movie. Or, laughing maniacally, I could rip my T-shirt off my body, expose my full, firm breasts (yeah, yeah, but this is *my fantasy*), and yell, "You'll never see these babies again!" The impassive, burly movers would stumble, drop their burdensome cardboard boxes, and run. Jump in their trucks and leave.

"Carly? Are you smirking?"

"Huh?" I lifted my gaze to his. Scott, freshly showered and shaved, was wearing tennis whites. Tanned and fit, his blonde hair glinting, he reeked of power, wealth, and sexual prowess.

"Are you smirking?"

I rolled my eyes and headed to the back of the house.

"Don't walk away from me."

"We're divorced now, Scott. I don't have to do this anymore."

He flew up behind me so fast I never heard him coming. He slammed me into the wall, jarring my head against the plaster, "Do you even care?" There were actual tears in his eyes.

"Let go of me or I'll scream, and those guys you hired to move your crap will be in here in a second, with a fun story to tell their wives. How they beat down some hedge fund douchebag who was pushing a woman around."

"Bitch." The word hissed out between the grinding of his teeth.

"Let go of me."

He did. Moving past him, I went out to the back deck and smoked cigarettes until I heard the truck leave. By then, my chest hurt and my mouth felt like a sewer. When the block was quiet, I went back inside, emptied the cigarettes down the garbage disposal, brushed, flossed, and gargled. I decided right then and there never to smoke again and to communicate with Scott only through business-like emails.

Until the Johnny Cash retrospective, I hadn't shed a tear. And now I couldn't seem to stop. The teakettle continued to shriek, a perfect soundtrack to my thoughts, and I moved quickly out of the hall and back to the kitchen to turn it off.

By the time morning color streaked the sky, I had done every yoga position I could think of, consumed endless cups of herbal tea, showered, then bathed. No use: my heart was still racing. I considered calling every person I knew - the kids, my friends who were still speaking to me since the divorce, the new post-divorce friends I'd made. My mother, even my brother--although his phone had been disconnected again. There was no one I could think of to say something that they all hadn't heard a million times before. And I couldn't call early in the morning to talk about the latest book I hadn't read or the newest film I'd almost made it to. My new obsession with Johnny Cash would freak out even his most hardcore fans.

There was no getting around it. I had to face another day on my own. The house was too clean to do anything to. It was time to get a job.

I looked through my closet for an appropriate employment-seeking outfit. Scary.

Three pairs of jeans; none stylish. Four stretched-out sweaters, one cream, one navy, one brown, and one black. A gazillion white T-shirts, bleached to transparency. A variety of necklines. Two peasant skirts; one turquoise, one white.

Two pairs of slacks; one navy, one brown. Good quality, classically tailored, and therefore still wearable even though they were eight and twelve years old respectively. A little black dress bought two seasons ago, timeless, and worn to every formal occasion since. A navy blue blazer, slightly frayed at one cuff, but easily hidden with many bangles. Jean jacket. Not a cute, styling one, either. Old school. Literally. I bought it my sophomore year of high school, which was in the late 70s, when it was referred to as a 'dungaree jacket'. Three pairs of cheap rubber flip-flops. Sneakers. Espadrilles. Navy pumps. Black stilettos. The underwear situation was even more pitiful, despite the lavender detergent.

Trying on every slack-sweater combo possible, I looked so unbearably frumpy, I considered tying one of the sweaters into a noose and hanging myself with it in my closet. In desperation, I stepped into the turquoise skirt (bought last season from a catalogue which had something inexplicably to do with Robert Redford), found the thickest white T-shirt I owned, laced up the espadrilles, and threw on the jean jacket. The look was aging suburban; decidedly unchic hippie. But at least I felt like me.

I slid silver hoops through my ears, then piled on many strands of glass beads and bangles. *They'd been doing it in Cosmo,* I thought defensively. Even women my age.

Now for hair. Uh-oh.

Better to focus on makeup. I swiped some gloss on and attempted mascara. *What do you know,* I thought to myself. *I actually have eyes again.* I looked into them to see if anyone else would be able to see how afraid I was.

I checked appliances and lights. Looked in my handbag to verify wallet, lip balm, car keys. Then I headed out into the impossible beauty of the day and started driving, with no idea whatsoever where I was going.

My phone went off while I was tearing down Route 117 toward Mount Kisco. The panicked thought that it may be my brother, Adam, trying to reach me after a short but none the less definitive period of being off the grid, impelled me to try answering while switching lanes, causing me to almost crash into the guardrail. The phone went flying. Pulling over, I tried to still the frantic thudding of my heart as I reached over to switch off the blare of "Open Road." My phone was ringing again; I retrieved it and flipped it open (yes I still had a "booty" flip phone, as Danielle insisted on calling it.)

"Hello?" I was proud of how normal I sounded.

"Where are you?" Danielle, sounding officious.

"Driving."

"Where?"

"Actually, I'm job interviewing today."

"That's great! Where?"

"Oh. I'm not sure--Mount Kisco."

"What's in Mount Kisco?"

"You know, stores. A lot of stores."

"Mother, please don't tell me your idea of job interviewing is walking around popping into stores and asking if they'll hire you."

"Why not?"

"Did you look online?"

"Yes. They're all admin. Or waitressing jobs. I don't have the skill set."

"You have a masters degree!"

"In fine art. I don't have computer skills and I can't carry three plates without dropping one."

"You can get an office job."

"I want to work retail."

"Great. Call an agency and have them place you."

"I'm not sure I'm ready for that whole thing."

"What about teaching?"

"I don't have education credits, Danielle. What's wrong with retail?"

"Nothing. But you don't even have a plan of action."

"Yes I do."

"Mother, you need to get out, meet people, network."

"I have been."

"Really? When?"

"Yesterday, in fact."

"Who?"

My eyes roved desperately around the car, searching for inspiration, landing on a card face-up on the dash. Supermarket Guy! I picked it up and looked at it for the first time.

"Michael D'Angelo." Michael D'Angelo--was he kidding?

"You're making that up!"

"I'm not, Dani, it says it right here. Michael D'Angelo, graphic artist." Hmmm. Never would have guessed. I figured he was--I had no idea, really.

"Are you going to call him?"

"Yes. No!"

"Call him, Mother. Right now. Then call me back."

I could visualize Dani flipping her hair around as she brought our exchange to its abrupt end. Since when had she gotten so bossy?

Before I could change my mind, I dialed Michael D'Angelo's number. It rang--and I didn't hang up.

"Michael here."

My throat muscles froze like rigor mortis had a death grip on them.

"Hello?"

"Michael D'Angelo?" I sounded like I was 80 years old, smoked a pack of Camels a day, and drank scotch every night of my life.

"Yes?"

"I um . . . met you yesterday . . . in the grocery store."

"Johnny Cash fan, right?" I could hear the laughter in his voice.

"Actually, my name is Carly."

"Hello, Carly." Still laughing, I could tell.

"I was wondering—I'm, uh--looking for a job. Do you know anyone who's hiring?"

"You called because you want a job?"

"Someone said I should tell everyone I meet--so."

"Carly?"

"Yes?"

"How difficult was it for you to make this call?"

"Not so difficult. It was sort of impulsive."

"So you weren't agonizing half the night over whether you should make it or not?"

"No. Pretty much never gave it a thought."

"I see. Didn't call your friends, tell them about our chance meeting, then spend an hour going over every possible scenario?"

"Nope."

"Just picked up the phone and asked a virtual stranger to hire you?"

"Well, you said call if I wanted to talk--and I'm not suggesting you hire me--but maybe you know someone who…"

"What sort of job are you looking for?"

"Well. Something where I can use my brain. Preferably a creative environment. Maybe I should see about becoming a museum guide?"

"What's your background?"

"Fine art."

"Graphics?"

"I dabbled, but primarily, I'm a painter."

"Have you shown anywhere?"

"Not in twenty years."

"Do you have a body of work?"

"Yes. Nothing very recent."

"What do you consider 'very recent'?"

"Twenty years."

"You haven't painted in twenty years?"

"No—I paint all the time--but nothing conceptual--just what I feel like doing."

"What other way is there to paint?"

"You know."

"Commercially?"

"I just paint--for me."

"Carly?"

"Yes?"

"I don't have a job opening, nor do I know anyone who does."

"Oh. Okay. Thanks for your time though. So, um, bye."

"Don't hang up!"

"Oh. Okay, what?"

"Would you like to have dinner with me?"

"Like a date?"

"So you have heard of dating?"

"Ha, ha."

"Would you like to? Have dinner with me?"

"I guess."

"Friday night?"

"This Friday?"

"If that works."

"It does. "

"I'll pick you up at eight? What's your address?"

"I'll text it."

I forced myself to send my address, waited for his response, which was concise and free of any embarrassing emojis, then looked in my checkbook and wondered if I could find a fabulous outfit for $79.00. I called my new friend, Allie. Also recently divorced. Also in my income bracket (big house, no money). But she was a fabulously sexy style-hound.

I explained everything--except how we'd met and why I originally called him—and asked her fashion advice.

She didn't hesitate. "Mandee's."

"Really? Danielle wouldn't be caught dead shopping there."

"Danielle's a fashion snob. Look, you have limited funds and need to look hot. Meet me there in fifteen minutes."

"But I was going job hunting today."

"Blow that, sister! You have a date."

Maybe they were hiring. I had no choice but to acquiesce.

Allie was already pawing through the racks by the time I got to Mandee's. She saw me and held up a silver halter and black mini-skirt, wiggling her eyebrows and grinning. Behind her, a much younger woman was clapping dressing-room rejects back onto their rightful hooks.

"That's not happening. I'm going on a date, not working as a call girl."

The sales woman shot me an evil glance.

I grimaced. "Not that these clothes are hookerish or anything."

The girl smirked. "Do you two need some help?"

Allie glared at me. "Yeah, please remove the stick from her butt!"

The salesgirl looked me up and down. "Size six should do it. Follow me."

Fingers flying, hangers clacking, her long pink nails clicking furiously, she whipped two garments out with a flourish.

I looked. I touched. Danielle would have scoffed at the gauzy cotton blouse because it didn't have the thick texture and soft feel of high thread count, but Danielle wasn't here. I liked the jewel-green color and the delicate smattering of silver bugle beads along the V-neck.

The clerk, sensing my approval, was also holding a pair of white denim jeans with complicated, tiny pockets and silver buckles.

"But--it's after Labor Day."

My new helper shook her head with the confidence of a bona fide Millennial. "No one follows that rule anymore."

Allie pushed me toward the dressing room. "Try it on."

Half an hour later, for $43.99, I left, armed with a date outfit and a job application. I hugged and kissed Allie, promised her I'd tell her everything, and watched her bustle off to meet the school bus. She professed envy of how much time I had to myself. I never told her how desperately I missed meeting the school bus.

CHAPTER THREE

"But remember the princess who lived up on the hill
Who loved you even though she knew you was wrong
And right now she just might come shining through
And the
Glory f love, glory of love"
- Lou Reed

Returning home, I hung the new clothes in the closet and changed into the jeans and T-shirt I used for gardening (a pink and grey leopard print V-neck I'd purchased from Canal Jeans when I was seventeen). I can still remember forking over the $5.00---cognizant that I'd be wearing more than six hours of babysitting on my back---but it had been my favorite for years. Scott had hated it on sight. Said it was trashy. And that was back in the 80s. Bitter Vituperative Woman took great pleasure in digging it out of the attic after Scott left. Happy to have it after a 30-year hiatus, I practically skipped down the stairs and out the back door.

Surrounded by late summer blooms tattered by the recent rain, I began the rhythmic work of gentle pruning and ruthless weeding.

Scott was after me to sell the house. Property taxes were high and he felt I didn't need it anymore now that Dani had her own place. The garden still had plants from seedlings I'd started the week we'd come back from our honeymoon. Cupping my hand under a bobbing hydrangea that had outlived my marriage, I left the flower to dry on its stalk instead of clipping it as I'd intended.

Every time Scott or his lawyer mentioned selling the house, I'd fought them like a cat in a corner. Dylan returning from school in his freshman year to the dissolution of our family seemed harsh enough; moving him from the only home he'd ever known felt unconscionable. I thought of the last telephone conversation Dylan and I'd had. He was anxious about the papers due, the reading he was already behind on, the tuition bill he didn't trust his father to pay, and the meager wage he was earning as a telemarketer.

I knew how much money Scott was worth, and how much money he'd moved around and hid before the divorce proceedings. I'd told myself I didn't care. I just wanted the house. I hadn't wanted to fight. Took the high road in some misguided sense of nobility. And truthfully, I was okay about it. But as the divorce party high wore off, I realized how badly I'd let Dylan down in the process.

* * *

When Scott and I told the kids we were splitting up, Dani cried. Scott reached out for her, and she'd let her head land against him for a moment before pulling away. Almost from birth, Scott had been able to soothe Dani. If she fussed, it was Scott who could calm her. As an infant, if she cried at night, Scott would get her, and she'd fall back to sleep on his chest. He always said it made him sleep better himself. If Dani fell, it was Daddy she cried out for, even though Scott was at work, and I was with her all the time.

She had been full of questions as a child and demanded so much energy from everyone around her, and Scott could match her long after I was depleted. Even now, when she had boy problems or work problems, it was her father she confided in. He was better at it; he'd listen and give practical advice, if asked. I, on the other hand, let all my anxieties break through, peppered her with questions, and offered her unsolicited advice. So when she pulled her head back from his chest and flinched away from his hand, I felt her loss like a kick in the chest.

Dylan sat quietly for a few minutes before saying, "Well, Mom, you deserve better, and I'm proud of you for going for it."

Scott looked like he'd been gut punched. "I suppose you think I deserve that."

"Yeah. I do. That's why I said it."

I saw it in Scott's eyes, then. I knew he would make Dylan pay for that the rest of his life. And the more I tried to protect Dylan, the more it would cost him.

My whole goal in life, as a young wife and mother, had been to ward off bad things happening by pretending to live in a television commercial.

If things looked perfect, I convinced myself, they would be. An illusion of control. My mudroom would rival any TV mom's. Our children had grown up in the financial heyday of the 90s. People were tearing down homes and rebuilding them for fun.

Scott was determined to find the most gifted carpenter in the county; he would need a pedigree. Names like Helmsley, Stewart, and Rockefeller began to be bandied about at dinner parties. Scott was doing his research. I let him worry about the library, family room, study. Even the kitchen and bathrooms became his purview. But I took the mudroom. That was the stuff of commercials and happy living.

The childrens' sports and outdoor gear were labeled with a handy little gun I'd picked up at a craft store. Every hand-hewn teak cubby had a matching label. My children learned how to read with those labels.

When my brother visited, there was always a furtive transfer of twenty-dollar bills from me to him as he avoided the worry in my eyes and I avoided the desperation in his. When those transactions were completed, I would enter my state-of-the-art mudroom that included a washer dryer. Not the family washer dryer which was installed in a neat little closet off the bedrooms, but a separate washer dryer for table linens, tea towels, and summertime sandy beachwear. There I would sort and launder, fold and carry, until the image of my brother's eyes had faded to neat squares of fresh-smelling linen.

Dani was an accomplished dancer and tennis player. She had a circle of girlfriends keeping her warm and bubble wrapped as they went from activity to activity. Whatever dramas unfolded among them, I wasn't privy to. I carpooled, but allowed them to turn up the music loud and sing along so we wouldn't have to talk. They slept over, but I allowed them to watch inappropriate movies the other mothers wouldn't so they would stay down in the rec room and leave me to my cleaning and sorting.

Dani seemed happy, and that was all that mattered. She was Scott's darling, protective of Dylan and me, and she seemed to understand the world at eight years old in a way I knew I never would. If there were scars, I never saw them - and I hadn't been looking, anyway.

Smoothing the soil with my hand, I considered that the real reason I was fighting to hold onto the house had nothing to do with Dylan. I was the one who couldn't bear to let it go. Selfishness, a thick putrid muck, filled me with shame. Digging my fingers into the moist soil, probing for the root, I plucked a hunk of crabgrass from the edge of the garden bed, its thin roots trembling in the air, before I tossed it away.

At 7:00, I unfolded my body, stretched, and went back inside. Another day fading. Another night to get through. Eating a yogurt while standing at the kitchen sink, I gazed through the window, watching shadows overtake the garden. Then I carried a glass of white wine up to my bedroom, dropped my clothes at the edge of my bed, and crawled under the covers to wait for sleep.

Crown Heights, Brooklyn in the 1970s revealed itself to me like a slide show of memory. We lived on the fifth floor of an apartment building across from the Brooklyn Botanical Gardens.

I remembered running down Washington Avenue; lettuce, radishes, leafy green carrot tops cascading from my arms, tickling my bare thighs. It must have been during the summer of 1970; I had been enrolled in the Brooklyn Botanical Garden's Children's Program. We'd each been given a small plot of earth, neatly edged, to grow our own vegetables. The earth was soft enough to dig in with a small trowel, yet my arms grew sore and my head hurt from the relentless beat of the summer sun. It was crowded, and the adults in charge were busy, but they'd show you with a deft twist, how to pull the tiny growth of leaf from the crevices of the tomato plant so the plant would grow stronger and faster. Each time I did it, never as smartly as they did, a pungent aroma rose, staining my fingers and flooding my nostrils.

I sat up in bed and peeled the curtains from the window. The vegetable garden fenced off in the southern corner of my yard was visible in the moonlight. The tomato plants shimmered silver. Most of the fruit was long gone.

Turning my pillow over, seeking the cool side, I closed my eyes and saw Franklin Avenue. This time it was winter. Litter covered the curb. Throngs of people walked the avenue. I felt small, inconsequential, afraid. I sat up. Why, I wondered, were these images haunting me? My life wasn't so great right now, but I certainly wasn't longing for my childhood.

During the evenings and weekend days, lines of drummers sat outside my building, playing bongos, congas, or steel. All day long, the air hummed with the beat. We played on the pavement, in the spray of the fire hydrant, and hopscotched with bits of broken chalk. We played Skully, a complicated game with bottle caps on tar. When traffic approached, we'd scatter out of the middle of the street, running for safety between the parked cars.

The Brooklyn Museum shared a parking lot with the Botanical Gardens. We seldom used the grand entrance on Eastern Parkway, entering instead from the back of the museum. I would lose myself in the cool, dim, interior. My favorite place was the colonial rooms: actual pieces of preserved homes; alcoves barred with glass so you could stand and look in. They were my first window into looking at other ways to live. I liked the simple ones best. They were utilitarian, neat, and safe. Everything I longed for.

One freezing winter morning, the year I turned five, my mother and I left my younger brother with a neighbor and went to stand in line for surplus food. The streets were crowded with people hurrying along the sidewalks, bundled in long colorless coats or green parkas called "Wolf Jackets". My mother pulled the shopping cart behind her, and my breath kept time with the squeaking of the wheels. We joined the line snaking out of the building, down the steps, and onto the sidewalk. We were the only white family: a fact I didn't notice at first.

My father had been gone almost a year. We had no idea where he was. He'd left to go on tour; we hadn't received word or money from him since. My mother had her part-time job at The Brooklyn Museum, but it paid very little.

We stood for a long time in the bitter cold. In front of us was a boy only a year or two older than me. He was holding a shopping cart similar to my mother's. I knew what was going in it. A large tin of peanut butter, a block of rectangular orange cheese, and split peas in a clear bag. Not a lot, but too heavy to carry. The little boy's hands were wrapped tightly around the cart. He didn't have any gloves. I had mittens, but they were too small. So was my jacket, leaving my wrists bare, the cold wind rendering them raw and red. His hands must have been much worse, clenching the chilled metal like that. He took turns blowing on one and then the other, alternating pockets.

Suddenly, a woman from one of the buildings began to yell from a window. "Who's that white woman in the line?"

I looked up at her. She was pointing at us.

"She don't need food stamps!"

People looked at us. Then they looked away.

Another woman appeared in the window a little ways below. "Rich Jew, probably stole them from her maid!"

People shuffled uncomfortably. There was murmuring down the line.

Suddenly something sailed past my ear, whooshing and hitting the sidewalk with a dull thump. A brown banana, the slimy insides spattered around the peel.

The little boy looked at me. He had moist brown eyes, tearing from the cold. I saw compassion in them. "You better go," he said.

At the same time the woman behind us patted my mother's arm. "Baby, get on out of here. That welfare peanut butter's not worth it." My mother nodded, grabbed my hand, and pulled me with her. Suddenly she stopped, took off one of the wool gloves she was wearing, and handed it to the little boy. Wordlessly, he put it on. My mother took my hand in her bare one, and we left.

I thought about that glove for years. Wondered if he kept it, or wore it. Imagined the two of them walking around, each with half a pair, one hand warm, one hand freezing. I remembered his moist eyes and chapped lips; the way his breath froze in the air as he said, "You better go."

Waiting at the bus stop, under a steely sky, I asked my mother why the woman yelled at us. "Because," my mother said, "this country has oppressed an entire group of people for 400 years, simply because of skin color--and people are angry--and they don't always know who to be angry at."

I found out years later that my mother took the long bus ride home, dropped me with a neighbor, and went back alone for the government peanut butter.

Falling asleep with images of my childhood behind my eyes, I thought about how far away it seemed and how I'd done everything I could to escape it. I couldn't have it threatening to come up now, like a whale breaching the sea.

The next morning brought sunshine and a heartbreakingly beautiful day. Clear skies; crisp but still warm enough for short sleeves. It reminded me, exactly, of the morning of 9/11. I guessed this kind of perfect September day always would.

Wearing a pair of my least worn-out jeans, a white T-shirt, and as many bangles and beads as I could pile on (as if they would offer some sort of barrier against the pale, plain glow of my skin), I fastened on jeweled earrings the color of the sky, threw on my blue blazer, and grabbed a butter-soft leather handbag, an expensive birthday gift from Danielle, purchased with her father's credit card, and an accessory she swore was chicer than chic and would be around for seasons to come. I looked like a little girl playing dress-up in her mother's clothes, but then again, I always did, unless I was wearing yoga pants and a tank top. Deciding not to worry about it, I jumped into the car, opened all the windows, and drove up Route 9 to Mandee's.

The same girl was there, looking very official with a clipboard while she expertly pawed through the racks.

She looked up when I entered: polite, professional, with zero recognition. "May I help you?"

"I was here yesterday?"

She nodded. "Sure: white jeans, green v-neck - I remember. How may I help you?"

"Oh. Um--"

"Everything o.k. with the outfit? Do you need accessories?" She eyed my layers of beads and necklaces.

"No. I was actually inquiring about a job?" I thrust the application at her.

She took it and glanced over it. "For you?"

"Yes."

"You want to work here?"

I nodded.

"We only have entry-level pay."

I nodded again. She stared at my hobo chic bag. I smiled weakly: "A gift from my daughter."

"Okay." She said it sarcastically, as if the fact that my daughter could afford a $900 bag would explain why I wanted to work there. Dammit, how did she know the bag was ridiculously expensive? I wouldn't have known in a million years, except that Danielle told me, expecting me to join her in glee at getting one over on her father like that.

How could I have explained that I would much rather have turned it in for Dylan's books? But Danielle wouldn't give me the receipt and I had no idea which store she'd purchased it in.

"So, are there any openings?"

The girl shrugged. "Sure. Turnover's high in September, when school starts."

I nodded wisely. She was about 24 years old, and pretty the way all young people are. Although she wore an unfortunate amount of makeup, she was tastefully dressed in black pinstriped slacks with a pink tailored shirt tapered in a flattering way at her waist.

She stuck her hand out. "My name's Janine. I'm the floor manager. Follow me."

She took me to the counter and thrust a stack of papers at me. "Fill these out. The ten to two shift is open. So's the three to eight."

"I'll take both."

She eyed me dubiously. "Let's start you on the ten to two and see how you do."

And so began my new life.

Of course, something that monumental doesn't feel so, at the time. The morning passed quickly as Janine "trained me." Poodle-like, I followed her around, trying to pick up on fashion lingo. I wished I'd paid more attention to Danielle when she'd spoken of the fashion-forward lingo of garments. Slacks, not pants. Tops, not blouses. Camis, short for camisoles; not to be confused with casual tanks. Accessories had a whole language of their own. The items needed to be properly wrapped and placed in the customer's bag. The shoes had an elaborate inventory system; you could only display one of a pair in the box and had to hunt through stacks of boxes in the storage room for its twin.

At break time, Janine and I went out back for a cigarette break. I eyed her Marlboro Light longingly. She offered the pack.

"Just this once." I took one and lit it from Janine's cigarette, dragging joyfully.

Janine looked worried. "How long has it been since you last smoked?"

I shrugged. "About a month. I quit the day my ex moved out."

"Huh? You decided to quit the day your ex moved out?"

"Well, technically, the next day."

"Funny. Most people would start--not quit."

"I couldn't start. I was already smoking."

She laughed. "You're kinda nuts."

"I think I'm getting a cigarette high. Whoa."

Janine rolled her eyes.

"You look like my daughter when you do that."

"Yeah? How old is she?"

"22."

"What's she doing?"

"Looking for work."

She laughed. "How's she feel about you working here?"

"She's supportive."

"You haven't told her, have you?"

"Nope."

We smirked at each other and smoked in silence. I watched the stock boys from the Stop & Shop break for their own cigarettes. The supermarket backed up to our store. I'd seen the same guys hundreds of times over the years. They were scenery, like piles of fruit and stacks of paper towels. Now, suddenly, we were on a cigarette break together. I tried to imagine smoking in the back of the Stop & Shop with Danielle. Impossible.

"What about you, Janine? You like working here?"

She nodded. "Pays the bills. Keeps my clothing budget down." She blew smoke rings. "I'm working my way through med school."

To my credit, I didn't look surprised. She started laughing.

"Really?" I asked.

"Nah. Just messing with you. I have a son, Jared; he's 15 months. My mom watches him while I work."

"His Dad?"

"Afghanistan."

"He's there now?"

She shook her head. "He was killed last November."

"I'm sorry." And to my horror, I began to cry.

"Hey, Carly, it's okay--"

"I'm sorry."

"I shouldn't have blurted it out like that--I'm just used to saying it now--"

"No, I'm an idiot. I'm sorry."

I wiped my eyes and accepted the tissue she offered from her purse. Took a last drag and flicked it into a nearby puddle, deep and dark, left over from the rain two nights ago.

"We'd better go in."

I nodded and followed her back inside the store, reeking of cigarette smoke and the peppermint gum she gave me.

Sleep, which I'd longed for all day, eluded me the moment my head hit the pillow that night. Maybe it was the physical and mental energy of the new job. Training to be a saleswoman was more difficult than it seemed. The last time I'd punched a register, I was 17, and it was at the Key Food a few blocks from our apartment. Or maybe it was the Brooklyn memories keeping me up. This time I think it was triggered by the smell of creosote flooding through my bedroom window. My next-door-neighbor had been repaving his driveway until the final glimmer of twilight had melted into night. Closing my eyes with the smell of the newly paved driveway filling me brought back a sudden image of standing with my brother on what we referred to as "Tar Beach", which was actually the roof of our six-story apartment building. On hot days, teenagers would sneak up onto the roof, carving sections for themselves where the neighbors would be least likely to hear them and call the super.

One hot summer day, when I was nine and Adam was seven, we'd climbed onto our fire escape to avoid the heat of our apartment. Our dad was long gone. Our mother was working all day at her part-time job at the museum, filing papers in the administrative offices. Even though it was only twenty-five hours a week, she worked three full days, Wednesday through Friday; a far cry from her days of kicking her legs up on a stage, the paint and glitter of her make-up replaced with a swipe of pale lipstick and pressed powder.

To educate Adam and me about her pre-children life in the theater, she would take us on subway rides across the Manhattan Bridge and uptown so we could walk with her along Broadway. Before we'd leave, she'd be animated, painting stories of her time dancing in various shows. I'd imagine air that sparkled, music magically accompanying us on our jaunt down the avenue, people smiling at us in recognition. But when we stood outside the theatre, my mother's eyes dulled with loss. All I could see were the gutters lined with litter and filth. The alcove next to the theatre emitted a stench of urine I recognized from every subway station I'd ever entered or exited. Instead of music, the air thrummed with traffic and men shouting. The tired marquee blared the name of whatever show was up at the moment. The posters along the exterior wall of the theatre looked frayed behind the streaked glass. Any glamour which existed from my mother's days on stage and in the crowded bustle of the dressing rooms had evaporated, and it was impossible for me to retrieve it. Broadway was no more or less magical than the Kenmore Theater on Flatbush and Church, which was a few blocks from our apartment in Brooklyn, a subway ride and worlds away from where my mother and father had met, fallen in love, and ruined her life.

I thought about our mother and the unraveling of her marriage. Young, sure, and beautiful, her physical presence intimidated the world of ingénues that populated the Broadway theatre world. She got the femme fatale parts. If there was a chorus line, she was the focal point because her legs were longest and could kick highest.

My parents met, married, and had me during the run of a popular Broadway show. My father sang the lead and my mother broke out of the chorus to be paired with him because they looked good together.

His height and tawny-blonde hair, thick and wavy, enabled him to escape the roles usually reserved for Italian singers and actors back then: gang members with chains and knives, wearing guinea tees and talking tough.

My father strove to lessen his Italian roots, changing his name from Gaetano Mancini to Guy Manning, which I thought a tad redundant.

But he was 19 when he did it, people liked him, the name stuck, and his constant reinventing of himself began.

I'd let my mother down for sure by being conceived, causing her to lose her place in the show. You would have thought the news of my conception, considered dire by my mother, would have been treated with horror by my father; but his narcissism allowed him to be delighted by the further propagation of his gene pool. The entire cast became enthralled with the marriage and impending baby.

My mother, while relieved to be able to take a break from the constant dieting and eight hour grueling rehearsals, became agitated at seeing other girls vie for her part. She began to watch with deep suspicion as my father, solicitous and enamored of her growing belly at first, became less involved and even a bit squeamish as she ballooned in front of him.

The excitement of the nuptials had worn off. She became no more than a married woman with the glint of a diamond chip set in a thin gold band squeezed around the swelling ring finger of her left hand.

Meanwhile, my father's life returned to normal. He went from punishing rehearsals to applauding audiences (a heady, seductive feeling for even the most jaded performer) and the inevitable reveling at Joe Allen's. In addition to the show, he'd picked up a gig at Gerde's Folk City as an emcee/singer. It was a perfect arrangement because the theaters were dark on Monday nights and it was a way for my father to make a few extra dollars. It was at Gerde's that my mother found my name.

As a child, I'd beg her to tell the story whenever I had her attention, and she always brightened when she spoke about it. She was five months pregnant, my father hadn't become disenchanted yet, and he loved bringing her around to show her off. He was emceeing that night, excited to introduce a sister act, two young female folk singers named Carly and Lucy Simon. The first song they sang was a favorite lullaby of my mother's -- 'Wynken, Blynken and Nod'. It was during that song that she felt me move inside her for the first time, making definitive flutters against the walls of her uterus to announce myself. My mother swore that Carly looked out from the stage and smiled at her; a beatific smile. It was a lifelong connection, my mother decided, and so she named me after her. For years after that, when my father was gone and I longed for him, I imagined living with Carly. She would smile at me, listen to me, and maybe take me shopping, not unlike a fairy godmother, freeing me from poverty. I imagined I would be cherished, and I wondered what that would feel like.

In reality, of course, my father was in and out of our lives, my mother alternately throwing him out and then giving him "just one more chance." It was during one of the "one more chance" periods that Adam was conceived in a desperate hope that another baby, especially a son, would bond him to her for good and settle him in Crown Heights, Brooklyn, which he considered to be the ultimate banishment from the world of Manhattan theatre life.

In the spirit of compromise, my father offered Washington Heights, where so many of his contemporaries were living, as a way to be near midtown without paying the rent, My mother, thinking of Adam and myself and the access we had to The Gardens, the museum, and the Brooklyn Public Library, refused to leave, tying us to Crown Street. And in many ways I'm not sorry, because I'm certain that even if we'd moved smack into the middle of the Theater District, my father would have taken off eventually; crying babies and the hunger of his children proving to be too much for him to bear.

After Adam was born, my father came home laden with presents for my mother - mostly costume jewelry from the play he had just finished. They were props (I found out many years later) used by the actress with whom he'd had a torrid affair during my mother's pregnancy with Adam. But for years, before my mother found out, she would tell me of that great evening when my father returned with jewels for her and a pink bear for me. I'd named the bear Daisy and kept it until the material wore through and the stuffing disintegrated, leaving me with two black button eyes and a scuffed nose. She described the way he'd draped her in jewels of glass and paste while she lay giggling on her bed. Sleeves of golden bangles were placed on her arm one by one, as he kissed his way from her wrist to her shoulder. She regaled me with this story until my dad had left for good and she was no longer trying to pretend he hadn't.

* * *

It seemed inevitable, when I thought about the fatal trajectory of my parent's love affair, that Adam and I would have been left to our own devices as children while my mother was out trying to earn enough money to keep us in our rent-controlled apartment. Adam and I spent that hot summer morning in whatever we had slept in the night before. In Adam's case, it was a pair of dingy, droopy underwear—-what my kids would now laughingly refer to as 'tidy-whiteys'. I was wearing a tattered penoir that my mother had discarded. It was white and gauzy and I thought it to be the most beautiful thing I'd ever seen. It was see-through, so I wore a tee shirt and a pair of pink shorts with a pattern of tiny yellow flowers beneath it. We were taking turns listening to albums. I had been playing Carole King's "Tapestry" over and over until Adam threatened to frisbee it from the living room window. He then played Jimi's "Electric Ladyland" from beginning to end six times in a row. We'd finally reached a truce, turned off the record player, and changed into the coolest clothing we could find—-in Adam's case, I remember him digging into the dirty-clothes hamper to find what he referred to as a "muscle shirt". In my case, I just took off the penoir. For breakfast, I made each of us a piece of cinnamon toast using the last two pieces of bread, which sat curled and slightly hard at the bottom of the cellophane bag.

The refrigerator was empty except for a bunch of tough carrots left over from the weekend's harvest at The Children's Garden, a jar of mayonnaise, a bag of sugar, a cylindrical container of oats for hot cereal (kept in the fridge so the cockroaches wouldn't crawl into them), and a small jar of Nescafé. The cupboard held a row of canned beans, tea bags, a rack of spices (including the cinnamon I'd used for our breakfast), Mazola corn oil, and a glass jar of white wine vinegar. We tried dipping the carrots in mayonnaise, which made us both gag. Then we tried dipping them in vinegar. Better. We ate until our lips turned white from the vinegar and our jaws ached from chewing. We were sitting on the fire escape of our fifth floor apartment, debating how much trouble we would get into if we threw our leftover carrot stubs over the railing. I was convinced that they would kill someone from this great height. Adam said I was being ridiculous, and was a chicken. He did, however, agree that people would know it was us if we threw it from our fire escape, and they might climb up here and kill us. Or they might wait for us downstairs and kill us.

Members of the Tomahawks lived in the building across the street. They found it hilarious that Adam would go over and engage in every elaborate handshake they could teach him. Adam told me the guys from the Tomahawks were cool and that if he were older and tougher, he would join them instead of their rival gang, the Jolly Stompers. A girl in my class lived in The Ebbets Field Housing Projects, where an aunt of one of the Jolly Stompers lived in an apartment on her floor.

My friend told me not to come around there any more because I kept taking the wrong stairway to her apartment. The staircase I kept using was the one she said The Jolly Stompers removed the light bulbs from so it would be dark and they could jump people. I took the stairs because the elevators were usually broken. She also warned me not to take the elevator in case a Jolly Stomper got on with me. I'm not sure the guys smoking and hanging out in the stairwells of her building were actually members of The Jolly Stompers, but she said they were, and that if they caught me, they'd stomp me until I bled to death. I imagined, because of their name, that they would be grinning and jolly while they did it; and for some reason, that thought made my potential murder even worse.

There had been a particularly bad street fight in the courtyard beneath my window the night before. I'd begged my mother to take the half screen out of our window so that I could close it, blocking out the shouts and thwacking of fists and flesh. The sound of breaking glass as bottles were tossed, the cursing, and cries of pain caused a physical sensation in my chest that made me think a Jolly Stomper didn't even need to stomp me to death - the sounds were menacing enough to crush the life out of me. Eventually someone called the police, and as the sirens wailed closer, the shouts intensified before the thudding of running feet receded, creating an eerie illusion of stillness.

Although daylight brought a hot, airless humidity, the recent violence kept me from joining the other kids on our block under the spray of the fire hydrant or for an enthusiastic game of ring-a-levio. I had lured Adam into staying home with me, in part so I wouldn't have to worry about him, and even more so because I was lonely. I had promised him he could have my coveted silver dollar. We had each gotten one from our father that past November, when he'd last visited. Adam, of course, had promptly lost his and had been maneuvering to get mine from me, ever since. I didn't really mind giving it to him. I would never have spent it, and rubbing my thumb over the shape of the head of President Kennedy or the intricate lines of the American Eagle made me inexplicably anxious. The silver dollar, carefully stashed in a secret hiding place in Adam's half of the closet, had rendered him my faithful companion until the evening hours when our mother would be home from work. We decided not to throw our carrot stubs from the fire escape, but chose instead to go up to Tar Beach and throw them onto the cement courtyard below where no one could see us, stop us, or - worst case scenario - seek retribution in the form of killing us.

We began the climb up our fire escape where I pretended not to notice the slight sway and jangle of metal ringing against metal, hoisting ourselves up and over onto the roof and walking across to the back part of the building. A few teenage girls had slicked themselves with a vicious-looking mix of iodine and baby oil and were lying on towels. Album covers glinted in tin foil wrapping, better to direct the sun onto their faces, the smoke of their cigarettes curling around them in a haze of knowledge and mystery. I stared at them, aching to wear the red, white and blue bikini one of them had on. She was glaring at me, one eye slanted closed from the smoke. "Shut the fuck up. If we get kicked outta here, I'll beat the shit outta you."

Adam gave her the finger, but he walked on tiptoe the rest of the way. Looking down at the courtyard below made my head spin and my stomach churn. I thought I saw spatters of blood from the fight the night before. "Throw yours." Adam demanded. I did, swinging my arm through the air and releasing the carrot stub from my clenched hand. It soared for a bit, then fell with an unsatisfying thunk onto the pavement below. He gave me a look of scorn: "you throw like shit." He tossed his far and wide, throwing it so far that we couldn't see where it had landed. - somewhere on the other side of the chain link fence separating us from the building next door, a tangle of weeds softening its blow. I imagined his stump of carrot imbedding itself into the earth, taking root, and an entire patch of leafy green shoots breaking through the following summer, a secret stash of carrots stuck forever in the ground below.

I don't remember anything else about that day - how long we stayed, or whether we climbed back down or took the stairs enclosed by the little hut-like structure jutting up from Tar Beach. There were other days which run together in my mind, when we took the stairs down two at a time and tumbled open the locks on our apartment door with the dull, gold-colored key I always kept in my front hip pocket - the one that made my fingers smell like metal; a bitter taste left behind when I slipped my fingertips into my mouth to chew on an errant piece of skin or nail.

I remembered Adam's smile, the crinkles around his eyes, and the warm boy smell wafting from his scalp and under his arm when he flung his carrot stub high in the air.

I remembered taking comfort in the fact that it was Adam and me against the world; that we would keep each other safe from The Tomahawks and Jolly Stompers and teenage girls with blood red oil, and our mother, who was sure to be tired and miserable and hungry after the hot walk home. I recalled how she'd come in and reach for the cabinet above the fridge: the one we hadn't searched for food; the one that held her bottle of gin, which she said was only for special occasions. Such occasions were becoming more and more frequent and no longer required the presence of friends visiting before the bottle made its appearance by her side.

Letting the memories swirl and collapse, I slid into unconsciousness and escaped into sleep.

The jangle of the phone woke me. Lunging across the bed to the side that used to be Scott's, I noticed that the clock read 3:16. Fumbling, I retrieved the phone. "Hello?"

"Mom?" The dulled voice of Dylan, when he had bad news.

"What's wrong?"

"I'm kind of arrested."

Kind of arrested! "Is anybody hurt?"

"Mom, promise you won't get mad."

"Dylan, you're scaring me."

"It was a fraternity prank."

I calmed down for half a second. "I'm going to kill you!"

"Mom, you said you wouldn't get mad!"

"You know how I feel about fraternities! Did it involve women? Did you guys do anything--"

"Mom! You're freaking out! I should've called Dad."

That did the trick. I imagined all the cops sitting around smirking at the freaked-out mom; the ex-wife. "What happened?"

"I was arrested for streaking."

Silence. I stretched it out for as long as my relief would let me. "Are you fucking kidding me?"

"It was for pledge!"

"You scared me to death because you wanted to play 'Old School'?"

"Mom!"

"You're right; you should have called your father."

"Well, I wasted my one phone call on you! Are you coming to get me?"

"I'll leave in the morning." But as much as I wanted to wait and teach him a lesson, I couldn't bear to.

I hung up. Got out of bed. Pulled on my jeans and t-shirt, and brushed my teeth. I ran downstairs, grabbed my bag, slipped my feet into garden clogs, and climbed into the car. I pulled out of the driveway just as the moon came out from behind a cloud.

I never wanted Dylan to live with the shadow of my fear. It's just that, from infancy, he looked so much like my brother. As he got older, because he had Scott's coloring, I tried to block it out; but his features, his expressions, and his lanky build and height were so like Adam's. Danielle looks just like Scott. It was easier to watch her grow. If she bumped, or bruised, I had complete confidence that she'd shake it off, just like Scott.

But Dylan was tainted with my memories and experience; and as hard as I tried, my anxiety spilled all over him. I don't know if Scott sensed it, and that fueled him; or if it was some other dynamic at work. But where I saw vulnerability and responded with a neurotic need to protect, Scott saw weakness, and tried to eradicate it.

When Dylan was 10 years old, he played for the 12-and-under team because Scott insisted that playing with an older age group would make Dylan perform better. Weeks of preparing for the tryouts resulted in his making the team, but the pressure was now on to make it off the bench ahead of older players.

One Saturday morning after breakfast, Scott was drilling Dylan in our backyard. I hovered in the kitchen, finding tasks that would chain me to the sink so I could listen through the open window. Scott was throwing the ball hard and fast, shouting at Dylan if he didn't catch it on the first try. When it was time for batting practice, he would pitch until Dylan could hit ten times in a row, starting over every time he struck out. I could see Dylan's face flush every time Scott roared *strike*.

When they'd been out there for two hours, I went out with a couple of water bottles. Scott turned on me. "What the hell are you doing? We can get our own water. This is why he's such a crybaby!"

It was an hour later and Dylan hadn't been allowed to take a break or get a drink of water. Scott kept pushing him from drill to drill, shouting at him the entire time.

"Dad, I need to use the bathroom." Dylan's voice was tentative, which just seemed to enrage Scott further.

"I need to use the bathroom," he mimicked. "You sound like a little girl. Ten in a row. Have you hit 10 in a row?"

"No."

"How many have you hit in a row?"

"Eight."

"What percentage is that?"

"80."

"You want to be 80 percent? Huh?"

"No."

"You think 80 percent will get you off the bench?"

"I guess not."

"You guess not?"

I turned to Dylan and said, "I need to talk to Daddy for a minute; would you excuse us?"

Dylan shot me a look. And it wasn't one of gratitude for the break. He was afraid.

When he'd gone inside, I turned to Scott. He was waiting for me, his arms folded across his chest. "Carly, you gotta butt out. I know you think I'm being hard on him, but I'm not half as hard on him as the world is going to be."

"He's a ten-year-old boy. You're humiliating him."

"And you're turning him into a mama's boy."

Dylan came running back out. He wouldn't look at me. "I'm ready, Dad. Ten in a row."

"About time," Scott said, and turned away from me.

Uncertain, I walked back inside. Scott was probably right, I told myself. I knew nothing about fathers and sons.

I began dicing carrots and grating ginger for a soup; a simple, yet time-consuming task that would keep me close to the kitchen window. Finally Dylan hit ten in a row. It was an hour later, and the noon sun was blazing in the sky.

"Go on," Scott encouraged. "Take your victory lap." Dylan sprinted around the base markers, red rubber mats that Scott had laid out early that morning. Sliding into home plate, Dylan caught a rock, ripping his jeans and gashing his shin.

"Come here," Scott commanded. "Let me see."

Dylan stood up without flinching and walked over to his dad.

"Does it hurt?"

Dylan shook his head.

Scott smacked him in the wound. "How 'bout now?"

"Scott!" I yelled through the window.

He rolled his eyes at me. "He's fine!" Scott held up his palm, streaked red with Dylan's blood. "It's a scratch!"

He looked at Dylan. "I gotta toughen you up extra hard. Undo the damage your mother's done. You wanna be a mama's boy--just say so."

"I don't."

"All right, then. Go inside and clean yourself up."

Basketball was the same. So was football. Each season held a complex set of challenges, taunts, and jibes for Dylan to overcome.

In contrast, when Scott was with Danielle, he'd swing her in his arms, calling her his angel or his princess. I worried this would create resentment between my children; yet it appeared to have the opposite effect. Danielle loved Dylan with a fierceness that seemed unusual for a sibling - at least, in the modern way of families. I didn't see that closeness, that protectiveness, in any of my friend's children. It reminded me, uncomfortably, of how I'd felt about my brother when we were young.

I pulled into the police station just as the first light crept across the sky. My maternal instincts clawed at me to run into the station. I imagined demanding a drug and alcohol test; an opportunity to obtain proof that I didn't need to worry about these.

Before Scott and I decided to divorce, we were trying to ride out our marriage in the wake of his infidelity. Naively, I believed my kids wouldn't find out about it. I'd underestimated the power of the gossip mill. One evening, Dylan and a few of his friends were hanging out on our back deck. I was coming up from the basement with a case of Gatorade. They couldn't see me around the bend in the hall, but I had a clear view of them, and their voices were louder and carried further than they knew. Ryan, a lifelong friend of Dylan's, whose baby diapers I'd literally changed, was making a crude thrusting gesture with his hips. He was laughing and saying to Dylan, "I heard your dad was banging that milf with the big tits."

I couldn't see Dylan. Or hear his reaction. I did see another boy shove Ryan and tell him to shut up.

After that evening, I noticed a change in my son. He walked off the varsity baseball team without a word of explanation. When Scott found out, they nearly came to blows.

Dylan's friends eventually gave up and stopped calling for him. He spent more and more time alone in his room or riding for hours on his bicycle. It never occurred to me to talk to him about what Ryan had said. I was afraid it would embarrass him. And I was too busy worrying that my son was turning to drugs, the way my brother had at that age.

Vigilant, I began to check for signs, hugging him too long as a surreptitious way of sniffing out the smell of weed or booze. Capturing his gaze in an attempt to see if his eyes were bloodshot or his pupils dilated. Monitoring whether he was eating and sleeping, in a way I hadn't done since his infancy. It was driving him nuts, and was evidence of my own descent into the land of Crazy Town.

One Sunday morning he woke and caught me standing over him, pushing up his sleeves and checking his arms.

"What are you doing?"

"Good morning," I said with the brightest, fakest, cheeriest smile in the history of motherhood.

"Were you checking my arms for needle marks?"

He looked angrier than I'd ever seen him. I turned away. "No." *He wouldn't know that,* I thought, *if he wasn't using.*

He grabbed my hand and I looked back at him. His gaze was steady now, and the anger seemed to have drained away, leaving him pale against his sheets. I registered that they were the same race car sheets he'd had since he was ten years old and made a mental note to go shopping for new ones. What kind of mother was I to let my 16-year-old son sleep on the thin faded sheets of his childhood?

"Mom."

"Yes?"

"I'm not Uncle Adam."

"I know."

"I'm fine."

"You seem so unhappy."

"I'm not."

"So angry."

He didn't say anything.

"Your father loves you. Just because he and I are having difficulties--"

"He's a liar. And a cheater."

"Dylan, that doesn't have anything to do with how much he loves you--"

"He's always going on about being a man."

"He doesn't mean--"

"He doesn't know the first thing about it. "

I didn't know what to say. But Dylan wasn't waiting for an answer from me. He was sitting up against the wall, his head leaning against a tattered poster of Michael Jordan. "A man isn't about how many other guys you can beat out. It's about standing up. Taking responsibility. He's full of shit."

"We'll be okay."

He shrugged.

"How about some pancakes?"

"Sure." But his voice sounded flat, as if it was coming from a smashed-up part of him.

I smiled, ignoring the flash of disappointment I saw cross his face, and went down to make the pancakes. Humming while I gathered ingredients, I thought of the smooth, unmarred skin on his arms.

* * *

Standing outside the police station in the half-light of early morning, I fought the impulse to walk up the steps and through the door. If I did, Dylan would know I'd jumped out of bed and raced up here. So I went to a local diner and sipped hot coffee, watching the air brighten and wishing that vigilance was enough to keep him safe.

Nearly an hour went by before I allowed myself to walk into the police station. A young officer was on duty. "We threw a scare into him, ma'am, but he's fine. Every year we haul a few kids in here for this prank. It's almost a ritual."

I caught myself glaring at him. I'd just driven four hours in the middle of the night with my heart in my throat because boys will be boys. I thought of how much worse it could have been, and forced a smile. "Thank you. Can I see him?"

Twenty minutes later, after the requisite paperwork, Dylan came out of the recesses of the building. Hair tousled, head hanging, he grinned at me.

"At least you have pants on."

That wiped the smile off Dylan's face and made the officer smirk. I walked out to the car, leaving Dylan to follow in my wake.

Without a word, I pulled back into the diner. Dylan ordered a vanilla shake, French toast, and bacon. My stomach rolled over. I ordered herbal tea. He looked up at me after shoveling food for a few minutes.

"Thanks Mom. I haven't eaten since yesterday morning."

I glared at him.

He shrugged and shoveled more food. "Sorry you had to drive all the way up here." He grinned. "Admit it; you're glad to see me."

I rolled my eyes at him. "Contrary to what you and your sister think, I do have a life."

"Yeah, but it revolves around us."

"You are not even remotely amusing. And I would take this more seriously if I were you. You'll have to face the school … come back to court …."

"The court thing is a fine, and I'll pay for it with my own money." He poured more syrup onto his French toast. "Actually, my brothers have a fund for it."

"That's revolting."

"And the school won't do anything. It's a slap on the wrist; they expect it." He grinned. "It's not like it goes on my permanent record." The last was a sarcastic referral to the threat I used to hold over his head until middle school, when he learned there was no permanent record.

"You're pissing me off more with every word that comes out of your mouth."

In truth, I was ashamed at how unmoved I actually was. I missed the ritual of caring for him. But I realized, with a twinge of guilt, that I had no idea what was really going on with him. I felt a nagging concern that he was far more involved in the whole fraternity end of things than he should be.

I dropped him back at school and watched a number of frat boys come swaggering down to greet me, still pumped with braggadocio from their successful night of pranks, looking pitifully like over-grown puppies. *They're just like my son,* I chastised myself. *Their mothers are probably equally horrified.* Even from the road, the smell of beer and stale sweat emanated from their living quarters. I regretted my decision to allow him (as a freshman with enough credits to be a first semester sophomore, thanks to AP classes) to stay in the frat house. It wasn't recommended by the powers-that-be at school, but the school administrators had gotten so used to caving in to the demands of helicopter parents that the freshmen were allowed all sorts of privileges that were ill-advised. Somehow, because I'd been preoccupied with my divorce, I'd allowed this to slip by me, and it was too late to do anything except regret it.

"Try to get some actual work done, okay?"

He hugged me, kissed my cheek, and grinned, "Don't worry so much. And Mom--I'm sorry if I scared you last night." I touched my hand to his face for the briefest moment and climbed back into my car. I wondered why he'd called me and not Scott. His father would have loved the whole frat boy thing. I pulled away, and through my rearview mirror, watched someone hand Dylan a beer, which he immediately popped open and poured into his mouth. I knew then, with a sickening thud in the depth of my belly, that I was seeing, from the distance of my rearview mirror, the scars across his soul.

* * *

As the roadway slid beneath my car at 80 miles an hour, I hurried to keep my date with my mother. It had been months since I'd gone to visit her. Of course, we'd met periodically for dinner or an art exhibit in the city, but I used every excuse multiple times in order to avoid the trip to her home, and she was starting to make noises about coming up for an extended stay with me if I didn't haul my ass down to her apartment in Park Slope.

My mother, Adam, and I had moved from Crown Heights to Park Slope the winter before my thirteenth birthday. My mother's part-time job at the Museum had become full time and she'd received a promotion and a raise - enough to secure a rent-stabilized apartment in The Slope. As Adam, my mother, and I collected boxes from the grocery and liquor stores, carefully wrapping the contents of our home in newspaper, I dreamt of our new life as if we weren't bringing every vestige of ourselves with us. Park Slope represented a new beginning; an apartment my mother had never lived in with my father, a place where we had never waited for him, first for hours, then for days, to show up when he said he would. The Slope shimmered with possibility and I couldn't wait to belong there instead of visiting friends or babysitting and then making the long walk home, first along Prospect Park West, then Eastern Parkway, and finally Washington Avenue.

We began our new life in the cold drab month of February, right in the middle of the school year. Adam and I knew many of the kids from our new school because for years we'd taken classes at the Brooklyn Museum and the Brooklyn Botanical Gardens. But there were plenty of kids we didn't know, and Adam spent the first month fist fighting the boys who called him a hippy because of his long hair. He was jumped day after day until he'd either kicked enough ass or gotten his ass kicked enough.

I was luckier, escaping the notice of the tougher girls until I'd unwittingly become friends with them and fell under their protection. Kids hung out on every block, claiming certain stoops. Social lines were divided along street corners and avenues, yet they were fluid enough that all you had to do was know one person in order to gain access and hang out. Adam fell in with the kids on First Street and Seventh Avenue. They were the kids who played frisbee in the Meadow and smoked weed in the tunnels of Prospect Park. And from then on the ass kickings and fighting seemed to taper off, which allowed the hardness in my stomach to soften. I found my way to the corner of Garfield and Seventh where we drank quarts of beer, blared boom boxes, and did the "Hustle," a complicated series of arm movements, turns, and lifts.

The city was broke, the streets were filthy, and there was violence everywhere I turned. But none of that was new for me or Adam and the move to Park Slope felt transformative; although, looking back, it was the beginning of the social divide Adam and I would enter for the rest of our lives.

* * *

It was late morning by the time I hit the Tappan Zee Bridge and I determined that I had just enough time to stop at home to change into something reasonable before continuing the trek to my mother's in Brooklyn. Managing to shower and throw on clean clothes in under fifteen minutes, I then dashed into the grocery store, hastily tossing random items I knew my mother would like into my cart. Selecting a pint of chocolate Haagen-Dazs, I thought about the summer she'd spent scooping ice cream when the Haagen-Dazs first opened on 7th Avenue and First Street in Park Slope. She was concerned that she would be scooping ice cream she couldn't afford to buy for her own children.

I didn't care about eating Haagen-Dazs. My friends and I were happy with the Carvel, a couple of blocks away. Only the rich parents of the children I babysat went to Haagen-Dazs. The job paid minimum wage and my mother was let go when the summer rush was over. Back then, we had no idea that one day the Haagen-Dazs ice cream store (before it's subsequent move west to President Street) would be considered nostalgic of the old Park Slope, before the "Hipster Invasion" my mother constantly railed against.

I understood, now, what that summer of scooping ice cream must have cost her when she believed we desired it above Carvel because she did. And I understood in a way I never knew I would, how lonely my mother must be living on her own, and how rare it was for someone to bring her a favorite treat. I threw a bag of frozen peas in, too, using the flawed logic that the two of them nestled next to one another in a plastic bag might lessen the possibility of melting during the hour-long trip to Brooklyn. Once I was on the road again, traveling down the Henry Hudson, I sent a prayer up to the traffic gods. I had exactly enough time to be on time.

At a stoplight, I tried my brother's cell phone. It was a new number; my mother had e-mailed it to me in the dead of night. She wasn't sleeping either. His message played. I left a voicemail I knew he'd never listen to. "Hey, Adam, just thinking of you. Call when you have a chance." Automatically, I checked the time. 3:30. He was probably awake by now. By rote, my mind began the machinations...was he in a detox cycle? Had he just used? In that case, he'd call me back hyper, giggling, spouting grandiose tales of success. My worst fear was when he called me with a thick, heavy voice. It made my bones ache just thinking about him.

Sometimes he looked okay: Standing tall, clothes clean and pressed, black jeans, short-sleeved tee. His signal to the world that he wasn't shooting up.

Scott used to tell me over and over again to let go. There was nothing I could do. I had no control over Adam's addiction. Intellectually, I understood. But letting go felt too much like giving up. Abandoning hope. Abandoning him.

I struggled with the thought of him holed up in his tiny apartment, which was spare and clean when he was reasonably well; nightmarish when he was sick. I thought about the last time I'd been to his place. The needles and bloody tissues littering the floor, the burned spoons scattered across the kitchen counter.

Heading into the Brooklyn Battery Tunnel, I promised myself not to think about it for the rest of the trip; a promise I knew I'd break multiple times.

Brooklyn had changed so much in the 25 years I'd been gone that it was barely recognizable to me. Rooftops visible from the BQE were the only constant. Faded brick and tar structures resembled the washed-out colors of a snapshot from the 1970s. On the streets below, however, trendy cafes and storefronts prevailed. Wrought iron tables and chairs with pots of ivy-laden geranium littered the sidewalks. The train station at Smith and 9th Street where I ran to work from school, not due to time constraints but to mitigate the chance of being jumped, now emitted young people in fashionable clothes pushing babies in strollers which cost as much as my first car did.

By the time I got to Park Slope, I was dizzy from the kaleidoscopic view of old meeting new. Circling Grand Army Plaza and shooting across Prospect Park West was a relief. The graceful architecture and burgeoning trees seemed soothingly unchanged.

Driving down Montgomery Place, I passed the stoop on which I'd consumed my first Colt 45 out of a paper bag, sipping it from a straw so it would "go to my head faster." My girlfriends and I, drunk and sloppy, had squatted between cars to pee, giggling uncontrollably until we were at risk of falling into the gutter. Straightening ourselves up, we smoked Newports on the steps of the Temple on Garfield and 8th Avenue, ignoring the glances of the adults walking by. We felt grown up and invincible. Brazen with our new breasts and tough stances, we were unaware that at thirteen we simply looked vulnerable with our cigarettes dangling from the corners of our lips and our bony hips thrust out in an approximation of womanhood. If Dani had behaved the way I did, I would have lost my mind and locked her in her room. I wondered why my mother never did; whether she ever saw us hanging out just up the block from her. Maybe she was too immersed in her own drinking or the guy she was seeing, or working two jobs so she could keep us housed and clothed and fed.

Driving down Garfield, I made the right onto Fiske Place. My mother was in a garden apartment in an old brownstone; one of the few that hadn't been renovated and cared for during the gentrification. I circled the block five times before giving up, and started driving up and down the streets of The Slope until I found a parking spot on 3rd Street between 6th and 7th nearly five blocks away.

The walk back to my mother's was a mixture of nostalgia and dread. The drugstore was still on the corner, but the candy store was gone. I remembered how we would torture the owner. He'd accuse us of stealing or reading his comic books. "Get outta here, girlie" were the only words he'd ever spoken to me. Of course, at the time we didn't realize that generations of kids had tortured him, motivating his bellowing and chasing us with broom handles. My girlfriends and I would huddle close amid the clutter of the store, sneaking into his pay-phone booth and pretending to make calls as we'd smoke the "loosies" we purchased; one cigarette for a nickel or three for a dime. It was a way to stay warm in the winter.

Cracked concrete and a rusty gate is what set my mother's home apart from her neighbors' well-maintained brownstones. Balancing the groceries and a bamboo shoot on a cheesy planter I'd picked up as a last ditch effort to be a thoughtful daughter, I managed to lean on the doorbell.

"Coming!" I heard the first round of locks tumbling and there she was, in the small vestibule behind the iron gate; taller than me, with a dancer's posture even though she was a few months shy of her 70th birthday. Her hair was a perfect platinum bob; her giant green eyes luminous even without makeup. She was still a beauty: possibly more so because she seemed impervious to other's opinions of her.

She took the plant from me and ushered me into her apartment. "Why do you waste your money on this crap?"

It smelled like Murphy's oil soap and I wondered if she'd spent the morning cleaning because she knew I was coming. The front room was dark and cool and she led me past it through the narrow hallway, the closed door of her bedroom shutting out any natural light, then into the kitchen with a wall of north-facing windows. I settled the groceries on the worn round kitchen table of my childhood. A familiar white Corningware teapot adorned with a blue cornflower was poised on the stove. It surprised me how comforted I felt at the sight of two mugs perched on the scarred Formica, teabags dangling over each edge.

With a flick of her wrist my mother turned the gas on, causing a clicking sound as the burner ignited and a steady blue flame licked the teapot. She set upon the groceries, exclaiming over each item. "Brie! You spoil me. HA! Haagen-Dazs! You know I won't set foot in that place—-they're on President Street now, y'know—but you got me Chocolate Chocolate Chip! You're all right."

Eventually, with mugs in hand, my mother sat across from me. "Dani tells me you're dating again. About time you got back in the saddle." She snickered at her own version of a double entendre and considered me.

"A date—-as in *one*. And I haven't gone on it yet."

"Well, good for you. Lose it or use it." She actually wiggled her eyebrows up and down.

"Stop it."

"Ha. You always were a prude, even as a little girl."

"I was hoping we could walk over to the museum."

"Really? I hate going there on my day off. Let's walk along the park instead."

"Sure."

That pretty much exhausted any safe topic of conversation.

"Have you spoken with your brother?" She smiled as she said it, opening her eyes wide, her mask whenever we spoke of Adam—-the one she put in place to hide the anxiety she felt. I recognized it because I wore the same one.

"Not recently."

"Mmmm. Well I'm sure he's very busy. He had a gig this summer in The Hamptons. Did he tell you?"

"He mentioned something—-"

"Very wealthy people. They had him staying in their guesthouse out there. Apparently they were so blown away by his talent that they found him a regular gig at their favorite restaurant, playing all original stuff. You would think Guy would do something for him—-big shot—-strangers look out for Adam better than his own father does."

The mug of tea was warm in my hands. I focused on that and willed myself not to say anything.

"What, Carly? You don't think Guy owes the two of you anything? Abandoning you the way he did. He's living high and mighty now." This, from the person who lectured me on Bitter

Vituperative Woman. But perhaps it was a cautionary tale, and one I had better pay closer attention to.

"Adam doesn't need his help, Mom. Anyway, Dad can't do anything in the Indie music scene. He's strictly Country. They're different connections." I had no idea whether that was true or not. It didn't matter anyway. My father would never help Adam because it would never occur to him to do so. And Adam would never be able to act on it anyway, because the only thing driving him was liquid poison shooting into his veins.

"Hmph. I don't know why you're sticking up for him."

"Who?"

"Your deadbeat father!"

"I'm not sticking up for him."

"If he wanted to help Adam, he could do it."

"The only person who can help Adam is Adam." I looked at the clock. I'd been there less than fifteen minutes and I'd walked right into it. The truth was, this conversation began the minute my car door slammed four and a half blocks away on 3rd Street and 6th Avenue. It was the only conversation we ever had. That, and my divorce.

"Oh, listen to you," my mother said, tilting her head back in that way she had which allowed her to slide her glance down at me. "Your life's not exactly bangin' right now. Dani told me what a hot mess you've been."

An eye-roll was my only response to that. My mother's absorption of colloquialisms isn't as much an affectation as it is a way of being, for her. Throughout the decades she grabbed words from the lexicon as readily as suburban housewives went from skinny jeans to flared legs and back again.

"Well," my mother continued, "at least Dani has it all going on. I take pride that you're a better mother than I was."

There was no way I was crossing that land mine. Virtuously, I took a sip of my tea.

"No man is ever gonna define that girl."

Not so virtuously, I took the bait. "Scott did not define me."

"Hmph. Well he doesn't anymore. And I give you a lot of credit for that." She stood up and took our mugs away, even though mine was half full and I was enjoying it. "Vamanos!" she said in terrible Spanish. But it was a peace offering. And I took it. Waiting for her to finish with the washing up of the mugs, the gathering of her wallet and keys, the practiced way she locked the doors, I made small talk—-mainly about new recipes I had found, which she had little interest in.

We began the walk up Garfield and she regaled me with another one of her favorite topics, which I endured because there was no danger of the past rising between us, or of my brother's illness. "See that one over there?" My mother pointed at a woman with a large baby strapped to her back in an elaborate pack and a toddler dangling from each arm. At a second glance, I realized they were all toddlers; most likely triplets. "Spent thousands of dollars getting in vitro. Told the whole friggin' Slope about it in her stupid blog, complete with her temperature and time of copulation. Now she whines about how difficult motherhood is because she has no time for "self-care". What the hell is self-care? Masturbation?"

"Shh. She'll hear you!"

"So what? She'd be thrilled with the attention."

"Why do you read her blog, if it irritates you so much?"

"Oh, it's a giant fucking train wreck, and I can't help looking." We spent the next hour like that, passing landmarks of my wild adolescence. The first time I'd been kissed, leaning against the black wrought iron railing of a home on the northeast corner of First Street and Prospect Park West. The playground on Third Street, where we'd been rousted by cops or rival groups of gangs looking to fight each other or anyone in their path.

One particular Saturday night in the middle of an August heat wave when the combination of close apartments and intense heat made boys angrier than usual, my girlfriends and I were lounging in the giant net erected for the purpose of small children to climb on during the daylight hours. We were passing a joint around when suddenly one of the guys shouted, in a voice thick with adrenaline and excitement, "All girls outta the park!" We looked above us at the slope of grass from the stone wall separating Prospect Park from the street.

There, against the night, were about thirty guys, bandanas tied around their heads, silhouetted against the sky. I'm sure if I'd have looked closer I'd have seen the outline of their weapons. Bats and chains, back then. But I didn't look. We tumbled over ourselves climbing out of that net and we ran. We heard the shouts; the thuds. And, eventually, the sirens. But they were too late.

By the time the cops and ambulances got there, one boy was dead from a bat to his head, and two others were put into the paddy wagon, their faces and heads already swollen from blows. The rest had scattered. Some of the boys found us later without the benefit of cell phones or texting; just a kind of radar friends seemed to have for one another back then. We knew which stoops we could hang out on and which would get the police called on us. My girlfriends and I were hiding in an areaway between two buildings, trembling (and in my case, nauseous with fear). The boys came tearing in, leaning against the grey stone buildings, fighting for breath. None of our friends were arrested or even hurt that badly, although one guy broke the knuckles on his right hand.

For the next two weeks, all people could talk about was the boy who'd been killed. He wasn't from "the neighborhood," as we thought of it back then. He was from 20th Street below 4th Avenue - what the hipsters now referred to as the South Slope. Which really pisses off my mother. Passing the playground, I was about to ask my mother if she remembered that incident. but she was mid-rant about something which had taken place in bloggerland about the Third Street Playground.

"Can you believe these foolish mothers want to ban ice-cream trucks at the playground because they are constitutionally incapable of saying no to their children? You know what, Carly? We may have been the "Me" generation or whatever of parenting--and granted, you kids saw too much sex and drugs and rock and roll or whatever--but not saying no--EVER--to little Johnny or little Henley or Anais or whatever stupid names parents are giving their poor kids these days--that is going to be the fucking demise of our civilization."

"Really, Mom? Spoiled children are worse than sexually traumatized, drug-addicted children?"

"Yes." And with a firmness of purpose my mother strode down Third Street, ending that particular conversation, leading the way right toward my car as if she'd known where I'd parked all along.

CHAPTER FOUR

"I hurt myself today
To see if I still feel pain
I focus on the pain
The only thing that's real
The needle tears a hole
The old familiar sting
Try to kill it all away
But I remember everything"
- Johnny Cash

The next morning, Adam called.

"Hey, Carly."

Alert, I listened for a clue. A call this early could mean he was coming down from last night. Or it could mean he was functioning well. Maybe he was going for an audition, or to the laundromat, or eating a healthy breakfast. My thoughts sped as quickly as any crack addict's.

"Hey!" I said too manically.

"You around today if I take the 11:40 outta Grand Central?"

And just like that, I was in a cycle of intoxicating hope.

I picked him up at the Tarrytown train station. His appearance alerted me that he was in a bad way. He was sallow and stooped, his clothes rumpled and stained, his face marred with scabs. I saw people avoiding him and giving him sideways looks. *He's not really like this,* I wanted to scream. *He's handsome and funny and smells of Irish Spring.* He got into the car; bleary-eyed and smelling of unwashed laundry and stale cigarettes. But he flashed me that familiar grin, and I immediately felt better.

"You hungry?" I asked.

"I could eat." He smiled.

"I picked up sandwiches. Italian Combo good?"

"Great. Yoo Hoo?"

I nodded. "Of course, and a Hershey bar."

We drove the short ride to my house and he filled me in on his life. "I had this great gig in The Hamptons. Stayed in an insane house, right on the beach. They have a place in Aspen too—-they're flying me out there—-putting me up in a cabin or whatever on their property. You should come out."

I pretended to believe him. "I'd love to. When?"

"Soon as I get settled---I'll call you."

We pulled into my driveway and I grabbed our lunch, leading the way around back. We settled in and I watched him try to eat, taking deep breaths before each bite, chewing slowly, and choking it down. He could barely manage a quarter of his sandwich, wrapping the rest for later. He drank two bottles of water plus his Yoo Hoo, and then wolfishly ate the Hershey Bar. I watched and catalogued his every move, trying to determine what all of it meant.

He smoked two cigarettes, then went into the house to use the bathroom. Twenty minutes later he came back out, his eyes soft, and patted my hand. "I just wanted to tell you, Scott's pretty much a dick. Always has been. And you're better off without him."

"Yeah," I said. "I know."

He nodded at me. "I gotta catch the 2:10. You okay to drop me off?"

"Sure."

We made our way to the car and drove the short distance back to Tarrytown. "How are the kids?" he asked.

"Dani's working---looking for something permanent. Dylan seems to be settling in."

"They're great kids. Take after you. They know Scott's a dick."

"He's their dad, Adam. I don't want them to know he's a dick."

Adam shrugged. "Our dad's an asshole."

"Ummm---are you trying to cheer me up?"

He laughed, "Nah."

I pulled up in front of the station.

"Carly, listen, I used my last twenty on the train fare up---I got a return ticket---but---"

"Sure---of course!" I said, reaching for my purse. I pulled forty dollars out of my wallet, leaving myself ten. "Here you go."

"Just till this gig kicks in, ya know?"

"I get it."

"Thanks. You're the best." Relieved, he jumped out of the car and blew me a kiss through the window. I watched him make his way up the train steps, slow and wobbly, like he was on a ship deck. I watched him as if I was on shore, and he was about to sail away to somewhere unreachable.

* * *

On Friday morning, I drove gratefully to my new job at Mandee's. Counting hangers and ringing up items seemed an ideal focus; the cigarette with Janine in the back of the store something to look forward to.

"Don't you have that hot date tonight?" Janine flicked her cigarette ash.

"It's hardly a hot date."

"Well, it's a date. The first one you've had since your divorce, right?"

I shrugged and tried not to think about tonight. I felt old and used up and could not imagine forming coherent sentences, let alone making any kind of impression that might lead eventually to an opportunity to have sex. It had been so long since I had actually enjoyed sex with Scott that it was surprising that I wanted to try again. But I did. Very much. My hormones, possibly because my eggs were screaming *last chance, last chance,* were in an uproar and I was in the distinctly uncomfortable situation of having the sexual desire of a 19-year-old in a 49-year-old body - which would be fine if I were having sex with someone who knew my 19--or even 30-year-old body.

"What are you wearing?" Janine blew smoke through her nose. I glared at her. "Oh yeah, the date outfit." She smiled. "Nice."

"Nice?"

"Sexy, but nice. Not like you're trying too hard."

"I'm not." I sounded defensive even to my own ears. Janine just eyeballed me and blew smoke out of the corner of her mouth.

"But you think it's okay?"

She nodded. "I picked it out, right?"

"Yeah, but you know me better now." A lot had happened in four days of working closely together during the slow season at Mandee's. We now knew each other's life stories.

She eyed me critically. I got a sinking feeling in my stomach. I'd seen that look in Danielle's eye and I knew what it meant. Reflexively, I began shaking my head.

"Come on, Carly, what are you doing with that--that hair?"

"What?"

"Have you looked in the mirror?"

"I'm a low-maintenance kind of girl, Janine--and at this point in my life--"

"You need highlights."

"Forget it. I don't have the time or money--"

"I went to cosmetology school before Jared was born--got my certificate and everything--but the hours were too long--"

"Forget it."

"They make an excellent over-the-counter product now; it'll take an hour, tops."

"No way."

"I get out at 4:00--what time is he picking you up--"

"4:30."

"Bullshit. It's a Friday night and he works in the city. He's not coming till 7:00."

"Eight, but I'm still not--"

"Knowing you, you'll be asleep when he gets there. Go home. I'll be at your house at 4:30. Mix us some Cosmos, and I'll work my magic."

"I don't think you should be drinking if you're--"

"I'll drink when it's done--go home - it's 3:00. Take a shower and shave your legs and whatever else."

She actually winked.

"Shut up."

She laughed. "Just don't wash your hair. I'll do it after, otherwise the color doesn't take as well."

"I don't know--"

"Trust me."

I didn't. But there was no arguing with her. The truth was, I needed a change. And the company.

I turned off Route 9 onto Bellwood, slowed down to 20 miles an hour, and opened the windows. The day was beginning to fade and cooler air brushed my skin.

I ran up the porch steps, fueled by the clock. Almost four. Janine would be there soon, with her beauty accouterments and endless energy. How did she do it? A grieving widow, single mother, living on a paltry Mandee's paycheck and meager Social Security - and she was always cheerful and proactive. I made a pact with myself that I was going to be more like her and less like the scared, remote jackrabbit I'd become. Even if it meant highlighting my hair. And, truth be told, I was secretly excited.

I was imagining my sleek glossy hair; pictured tossing it around like the women at Scott's country club. Maybe I would suddenly become like them: confident, untouchable, and resistant to my own shameful memories.

CHAPTER FIVE

"I have phrases and whole pages memorized,
But nothing can be told of love…."
– Jalaluddin Rumi

Nice hair, Red."

"Don't ask."

"Was it this color when I met you--"

"No. Can we go now?" I was standing on the porch, keys in hand. He was still on the steps. I'd been waiting outside. I didn't care if it made me appear over-eager. It was better than sitting inside, staring in horror at the mirror.

"Seriously, your hair's really red."

"Good, you're not color blind."

"Not copper exactly. More like…Titian."

"Shut up."

"So, what happened?"

I was striding toward his car, but stopped. "Look, if you're embarrassed to be seen with me--"

He grinned. "No way."

I glared at him. He grinned wider. White, even teeth, a slight slant to the bottom of the left front tooth. Cute. But I wasn't in the mood. "Most guys would pretend to like it."

"Most women would have cancelled the date. Or worn a hat."

"Hmph. I'm not most women." I glared harder. Looked into his eyes. Almond shaped. Warm. Thick black lashes. I felt a tiny pull, deep inside. *Say something nice,* I told myself. *Charm him.* "I hope you're driving, because I plan on drinking."

He opened the car door and ushered me in. "Works for me."

We took off and he blasted John Legend. "Too loud?"

I shook my head and smiled without thinking. He smiled back. Our gazes held. For the first time in a long time, I felt like I had a shot at something resembling fun.

I left my window open, figuring the wind couldn't do any further damage to my coif. I let go of the image I had concocted of myself: sleek, silky, sophisticated, with salon-lady hair and trendy clothes.

Instead I had hair the color of beets right out of the ground, and I sported clothing picked out for me by my 24-year-old boss. There was only one thing to do about it. Strut. Act like it was intentional. Pretend to be a free spirit. After all, he didn't know me, and it was a chance to reinvent myself.

The wind felt clean and John Legend was vibrating a beat through my entire body. I looked at Michael out of the corner of my eye. He was concentrating on driving. The car was fast and black and shiny. I had no idea what it was, but I liked the power of it beneath me. He turned and caught me looking at him. He grinned at me again and reached over and brushed his thumb lightly across my cheek. Then he laughed. His touch was unexpected, erotic, and had me reeling, so I turned my head and watched the Hudson River swell into view.

I hadn't been on a date since high school. And those hadn't gone so well. I'm not sure they even counted as dates.

* * *

One sticky summer night in particular, I was almost 14 and preparing to go to a party on Fifth Street and Seventh Avenue. I wore a navy blue tube top with bands that circled my upper arms, cut-off denim shorts, and what we called "Chinese Slippers": black canvas shoes styled like the Mary Janes of my childhood, but with a thin rubbery sole. I had to go all the way to Chinatown in order to buy them. My nails and lips were a bright fuchsia and I had on navy blue mascara. Adam tried to block my way; telling me to change my clothes - that guys would get the wrong idea about me. I shook him off and headed up the long avenue block to meet my girlfriends.

I ignored the sounds of catcalls and whistles from the guys on stoops, in cars, and standing in front of the bodega. I had discovered that they carried on the same way whether I wore baggy sweatpants and sneakers, short-shorts and heels, or a paper bag over my head. I discovered that if I stared straight ahead and pretended not to hear them, they usually shut up after awhile. One guy in a car was particularly aggressive and was driving slowly alongside me, shouting filthy things he wanted to do to me. I wouldn't look at him, but I had the impression he was really old; like thirty. I was beginning to get nervous. I also knew that the guy could drag me into his car in the middle of the street in front of all those witnesses, and no one would really give a shit. They'd figure I knew him, or deserved it, or both.

I turned around quickly, and started heading down the block, figuring I'd walk up Garfield instead of First Street. He took off after my sudden about-face and I had to pass the old couple riding behind him. The old lady leaned out of the car window and yelled at me: "Hey, disgraciada! What's the matter with you, walkin' around like that! You should be ashamed. You look like a *boutana*." I ignored her, too, and walked the long way to Seventh.

By the time I got to the party it was in full swing. The guys were clustered around the keg. Blacklight posters glowed eerily on the walls and a strobe light throbbed to "Bohemian Rhapsody".

My detour meant I missed meeting my girlfriends on the corner and I was now stuck having to walk in alone.

Awkward and unmoored without my girlfriends, I wasn't sure what to do, so I made my way over to the keg. Tito, handsome and reputed to have done time in reform school (as we called it back then), winked and gave me a beer. He slid his arm around me, letting his hand rest against my ass. His touch burned. I felt my cheeks flush with shame, but the pressure of his body against mine felt oddly comforting and I loved the smell of his shoulder-length hair, silky and black. He leaned over and kissed the back of my neck right underneath my ear, and a shot ran through my body. I had never felt anything like it before, and I spent the next 35 years of my life wondering if I ever would again.

Suddenly, I felt myself wrenched away into the throbbing space under the black lights in front of the dance floor. My girlfriend had me by the arms.

"What the hell is wrong with you? Do you want people to think you're a slut?"

We formed a circle and began dancing to Donna Summer's "Love to Love You". Alternately embarrassed and intrigued by the moans and groans the boys assured us was an actual orgasm she was having during the recording session. I let the sensuality of the music, the throbbing strobelight, and the beer I'd chugged, envelop me. The boys kept trying to break in and dance against us, but we kept to our circle.

When the music changed to a slow dance, everyone started pairing up. I pushed past a couple of guys who were trying to pull me toward them.

"Bathroom," I mumbled, and staggered into the hallway, the tight jeans and 12-ounce beer creating pressure so painful I could hardly walk, I had no idea where the bathroom was, and the room was weaving.

I opened one door and found myself in a bedroom with couples writhing all over each other in various stages of undress.

Shocked, I pulled the door shut and turned quickly down the hall. Next, I walked into a closet that held a strong odor of unwashed clothes and wet wool. Rearing back, changing direction, desperate, I found a line of four girls. They turned and glared at me, the one in front of me swinging her hair and lashing me across the face with it. Her long red nails arced ominously through the air. I stood flat against the wall and stared at my feet. They all went in together. There was a lot of laughing and noise. Pot smoke seeped beneath the door. Every once in a while a toilet flushed. Finally, the door opened and they pushed past me. I locked myself in. It was cramped. Tiny black and white tiles, with brown-pitted grout. It had a filthy toilet, a chipped sink with hot and cold spigots, and a slimy shower curtain. I used the toilet without sitting down and held onto the bathtub while the black and white tiles shifted and swayed below me.

I tried running cold water on the inside of my wrists, then splashed my face, unconcerned about the heavy makeup I'd carefully applied earlier. I did the best I could to rub the mascara from beneath my eyes, then opened the door.

A solid force pushed me back, my calves hit the tub, and I would have fallen backwards, but his arm was behind me, pulling me forward. I recognized him as one of the guys from the neighborhood. We weren't friends, but I'd seen him around. He was big, with sandy-colored hair and deep-set blue eyes. My friends all thought he was cute, but to me he seemed arrogant and cold, and I'd never really liked him.

He had kicked the door shut and turned the lock in what I'm sure he thought was a very smooth move. He smirked at me. "I like that dance you were doing for me out there."

"It wasn't for you."

"Come on, you saw me watching you."

I hadn't actually seen him watching me, but I didn't know what to say. When I didn't say anything, he reached for me and shoved his tongue against my lips. I pressed them together and pushed, but I couldn't budge him.

"Come on, baby, you don't gotta play hard-to-get with me."

"Let go of me."

"What? You worried I ain't gonna respect you or something? I'm not like that. You'll be my girl."

He was panting and thrusting. His hands were everywhere. He was squeezing one of my breasts so hard that tears sprang to my eyes. He had my shorts unbuttoned and was attempting to tug them off me while I was trying to push his face away from me.

I was squeamish about doing what I needed to, but I panicked when I felt him press his naked and erect penis against my thighs. Squeezing my eyes shut, I rammed my hand between us and beneath him, grabbing and twisting his testicles. His eyes widened in pain, and then he was off me and pulling away. I released him and pulled my shorts up while he folded in on himself. Somehow I climbed over him and made it out of the bathroom.

I learned from that experience. Having no father sent a signal into the world: she is not precious---take what you want. And I made a decision right there and then, that none of them would get a thing from me. Dating was out. Studying was in. I must have gotten out of the apartment and walked the few blocks home, but all I can remember was rubbing my hand against my jean shorts in an attempt to get the stench of that boy off of me. Some of my skin came off, leaving a raw wound at the base of my palm; a wound I opened and reopened many times over the years, when I'd inadvertently find myself rubbing it against surfaces as if trying to remove a stain.

Because I'd met Scott my freshman year of college and dated him exclusively until the day I married him, my dating experience was pretty much non-existent. I had borne two children, had sex twice a week for 29 years, and had never experienced an orgasm. I wondered if there was any way Michael D'Angelo could tell.

* * *

Gliding to a stop, we sat at a red light. Michael turned his head and caught my gaze. I felt an unfamiliar tug deep inside my belly and further down, mysterious and alien. It scared me that maybe Michael knew how frigid I was, and that some sick part of him liked it. Simultaneously, a thought bloomed, weak and thin in the dark depths of my mind, that he was responding to the new, bold, pretense of a self I was showing the world, and that maybe I had buried my damaged self for good.

The interior of the restaurant was dim, intimate, and anonymous. Art deco furniture and paintings were scattered about, the bar had a sexy red luster to it, and although it was three deep, Michael somehow managed to squeeze us into a secluded corner of it and had drinks in our hands within moments. He was sipping a gin martini and I was gulping a cocktail that the bartender promised I would love.

The sheer force of the crowd had me wedged against him, his knee between my thighs, causing a friction and a fullness that was making it difficult for me to draw a steady breath. Our stomachs were flush and my breasts were pressed against his chest. He had one arm around me, the other held his drink, and our lips and eyes were level. He said something. I laughed, and I felt an unfamiliar, almost alarming flood of moisture and warmth. Heady from the new sensation I was experiencing, not to mention the very strong drink and the tickle of Michael's breath against my throat, I let my eyes shut, squeezing out the crowd, and gave into the press of his arm against my back, balancing against his hips and thighs.

Our hostess came over and tapped him discreetly on the shoulder, forcing Michael to pull his lips from the pulse of my neck. He had been whispering questions in my ear, and I had been whispering answers to the best of my ability. At first they had been simple ones: "Chocolate or vanilla?" "Yankees or Mets?" "Ocean or lake swimming?" "Sunrise or twilight?"

His last question had been "Religion or spirituality?" The hostess was waiting and my usual reaction would have been to immediately follow her, but it was too difficult to pull away from him, so I left her waiting and leaned up to whisper against his ear.

His scent, Ivory soap on warm skin, filled me, and I felt him shiver as I gave my answer: "Neither."

"Hmmm." He looked at me with what seemed to be compassion, causing me to feel bereft in a way I hadn't known I was.

"What about you?" I whispered back.

"I'm open." The hostess interrupted us for the second time. As she stalked to our table, we followed, Michael's hand on the small of my back.

Wine, warm olives, and thick crusty bread were placed in front of us and Michael leaned back in his seat. "Should we get the whole how-my-marriage-ended-thing over with?"

I grinned. I was dying to know how anyone could let a hunk of burning love like Michael out of her grasp. "Sure. I'll start. Married the wrong guy. Your turn."

"Ha. Not so fast. What made him the wrong guy?"

I had certainly gone over it a million times in my head, and my girlfriends had heard the gory details, but I had never spoken this part out loud before. "I guess that all the things he loved the most about me, I considered my worst detriments--and all the things I loved about him were the traits he eradicated as soon as he could."

"That requires an anecdotal explanation."

"Okay. Scott loved that I was organized; a planner. He also loved that I was content to be a stay-at-home mother."

"Those don't sound like detrimental characteristics."

"Not at first, but when the kids got older and I wanted to try new things, he became more controlling. " Michael didn't give anything away. I wondered if his wife was telling some other man the same things about him. I tried to imagine another woman having this conversation with Scott, but it was impossible; he'd never have it.

"When the children were young, while they were napping, I would clean all the grout in the house with a Q-tip and bleach. Scott loved that about me; bragged about it to his mother. Even with rubber gloves, the skin was peeling off my fingers in raw red strips. When a friend of mine convinced me that a spray bottle and scrub brush could do the same job, he became sullen. Said my friend needed to mind her own business--asked me if I'd ever seen the state of her guest bathroom."

Michael was looking a little ill at this point, it felt as though somehow I was betraying my younger self. "Your turn."

Michael stroked the palm of my hand with his thumb, causing an instant and contradictory reaction of relaxation and supreme stimulation. Smiling at me as if he knew what he did, he placed my hand gently on the table lifted his glass and sipped his wine.

"I'm going to tell you my side of the story--and I hope it doesn't change how you feel about me."

"Are you a hound dog cheater?"

"If you're asking if I was ever unfaithful to Elena, I was not."

Elena. I imagined a petite brunette with full lips, cat eyes, black curls, and a body built for sex.

"El and I were married at the age of 23. On the night of our 20th wedding anniversary, she made an elegant dinner and invited four couples over; our closest friends. Our twin boys were away at school. I made a toast I thought she would love and presented her with a necklace of emeralds. She graciously accepted, everyone applauded, and then she made her speech.

"El had always been shy, and she didn't like being the center of attention. I probably shouldn't have given her the gift in front of everyone. I had tried to give it to her earlier, but she was so nervous about the party, and I really wanted her to have it during the evening - to see it at her throat. Anyway, she was kind of flustered and she gave the standard speech— thanked me, said how grateful she was for the boys, thanked everyone at the table for coming and for the years of friendship—-the usual stuff. And then she said that she needed to spread her wings."

"That's understandable."

"I didn't know what to expect. She had never told me of any plans she had; she was so content gardening, she sat on several boards--I couldn't imagine what it would be. So I thought somehow that she was going to plan a trip--a lengthy one--without me; and I promised myself I would support her because, after all, she never took anything for herself. But she wasn't planning a trip at all. She said she was going to take singing lessons."

"What did you say?"

Michael's face flooded with heat. I could see it was difficult for him to meet my eyes. But he did. "I laughed."

"Uh-oh."

"Every woman has that reaction."

"This is your big first date ice-breaker story?"

"Gotta get it over with."

"So then what happened?"

"Nothing. She looked at me for an instant. No more than a heartbeat. And I doubt that anyone else saw it, but her gaze was full of hatred."

I swallowed more wine and gave him a pitying look.

"It was the craziest thing. We finished the evening as if nothing had happened. Folks stayed till the early hours of the morning and we all cleaned up together, had coffee, dessert, and after-dinner drinks, laughed, played a few rounds of 'I never' (or something equally stupid), then eventually sent our guests away. We went upstairs, I undressed her, we had sex with her necklace on, she kissed me afterward and thanked me again for it, and I thought the moment had blown over."

Who does this? I thought. *Who tells a woman on his first date about making love to his wife and what she wore?*

But Michael just rambled on like he hadn't said anything remotely creepy. "The next day when I went to work, El seemed fine. I called her a couple of times during the day, just to check in - never reached her, but figured she was just busy. Came home that night to an empty house, which was highly unusual--not that it would be empty; just that she wouldn't have mentioned it to me. Went upstairs to change and that's when I saw…."

"What?"

"Her closets, drawers, jewelry chests, vanity--emptied. Not one personal item was left in the room. The rest of the house was intact. She left me a note saying, "I emptied all our joint accounts. You can keep the house and your pension plans. Please keep me on your healthcare until I find a job--after that, I don't want a dime from you. Please continue to care for our children as if I still loved you."

I was torn between horror and admiration.

"Here's what I learned from that, Carly. You can't ignore a wife. You can't just go through life thinking about someone else as if they're nothing more than an extension of yourself … oh, my extension is hungry, I'll feed it; it has an itch, I'll scratch it. Doesn't work. I should have paid closer attention. I should have listened. And I should have asked more questions. But I just wanted the path of least resistance. And it took me straight to divorce court. I sold the house, wound up in a man cave condo with nothing but a recliner, a giant flat screen, a freezer full of steaks, and a fridge full of beer. I was never alone, 'cause there was always some other poor slob who'd fucked up, staying with me until he figured things out. And my sons were really good about visiting. I never trashed their mom. I tried really hard to explain her side of things to them, but it was tough on them. They were mad at her. They had no frame of reference, so they blamed her."

"Did she date?"

"Well, that's when things got ugly. She'd always been so shy. And so proper. Here's our anniversary picture."

I hurt myself trying to get to it, even though I threw him a withering look and said, "Who does this on a first date? You bring pictures of your ex-wife - are you some kind of weird creeper?"

He laughed. "Listen, I'm just doing it all up front now--and you practically killed yourself trying to get a better look."

Of course he was right, so I abandoned all pretense of taking a higher road and grabbed the picture, as well as the reading glasses he had used to look at the menu, and studied it. She was nothing like I'd imagined. Michael was beaming, looking remarkably the same as he did sitting across from me. Elena was petite, but with blonde anchor-woman hair, wide blue eyes, remarkably childlike, full lips, she didn't look a day over 30 even though she must have been 45 in the picture. She was wearing the necklace. A stunner. She wasn't smiling, but she had a vulnerable look, and she was beautiful. I wished I'd never seen the picture. Then he whipped out another one. "This is a photo of her two months after she left. A friend sent it to me."

It was difficult to fathom that she was the same woman. Her hair was cropped into a spiked pixie and had been dyed black. Her baby blue eyes were rimmed like a raccoon's and her lips were pale and shiny slashes of color like wounds on her cheeks. She was dressed head to toe in a black leather cat suit, a large silver cross dangling between her breasts.

"Singing lessons, huh?" I'm not proud of the snide tone that was in my voice.

Michael laughed. "When I met her, she had just graduated from Julliard. She was a classically trained pianist. Two months after leaving me, she became the keyboardist for an all-female rock band with some ridiculous name."

"Let's hear it."

"Rocked Out Milfs."

"Whoa."

Michael frowned, "A cliché from hell."

"Well, Scott has a girlfriend our daughter's age. He's a walking cliché too--which, I guess, makes me one."

Michael lifted his glass, "To the clichéd."

I clinked my glass against his, leaned over, and kissed him softly on his lips, tasting his surprise, his eagerness, and the promise of something I had never known.

Dinner was, I'm sure, delicious. But I don't even remember eating. The drinks had gone to my head, and watching Michael and feeling his touch on my hand or arm, his gaze on my face, was making me delirious. Several times our knees caught and locked under the table, flooding me with longing.

"Do you want to get out of here?" he whispered. I nodded. The next thing I knew, he had my hand and was pulling me through the crowd and into the cold air. At some point he'd paid our bill and gotten our jackets. As he wrapped mine around me, he lifted my hair in a single movement and kissed my neck, right below my ear. Liquid heat shot through me and I felt my knees weaken. Thirty-five years exactly. It's as if he knew exactly where to kiss me. His lips moved against my neck and I knew he was smiling. I turned into his arms.

We stood like that for a moment, swaying into each other. His strength and warmth flowed into me and for a ridiculous moment, I wanted to let go and have him catch me.

"Carly?'

"Huh?"

"Were you named for Carly Simon?"

I nodded," Winkin' Blinkin' and Nod"

"Can you sing?"

"Only off key."

He laughed. And I leaned against him. But I wanted to say my childhood was off limits.

"What now?" He asked me. "Live music, another bar, walk down by the water?"

I didn't want to share him. "Let's go to the water."

Walking next to him hip to hip, his arm wrapped around my waist, felt right. Our strides matched, our bodies fit. When we got to the docks, the wind was harsh, and I turned into him for relief. Our eyes held, and his gaze was steady until his eyes closed. This time his kiss was deep, slow. As if his tongue was inside my mouth and everywhere else on my body at the same time.

It was too much; my knees buckled. I wanted to pull him to the ground and strip away everything until all I could feel was his skin against mine, his heat burning me. *Stop,* I told myself, *before you humiliate yourself in front of this man.* I pulled away harder than I needed to, throwing myself off balance.

He steadied me and laughed, "Hey now, I got you."

Forcing myself to straighten up, I asked him what time it was.

"If I tell you, are you going to make me take you home?"

"No--yes! If it's late--is it?"

"A quarter past one."

"Time to go!" Ridiculous, I know. I had no obligations. But I didn't trust myself around him anymore.

He laughed, but I saw something in his eyes - disappointment? Realizing I was acting like a sixteen-year-old trying to figure out if a guy liked her or not, I felt a wave of shame.

On the way home, he pulled me against him. At first I resisted and tried to walk straighter. *Just these couple of blocks,* I told myself. *Let me have these few blocks to lean into him, pretend I belong to him, and he belongs to me.*

Car rides have always struck me as a way to bend time. Maybe it's the phenomenon of moving through space at high speed, covering distances in a way that's impossible for humans to achieve on their own volition. Music has a potent effect on my sense of time as well, transforming a five-minute car ride or a three-hour road trip into a rabbit hole of sorts; an escape. Radio blasting, the open window allowing the chilled night air to rush over me, and Michael's hand gently resting on mine created a powerful aphrodisiac. The combination disoriented me and I couldn't tell if we'd driven home in 30 seconds or thirty days. I had this horrifying urge to cry. So I did what I always do when I am overwhelmed by my own interior life. I stilled myself.

Michael turned the car off. Slowly the nighttime sounds resonated; crickets, a rustling of the autumn leaves in the trees, the distant roar of the train on the tracks along the Hudson River. Michael left the warmth of the car and I watched him in silhouette as he walked around the front of the car and opened my door.

Unfolding my legs, I felt myself lift away from the car and into the cool air. His arms went around me and I leaned against his body. Hard, compact. His knuckles brushed my cheek and his thumb slid down my throat, sending shivers through me. Kissing me, his smile was bright against the night. "I'll watch you go in; make sure you're safe."

It took more strength than I guessed I had to walk away from him. But I did it.

"Carly?"

Stopping along the garden path leading to the side kitchen door, I turned my head to look at him. He'd left his jacket in the car and was shrouded in lamplight from the street pole. I could see the definition of muscle in his arms, which were folded across his chest. His stance was wide and he looked strong, but there was a question in his voice.

"Yeah?"

His grin was wide, confident. "I'll call you tomorrow."

"Okay."

He laughed. "I'll go when I see a light on inside."

"Okay. Good night."

"Goodnight."

I forced myself not to look back, but hurried into the house, turned on a light, and held my face pressed against the inside of the kitchen door, listening to his car door slam and the roar of the engine as he pulled away.

Somehow I made my way upstairs to my bedroom, the wing flutters in my stomach propelling me through the air. Stood in the middle of the moonlit bedroom with the answering machine (yes, I still had one) blinking a frantic tattoo. I tried to settle down by simultaneously using every meditative yoga technique I'd ever learned, resulting in an unfortunate moment face down on the rug. The answering machine maintained its visual alarm. Against my will, I pressed the 'play' button.

"Mom, where are you?" Dani's voice. "It's 1:30! Are you home from your date? Oh my god, are you alone? Call me!"

I rushed for the button before the series of beeping and automated time systems pounded their way into my brain. Wriggling out of my clothes, I fumbled for three aspirin, washed them down with tepid tap water, and slid naked under the covers, smudged mascara and all. It had been about as perfect an evening as I'd ever had - which scared me more than anything had in a very long time.

* * *

Yoga was not an easy thing to practice at 8:30 in the morning with a head the size of a watermelon, a queasy stomach, and a plethora of shame. I couldn't tell whether I felt elated or suicidal, so I decided to forget about the useless pursuit of figuring out my state of mind and focused instead on the dusty, sunlit yoga studio I'd been attending for twelve years.

We were cramped in a small room at the top of a local church. On a positive note, the floor to ceiling windows high above the village let in plenty of light, despite the layers of polluted grime or the dreariness of the day. Even on an overcast morning like this, enough natural light streamed in to warm the creaky floorboards. A wall of mirrors made the studio appear larger than it was, and the brightly colored yoga mats provided rectangles of cheer in an otherwise unadorned room.

Hester, the yoga teacher (or guru, as too many people thought of her, and as she no doubt thought of herself), was sitting placidly in her usual place in the front of the room perfectly centered (or composed, depending on your orientation). Her short hair, shaved around the back and sides and colored a deep indigo this week, had tips of acid orange, like punctuation marks. Her yoga pants and spaghetti strap camisole showed off her wiry muscles, super flexible build, and tiny pointed breasts. Knobs of bone protruded from her wrists, and her quick-bitten nails made the backs of my knees and insides of my wrists hurt. As long as I can remember, these are the two parts of my body where I feel other people's pain.

Charcoal eyeliner marked Hester's otherwise-bare face. Lines etched into her forehead and at the sides of her mouth were the only indication that she wasn't as young as she appeared at first glance. I, of course, couldn't have done a fraction of her yoga moves when I was 17.

I looked around the room. It held the usual suspects. Melissa Cameron, Caroline Logan, and Pat Donovan were stretched out in an assortment of delectable poses. With the exception of Pat, who was friendly to me in an absent, I'm-nice-to-everyone way, the women had shunned me since my divorce. Melissa's husband worked with Scott, and for some unknown reason, she was uncomfortable with me. I didn't care if she went to dinner with Scott and his flavor-of-the-month, underage bimbo (I know: I was Bitter Vituperative Woman; probably the real reason none of them can stand me). I'm sure my post-divorce ejection from the club was a source of relief for her. She wasn't the only one who found it offensive that I was a member of the Country Club, yet didn't wear the right clothes and jewelry, didn't get my hair done, and didn't apply makeup the right way. My new hair color would probably cause her to have a bird. Also, I'd kicked her ass on the tennis court, and that pissed her off to no end.

I was a lowly Brooklyn girl who'd grown up playing handball, and I'd ruined her idea of what was right with the world when, after a few lessons, I became an ace tennis player. At least, that's what Caroline always said. But in retrospect, I've been rethinking that, because Caroline's a liar. She was my former tennis partner; the one that was fucking Scott for six months while she was reconciling with her husband. The truth is, I'm not even that mad at Caroline. My marriage was over long before my husband took up with her, and I know how charming and persuasive he can be. But I was enraged when I found out. And truthfully, I didn't handle it in the most ladylike of fashions. My behavior gave a lot of people plenty of dinner-party conversation and entertained the neighborhood for an entire summer. It must have deeply embarrassed Dylan, although I think it raised Danielle's estimation of me considerably.

For a while, rewriting this story in my head with a better outcome was a favorite pastime of mine; especially while swilling white wine and listening to old Dinah Washington LPs, which is how I survived the first month of our decision to divorce. It was a decision that left us living in the same house for a year and a half. My behavior, I'm sure, made it much easier for him to leave.

The thing about the altercation with Caroline is that we both came out of it scathed and ridiculous. In my obsessive replaying of it, I am alternately dignified, leaving her speechless with a perceptive, witty, and deeply cutting remark in front of all our friends, or… I knock her out with one clean punch after she tries to start a drunken brawl with me in a local restaurant populated by everyone we know, who of course cheer for me and buy me countless rounds of drinks while she stumbles out, disgraced, disheveled, and somehow (I'm not sure why), with wet hair plastered to her head, revealing to all the world that without her salon blow-dry and careful makeup, she looks remarkably like a weasel.

In reality, the altercation was unplanned and extremely unfortunate for both of us. I had gone running. It was a perfect spring day. I was angry all the time, couldn't eat, and I ran compulsively. I'd been down through Kingsland Point and was running along the narrow, pebbled parking lot, intending to end at the river's edge to stretch, when I saw her. She was trip-trapping off the train station platform in trendy heels and a cute little dress. Her hair was perfect; she had sunglasses on, swinging her matching handbag and tooting her car keys so her fancy new car would start its engine while she was still on the platform. It seemed to me at the time (and I realize now how wrong I'd been about it) that she was completely untouched by the scandal and ruin that had become my life. The humiliation Dylan felt didn't affect her daughter, who was younger and went to a private school across the bridge, but my son was still attending the local high school and he was being treated to blow-by-blow descriptions about his father that he shouldn't have been. And there she was, traipsing along like nothing had changed. The bottom hadn't fallen out of her world and left an aching, raging pit where her torso used to be. That it seemed, was my lot.

I, of course, had no way of knowing how she viewed me - the wronged one; the one everyone, even her best friends and my mere acquaintances, were siding with, against her. I was the non-slut. The brave, strong person who had the bad luck to marry a jerk who'd used and abused Caroline because he could; because she was a woman with a worthless sense of herself. To this day he's getting locker room slaps on the back from everyone except her ex, who'd finally had enough and moved back to New York City where he was forced to become a weekend dad.

But when I saw her on that platform, none of these thoughts were accessible to me. All I saw was the source of my pain, humiliation, and misery. True; not the major source - but Scott was the father of my children, and there wasn't much I could do to him without having my children suffer for it. At that moment, Caroline just seemed like fair game. She halted when she saw me and reared back like a deer in the headlights. Ordinarily, that sort of reaction would elicit compassion in me; a desire to comfort even my worst enemy. But that day, it just spurred me on.

I stopped at the foot of the stairs, leaving her unsure of whether she should remain teetering at the top of the six steps to the parking lot or come closer to me.

Still out of breath, I remember balling my fists and planting them on my waist. "If it isn't the slut of Sleepy Hollow," I said (not my finest or wittiest moment).

She wrinkled her nose and looked down at me. "Carly, I don't know what to say. I'm sorry."

"Sorry you got caught, maybe."

"No. Sorry I hurt you. It was a terrible thing to do."

"But you did it. And lied right to my face - pretended to be my friend, sat in my kitchen, took my daughter for manicures! Why? To pump her for information about her father?"

"Of course not!"

"Oh, did I offend you, Caroline?"

"How is this productive? We all need to move on. My life is in shambles too, if that's any consolation to you."

"It's not." But it was.

"I don't know what else to say." We stared at one another for a moment. The air around me hummed with some undefined energy. We were alone, seemingly isolated in this very public spot, and I felt my mind detaching itself from my body. Then she said two simple words. "Please move." My undoing.

I watched my arm reach up and grab the front of her dress.

As if from outside of myself, I watched her body as I dragged her close to me, her face a panicked mask, her arms flailing, her fingers clutching the air. I remember thinking *this is what every wife who's been cheated on really wants to do to the other woman*. I'm not sure what happened next, but it definitely involved some rolling around on the pebbled driveway. Fighting my way above her squirming body, I straddled her and pinned her arms to the side of her head. She was crying and trying to cover her face, but I held her down until she looked at me. She bucked against me, and her eyes and nose were streaming tears and mucus. Repulsed by the feeling of her bony pelvis beneath me, I jumped off her. That's when I saw the car keys. Her ridiculous car was still running. I picked them up and stood over her.

"You're a lunatic!" She was struggling to stand up, smoothing her dress and hair and gathering her handbag. Then she saw me with the keys. "What are you doing? Give those to me! Carly! Don't you dare!"

It was like a song in a movie, her frenzied voice, as I walked calmly over to the precipice above the Hudson River. Arcing my arm through the air, the keys left my fist, rendering me weightless and strangely peaceful as I watched them disappear into the Hudson. I gleefully passed her still-running car and walked back over the train trestle platform, jogging the couple of blocks home, imagining I could still hear her faint crying, like background music.

* * *

There was a part of me that believed I should leave the yoga class; move on without the constant reminder of the way Caroline's and my life were forever entwined. But a bigger part of me wanted to stay. I'd had enough changes in my life and I didn't want to find another practice. If I made the others uncomfortable, too damn bad. And if they made me uncomfortable, it was nothing next to the low-grade misery of being married to Scott. So, I figured, either way, I'm in a better place. Om.

But for all my bold talk, I found myself looking desperately around as I set my mat up toward the back of the class. Where was Joanna? She was the one person I truly liked in the class. She was my age; a local woman who'd grown up here, moved away for twenty years, and came back last year. We were like magnets, drawn together by our alienation in a familiar environment and our world-tilting change of status as misfits in suburbia.

Relief spread through me like a slow burn when Joanna raced in and flipped open her mat next to mine.

"Namaste." Hester opened her eyes for the first time in at least 15 minutes. Her gaze fixed on Joanna and me from across the room. We weren't focusing on the guru, as expected, and she knew it. I'd confessed to Joanna that I was going on my first date since the divorce, and she wanted details.

During our brief conversation about it at the end of our last class, I'd sensed Hester moving around us, trying to hear what we were talking about. For some reason I was reluctant to let Hester know anything too personal about me. I didn't want her judging me--it was difficult enough to let go during the class—and she'd already heard enough gossip and intimate details of my life from Caroline and the others.

Joanna wiggled her eyebrows and mouthed silent words at me: "How was the date?" I smiled. Couldn't help it. An honest-to-God giant smile that I can't remember feeling in months.

"Namaste." The class (all but Joanna and I) answered. Hester glared at us. "*Namaste,*" she repeated.

"Namaste" the class dutifully answered for the second time, and this time Joanna and I joined in, our eyes respectfully on Hester.

And we were off in a competitive haze of meditative, body-twisting moves masquerading as spirituality and health.

Hester moved among us, rearranging various body parts, making corrections, laying hands on our hips or the space between our shoulder blades.

Joanna, to me, was the only one of us who seemed to truly transcend through yoga. Her moves, while nowhere near the most advanced, were graceful; and she moved effortlessly from one position to another, her feet gliding silently and her placement flawless, the light whoosh of her breath propelling her through air and space like a sculpture on a moving axis.

Joanna never looked around and seemed impervious to Hester and the other women, yet when we made eye contact and she flashed a smile of pure joy, a small spot of happiness took hold in me.

If Joanna had heard of the incident between Caroline and myself (which she had to have), she never once mentioned it. By tacit agreement, the other women and I, Caroline included, were civil to one another without really speaking. It couldn't have been comfortable for Hester or Joanna. But, as I said, Joanna seemed to transcend all worldly things during yoga, and Hester seemed to relish being the major focus in the room and also delighted in singling me out for praise of my accomplishments even when I was clearly undeserving.

Maybe it was just my imagination, but I can't believe Hester didn't notice the sulky glares of Caroline and Melissa when she praised a position I achieved or a new level of difficulty I attained. As much as I hated the undue attention, and was ashamed of it, there was nothing I felt I could do without appearing disloyal to Hester who, after all, was showing, in her own small way, allegiance to me. That was perhaps what I resented the most about Scott's unfaithfulness: that I had somehow been reduced to the object of people's pity, or that I was a person in need of defending. There was nothing I could do except ignore it and train my mind as much as possible to live in the moment, pray for clarity and strength, and shift all my petty thoughts into a lock-box in my mind. Easier said than done.

The class was an exceptionally difficult one. "Deep cleansing breath in through your nostrils--exhale out through your teeth--shhhhh!" Like an angry cat, she pushed the air out through her teeth, and we all followed suit.

Caroline glared over at me. "Hester?"

Hester floated over. "Yes?"

Caroline fidgeted and threw me another dirty look. "Could you instruct the other students not to take in more than their share of oxygen--and, more importantly, not to breathe out too much carbon dioxide? I read somewhere that it's dangerous for the rest of us and is actually a contributing factor to the rise in lung cancer."

Hester narrowed her eyes. "Excuse me?"

"There are some people in this class who are breathing in too heavily, taking more than their share of air, and--"

"*Some people*? Would you care to be more specific?"

Caroline tossed her hair extensions back and adjusted her top over her silicone breasts, which strained against her skin in a way that looked painful. "Really? You're going to make me say who?"

"Well, I can't tell them to stop breathing unless I know who it is."

"I never said to stop breathing--just not to take so much breath."

"Are you under the impression that there is a finite amount of oxygen in this large room? And that someone's exhalation is so toxic that you are put at risk of lung cancer."

"Well, I did read it somewhere."

"What publication would that be?"

By now, we had all stopped pretending to be working and were watching the two of them.

"Well, I don't remember specifically; just some health publication."

Hester smirked. "I see." She looked around at us. "Did I say to let go? Back up in plank; full plank, everyone."

Obediently, we returned to a plank pose. Hester began her inventory of us as she walked around the room. "As your yoga instructor, I am aware of certain toxic emotions in this room which are clearly manifesting themselves in Caroline's belief that Carly is breathing more than her fair share of air and sending out toxic lung-cancer-inducing emissions of breath."

I felt everyone in the room tense, even Joanna. Hester continued. "I want everyone in the room to continue working. You know the sequence. Carly and Caroline, please come with me."

Joanna looked over at me. "This is bullshit; you don't have to go."

I shrugged. "May as well get it over with."

Hester walked purposefully across the room, as if she were exiting a stage. Caroline stalked past me and I followed, wondering if the entire rest of my life was going to be made up of a series of petty humiliations.

Hester ushered us into her airless office, which was filled with discarded equipment, stacks of dog-eared file folders, and boxes of environmentally friendly but exorbitantly priced water bottles. We all bought these bottles out of a sense of obligation--not to the environment; there were certainly less expensive models out there-- but out of an obligation to Hester, who constantly told us that the only way she could continue to serve us is to charge three times what other yoga instructors charged, in spite of their newer facilities with better amenities, and to gouge us on prices for mats, water bottles, yoga wear, and T-shirts.

Hester turned to face us. "Carly, Caroline; both of you know how much I give to our practice, not only physically, but spiritually as well."

We nodded respectfully.

"I have said many times that yoga practice is performed on many levels, and my commitment to you as a teacher is given on many levels as well."

I found myself obsessing that she'd used the word "many" three times, causing me to reflect on the fact that in spite of her scholarly tone and careful enunciation, Hester was not always as articulate as one would expect from such a guru-like figure.

Hester breathed in deeply, causing her diaphragm to swell impressively. "My practice is such that I cannot have negative energy poisoning the class. We must work in a place of positivity. I pride myself on being able to help all my students, not only during the pursuit of physical strength and flexibility, but also on a spiritual journey. As you know, I use guided meditations as a tool. I have traveled extensively through the Far East and have witnessed first hand the effects of karma on the body."

I was having the distinctly disloyal thought that Hester was quite full of herself and seemed to enjoy the sound of her own voice in a distinctly non-transcendent way. Caroline was fidgeting and I could tell she was sorry she'd opened her fat petty mouth. She seemed about to say something, but Hester put her hand up to stop her. "Uh-uh. Now is not the time. I am going to ask you both to vent your frustrations, not to one another, but to me, and I will assist you in a cosmic release of the poisons of anger, jealousy, and greed into the universe."

Caroline and I looked at one another in horror. I tried to form words in my head to ward this off; something like, *this is making me uncomfortable*--or *what the fuck*??? But instead, Caroline and I found ourselves nodding in agreement. Maybe it was the confidence Hester seemed to exude that perpetuated the guru-like hold she had over us. It felt unhealthy, but I think I hated myself so much that it seemed appropriate - or at least, familiar enough to go along with.

"Caroline, express the poisonous feeling of anger and jealousy you feel toward Carly."

Caroline stammered, "I don't--"

Hester gave her a disgusted look. "No judgment from me, Caroline. Just a healing cleansing of the spirit. It is clear you harbor anger, resentment, and jealousy of Carly, and it is imperative that you express them to me at this time."

"Hester, I can't--it's not like that...."

Hester allowed a slight snarl to escape her lips before regaining her composure. "Fine. I will help you by telling you what I observe."

As completely fucked up as I knew this was, I couldn't help leaning forward with fascination. Hester didn't disappoint. "Caroline, you frequently glance over at Carly during class and attempt to compete by extending your leg higher or arching your back deeper. I have overheard you on numerous occasions commenting unfavorably on the clothing Carly chooses to wear to class. And I know all about the physical altercation the two of you had last spring. I also know about the sexual affair you engaged in with Carly's husband. I practice a spiritual life in such a way that I have no judgment about any of these events. And I believe that the physical manifestation of sexual intercourse is irrelevant without a spiritual connection, so for me, the sexual relationship was meaningless and therefore negated--so if it were my husband you were fucking behind my back, it would not have bothered me. However, I am aware that Carly may not feel the same way. Our social norms have positioned you as sexual competitors, and that is manifesting itself in my classroom."

Caroline and I looked at one another. I wondered if she found this conversation as wacky as I did. I also wondered, in spite of myself, how much truth there was to what Hester was saying. As if Hester could read my thoughts, she smiled beatifically at me. "You, Carly, work very hard in class, you are focused, and while you are not the most graceful or flexible - or that strong, for that matter - you are dedicated and courageous in not allowing Caroline's anger and jealousy to interfere with your practice."

What was I supposed to say to that? Thank you? I thought of an expression Danielle used, "sucks to be me." Of course, when she said it, it sounded wry and amusing. If I were to say it, I was sure it would come off as pathetic. And Hester was wrong about me. I was competitive and angry with Caroline; I was just equal parts stubborn and prideful--probably high on her list of poisons in need of spiritual cleansing.

Hester bent over and began rummaging around in a cabinet. Of course, her foot was perfectly pointed, and she made even this simple task look balletic. "Aha!" She stood up, holding what looked like an elaborate, multi-colored feather duster. She began waving it around our heads and bodies--first Caroline, then me, then the air between us. As she waved, she chanted, "Shanti," which means 'peace', a word used in Hindu prayer. Hester enjoyed the word and employed it as a salutation, signing her e-mails with it or signifying the end of class with it. Like the word 'om', shanti had made its way into the suburban mother's lexicon.

Hester's face was a mask of spiritual rapture as she twirled around and between us, brushing the air and our bodies with the feather duster. Guttural sounds emanated from her, culminating in deep chants of "shanty" as she brushed our foreheads, throats, hearts, and at one horrific moment, hovered over our vaginas with the feather duster.

Inexplicably, I thought of the long-ago subway rides my mother took us on to go to Hatha Yoga in the West Village. My brother and I would stand at the window of the first car with our noses pressed to the grimy glass, thrilled as the graffiti-ridden subway tunnels would give way to the glorious freedom of hurtling across the Manhattan Bridge. We would exit at West 4th Street and make the short walk to Hatha Yoga (which smelled suspiciously like the food co-op we belonged to in Park Slope. Many years later, I identified it as the pungent aroma of weed).

My mother had acquired a part-time position as their weekend receptionist in exchange for children's classes for us and adult classes for her. My brother and I tried unsuccessfully to transcend the pain of tight ligaments and joints. "Just go as far as you can; you don't need to look like me." The teacher instructed in a flute-like voice, her long legs wrapping effortlessly around her neck. Now, more than 30 years later, I was receiving praise for doing exactly that: going at my own pace and giving myself credit for merely showing up. There, in Hester's sad office, I experienced a vivid memory of my mother standing at the kitchen sink in our Crown Heights apartment chanting *om shanti, o-hm shanti, oham shanti, ooohhhmmmmm,* while she washed dishes.

Hester finished her spiritual air cleansing of our poisonous thoughts and stood smiling at us. Caroline looked as traumatized as if her balloon breasts had mysteriously combusted and, I must say, I was feeling pretty shaky myself.

"Go!" Hester waved at us with the giant feather-duster cleanser. "Go with om." Like obedient students, we filed out of her office, me behind Caroline, took our places back at our mats, and joined in at the end of what must have been the 10th round of 'Sun Salutation'. Joanna rolled her eyeballs at me and I threw my graceless self into the pure joy of moving through space, freed of any worries about what anyone would ever think about me ever again.

In truth, I cannot say I had transcended to a higher plane; nor was I developing a stronger spiritual life. I was simply too busy trying to dodge the bullets of memory unleashed by the vestige of my safe suburban life.

* * *

Sixteen hours had passed since my date with Michael, and eight had passed since the yoga debacle. When I wasn't obsessively thinking about Michael, I was thinking about the fiasco with Hester and Caroline. I considered never going back to that soul-sucking studio--but the next moment, I worried that I wouldn't see Joanna anymore; that without the studio, we would drift off into the ether of our separate lives.

In an effort to stimulate the part of my brain that actually functioned with curiosity and wonder, I drove over to the public library. It was almost closing time and it was fairly empty. I took some time to peruse the small gallery where rotating exhibits of local artists were presented. For years, I had thought about applying, but was too lazy or too scared (or too something). Most of the exhibits were by painters who had been tutored by a talented local woman who taught everyone to paint in exactly the same technique; so no matter which artist you looked at, people immediately said "oh, that's a Babz Shlossinger student". The paintings were lovely, restful to look at, and hung in almost every home I'd been to in Sleepy Hollow.

The current artist was someone new whose work I hadn't seen before. She worked in mixed-media collage. My favorite piece was a woman, conceived from bits of paper, lace, and corrugated cardboard; her simulated hair jutting in a variety of directions as if some unseen breeze assailed her. Paper eyes slanted closed as if facing the sun and her dress was a blend of muted threads of color. Something about her expression evoked a sense of solitude--not loneliness; just solitude - a state I recognized, but didn't know.

I heard the bell signaling fifteen minutes to closing, so I ran to the stacks and grabbed the book of letters John Adams had written to Abigail. It was a book I would never have chosen in a million years - and the perfect antidote to myself.

Arriving home, I resigned myself to a quiet dinner of spaghetti squash with olive oil and Parmesan. Having bought the squash, I felt compelled to make a meal of it. I also accepted the reality of making good on my literary choice.

The answering machine was blinking. My heart pounding a sickening thump from my chest to my throat, and with the push of a button, Michael D'Angelo's voice filled the room.

"Hey, I've been thinking about you all day. And I bet you've been thinking about me too; admit it!" Then he laughed…and I did, too.

But I didn't call him back. I wasn't brave enough.

Instead, I let the voicemails run through. Joanna called, checking in to see how I was doing after "the incident" as she referred to it. Robo calls telling me who to vote for in the next election. And a frantic Danielle saying if I didn't call her back immediately, she would be forced to jump on the next train home. It felt ridiculous to be calling my daughter to tell her about my dating life. I was still mulling over the evening, on my own--and talking about it felt precarious, the way I used to feel if I blew a dandelion wish and there were stubborn bits of fluff clinging to the colorless orb in the center: not unlucky exactly--just as if I had wasted a wish.

I wasn't entirely sure how Danielle had gotten wind of my date. Even as a young child, she listened closely to my conversations and intuited things about me, which I hadn't even recognized myself yet.

Once, when she was about four years old, I discovered her in the tiny potting room off the back porch. She had my gardening clogs on, and nothing else. It was during a brief but embarrassing time of exhibitionism which regularly involved her turning up naked at the house next door, which was occupied, of course, by a lovely woman who never lost track of her three daughters; all of whom were dressed in matching outfits and coordinating hair accessories. I'm ashamed to admit that in a petty and malicious way, I actually found excuses at varying times to see if I could drop in and surprise her, sure that when no one was watching, there were grape-jelly stained T-shirts and kitchen counter clutter… but, no such luck. Danielle was wearing the clogs and puttering around the shed with earth and a cultivator, saying: "Time to plant the flowers. I don't really like to, but I have to!"

I swear I had never ever uttered those words out loud. Not to myself and not to anyone. I wanted the entire world to think I loved gardening. It was part of the image I had created for myself, and I wanted to believe it. I wondered if she had heard a TV mother say it (another bad-parenting technique--TV babysitting--and not just videos or PBS, but actual cartoons). But I knew she hadn't, because it was exactly the way I felt all the time.

"Hi, Dani-bear; whatcha doing?" I'd asked her in my most casual voice.

She looked up at me with those clear blue eyes and said, "Being you."

"But, Dani, you know Mommy loves to plant flowers."

"No you don't, Mommy. You make this face when you do it." And she thinned her lips in a perfect imitation of my own mother. It was so horrifying that I almost gasped out loud.

"No Dani-bear - that doesn't mean I don't like gardening. It's just my thinking face."

She shook her head and glared at me. "THAT is a lie." She turned around and went back to her angry stabbing of the dirt with the cultivator.

From then on, I made a point of gardening with a pleasant face, using music to help me. But I always knew she saw right through me.

Danielle answered on the first ring, which was completely untypical. "Finally!" she practically shouted into the phone. "I only have a minute, so spill it fast!"

"I have no idea what you're talking about."

"Save it, Carly. Two of my girlfriends were at the bar last night and said you were there with a hot guy…well…," she clarified, "hot for an old guy. They said your hair was a really weird color and you were practically sucking face with the dude at the bar! Totally unacceptable, by the way - and I'm proud of you."

Since the divorce, Danielle had developed the extremely annoying and smart aleck habit of referring to her father and me by our first names. She didn't do it all the time, tending to save it up for particularly awkward moments.

"Oh. Well it's true about the bad hair, but we were absolutely not sucking face. And that is a disgusting term."

"Whatever, Carly. Spill it: who is he?"

"I thought you had to go?"

"I do, so talk fast."

"He's a friend, Danielle; that's all."

"HA! Fine, don't share. I just hope he isn't some serial killer. How did you meet him? The girls didn't recognize him from the club or the neighborhood, or as any of the other sad-sack divorced dads around town."

"Knock it off, Danielle."

"Please don't tell me you met on Match.com."

"What if I did?"

"Ha. You would never. So who fixed you up?"

"Nobody. We met on our own."

"You never go anywhere!"

"I'm hanging up now."

"Okay, fine. But do me a favor: if you're going to be pulling any more all-nighters, just text me so I don't have to worry."

"Bye."

"Mom, seriously. I worry."

Suddenly, I heard it. Fear and anxiety, seeping through the veneer of sarcasm and bossiness. It had been there for a while, I supposed; yet I had been so invested in believing the divorce didn't have a real impact on her that I had failed to notice.

* * *

If play is children's work, then I prepared relentlessly. All I had ever wanted to be was a mother. A wife was certainly part of being a mother, but it was the mother part I practiced for. Co-opting my little brother and as many friends as I could, I set up house. Sometimes it was the tented home in my mother's bedroom, where I dragged every blanket and sheet I could to build the house of my dreams. Other times, the courtyard behind our building lent itself to a wonderful modern home complete with a sunken living room like the ones I saw on television. My favorite was the Rose Garden in the Botanical Gardens. The white lattice nooks became my cottage; the mossy rocks, my bed. Gathering fallen petals, I tore them into bits and fed them to Annabel, the worn Raggedy-Ann doll I carried with me everywhere I went.

When my children were babies, I was tired, over-worked, and too much of a perfectionist. Not that you could tell by the way I did things; because nothing ever looked perfect, much to my chagrin. Despite the internal raging of my thoughts, I remember experiencing the most sublime moments of joy.

These came from simple things: preparing a colorful meal of softened carrots, tiny green pearls of shelled peas, elegantly cubed chicken, and watching the childrens' chubby fingers lifting the food, and their intent looks of pleasure as they stuffed it between their pursed baby lips.

Slow meandering walks near the duck pond and reading *Good Night Moon* ten times in a row all counted as among the happiest moments of my life.

Even later, sitting and watching their various sport or dance activities, I was truly happy. And I was never lonely or bored. I had a rich internal life, which allowed me to once spend an entire afternoon following Dylan up and down the steps as he learned to navigate them. Motherhood and suburban living had catapulted me far from the fears of my own childhood, and for a time I'd been happy. I hadn't known those fears would resurface like a dirty tide the moment I found myself truly alone.

CHAPTER SIX

"The essence of all beautiful art, all great art, is gratitude."
- Friedrich Nietzsche

During the spring of 1969, my father had his first hit record. Although we hadn't heard a word from him in months, he showed up one weekend. He may have been between women at the time, or he may have wanted to visit us and realized the only way to do it was to romance my mother. She was still falling for his sincere-contrite act, back then. He pulled up in a long, shiny, powder blue Cadillac convertible. It was the nicest car I'd ever seen and the boys on the block stood around and whistled while he parked. He threw the biggest of them five bucks to make sure nobody sat on it while he went upstairs to get Adam and my mother. Five dollars was a fortune to a kid back then and I was awestruck and embarrassed by his showiness; but I followed him faithfully, my friend's eyes burning the place between my shoulder blades in a smolder of jealousy and (I was certain) a promise of retribution. I remember thinking that maybe this time he would stay and I would have nothing to fear from any of them.

That warm spring day was our first visit to a restaurant, unless you counted the Wetson's fast food hamburger place on Empire

Boulevard or the pizzeria around the block on Franklin Avenue. My father took us to Jahn's on Flatbush Avenue, where a waitress in a cute uniform came over and wrote our orders on a pad. There were shiny menus with lists of different kinds of milkshakes and ice creams. Adam ordered a cheeseburger, French fries, and a root beer float. I had a hamburger, French fries, and a chocolate malt. My mother had a Tab and smoked cigarette after cigarette which my father lit with a square gold lighter that clicked before spurting a tiny blue flame.

My mother would rest her hand on his and inhale while looking into his eyes. It was summertime and she was wearing a short silky dress with an emerald green and white geometric print that she'd gotten at Goodwill. She said it was real silk and she couldn't believe the things rich people discarded. She said the lady who'd owned it probably didn't like to be seen wearing the same thing twice, and that it was important to go to the Goodwill near the wealthiest neighborhoods to get the best stuff. She'd taken two subways all the way to the Upper East Side to get that dress. Large square plastic earrings in the exact same emerald green shade completed the outfit.

For two months, we lived a life of luxury and hope. My father doted on my mother and we had a cupboard and refrigerator filled with groceries; some of them lasting even after my father disappeared again.

To amuse myself, I would take turns playing at being the waitress or being my mom. If I were the waitress, I'd use my school memo pad and a school pencil. I would make Adam and his friends sit at the kitchen table and place orders. All of them had to order grilled cheese and chocolate milk because that was all I knew how to make. I would write down their mandated order on the pad, sashay around the kitchen gathering the ingredients, then fry the government cheese sandwiches in the small cast iron frying pan before sashaying over and sliding them expertly in front of them.

"Just make us food," Adam would say. "Don't write on that dumb pad."

"You play, you pay," I'd answer. Which made no sense, but I'd heard it somewhere, and I liked saying it.

When I was being my mother, I would do that alone in front of the bathroom mirror. I'd wait until she was out with my father, then I'd sneak in and get a cigarette butt from the ashtray, her green earrings (if she wasn't wearing them - her gold gypsy hoops, if she was), her lipstick, and eyeliner.

I'd carefully line my upper lids, letting the corners wing up, then would paint my lips with her waxy red tube of lipstick. After carefully blotting them on a single square of toilet paper, as I'd seen her do countless times, I'd stare at the transformation in the mirror. There was nothing I could do about my limp hair, so sometimes I'd wrap it in a twisted-up towel and pretend I was in my "dressing room." Then, I'd put the smoked down cigarette butt in my mouth and practice cupping imaginary hands, holding a lighter. I'd practice smiling at myself with the cigarette between my grown-up teeth in my little kid face. I'd bat my eyelashes, swat my hand at my imaginary boyfriend, and throw my head back with pretend laughter until inevitably Adam would pound on the door, demanding to be let in.

Watching my mother fall in love with my father, I was falling in love with myself - trying on the idea of becoming a woman, realizing that the mysterious hold my mother seemed to have over my father during that period would someday become available to me as well; and it was something I could practice.

Adam and his friends were a most unappreciative audience. At six years old, all they cared about was food. Once I'd fed them, I was useless.

The older boys on the street were intimidating. I wouldn't say hello, let alone smile at them. The boys my own age thought of me as one of them, because I was. We played street games together, hopped fences, raced, and fought. I was no more a girl to them than they were men to me, and the thought of one of them putting their grubby fingers on that beautiful gold lighter just seemed repulsive to me.

So it was my mirror and me.

On the last night of my father's return, my mother was in a rare and wonderful mood. It was late spring and all the windows in the apartment were open, allowing a breeze to stir and carry her perfume. She was beautiful in an elegant black shift, her hair, still a honey-rich brown, piled high on her head. Many people over the years exclaimed about my mother's eyes. Green as a cat's, they would say. Bewitching. I knew what they meant, and that night, they were glowing beneath a heavy fringe of eyeliner and lashes. She was holding a gin and tonic. The sound of ice cubes clinking against glass usually gave me a thudding stomach, but that night they just sounded musical.

When my father came home from rehearsal, he was carrying a large bunch of purple lilies and a box of chocolate-covered cherries. He made a big show of swirling my mother around the apartment from room to room. It was like watching a movie.

Before they left, my mother placed her hand on my cheek and bent down to kiss me goodbye. "Are you sure you don't mind staying home with Adam for a few hours?"

"I'm happy you're gonna have some fun."

"My sweet girl." And with a grand gesture, she took the box of chocolates and presented them to me. "Have as many as you want, both of you; but don't eat yourselves sick."

My father winked at me, which I took as permission to do exactly that. The delight of biting into the creamy chocolate just to have the rich cherry syrup flood our mouths was heaven. I didn't feel a bit guilty not saving any for my mother because I knew that when she was in love, her only diet was lettuce, a tiny bit of canned tuna, Tab, and her unfiltered Pall Malls.

When the box was finished, I made Adam accompany me to the bathroom to wash our sticky hands and faces and brush our teeth. Both the cold and hot water taps spouted icy, so we did as perfunctory a job as we could.

Determined to preserve my mother's good mood, I cajoled Adam to get in bed and lulled him to sleep by running my fingernails up and down his back until his breathing was normal. Slightly nauseous from the chocolate gorging, I crawled into my own bed and waited for sleep.

The crash that woke me may have been the apartment door swinging open or the dishes my mother threw at the door one by one, destroying the set we had purchased by saving green stamps for two years.

I jumped up and ran outside. My mother was standing in the foyer, hair wild, ruined makeup staining her face. Her fists were clenched at her sides, and she was trembling. I wanted to run to her, throw my arms around her, and make the terrible shaking stop. But I was afraid; afraid she'd turn the anger brimming out of her on me. Burning with shame at my own cowardice, I ran instead to the living room window, just in time to see the blue Cadillac turn the corner. Silently, I crept back to bed, leaving my mother to clean up the broken bits of dishware all by herself.

* * *

Falling in love was intoxicating. Poisonous. I'd done everything differently than my mother, but I'd wound up exactly as she had.

What I experienced with Michael after our first date (excitement, lust, hope) seemed dangerous. I'd never felt that sick heady feeling of love with Scott. From the beginning, he'd been safe. I'd loved him for his confidence and because he loved me. Perhaps that was the way I'd betrayed him, and his affair with Caroline had been my comeuppance. It seemed that love in any form was not worth the risk. I kept thinking about the cardboard and cut-paper woman I'd seen at the library art show - her upturned face, eyes slanted against the wind or sun. How comfortable she seemed in her solitude. And I knew that if I wanted any shot at moving past the limbo I'd created for myself between my old lives and the new unknown one I found myself in, I was going to need to understand how to do that and be alone with myself to bask in the wind and the sun.

My college roommate Leila had a "summer cottage" she used occasionally to escape the brutal heat of New York in the summer. Miraculously, it was only 30 minutes away from me in Northern Westchester. I called her, and she told me where I could find the hide-a-key.

Morning light seeped slowly into my bedroom, weak with fog and the promise of impending rain. I welcomed the day in any form and made my bed around the still-sleeping Bridey, only having to lift her once to settle her back down on the smartly folded coverlet. Ten minutes to brush teeth, run a comb through my hair, slip into my softest jeans and T-shirt, grab my handbag and the small suitcase I'd packed the night before, and lock the door behind me.

Thick blue-grey clouds tainted the air with moisture, causing heaviness in my chest, but I slid into the car, opened the windows despite the humidity, and took off up the Saw Mill, letting the speed revive me.

I stopped in a quaint town several miles north and shopped the expensive but abundant markets, filling my basket with bright autumn vegetables, a loaf of fresh-baked bread, Irish butter, a tiny wheel of brie, fig jam, and a small piece of wild salmon. After a hummingbird beat of hesitation, I placed a large bouquet of sunflowers tied with raffia into my basket and didn't even blink at the woman when she totaled the amount in a casual manner. I swiped my credit card, held my breath until it went through, and smiled gregariously at her when I left. Impulsively, I went into the tasteful wine shop next door and bought a lovely bottle of cabernet, for which I paid sixteen dollars in cash.

I pulled up to the "cottage," which was actually a three bedroom cape surrounded by a birch grove overlooking a smooth-stoned brook. As I stretched, a flight of birds sailed above me, one lone cry sounding out; the distant beat of wings echoing the beat of my heart.

My skin lifted in response to the first chilly drops of rain and I smiled as I found the copper-colored key in the spot in the garden, right where Leila said it would be.

The house smelled faintly of lemon polish and bleach. I began to think about what sort of thank you gift to send her; a welcome diversion from thinking about the fact that I'd never called Michael back. And with every hour that went by, my chance to do so was slipping further and further away. I was caught between regret and relief. But relief, it seemed, was winning.

After putting away the groceries, I found a tall sky-blue ceramic pitcher, which held the sunflower bouquet perfectly. Setting it on the kitchen table, I stepped through the French doors and into the rain. The field behind her garden was filled with late autumn wildflowers and leaves just beginning to turn. My arms full, I came back in, reveling in the feeling of damp skin and hair and the slight chill spreading down my back; an easy, temporary discomfort - one that could be assuaged. Letting the damp seep deeper into my bones, I made an elaborate arrangement for the living room table before going upstairs to unpack.

I didn't even peek inside Leila and her husband's bedroom. I told myself it was because I was respecting their privacy. But the real truth was, I couldn't bear to see the evidence of couple's life - especially, a happy couple's life; anything that might reveal a shared sensuality, or rituals of a marriage that worked. I felt small and petty, but comforted myself with words of praise for the restraint I showed in not snooping. While the tub filled, I poured in some of Leila's honeysuckle bath oil, piled my hair in a messy knot on top of my head, and dropped my clothes to the floor. I tested the temperature, and when it was hot enough, I slid gratefully under the water.

Hot water had been a scarcity, growing up in rental apartments; and even years of suburban living with a generous water heater and the bills to match had not rendered me heedless of this fact.

I had grown accustomed to comfort and ease in a way my mother had never had the opportunity to enjoy. She was barely twenty years old when I was born at the forefront of the Cultural Revolution. My mother entered the sixties with an explosion of her body, propelling not one but two children into the world at a time when doctors allowed women to labor strapped to a bed, then knocked them out with general anesthesia just as the baby crowned. Exhorting a mother to push was an inconvenience easily dispensed of with a jab of a needle. Despite the way women were treated in the birthing rooms, my mother considered the 60s a time of unprecedented freedom, and she was eager to leave behind the stifling social mores of the 1950s, entering an era of idealism and rebellion with all the wild beauty of a Pollock painting.

Communal living, while not something directly participated in by my mother, was of great interest to her. Although she maintained our apartment in Crown Heights as our own, there were various transient friends of hers (or friends of friends) who would sleep on the lumpy cot in our living room, which we used in lieu of a couch. It seemed I lived in a world alternating between a lack of privacy and a deep sense of loneliness; a feeling I'd erased during the years of my marriage and raising children.

Those years of bearded men in and out of my mother's bedroom, the strangers wandering naked from their perches in their living room to our shared bathroom, the loud parties night after night, and the lack of any kind of household order were images I'd stuffed into a messy corner of my mind, whitewashed and forgotten like an old, painted-over canvas. There was nothing real there that could hurt me; just vague memories or ancient scraps of sensation that hit me in moments of weakness - things best left undisturbed and forgotten.

Yet there were moments of sheer beauty back then as well: moments I held onto and integrated into my being. The Metropolitan Museum of Art, for instance. I loved the abstract collection best and can remember standing in the clean, cavernous gallery, the hush of the room its own kind of roar, standing beneath the freedom of Pollock's "Autumn Rhythm (Number 30)". How I was torn between the fierce desire to never take my eyes from it, or to move wildly around the room in an impossible attempt to dance each brush stroke into the air. My mother watched me as if she understood, and I wondered if that was what she had felt when she'd spent her time dancing instead of filing cards and taking care of us.

In the spring of 1970, my mother had me meet her on the front steps of the Brooklyn Museum. Smiling triumphantly at me, she held up two tickets. "Look what someone gave me-- I'm about to change the way you think about dance forever." With her pulling me by the hand, we practically flew down the subway steps and took the short ride to BAM (Brooklyn Academy of Music). I watched Judith Jamison move in a way I'd never imagined possible. It was as if she was dancing outside the parameters of her body, and I could feel it. Alvin Ailey was transforming the world of dance, and in the process, he'd transformed me. I too would experience that flight through space; that majestic grace. The YMCA on Atlantic Avenue had free lessons--all I needed was a subway token and a bag lunch, both of which my mother cheerfully provided. Tragically, I was introduced to my two left feet. I finished the classes through sheer will and determination. Seeing how discouraged I was, my mother enrolled me in a painting class (also free) offered by the Brooklyn Museum. There, I discovered, I could paint the feeling that Alvin Ailey's choreography elicited in me. It may not have been the form of expression I would have chosen, but it was the one that chose me.

The bath water flooded my skin and bones with warmth and lightness and my hair lifted from my scalp and infused the top of my head with a slow, ticklish heat. When I emerged, parting the water with my face and surfacing into chilled air, I wondered if it was possible to paint an absence of heaviness; a state Judith Jamison's long-ago dance had, once upon a time, inspired in me.

Three days went by and I didn't speak to a single living creature. My voice was superfluous, and I didn't use it to keep myself company. I never turned on the television, so the only face I saw was my own, in reflection or those in paintings or photographs scattered around the house. Music was my constant companion--but I even grew weary of lyrics and so began to search out classical and jazz favorites. Once, I peered into the recesses of my mouth, trying to gauge if my throat appeared as dry and crusted-over as it felt.

Food was simple, yet delicious. There were layers of the flavor in figs, which I had never noticed. The creamy texture of cheese suddenly took on a sensuous cast I had never before experienced. The swirl of wine on my tongue and the warm slow trickle in a swallow became almost unbearable--and the tiny groan I emitted cracked my throat.

Yoga, for the first time, became a slow, sensuous act allowing every nerve ending in my body to hum as I moved on the sunlit wooden floor from pose to pose without mirrors or other bodies to distract me, the soles of my feet rooted firmly to the wooden floor, hands opened to the sky. In that moment I felt the fused joints of my hips loosen, space opened between each vertebrae, and something else. It happened while I moved through the three stages of Warrior. My breath flowed through me in a way I'd never experienced, and I was able to move through the poses with a fluidity I'd never experienced before. It was during Warrior III that I felt the surge of adrenaline. And with it came the memories.

I don't remember coming out of the pose. The next thing I knew, I was lying on my back, my palms protected by fists, my breath ragged. The memory unspooled behind my tightly shut lids. My mother, brother, and I were at the yoga studio. I'd been sitting at my mother's side, behind the reception desk where she was working in exchange for taking classes. I watched other women my mother's age come in, bangles clattering and suede handbags swinging as they ordered her around. Feminism hadn't quite reached across the racial or socio-economic brackets.

Sometimes they would come in with their children and they would argue with my mother about the no eating or drinking rules, as they would try to feed their children snacks. "It's an hour-long class," my mother would reason, "and there are no food or beverages allowed in accordance with–"

But she couldn't finish her sentence before one of the myriad of harried mothers would shove raisins at her child and say impatiently "What is this? A police state?" (or some other inflammatory line, which instantly caused my mother to back off).

Eventually it quieted, the dreary winter light faded from the filthy windows, and my mother disappeared gratefully into the depths of the studio with a stern look, letting me know she expected me to color quietly for the hour-long class she would be taking.

Another student came and took her place. He was young; probably in his early twenties. His hair was light brown and fell in soft waves to his shoulders; he had a wispy beard, long fingers with large knuckles, and sad blue eyes. I found him very handsome and stared raptly at him for a full five minutes, which didn't seem to unnerve him in the least. I thought he looked exactly like Jesus Christ - actually, like the painting of Jesus Christ in one of my mother's art books, which showed Mary Magdalene washing his feet. And while I knew he wasn't actually Jesus Christ, I felt the same rush and swell of emotion that I'd had when looking at that portrait in the art book.

Forcing myself to continue with my coloring, I kept my eyes down for a whole section before stealing another glance at him. I was trying to figure out if his eyes were the color of a blue marble or a green one. I had just decided they were a mixture of the two when he caught my eye and smiled.

Standing up so rapidly my head swam, I muttered something nonsensical, then ran toward the last place I'd seen my mother. After pushing through a few doors, I found myself in the women's locker room.

My mother was there with a tall man. They were standing hip to hip. Their lips were touching but not pressed together and he was blowing smoke into her mouth. She reared back, inhaled sharply, and held her breath while his hands roamed over her, cupping the swell of her backside, hovering up her body, and landing on her breast in a way that looked aggressive and painful to me. She, however, smiled and leaned against him. I averted my eyes for a moment, but when I looked back they had separated and he was handing her a baggie filled with what looked like dirt. I'd seen my mother and her friends spread that dirt out onto the top of record albums and sprinkle it onto what looked like squares of rice paper. I knew all about rice paper from my weekly art class at the Brooklyn Museum. I'd also seen my mother and her friends tap that dirt into the bowl of a blue clay pipe she kept in the top drawer of her bureau (with an admonishment that I was to leave it alone).

The following week, when my mother went to work at the museum and I was babysitting Adam, I picked up the blue clay pipe and my favorite gold cigarette lighter next to it. I began my search. The bag of dirt was hidden beneath an old wool cardigan of my father's in the bottom drawer of my mother's dresser. I also found the little squares of rice paper. Reasoning that the clay pipe would be easier to manage then the complicated record-album-rolling-licking-lighting display I'd seen during the frequent parties in our living room, I packed the dirt into the pipe and called Adam away from the elaborate war he was setting among his small army soldiers. It took us a while to figure out how to activate the lighter, which had a childproof mechanism on it. Adam was a keener observer than I and he figured it out faster than I could. When the faint glow of red lit the dirt in the small bowl, I placed my lips around the end of the pipe and took a deep breath, inhaling the way I'd seen my mother do.

Burning my mouth and chest, I coughed for what seemed like an eternity and eventually began to gag and almost throw up. Learning from my mistake, Adam breathed it in much more gently and held the smoke expertly in his mouth before taking it into his lungs and blowing it out slowly. He coughed and sputtered too, his eyes turning red and watery, but not as badly as I had. He offered the pipe back to me with a slow smile, but I shook my head and waved it away. The glow had faded to black and the acrid smell permeated the room, making my head hurt and my stomach roil. Gently, he placed the lighter against the bowl and tried again, a slow smile spreading over his face. He spent the rest of the afternoon glassy-eyed and smiling. He looked like he was floating, and I envied him. Unwittingly, I had fired the shot that would begin his life-long pursuit of that first taste; that elusive sensation he once described as a "lightness of being".

That memory was enough to transform my experience as effectively as a shade being drawn against the light. Pleasure evaporated. Figs were gummy and tasteless, cheese was rancid and pungent, wine as sour as bile reflux. Bathwater was tepid, and an Indian summer had rendered the outdoors a humid, rotting, insect-filled hell.

Packing my things took all of fifteen minutes. Another half an hour was required to scrub all traces of myself from Leila's beautiful home. Soon I was back home, facing a disdainful Bridey. Other than canceling Bridey's pet sitter, I didn't tell anyone where I was. I wasn't due back at work and there were no demands at all on my time, yet I craved an act of physical and mental discipline; a respite from the tsunami of memory and guilt. Propelled with a need greater than my fear of inadequacy and failure, I headed to the fly-infested, stifling, leaky art studio above the garage, which I'd successfully avoided for the better part of a decade.

The paint swirled and accumulated of its own volition beneath my brush, letting the ache in my muscles transform into color and shape. I blended, re-blended, scraped, and diluted until the layers were exactly right; until I had achieved the impenetrable depth and luminescence of the night sky visible above me on my midnight walks.

Building my first square of color took almost two weeks of layering cyan, red, and touches of yellow, allowing each to dry.

I hiked the woods, crossing Route 9 into the Sleepy Hollow Cemetery and up into Pocantico, my camera around my neck; yet I never took a single picture, knowing that somehow I'd be unable to capture the colors I was searching for. The beauty of paint is that you can find it through trial and error, and you can collage an image on your canvas that comes from experiencing all of the world as you walk through it, seeing, touching, and tasting it. Also, by experiencing it through dreaming, imagining, and conjuring it. The canvas can take it all. Hit after hit of bristle and pigment create something that is both real and unreal; imagined and true.

I was searching for the correct mixture of white to create the bony eye socket I was painting into the night sky. The viewer of the painting would never see the color of the bone. It would be covered with brownish tendons, flesh, sclera (a bluer white than the bony socket), infinitesimal red veins, and lashes; so no one would ever see that white bone. Yet I would know it was under there, and it had to be correct or I wouldn't be able to keep going.

I found the perfect rock, the size of a quarter. I'd almost missed it because it was off road. A red-tailed hawk had captured my attention in the open field, soaring in broad wide circles. Without meaning to, I drew closer, mesmerized by the powerful rhythmic motion of its flight. My foot landed unevenly on the ground below, and I looked down automatically. There it was, nestled in the brown-green grass. I picked it up and held it in my palm, feeling its weight. Placing it back against the burned grass, I stared at it, memorizing the color. I knew enough not to take it with me, aware that once it left this place - this light, the bed of dirt and grass—-it would be rendered a different shade of white. Photographing it would be no better. Ruing the weight of the useless camera around my neck I stepped back. The hawk was gone; perhaps with its prey or maybe in a nearby tree, watching over its territory. I hurried home to my studio.

Another week for the white bony socket.

The flesh covering the eye socket was pale and grey and left me wondering if I had painted the eye of something living or partially dead. I'd used ultramarine blue, mixing umber until it turned the pigment of skin I wanted.

The sclera was challenging as I tried for the correct amount of light to make it glisten. Frustrated by failure after failure, I left the studio and went into the kitchen. I knew I had a quart of milk (it had started to sour, not spoil) just a few days off it's due date, and fine for my purposes. Bargaining with God, I opened the drawer where I kept eggs and found four of them.

I now owed God.

When I cracked them, the yolks were flat against the whites, letting me know how long they'd been sitting in my fridge without anyone to cook for. I whisked them into the sour milk, added maple syrup and vanilla, whisked some more, and realized I had yellowed it too much with the vanilla and syrup. Upset for a moment, I rethought it and knew that the sclera I wanted to paint would not be either the blue white of a healthy person or the newness of a child's eyes. The syrupy vanilla color was perfect. Putting the mixture into a baking pan, I slid it into the pre-heated oven at 400 degrees. While it baked, I paced restlessly and attempted a Vinyasa flow of down dog and plank, but my heart raced throughout, throwing off the rhythm of the flow. I began a somewhat frantic search for an old stale pack of cigarettes I thought might be tucked away in a drawer. Slightly relieved I hadn't found them, I heard the ping of the oven.

Pulling the custard out and placing it on the counter, I felt my shoulders settle and my heart slow. Without waiting for it to cool, I walked out the kitchen door, across the overgrown path to the garage, and up the rickety steps to my studio and began to remix the paint until it was the color and texture of the custard.

Another week of waiting. The sheen I was after still wasn't there, so I thinned paint glue with water and applied a careful wash over the sclera.

The yellow cast of the sclera affected the red of the veins, and it took me a while to find the right hue. I had to add more ochre than I'd originally thought. My hand quivered and my arm shook as I began tracing the roadmap of veins from the edges of the eye to the center. I knew the orb of eyeball would be placed above the center and I wanted to compensate by making the exterior lines of vein thicker; almost tubular. Building paint that thin and fine was proving to take more muscle and fine motor skills than I'd anticipated, and I needed to take frequent breaks. These breaks consisted of staring through grimy windows, knowing the light would be vastly improved if I took some vinegar and water to them. The filthy glass served the purpose of muting the full autumn glory, which seemed somehow appropriate to my mood.

At some point in the process, my vacation ended, and I went back to work. My days began at dawn, and I'd paint until I had to get dressed for work, trying futilely to rub all traces of color from my hands. I would wait anxiously for my shift to be over so I could rush home and make the most of what was left of the natural light. Janine noticed how distracted I was and tried to lure me into conversation during our breaks (during which she smoked and I sometimes lit her cigarettes for her in lieu of smoking a full one).

I couldn't explain to her what the process of this painting was doing to me: how exquisitely painful everything felt; how every change in light outside the large block of fluorescence we were living in contracted the space between my left breast and my rib cage. How the thundering of my heart would beat in my ears while I sorted racks of synthetic color and inhaled the chemical of the clothes fresh from the factory; how obsessed I was with imagining brush strokes against canvas and whether or not a movement in one direction or another would create the effect I was trying to obtain.

She thought I'd made a mistake not calling Michael back - that I was pining for him. There were random moments in which I'd remember the shiver he'd sent along my body when his breath whispered against the side of my throat, but I released those thoughts, relegating them to a road not taken and forgetting about it as soon as I stumbled up the steepness of the one I'd chosen.

One rainy Saturday morning, I woke up with a weekend stretching before me, with nothing and no one to answer to except my studio.

I began the process of mixing yellow and magenta, then subtracted light with a touch of black until I was satisfied, covering the infinitesimal delicate red veins, rounding an orb, and adding an invisible fringe of lash, painstakingly blended into a ghostly film of Milky Way.

Finally it was drying in front of me, leaving me spent and free, for the moment, of all other sensation or knowledge.

I named the painting "Mercy."

CHAPTER SEVEN

"When it was dark you carried the sun in your hands for me"
– Sean O'Casey

Back at work the following Monday, I looked, for the thousandth time, at Michael's last text. He had sent it right after I finished the painting--as if he were privy to some uncanny knowledge of me. It read, "Any life is made up of a single moment, the moment in which a man finds out, once and for all, who he is." – Jorge Luis Borges.

I sent nothing back. Nor did I call. How could I? How could I ever explain how completely he seemed to know me - and how frightening I found that? It was either an illusion (and in that case, when he uncovered the real me, he would run screaming from the room)… or he really did have some unworldly understanding of me, and still wanted me - and how messed up was that?

Janine caught me looking at the text again. "Call him, Carly. You know you want to."

I flipped my phone shut and shoved it back into my pocket. The sound was off, and I never carried my phone in my pocket. I just liked looking at the text - a single moment of truth in which I discover who I am. When would that defining moment come?

Or had it happened? Was it a memory…or had it happened the moment I'd finished "Mercy"? And who was the mercy for? Myself? Was I, after all, worthy of mercy? I longed to ask Michael about it, and to discover what his single moment was. But how? How could I talk to him now, after I had let so much time lapse? It didn't seem possible.

Janine looked at me for a long time. I didn't like the sub-text in her stare. Then she spoke it: "You are sabotaging the first good thing to come your way in a long time."

"Thank you, Dr. Phil," I said, in a pretty good and extremely annoying rendition of the way Danielle speaks to me.

"Puh—lese, I am not that creeper. Call me Chelsea."

"Who?"

"Chelsea Handler. She is the only celebrity I would ever take advice from."

"Not Oprah?"

"Hell no!"

"Dr. Drew?"

"He's an ass."

"Well, who's this Chelsea, and what did he write?"

"She. *Are You There, Vodka, It's Me, Chelsea.*"

"Like Judy Blume?"

"Uh huh."

"And it's a self-help book?"

Janine snorted. "Like I would ever read a self-help book. No. It's just funny."

"What would she say about my situation?"

"She wouldn't give a shit."

"Oh.

"But if she did, she'd say, 'you need to go out and get laid'. Get Michael to give it to you good."

"Oh--well."

"Carly, you're blushing. Pathetic."

"Janine, that is just--I don't know--"

"What?"

"Cheap."

"Ha! What do you think your ex is out doing?"

"I don't care what he's doing."

"Good for you."

We went back to sorting racks. When I looked up, Janine was smirking at me.

"What?" I attempted a gruff tone to see if I could get her to back off. Yet there was a part of me that was fascinated by this discussion and the idea that I could just call up Michael and "do him."

She grinned at me. Pure mischief. "You know you want to."

I couldn't help it, I laughed.

"Just do it, Carly. You owe it to yourself."

Chimes rang out, signaling new customers entering the store, and I turned away to greet them, but not before Janine made ridiculous eyebrow contortions at me, which I ignored in order to regain my composure as a sales representative.

* * *

After work, as I was walking to my car, I bumped into Ally in the parking lot. She was navigating her children toward the ice-cream shop. Somehow, she managed to throw her arms around me without letting go of their hands.

"Woman!" she shouted. "You owe me details! Where have you been?"

I laughed. "Working, painting…"

"Well, those texts were very mysterious. How was the date? Did you look super hot?"

"Mommy!" her daughter shrieked. "Ice-cream!"

"You always talk!" Her son pulled her arm.

"Go on," I waved. "We'll catch up later."

She grimaced. "We're moving. Back to the city, I'm happy to say."

"Oh."

"Don't be sad, Carly! You can visit me there. We'll go to museums--have drinks--"

"Our mother is mean!" her little boy said.

She tugged his arm. "Stop it! You're lucky to be moving to the city!"

"ICE CREAM," her daughter shrieked in a voice high enough to make my eardrums bleed.

"I'll Facebook you," Ally said.

"I'll call you!" I promised. I wasn't on Facebook and didn't have any plan to join.

Wanting to be happy for her, I mustered a bright smile and hugged her goodbye. But in a selfish way, I felt like crying. She was the one who got me through my divorce; organized girls' nights out, and let me cry without saying things like *you're free to date now,* or *take him for every cent he's worth.* She never gave me advice unless I asked for it, and she seemed to understand everything I couldn't say. Now she was moving on; starting over. And I was truly happy for her. But I also felt like a needy little brat. I wanted to shout *don't leave me* in an eardrum-splitting wail to rival her daughter's. And yet, I knew she needed to let go of me. I was a reminder of the life she was leaving behind. It was time to put on my big-girl panties and set her free.

* * *

Days later, when it had fully dried, I took Mercy, swaddled gently in bubble wrap, over to the frame shop. Torn between desperation to see Mercy framed and shame at having no shame, I was about to prostrate myself to get it done.

Struggling through the frame shop's door with the large and unwieldy Mercy, I was grateful to see Karen run to help me: all five-feet-two-inches and about one hundred pounds of her. Her hair was pure white, framing her face, setting the black brows and even darker eyes in stark contrast. Unadorned except for a tiny glint of gold in her right nostril, wearing her usual uniform of black T-shirt, worn black corduroys, and black high top converse sneakers, she looked unchanged and welcoming, and I felt a surprising tightness in my throat as she greeted me.

"You've been busy--let's see this baby."

The awkward reality of my bringing a painting in for framing that I had no ability to pay for was temporarily mitigated by the business of settling Mercy in for her first viewing.

Framing an artist's work is a large chunk of Karen's bread and butter, so by necessity, she had become accomplished at praise--not too much to seem obsequious, but enough to induce excitement and pride in the artist. If the painting didn't move her, she would compensate by having deep technical discussions about the process of framing.

I had experienced the gamut of her responses over a twenty-year period, so I was anxious to see, which one, from her stockpile, Mercy would evoke.

Never had I seen Karen go still. She seemed almost furious in her attention, and I wondered if somehow the piece was offensive.

Propped on the counter, Mercy took on an entirely new dimension. When I conceptualized the orb, I imagined it would be looking down upon me, but I had failed in this mission and the effect was to have it gazing right at me… and while I expected to be disappointed by this perspective, I wasn't. Mercy's gaze was a bright burn; a reflection in the abyss.

Karen turned toward me, clasped my hands in her rough ones, and kissed me gently on the cheek, almost like a lover saying a final good bye.

"This is your best work, Carly. The piece you've been waiting for."

"I ... ummm ..." There was no way I could respond to that. It was too much. "I had different ideas for framing it."

"Tell me."

"Well, the subject was seen through a skylight, but I don't want a literal interpretation of that..."

Karen nodded, waiting for me to continue. I knew she had a million ideas swirling in her head, but she didn't want to influence me. She wanted to understand my vision first, which, of course, I couldn't articulate sensibly at all.

"Nothing too trendy...a modern material, but nothing cold, and nothing that evokes aerospace--rockets or airplanes--"

"Are you against scavenged material?"

"No--I just don't want it to be wood that evokes a window frame, and I would like it to float..."

"You want a loose boundary."

"Exactly! But a definitive one."

Karen disappeared into the back. Rummaging noises, some clattering, and then she called out, "I'll be right back," and I heard the screen door into the back parking lot open and shut.

An unnerving ripping sound was coming from out back. I was about to go investigate when Karen came struggling in. I rushed to help her with pieces of battered, blackened material which looked suspiciously like roof gutter. I looked at her. She gazed calmly back at me. "They were loose."

"Karen!"

"They were loose."

She pushed past me and began setting up. "Of course, I'll have to cut them down and finish the ends, I'm thinking about four to six inches of floating paper behind the canvas--how does this silver look? The sky really pops--and the jagged, familiar yet unrecognizable material to frame it...a reference to a roof above... without impairment to our vision; solid, but transparent..."

She was brilliant. She had discovered the perfect container to hold the uncontainable.

Excitement quickly gave way to a familiar post-divorce anxiety. Finances. This frame job was going to require sawing and soldering and apparently an entirely new roof gutter for the shop--it would be expensive.

"It sounds expensive..."

"Not too bad. I'm not charging you for materials, obviously."

"You need to replace--"

"I was doing that, regardless."

" —-the labor."

"We've done worse damage, you and me. I figure it will run around $650."

A bargain, actually, for a piece this size. But still - it was six hundred and fifty dollars I didn't have, and I would have to log many more Mandee's hours to get it.

"Karen, it's a great price. Generous, really. It's just ... since the divorce..."

She nodded. "I get it."

We sat in silence for a while. Strangely, it wasn't awkward. It was the same silence we engaged in when trying to decide on matte color or frame materials.

"Jordan quit."

"Really?" Jordan was the 26-year-old multiply-pierced art student who had been working for Karen the past three years.

"Yep. She's following her boyfriend out to Santa Fe."

"Will she show, out there?"

"She's planning on it."

"So that's a good thing."

"Yep. Her hours were Wednesday to Friday, three to eight, and ten to six on Saturdays."

"I could do that." It would mean coming right here from Mandee's, but that was convenient--and what else was I doing? I could paint on Sunday and Monday. And I wouldn't even have to change my yoga schedule.

"I'll train you on the specifics, but you know everything you need to."

With a smile and a handshake, it was done. I had managed to obtain two jobs in a little over a month. Danielle was going to be extremely impressed.

Sleep that night came easier than expected. The exhilaration of finishing Mercy was tempered by putting her in Karen's hands--like the nurse in the hospital taking my milk-fed blissful baby from my swollen nipple, when I commanded a much-needed rest. Exhilaration was uncomfortable for me. I craved complacency. Giving Mercy over to Karen allowed me to close my eyes and imagine my next painting--the thank you gift for Leila. It would be the view of the red maple from her kitchen window, a smolder of leaves in late October sunlight. I visualized which paints I would mix for that specific illumination; the tiny brush strokes needed for each leaf. Maybe, I thought before drifting off, I would see it in my dreams.

Instead, I dreamt of climbing fire escapes at night - one after another, from my building on Crown Street, over the courtyard and up onto the buildings along Washington Avenue; scrambling, fearful, and certain that each one would bring me home. But they never did. I was encumbered with heavy clothing, and toward the end of the dream, I was carrying my brother. He was slipping and I feared he would fall through the iron steps and be crushed against the pavement below. Holding him against my chest, I tried sinking flat against the platform, wondering if I could hoist him, then myself, over the low barrier to the roof where we could lie in safety against the wide expanse of tar and gaze up at the midnight sky.

Longing to lie down, I relaxed my hold and felt him slide away from me and I woke up gasping, alone in my room, my throat on fire and the distant sound of the train rattling the radiator. The two a.m. Amtrak hurtled by, saving me from my dream.

Daybreak, in late October, is the most beautiful light in the world. There would be no more sleep for me after that dream, so at first light I stretched, layered myself in cotton and wool, prepared a thermos of hot coffee, and walked down to the railroad tracks overlooking the grey-green expanse of river. Clouds were rolling in, lit by the ascending sun, turning the sky a raw, meaty pink.

I had my camera slung around my neck, a sketchpad, charcoal, and soft sunrise-colored pastels. But I couldn't touch any of them. I placed the supplies on a rock to protect them from the sodden ground and removed the weight of the camera from my neck, nestling it on my backpack. Wrapping my scarf tighter around my neck, I opened the thermos of sweet black coffee and sipped it.

When my cell phone rang, I considered not answering it; especially when the ring tone ('Fuck You Too'--yeah, I know it's called 'Forget You', but I prefer the first name, and that's the part that plays--and yes, it's very rude and immature--but so am I). "Hi, Scott."

"Hey. Just checking about Thanksgiving."

"What about it?"

"We agreed we would have it together, as a family."

Scott and I, in a haze of guilt about the children, had agreed that for the first year of our divorce we would have all the holidays together as a family so the children would not feel torn between having to choose which of us to celebrate with. It had seemed like a good idea at the time.

"You're welcome to come. My mother and brother are coming, too."

"Do they know I'll be there?"

"Yes."

"Will they be civil to me?"

"I assume so."

"I'd like to bring a guest."

Now we were getting to the real reason for the call. "Really, Scott? You'd like to bring your flavor of the month to Thanksgiving dinner?"

"I'm seeing somebody seriously now, Carly."

"Is she old enough to drink?"

"I think you'll like her."

"Scott, I don't need to like her; you do. She's your girlfriend."

"Fiancée. Her name is Merry"

"Mary? As in the virgin?"

"*Merry*." His voice softened, as if I were still his confidante; the recipient of pillow talk. "I never expected to feel like this again, you know? It just—happened."

"Um. Okay, well this should be interesting. Dinner's at three. See you and the merry virgin then."

"*Merry*! Short for Meredith—-and the kids love her!"

I placed the phone down gently and stood looking out into the yard. It was beautiful: a topsy-turvy world of leaves on the ground and a sky absent of color above.

Slipping into my garden clogs, I went out the front door with a trowel and burlap. It was past time to bring the Dahlia bulbs in for winter. Engrossed in my work, I didn't see anyone approaching, so it startled me to feel a hand on my shoulder and a familiar voice say my name. Sharon Barlow. She and her husband Frank were our pre-divorce best friends. Scott had gotten them.

I stood up and returned Sharon's awkward hug.

"Carly, I was hoping I'd bump into you."

I just smiled at her. I didn't know what to say to that.

"Do you remember that night at the club? We were in the ladies room?"

I knew the evening she was referring to. It was years ago, before I had any knowledge that my marriage was in trouble.

Sharon had asked me if I was happily married. We were applying lip gloss and I'd caught her eye in the mirror.

"Sure", I answered. "Aren't you?"

"No," she said, looking away. "I'm not. There's just--nothing between us."

"But," I rushed to assure her, "you're so cute together. Frank adores you! And you throw the best parties." Idiotic, I know.

"Carly, that isn't happiness. Define a happy marriage."

"I don't know. It works well enough, I guess--I mean, we have our problems like everyone else--but..."

"But what? You love him?"

"Of course. He's my husband."

"Really? That's what you love about him?"

"Well, I don't know--I'm used to him."

"Wow. There's an endorsement for marriage."

"Where is this coming from?"

Sharon gave me a sideways look in the mirror. "There's a cute guy at the gym--he's been flirting with me."

I shrugged. But I was shocked. "So, flirt back." But I didn't mean it. *That was a slippery slope*, I thought. It would lead to embarrassment, recriminations. So much safer to ignore it.

"I have been, and it's amazing. I feel--on fire."

I watched her in the mirror. She did look beautiful, as if she knew she was desired. "Your eggs," I told her. "They're dropping indiscriminately. They know it's their last chance. It's not your fault."

She laughed. "Carly, I'm happy about it. I'm thinking about leaving Frank."

"Don't be hasty!" I practically yelped. "This thing will burn itself out and you'll be sorry."

She shrugged. "Maybe." Her lip gloss was perfect. She shook her hair over her shoulders. "Hair extensions. Frank didn't even notice--but my guy loved them."

"You look great." And I meant it. She did. But I was sorry for her. She seemed--unsteady. And that was frightening to me. The funny thing is, she and Frank are still together. As far as I know, that flirtation never amounted to anything more than that.

Looking at Sharon now, there was no sign of the hair extensions. Even the duck lips from the collagen applications had subsided and she had the same wry sideways smile I remembered and missed during those years of non-moving puffy lips. There were new lines around her eyes and on her forehead and the creases on the sides of her mouth were deeper. She looked more beautiful than I'd ever seen her.

As much as I longed to haul her into my kitchen for tea and to catch up with everything that was going on in her life, I felt frozen with indecision. So much time had passed. It was as if we were strangers, despite the familiar pressure of her hands as she grabbed one of mine in both of hers.

"Carly, I need you to know—-you helped me so much, that night. All our other friends were pushing me forward. Either they wanted me to join them in cheating on their husbands, or pave the way for them to do it. But you were shocked. And you had such good common sense. And I realized, *what am I doing*? I love Frank, so what if he's a little boring? We have a life together."

"I'm sorry I haven't called," Sharon gushed. "It's just been so awkward for the boys. Scott and Frank do business together, and I can't rock that boat. You understand, right?"

NO! I thought. *I don't. We raised our children together. We drank endless cups of tea together, hosted dinner parties together, went on family vacations together. I DO NOT UNDERSTAND AT ALL!*

"Of course." I said. "It's been difficult for everybody."

"Oh, Carly." She pulled me close. "This has been the hardest thing I've ever gone through. When you and Scott split up, it threw everyone for a loop. Nothing's been the same. And I miss you."

"Oh," I said, as brightly as I could. "Well, here I am."

She pulled me to her again, wiped her tears, promised to call (even though we both knew she wouldn't), and walked away.

In a moment surprisingly absent of fear, I understood something which had been pressing against my consciousness, seeping through in memory and dreams. My grand scheme, concocted as a small girl in the grip of deprivation and loss when my father walked out on us, hadn't worked out. I had planned to grow up to be a good wife. I'd made an unspoken promise to raise my own children with security and safety, tucking them into beds with matching sheets and top sheets and coordinating quilts. Hot water would be plentiful for regular showering. Food would line the refrigerator and cabinet shelves. Their clothes would be bought new from department stores instead of handed down or collected from a John's Bargain Store bin. I would cross tunnels and bridges, heading into the leafy suburbs, as far away from Brooklyn as I could get. My plan, executed perfectly, had failed. And it was time to let go of the bits and pieces of it. I needed to move forward in a new direction. Sharon said I had helped her, and unwittingly, she had just helped me. Even if it meant we were lost to one another.

Before I could change my mind, I went inside and called the realtor who'd been drooling over my house since the day the moving truck took Scott to his bachelor pad in New York City. I gave her the listing and set myself free.

CHAPTER EIGHT

"Your living is determined not so much by what life brings to you as by the attitude you bring to life; not so much by what happens to you as by the way your mind looks at what happens"
– Khalil Gibran

It had been two weeks since I decided to sell the house, and I had done precisely nothing...except hire a man with a van to cart out a lifetime of detritus from the attic, garage, and crawlspace beneath the house. The consequence of such a junk-free house made me reconsider the idea of selling at all, but another weekend spent alone, prowling the large dark rooms, had me re-convinced to put it on the market. I imagined a light, airy two- or three-bedroom somewhere in the inner village and an end to the pit in my stomach whenever I sat down to pay the bills.

All the clearing and sorting had provided an excellent distraction from the thought of Thanksgiving, which was now eight days away.

Which in turn, was a perfect reason not to attend "girls' night out".

I had just delivered this indefectible excuse to Janine. We were standing in the grimy back alley of Mandee's, gleaning whatever warmth we could from cardboard cups of steaming coffee.

Janine slid a Marlboro Light out of her pack and brandished a blinged-out lighter while she laid a guilt trip on me. "Have you met me? I am a single mother with no date and a free babysitter Friday night. If you don't come out with me, you are officially the worst friend ever."

She managed to light her cigarette, blow smoke out of the side of her mouth, and glare at me in one fluid motion.

I took a sip of my coffee and eyed her right back. I knew she had a bevy of girlfriends to go out with.

"No. Uh-uh." She waved her lighter around for effect. "I know what you're thinking. My son has to be at playgroup at nine am. I can't be going out with my slutty friends! They'll be partying all night! I need an evening out with good food, a nice bottle of wine, and a few laughs."

"Hmmph. You sound like you're fifty years old."

"Maybe I do--which is why I need an old lady like you to hang out with me."

"Wow. Flattery isn't your best attribute."

"Flattery would never work with you, Carly."

"That's flattering in and of itself."

She grinned her most evil grin. "Do you need a new outfit? 'Cause you can't keep wearing the same thing you bought last time--you can't just throw a cardigan over it and wear boots instead of sandals. Ew."

"Whatever," I said in my best Danielle imitation. Janine rolled her eyes, flicked her cigarette to the ground, and crushed it with the pointed toe of her hot pink pumps. I found myself wishing I could wear them.

She must have seen it in my eyes, which annihilated any hope of a quiet pity party for myself, home alone on Friday night.

In between customers, Janine began shoving me into the dressing room, armed with ridiculous outfits.

"Put this on- - - and these!" she barked at one point. And I found myself in a sequined skin-tight mini dress with giant red platform heels.

"What?" She turned her hands up in the universal symbol of innocence. "Red and silver are gorgeous together. You can't do silver and silver. That's tacky."

"Really? Silver shoes would put me over the edge? A 49-year-old woman in a dress even a Kardashian wouldn't wear isn't the problem?"

"Carly, you look HOT in that dress."

I don't understand why I put it on in the first place. Janine's bossiness had a scary effect on my judgment.

"Janine, there is no way I will ever wear this. Ever."

"Fine!" She thrust a pewter-colored silk (faux silk, but smooth and cool and lovely in its own way) dress at me. "Put this on." It draped nicely and hit me at the top of my knee, which she well knew was my preferred length. I began to suspect the sparkle dress was a ruse to get me to appreciate this one.

I looked at her and couldn't help smiling. She smiled back and kicked off her shoes. "Try these on."

"Pink and grey?"

"Live dangerously," she said in her most sarcastic way. In spite of myself, I slid into them. They fit, I could walk in them, and I was in love. "They're yours." Janine winked at me and slid her feet into the red ones, which had made me look like a sad and aging call girl, but made her look--confident. It was, I realized, all in the strut.

Unfortunately, the store was pretty empty for the rest of our shift, so I was draped in a variety of large hoops, statement rhinestone necklaces, imitation animal print hand-bags, and loud bracelets that bumped painfully against my protruding wrist bones.

"Enough!" I shouted. "I will take these silver hoops and this giant bling-ring, and that is it!"

"Fine." She swooped the rest of the stuff away, and I realized she'd scored a victory by getting me to wear the ridiculously large "pointer" ring. I could tell by the smug look she wore until the end of our shift.

While driving toward home (which takes about 8 minutes), the lightness Janine had inspired in me began to dissipate, leaving me with a mixture of excited anticipation and gnawing anxiety.

I took comfort in the notion that the change in my mood was no more than an echo of the natural world around me. November light has a way of dramatically shifting, and the day had been spectacular in its variations of wind.

I drove home along the river just as day began to descend into night. The fading light over the river was something I'd been trying to capture on my color palette, and I'd been unsuccessful and frustrated. But there was something about this light that gave me hope, and I wondered if I would be able to capture it if I added a touch more violet. The flat quality of the small painting I'd been working on was, I felt certain, something I could alleviate with more light and texture, and I wondered if I had time to head into the studio before getting ready. Positive I wouldn't be able to concentrate on anything else until I'd tried, I allowed myself an hour in the cold studio, squeezing, mixing, and applying paint in an approximation of the sky above the mountains and the Hudson River. It would be impossible to tell until it dried if the violet had been exactly right or a terrible mistake. I was stiff and sore from the cold, and I headed across the garden toward the warmth of the kitchen.

* * *

Bridey, as expected, vibrated against me, winding in and out of my legs in a touching display of gratitude. Bending down, I kissed her tiny triangular pink nose and scratched her ears.

The phone rang sudden and loud.

"Mother?" It was Danielle. And she was using her officious voice. "Please tell me you didn't invite Dad's--whatever she is--to Thanksgiving dinner."

"We're still a family."

"Ugh. What's-her-name is awful. She wears twinsets and speaks with a fake British accent."

"How do you know it's fake?"

"She's from Ohio."

"Maybe she went to boarding school."

"That's ridiculous, Mother. And why are you defending her?"

"Has she done anything to offend you?"

"She wears pearls with her twinset. She looks like a suburban housewife from the 50s."

"Ha. Just what your dad always wanted. Good for him."

"She's twenty-five."

"Dani, I'm sure you're exaggerating."

"I saw her license."

"Oh. Well."

"It's disgusting, Mother."

What was I supposed to say to that? *It sure is, especially for her? She clearly has a daddy complex and she's fulfilling it with your daddy*? I said, "Dani, I didn't know you felt this way. He told me you love her."

"He is such a liar."

I felt like saying, *no shit, Sherlock*. But I said, "Dani, honey, I'll tell him not to bring her. I don't want you to be upset."

"No, you can't. It will make you look petty. And he knows it. God, he's such an asshole."

"Oh, Dani. "

"He is, Mom. Don't defend him."

"I'm sorry that you've been exposed to…this ugliness."

"It isn't your fault. You were 22 when you married him and I'm sure you thought it was a good idea at the time."

I snorted.

"It's gross. Dylan drools over her. Thinks she's *classy*, ew."

"Well, at least he won't be unhappy she's coming."

"Oh, are we looking on the bright side? Okay. I won't have to take a break from my diet. I'll be too nauseous to eat."

"Dani, are you dieting? You were so thin the last time I saw you."

"Don't worry; in my industry, I'm practically obese. And I eat more than anyone I know. I was only kidding about taking a break from my diet. I take breaks all day long. Pizza breaks. Chocolate chip cookie breaks. I'm awesome that way. Oh, Mom, make your chestnut stuffing. The "fiancée," as Dad disgustingly refers to her, is deathly allergic. Gotta go. Love you!"

I woke up the next morning and my conversation with Dani was the first thing that popped into my head - that and the fact that it was now seven days until Thanksgiving. Immediately, I began to imagine all the things that could go wrong. Scott picking on Dylan, my mother being rude to Scott, Dani feeling torn between her dad and me, a dry turkey, lumpy gravy, Scott's criticism, Adam shooting up in the bathroom—-the possibilities were endless. I decided to see what Joanna was doing for Thanksgiving. Neither she nor her boyfriend, Jake, had family to go to. Maybe everyone would be on their best behavior if we had "company". But what if Jake and Joanna weren't a deterrent and instead were to bear witness? What if Jake caught Adam shooting up and had to arrest him! He is a cop, after all. I would just have to warn Adam not to use while he was here. I threw the covers off and tried to literally and figuratively center myself in the middle of my bedroom while Bridey quietly judged me from the foot of the bed.

Let it go, I chanted, breathing deeply as I stretched from downward dog to plank. *It will be ok,* I told myself, stepping under the steaming shower and distracting myself with scalding water and the pinking up of my flesh. *Don't let Bitter Vituperative Woman take hold of you,* I warned as I slid into my warmest sweater with the least amount of pills and pulls. *You can't control everyone,* I reminded myself as I rejected the comfy Uggs I had splurged on for the more stylish, but slightly pinching, black leather boots with the moderate heel. I rubbed the spot on my stomach right above the place the pit had settled, shoved myself into my coat, grabbed my car keys, and went out into the wet morning.

Keeping busy was simple. Errands I had been putting off, my usual shift at Mandee's, a few hours at the frame shop, and I was home again, facing my makeup mirror. Friday night came quickly, with no reprieve.

I piled on two extra coats of mascara and put highlighter in the corners of my eyes to make them "widen" - advice I read in a women's magazine online at the drugstore. I had actually gotten off of the line to pick up the magical powder and some other embarrassing impulse purchases like press-on nails, feminine hygiene wipes in a delicate floral scent, and lip plumper.

Fully armed in drugstore war paint and pushup bra artillery, I went downstairs to wait for the car service. Janine and I agreed that we wanted the option of multiple glasses of wine and didn't want to wind up splashed across the newspapers as drunk-driving housewives.

The car smelled heavily of cologne and air freshener. The driver was on a headset, arguing with someone (his daughter, I think; about a concert she wanted to attend). He was punctuating alarmingly with his hands while driving and changing lanes along the narrow ridge of Route 9 without so much as a glance in his rearview mirror. Depositing me in front of the restaurant, he demanded 28 dollars for a ten-minute ride and raced off. Grateful to be out of the car, I lifted my face up to the gentle mist falling from the sky. Who cared if my hair frizzed and my carefully-applied mascara ran? I stood there letting the nausea and profuse underarm sweating engendered by the car ride from hell subside before going inside.

Inelegantly, I maneuvered through the restaurant, shrugged off my coat, and searched the bar for Janine. I wasn't disappointed. She had obtained two prime seats at the three-deep bar, holding a cocktail and looking fabulous in an outrageously short skirt, thigh-high boots, and a sparkling cowl-necked sweater the likes of which I hadn't seen since the early 80s.

Squeezing in next to her, I gratefully accepted a pale pink cocktail, clinked glasses with her, and sipped.

"You look gorgeous," Janine said, loud enough for the two guys next to her to turn around and appraise me themselves. Clearly unimpressed, they turned back to their buddies.

"Shh," I said.

She just laughed. "Our table should be ready in about half an hour, plenty of time to get our drink on."

As if on cue, the bartender was back in front of us, grinning at Janine. And she was smiling back.

"Hey, pretty ladies," he said to both of us while staring at Janine. "Ready for another?"

"I'm just starting on this one."

Somehow he managed to bring Janine a new glass frosted and chilled, pouring her a drink without breaking his gaze. *Hmm,* I thought. *Sexy.*

When he left to tend the other side of his bar, Janine turned to me with an evil grin. "Hot, right?"

"Yes. And totally into you."

"You think?"

"I *know.*"

"His name is Gary. We went to the same high school. He knew my husband."

"Okay."

"I feel disloyal."

"You're going to feel that way no matter who you date."

"I don't think Tommy liked him much."

"Why not?"

Janine shrugged. "Tommy was into sports. And Gary wasn't. He was kind of nerdy. And he played in the marching band. I don't know. It sounds so superficial." She looked over at Gary, who was handling a rowdy group of women clearly having their girls' night out. "Gary's super-smart. He's going to grad school. This bartending gig is paying for it. Physics."

"Wow."

"He didn't have that body in high school. Late bloomer, I guess."

"It happens."

"What if he asks me out?"

"You should go."

"You think?"

"Absolutely. If there's anything left of him." I jutted my chin as a woman whom I knew to be the president of the Hockey Boosters took Gary by his T-shirt and dragged him into a lip-lock, her enormous wedding rings glinting in the bar light.

Boisterous yelps from the rest of the booster squad and a few catcalls from the aging bros erupted next to me. The bar scene was getting ugly and I yearned for our table and a crisp glass of Sauvignon blanc. I placed the strong sticky cocktail on the bar. Janine rolled her eyes. "I'm starved. Let's go eat."

I saw Gary turn around and catch Janine's eye before we made our way around to the hostess. I allowed myself a tiny wriggle of hope for Janine. A tiny swift breath inside me whispered, *you too. You can have it, too.*

Just then, as if God had heard me and decided to play a horrible joke, we bumped smack into Michael D'Angelo and his date.

How do I know it was his date and not his sister? Or cousin? Because I know he's not Creepy Incest Guy. And this woman's breasts were forming an indentation against his arm. Small, curvy, and blonde: my worst nightmare.

"Hey," I said, backing off his shoe. "Sorry. Crowded..."

"Carly." His eyes seized mine.

Janine stepped forward, aggressively sticking her hand out and grinning from ear to ear. "Janine."

"Yes," I repeated in a semi-stupor. "This is Janine. Janine, this is Michael. D'Angelo."

Michael shook her hand, dislodging his date's breast from his arm. "Pleasure to meet you. Pammy, this is Carly and, umm, Janine."

We stood looking awkwardly at one another.

"So...," We all said at once, except Pammy who was pouting her lips and looking up at Michael from (based on my recent perusal of magazine articles about makeup application) expertly-applied lashes. In fact, they may have been individual lashes stuck on with tweezers and glue. Impressive. I would certainly have lost an eyeball attempting it.

"We were just leaving. Hope you enjoy your dinner. The food is really good." Michael lifted his hand, as if to touch my hair, then caught himself and pulled away, "You, um, changed your hair."

This was true. Janine had dragged me to her salon and pinned me to the chair for two excruciating hours. My hair was now the same honey-color as it was when I was six years old. It swayed around me and brushed my cheeks and neck and the very top of my shoulders with a light sensuous tickle. I'd taken to wearing wide V-necks just to feel it, and I was dangerously close to becoming one of those people always checking shiny surfaces to catch a glimpse of themselves.

"Well," Michael smiled at me, causing an unfamiliar hitch in my breath, "it's an improvement." With that, he extricated himself and Pammy, leaving Janine and me to make our way to the table.

"A glass of Sauvignon blanc, please." I used my brightest voice for the waiter. I couldn't look at Janine. Horrifying as the meeting was, this was worse. I actually felt tears pushing up behind my eyes.

Janine put her hand over mine. "A part of you thought he was going to wait it out, right?"

"Don't be kind. I'll cry. Say something mean."

"He's short?"

"Not about him! And he's not short!"

"She looks like a troll?"

I grinned. "I meant about me being an ass. But thanks."

My wine came. It was perfectly chilled. I sipped delicately, letting the flavor burst over my tongue, waiting for numbness. "I am an ass. He was the first good thing to come my way in so long and I sabotaged it."

"You weren't ready."

"He's cute, right?"

"For an old guy."

I laughed. "I hope he and Pammy are very happy together."

"No you don't."

"Okay, I'm a total bitch. I don't."

"He's still into you."

"They were glued to one another. Must be his M. O.," I said, bitterly and vituperatively, remembering the way his hips had lined up with mine at the bar and the shiver I'd felt when his lips brushed the side of my throat when he'd helped slide me into my coat.

"She was glued to him. Not the same."

"Whatever. It's done now."

Janine gave me the eyeball. "We'll see."

Just then the group of booster moms made an entrance, sparkling with enough gloss and glitter to rival any young pop star. Their voices, trying to outdo one another, rang out in the quiet dining room.

After a few minutes, Janine gave up on any pretense of surreptitious glances and just turned to watch them.

Barbara, the president-hockey-booster-mom, was on top of the table badgering the waiter to turn up the music. I felt sorry for him. The hockey moms were spending a great deal of money, having already run up a bar tab that would feed the waiter-guy's family for a month. They were so wasted they didn't realize that the other restaurant patrons weren't finding them as amusing as they found themselves.

A slightly overweight, but sexy-looking, brunette clambered onto the table next to Barbara. The others hastily began moving dishes out of the way. A tall skinny blonde with Barbie boobs and collagened duck lips began egging her on.

"Go, Christie, it's your birthday! Go Christie!"

Soon the others began chanting with her and Christie began to crawl around on the tabletop doing a terrible approximation of Baby from *Dirty Dancing*. Barbara took one look at her and decided to up the ante. She turned to the waiter, who looked like he might break down sobbing any minute.

"You!" She pointed at him and wiggled her hips, then her breasts, in a most riveting shimmy. "I wanna fly!"

"Do it! Do it!" The hockey moms began chanting.

Barbara poised herself to leap off the table into his outstretched arms while the brunette crawled over to him and was busy making growling noises and trying to bite his earlobe. He was trying to avoid her by pulling away from the table and she was perilously close to falling off. From our seats, Janine and I had a full-on shot of her flesh-colored Spanx. The duck lip lady was jumping up and down, clapping and screeching,"fly, fly!"

Eventually reinforcements came in the form of the front-house manager. Deftly he coerced Barbara from the tabletop without breaking any dishes or bones, although I did see her Louboutin boot land sloppily in a bowl of salsa. He then managed to flatter them and shut them up at the same time by offering them the private room in the back of the restaurant, which was usually rented out for parties; but they could have it gratis.

Barbara and the other women were torn between the offer of VIP service and keeping an audience. Looking around and perhaps seeing the hostile glares directed at them through their alcohol-induced haze of euphoria, Barbara made a decision. "Will you and that hottie bartender be joining us?"

And with that question, the show ended. The women filed out, laughing, leaning into one another, and sloshing cocktails they refused to hand over to the beleaguered waiter to carry on his tray.

Janine rolled her eyes. "I can't compete with them."

"You don't have to. Gary will go in there, humor them, and earn a semester of tuition. But he isn't interested in hitting any of that."

"Did you just say that?"

"A lot of young guys are into the whole cougar thing, but he isn't. Believe me, I know the difference. You won't see him tonight. He has his hands full with them, pun intended, but he'll call you, I promise."

"Huh. We'll see." Determined not to waste her evening out, Janine smiled and whipped open the dessert menu. "I'm excited for crème brulee!"

I laughed and picked up my menu, I felt warm and light from the excellent wine and pleasantly full from the fish and vegetables I'd eaten; and if I felt a twinge in that spot beneath my left breastbone when I thought of Michael kissing Pammy good-night (or worse, sleeping in her bed), well, I'd pushed away worse pain.

"The apple crisp, please? With chocolate ice cream."

"One crème brulee and one apple crisp. Wonderful choices." The waiter smiled at us, and whether it was deep gratitude that he wasn't in the back room with the moms gone wild or if he just had a polished professionalism to him, it didn't matter to us. Janine and I smiled, raised our glasses, and toasted one another.

Ridiculous fantasies popped into my head as soon as Janine and I parted. The much-improved car ride home lent itself to the daydream of Michael waiting on my front porch when I pulled up.

"I couldn't stay away," he'd whisper urgently but smoothly. Like an erotic tango, we'd get ourselves into the front door and he'd take me right there in the dark, cold hallway up against the wall.

When the car service dropped me off to a barren front porch, I shook my head at myself. Unlocking the front door to a needy and winding cat, I fed her and went upstairs to wash off my makeup and brush my teeth. I stripped my clothes into a heap on the bathroom floor and slid beneath the covers, waiting for exhaustion and disappointment to dissipate into sleep. Soon Bridey came up and leapt onto Scott's side of the bed where she curled up and purred herself to sleep.

Waking before dawn, I wrapped myself in layers of clothes, prepared a thermos of coffee, and strode out to the dark morning. The air was crisp and I walked quickly, the thermos tucked against my ribs, radiating warmth through my jacket.

I was embarrassed to be inside my own head. Three times I thought I saw Michael. Once it was a tree, once a forgotten Halloween scarecrow at the edge of someone's lawn, and once, a woman walking from town to nanny a neighbor's child.

As morning broke, I was striding along the Hudson River. Below me was the spot Caroline and I had rolled around, grabbing each other for purchase to beat the other down.

I averted my gaze and made my way down the path toward the point. Unbidden, a full fantasy popped into my head as if a memory, vivid and bold.

Michael is waiting for me on the point. When I walk up to him, he touches the side of my face. When he speaks, his eyes are holding mine. "I've missed you."

I don't have to answer. He is magical Michael, reading only the thoughts I want him to without any messy explanations from me. He knows what is in my heart. He did, after all, text me the Borges quote: the single moment of truth when a person discovers who they are.

Then the fantasy took an ugly turn, without my being able to control it. *What the fuck?* I wondered. *Can't I even control my own daydreams?* I push my lips to his, but instead of feeling his kiss, I hear myself say, "Want to come to Thanksgiving dinner at my house?"

He looks at me with the same compassionate knowledge he had during our first meeting in the grocery store. "Oh, I get it, your ex is coming and he's bringing someone."

"His fiancée," I mutter pathetically. "She's 25."

"And you want me there for moral support? To show him you're still desirable?"

"Uh-huh." I agree, equal parts stupid and grateful.

He grins, slow and sexy. "Yeah, well, I'm not that guy."

"I understand," I whisper.

"And I didn't deserve the cold shoulder you gave me."

"Agreed," I say.

"Next time, woman up and be straight with me."

"I couldn't trust myself to talk to you. I knew I'd see you again"

"How is that a bad thing?"

"It just is."

And that was as far as I got. I would try to start over. But it always went south. Even my daydreams sucked.

I headed across the sparse sand and rock and reached the point. No Michael. I balanced on the point, untethered, as if the wind could lift me up to the turbulent sky and release me into the choppy river. My mother's words came back to me. It was during a conversation right after my divorce: "Carly, consider medication. I don't like the way you're speaking - some anti-depressants, maybe?"

But the thought of all the side effects, and the image of my brother jonesing on the floor in a fetal ball of aching bones and clammy skin, caused me to reject the idea for the gazillionth time.

Sitting on the point overlooking the river, a merciless wind brushed my skin raw. Now and then breaking waves cast a fine cold spray, causing me to clench my hands around the thermos and sip.

"Just lean forward a little bit," the voice inside me whispered, "and let go, and then it will all be over. It won't be quick; it will hurt you and scare you, but you can take pain. You know fear. You can handle it, because then it will all be black. Smooth, silky, sexy, black nothingness. Blissful sleep for eternity."

"Whoa," I said out loud to clear out the horrible little voice and regain my footing. Even Bitter Vituperative Woman is better than Crazy Dark Little Girl. She'd been with me for a long time. But I was stronger than she, and there was nothing she could bring that I hadn't flung back at her.

* * *

Once, right around the time of my tenth birthday, my mother was taking us home from one of our pilgrimages to Broadway. We'd gone to see a friend of hers who was dancing in Pippin. My mother nearly swooned when first Ben Vereen, then Jill Clayburgh, stopped and chatted to us outside the dressing rooms (which were smaller and messier then I'd imagined.) Ben Vereen had placed his hand on my brother's head and my mother joked that Adam had been anointed the next star of his generation. I'd been captivated by the show and felt strangely disoriented meeting them in the cramped and narrow corridors back stage. They were as ordinary as any two people on the street, although their faces were thick with greasepaint and there were half-moons of sweat staining the fabric of their costumes. Perhaps my mother felt the same disenchantment I did, or perhaps the reality of leaving the theatre and returning to her drab and desperate life as an impoverished single mother set in, but as soon as we headed down the subway stairs, her mood shifted and she grew irritable and sharp.

At one point I was dawdling, lost in a reverie of floating jazz hands, Ben Vereen's handsome face, and a desire to live in a world where there was "magic to do—-just for you". I was imagining myself moving effortlessly across the stage, my hips undulating, holding my palms up, fingers spread at a forty-five degree angle from my hips in my best Bob Fosse approximation when my mother, her lips thin and eyes flashing, grabbed my arm and pulled me behind her. "Wake up, Carly," she'd hissed. "We're in the god-damn subway—-not la la land." Adam winked at me behind her back and made the toking sign, pinching his forefinger and thumb to his pursed lips—-a signal that he'd scored and was high. He'd become adept at finding my mother's leftover joints (what her friends referred to as roaches); another reason for me to find the whole thing repulsive. Adam would hide them in little bits of tin foil and carry them around with a book of matches in his pants pocket. He was eight years old. He must have gone into the bathroom stall and lit one up while my mother was talking to the women backstage. I'd created a monster the day I'd introduced Adam to my mother's "dirt" and pipe, and I had no idea what to do about it.

The other thing I remembered about that day was that I'd been foolishly hopeful and naive enough to think we might bump into my father.

A month or two prior, he'd been touring with a show which had failed to make Broadway. It ended in Chicago, and he'd been stuck there trying to find work. I heard my mother shouting on the phone with him right before she'd called us in, tight lipped and pale. "Your father wants to say hello."

"Hi, Daddy," I'd said.

"How's my favorite girl?" I'd been relieved by the heartiness of his voice. For some reason I always imagined him alone and sad, eating cold Chickarina Progresso soup from a can when he was on the road.

"Good," I'd answered. "Are you coming to visit soon?" Wrong question. I bit the inside of my cheek in self-retribution when I heard his voice grow hard. "You sound just like your mother. Put your brother on, I don't have much time."

I'd passed the phone to my brother and watched him closely for a sign of the right way to act. He was smiling and cool and regaling my father with stories of a stickball game he'd played that day, leaving out the part where he'd copped a joint from the kid across the street in return for delivering a dime bag to the teenage girls up on tar beach.

After Adam hung up, he looked at me. "He's coming to Broadway soon, Carly—-he said we'd see his name in lights before we know it." Sick with relief and longing, jealous of Adam's easy rapport, I just shrugged and went inside to turn on the television. It was Friday night and almost 8:00—-time for The Brady Bunch, my favorite show with a happy alternate universe in the suburbs. I had designs on it, even then.

But I'd taken Adam's words to heart, and believed that the next time I went to Broadway, I'd bump into my father there. And I'd know exactly the right thing to say.

Wherever my father had landed to find work, it hadn't brought him back to New York; or if it had, he hadn't called or visited. His name was not yet up in lights and we hadn't bumped into him there. Despite the afterglow from the music and dancing that *Pippin* had elicited in me, the sweltering subway, my mother's sour mood, and Adam's red eyes and high smile had all conspired to bring out Crazy Dark Girl.

My mother, lost in her own thoughts, relaxed her usual vigilance of me. I crept closer to the edge of the subway platform, listening to the little girl's voice inside of me. "Go closer, no one is watching," she whispered. "Put your toe over. Go on. If you fall, it will be quick. *Splat* in one second. You won't even feel it. Touch the third rail." All us kids knew the lore of the drunk guy that peed on the third rail and electrocuted himself through his penis.

"Carly!" My mother screamed. Pulling me back, she slapped me hard in the face, the sudden sting welcome.

After that, people gave us a wide berth, the young mother with her two disheveled, odd children. I registered the different glances. Disgust. Anger. But the worst was the woman with straight gleaming hair and blue and white checked maxi-dress. She looked right into my eyes, revealing her pity. And I felt the shame bubble up inside, forming a lifelong tumor in the pit of my stomach.

Placing the thermos down, I grabbed onto the rock, holding tight against my own impulses. Crazy Dark Girl was just an alternate way of being, like Marcia Brady, Laurie Partridge, or Penny Robinson from *Lost in Space* had been years ago. She had no sway over me and my fondness for her was the same way I felt about those fictional characters. They helped shape my ideas about myself when nothing about my internal life matched the reality of my surroundings.

Leaning into the mist, I smiled up at the brightening sky. Stretching my arms above my head, I laced my cold damp fingers together, lifting my ribcage an inch above my hips. Bending forward slightly, I felt my hip sockets open. My shoulders released, sending warmth up and down my arms. Calm settled over me just as color seeped into the horizon.

Walking home in the early morning light, the soles of my feet pressing against solid ground, my body buoyant through the chilled air, I felt, for the first time in my life, not invincible; but safe.

CHAPTER NINE

"The have together, since the beginning of time, side by side, step by step."
– Jalal ad-Dīn Muhammad Rumi

Courageous after my epiphany at the river, I decided to go back to yoga. I missed practicing in the big dusty studio with the stained glass windows overlooking the Hudson. So I called Joanna. Not giving me a chance to change my mind, she offered to pick me up and was outside my door before I'd filled my water bottle.

"You look great!" Joanna said when I got into the car. She was normally quiet and reserved - one of the reasons I liked her so much - and this outburst was tantamount to gushing.

"Thanks. It's the hair."

"I saw you strut when you came down your porch steps."

"It's a residual strut from the red hair. Now I strut with awesome hair."

Joanna smiled and turned the radio up: a pop song about being fancy with filthy lyrics and a great beat. "This is your jam now."

"Ha!"

But the song was catchy, and put me in a good mood in spite of myself. Pulling into the parking lot, Joanna looked at me.

"Just concentrate on yourself. Hester's a narcissistic self-styled guru and those other women are ridiculous. Don't let them get to you."

"I'll just breathe."

She laughed. "Yeah."

The familiar smell of mildew, mothballs, and Pine-Sol rose up as soon as we entered the studio. The women were lined up on their mats when we got there, and I found myself engaging in an ancient habit of deciphering their gazes; a condescending sneer or a pull-back of revulsion; pity in the guise of compassion.

Be free, my new voice whispered. *Who gives a shit? What she thinks is not your business. And you are not her business.*

Hester made a startling beeline for us. I felt myself tightening. My hope that she'd just treat me as if nothing had happened dashed like the early-morning waves against the rocks.

She grabbed my cold fingers and, attempting to stare into my eyes, she whispered, "Namaste."

Joanna placed her mat down without glancing Hester's way, embodying a message to me to ignore Hester and get on with my practice. I tried. But my newfound confidence was quickly eroding and, as we began Sun Salutation, I was aware of everyone's glances at me, then at Caroline, when they thought we weren't looking. My body began to react as if concrete had been poured into each joint. Blowing shallow breaths into the air, I attempted to muscle my way through the class.

By the end I was anxious, exhausted, and desperately trying to leave with a minimum of fuss. Caroline stepped in front of me. "Carly, do you have a minute?" Her lips pulled inside her mouth.

"Ummm."

Joanna came and stood next to me. Caroline glared at her, then turned back to me. "You can call off your guard dog. I just wanted to say---if this is too uncomfortable, I could find another class. I don't have to keep coming."

"No," I answered quickly, almost involuntarily. "That isn't necessary. We're adults. I think we can handle a yoga class."

"Okay. If you're sure." I looked at her bevy of friends who were alternately staring and averting their gazes.

Hester came gliding over. "Do I sense a moment of reconciliation?" She beamed in a way I can only describe as nauseating.

Caroline and I moved apart. "We're good," I said, and Caroline nodded quickly.

Joanna and I practically ran to the car. Pulling out of the lot, she turned to look at me. "Is there any way in the world we can justify vodka this early in the morning?"

"I ask myself the same thing on a daily basis."

"And?"

"No."

"Wine?"

"Not even Nyquil."

"You've asked yourself about Nyquil?"

"Uh-huh. And vanilla extract."

"That's wrong."

"Agreed."

"How about the Tea Shoppe?"

"Fine."

We sat across from one another, two suburban women in yoga clothes sipping delicate expensive tea, mid-morning. I felt like a cliché. Which of course, is what I had aspired to be my entire life. Safe. Conformed. To be original invited attention, and that, I learned early in life, was an invitation to danger. Better to be overused, worn out, or even dismissed. Staunching possibility for myself had seemed preferable to attempting anything out of the ordinary. And yet, just that morning, hadn't I experienced joy over the seam of color breaking through the sky and the river spray on my face?

Joanna placed her mug of tea down gently. "Let's find another studio. Hester's on my last nerve."

Hester was expensive, the studio was dilapidated in spite of its beautiful view, and I was beginning to suspect that her practice was not as advanced as she let on. But I'd been taking class with her for 10 years, it was familiar, and despite the huge upheaval in my personal life, I was not someone who welcomed change. I didn't trust Hester, but she was familiar, and I couldn't shake the idea that I was stuck with her. Due to some mysterious whim of the universe, I deserved her.

"Okay." The word just popped out of my mouth.

"Consider it done." Joanna smiled at me and I smiled back.

Later that day, armed with a list and grocery bags, jubilant after securing a spot in the brutal jungle of the Whole Foods parking lot, I began shopping for Thanksgiving.

The produce aisle, usually my favorite, was clogged with competitive, angry women and a couple of confused old men who probably forgot it was a big Thanksgiving shopping day and had ambled in for their weekly stockpile of overpriced jewel-like vegetables and fruits.

Two women were in a standoff with their shopping carts locked together like a pair of rams, both trying to navigate the narrow corridor near the sweet potatoes.

The body lotion/makeup aisle was unusually empty. Shoppers were focused on the big meal they were preparing for, leaving the body scrubs and beet-colored organic lipsticks untended. I stood for a moment, reveling in the surprising freedom of not having a clock to watch. I could cook all night if I wanted to and not have to stop to prepare other meals or take care of anyone except Bridey and myself.

Taking the time to sniff tester bottles, I selected a sugar scrub at a bargain sale price and placed it in the cart among the Swiss chard, dried apricots, and chestnuts. This aisle I deemed as having a sensuous, exhilarant energy. It was restorative.

The dairy aisle was frantic with shoppers flipping open egg

cartons and grappling over the grass-fed milk. The meat aisle was thick with people clutching scraps of numbered paper, waiting anxiously for their turkeys. This line, I knew from experience, was nothing compared to the organic farm stand lineup at Stone Barns. The stately, beautiful preserve housed an equally stately, beautiful restaurant with gardens and animals to produce milk, butter, and even meat. For hundreds of dollars per person, waiters traveling from as far away as Queens and Long Island would present radishes and wild sorrel arranged on thin, delicate nails hammered into blocks of salvaged wood. The cache of Stone Barns included a farmer's market where you could purchase exclusivity. The lines were acres long and people huddled in thick coats, hats, scarves and gloves clutching mulled apple cider and making cheerful small talk, virtuous in the knowledge that their food would be more wholesome with less of a carbon footprint than their less sophisticated neighbors who weren't buying their turkey from the farm. And everything was hunky dory. Until it wasn't. Because administration assembly line customer service was not a priority. So a person could order a 14 lb turkey, but all the farm did was take your name for a turkey. So if the 20 people before you wanted 14 lb turkeys and they ran out, you were stuck with a 20 lb one. And things turned ugly fast. Once the customer learned there were no threats, cajoles, or reasoning to sway the farm stand people, they turned on one another, demanding to see proof that one or another had actually requested a 14 pounder. Rumors began to swiftly circulate that one or another person had requested a 20 pounder but some guests had canceled, leaving her with the need for a 14 pounder, and so she had taken someone else's bird. Unable to face the stressful (although somewhat entertaining) scene this year, and unwilling to wait in the Whole Foods line, I was throwing caution to the wind and buying a previously-frozen Butterball.

A man in his late thirties with an infant strapped to his chest was pointing his finger at the cashier, a stooped older man in his late sixties. "Listen, Man," the father was saying. "You let that lady cut the line. You've got one job: to check us out in an orderly fashion. By letting her cut the line, you have created DISorder. Not cool, man; not cool at all." Clearly the cashier had been well trained in the "customer is always right" philosophy. He just pushed his glasses further onto the bridge of his nose and stared the father down. "My apologies. In order to keep the line going, would you like to step down and have your receipt validated for parking?"

Angry Dad had no choice but to collect his groceries and accept his validated-for-parking-receipt while I placed my items on the belt and exchanged smiles with the cashier, who winked at me, rendering me a willing co-conspirator against Angry Dad.

Leaving the parking lot was almost as hairy as trying to enter. A white-haired grandmotherly woman gave me a stiff middle finger for some reason. I must have pissed her off because I took too long to load my groceries or back out of my spot. I waved maniacally at her and blew her a kiss before maneuvering out onto the street.

When I returned home, I decided to live dangerously, and turned on every lamp on the first floor. I'd take my chances at the end of the month when the electric bill rolled in, and would cut back on the yogurts, eschewing a favored brand for whatever was on sale. After putting away the perishables, straightening and storing the shopping bags, and assembling all the items needed to begin cooking, I found myself standing in the middle of the kitchen, turning around in a circle as though searching for something. I realized with a start that I was lonely. No one would be coming in demanding food or attention. I had never prepared a Thanksgiving dinner under such circumstances before, and I was at a loss.

Christmas carols, I thought. And began playing them. I chopped and stirred to "The Little Drummer Boy." Rolled out piecrusts to "Coventry Carol." Split and roasted chestnuts to "Baby It's Cold Outside." Dean Martin, Tina Turner, June Carter Cash, Sheryl Crowe, P. Diddy - everyone had a cover of at least one Christmas carol, and I was making my way through them all.

Christmas carols didn't make me nostalgic. They didn't remind me of the children being little or of sitting with Scott on the couch, his hand stroking the instep of my foot when he lifted it to put more wood on the fire. Christmas carols didn't remind me of my own childhood in Crown Heights, the dreary march to the corner bodega for a spindly tree we couldn't afford, the decorations scavenged from other people's rejects, or the disappointment in my brother's eyes when the scarcity of presents was revealed. Christmas carols felt public; sanitary.

I missed Dylan. He wasn't coming home until Thanksgiving Day. He was one of those kids who didn't want to be home until he had to. *Be happy for him,* I told myself. He was staying at a friend's house up north. I knew, without him telling me, that he was staying there because that friend lived in a town where the kids could go and drink in the local bar owned by his friend's uncle. Dylan had let that slip long before we had started discussing Thanksgiving, and I'd filed it away. Wednesday night was the biggest party night of the semester. I remembered that from Dani's college days although she was always in the city.

Strangely, I didn't worry as much about her. She wasn't a big drinker and she seemed so wise and confident, surrounded by other glittering people from the fashion world.

But it was different for Dylan. I worried, of course, that his drinking would escalate; that he'd wind up suffering like my brother. That he'd get into bar fights. That he'd get arrested. Endless lists of fear and worry settled like familiar food against the lining of my stomach.

Whatever damage Scott and I had wrought with this divorce was done. And if I were to be completely honest with myself, which was more painful than having a root canal, our home hadn't been a happy one even before the divorce.

This Thanksgiving would be different. A long time ago, I'd attempted to create certain Thanksgiving traditions. China so thin you could see through it, twenty-five years of marriage carved into the delicate patterns, and carefully-made place cards so everyone would know where to sit. Particular foods—-a favorite for each person in attendance. - and a carefully set dining room table. This year we would eat the same foods at the same table, on the same plates; but all pretense would be gone. My brother would probably be detoxing on the couch, just as he had for the past six years, but I no longer had the energy to pretend he wasn't. Scott would be here with someone other than me - someone he's screwing. And he won't have to hide it. Dani, will be too thin and won't eat, but I can no longer pretend it's a phase. Dylan will try sneaking beer with a wink from his father and they will both ignore my silent, resentful hostility.

But this year, I don't have any more room left for fear. If my son develops a drinking problem, he will have to take care of it. I can't police him from four hours away at college, and the truth is, I didn't want to any more. I just want to see him - make his favorite food and listen to him laugh. My mom, as usual, will be seeking reassurance from me that everything is fine. And any other year, I would have bent over backward to pretend it was - lied to myself and swallowed my worries, letting them burn rancid inside me. Now, the pressure was off. My family life had fallen apart and we were in the midst of reconfiguring it imperfectly, so my mom wouldn't be getting any reassurances - just the truth. Knowing that gave me a light tingling sensation. Although the feeling was a new one, I recognized it. I had seen it; tried capturing it with paint on canvas. It was the seeming stillness of the grey-green river beneath a violet sky; the elusive, glorious absence of tension. Calm.

* * *

Thanksgiving morning broke cold, bright, and gusty. Leaves scuttled across the back deck, causing Bridey to bat at them from our side of the sliding glass door. I had painstakingly laid the dining table the night before. Checking to make sure the dishes hadn't suddenly exploded, I found everything as I'd left it. On impulse, I turned on the overhead chandelier despite the early light, and watched the sparkle of electricity and glass.

In a tattered robe, sucking bits of warm bread doused in butter and chopped onion off my fingers before washing my hands, I let the warm water run over them longer than necessary, then stuffed the turkey and wrestled it into the oven.

Looking around, I realized there was nothing left for me to do until later in the day. I considered going for a run, knowing it would help the soreness in my legs and hips. Rejecting the idea of all that healthy exertion, I considered getting into the studio and mixing some paint. My last effort had, in fact (once the paint dried), been unsuccessful.

I thought about daybreak down at the river yesterday morning; the golden cracks topping an indigo sky. I speculated that the right combination of ochre, crimson, and azure might provide what I was looking for. Checking the time, I thought about crossing the windy yard to go to the studio. Capturing that sky would give the painting the dimension it was lacking, and it was a technical challenge I ordinarily welcomed. I knew that if I crossed that yard, I could leave the sparkling Thanksgiving display behind and immerse myself in the bending of time that painting provided. Once I started working, muscle soreness would dissipate. Regret, fear, and shame would evaporate into the cold air. But I knew that the fine work required after the colors were mixed (assuming they could even be conjured) would be tiring. It was a small painting that required a type of resilience I wasn't sure I could muster, given that in a few hours my family would be under one roof for the first time since the divorce.

Thoughts of a warm bath with grapefruit scent and chamomile oil took hold; the *Pachabel Canon* I could play while the water took me in. *Perfect,* I thought. I'd feel good, look good, and smell good.

On the way upstairs, I thought about calling Michael; about what it would be like if he was the one I was anticipating, instead of the visit from Scott I was alternately dreading and spitefully plotting for. *What if,* I wondered, *I'd answered that last text of his with the Borges quote "Any life is made up of a single moment, the moment in which a man finds out, once and for all, who he is."*

And it was that thought which led me to lie down for five minutes instead of running a bath. I slid out of my robe, letting the comfort of my bed seduce me with the promise of oblivion in the guise of sleep. And that is how it came to pass that three hours later, the racket of car doors, friendly and not so friendly greetings, and a ringing doorbell were the intrusions which went in after me, hauled me from my dreams, and presented me with a heart-thumping reality. I was lying amid tangled covers while my family, along with Joanna and her husband Jake, were trying to get into the house.

What I must have looked like whirling around, naked and desperate! I ran to the window, wrapped myself in drapery, stuck my head out, and yelled, "Yoo hoo! Up here - just getting ready; be right down, Dylan, let them in through the garage, honey!" That's right. I said "yoo hoo". Never used that expression in my life. All I can think is that it must have been the drapes and my interpretation of something Scarlett O'Hara might have said.

Pulling the first thing I touched off a hanger, a shapeless grey tunic, I layered it over leggings and the Ugg boots, making me look like an Australian grandmother in her pajamas. Using up precious seconds, I forced earrings on (big chandelier ones to over compensate for the Australian grandma outfit), combed my tangled hair as best I could, pulled it up in a messy topknot, layered two coats of mascara on for confidence, brushed my teeth, smeared some gloss over my lips, and headed down to face whatever the rest of the day brought.

"Mom," Danielle hissed as the entourage poured into the house in awkward unity. "What are you wearing?"

Dylan rushed over, lifting me in a bear hug. "Smells amazing in here, Mama!"

Hurrying to the kitchen to pull out the platters of appetizers and pour drinks gave me a few minutes before I had to turn around and face Scott and Merry. Dimly aware of my mother and Joanna flanking me, I saw Jake distract Dylan with some new electronic gadget and I felt, more than saw, Danielle's eyes narrowing from across the room. Taking a deep breath, I ignored the ridiculous little-boy gaze in Scott's eyes, as if he were presenting his new girlfriend to his matriarch. I had to ignore it because it was seriously pissing me off. *Be a man,* I wanted to shout. *Introduce her like a man. No wonder Scott's dating a child,* Bitter Vituperative Woman spit in my ear. *He is an effing child.*

Danielle hadn't exaggerated. Merry did indeed have a blonde bouffant and was wearing a salmon-colored twinset, and loops of faux pearls. What Danielle had failed to mention is that Merry had paired this getup with a pair of micro-booty shorts, fishnet stockings, and six-inch-heeled "come-fuck-me" boots that rode above the crest of her knee, making her look like a cross between a dominatrix and a librarian which was, as I unhappily knew, Scott's deepest fantasy (and probably at least fifty percent of the cause of our sexual dissatisfaction, as I was pretty much one hundred percent a librarian and not of the sexy, "pull off my glasses, let down my hair, and hike up my skirt" variety).

"Carly," she said as she pulled my rough hand into her slender smooth manicured one which glittered with a five-carat princess-cut diamond nestled on top of a band of sparkling stones. "I have heard so many wonderful things about you, and I have to compliment you on your beautiful children!" She uttered a darling tinkly laugh. "Scott gives you all the credit." She wrinkled her nose in a way I can only describe as adorable. "He admits he was never home, working all the time." Suddenly self-conscious, she inadvertently glanced at her ring and released my hand. Quickly recovering, she said in her Madonna-like British accent, "Anyway, thank you so much for having me; it means the world to us."

Scott beamed proudly at her. I stood smiling in a way which I was sure would crack my back molars and waited for someone to rescue me. No one did, so I did what any suburban mother and former housewife would do. I thrust a platter of canapés at her. "Salmon roll?"

"Why yes, thank you." She smiled again and popped one into her mouth. "Mmmm." She rolled her eyes in ecstasy and turned to Scott. Joanna shoved me out of the way and took the platter from me to pass around. I made myself busy in the kitchen and let the ensuing chatter rise above and around me.

My mother was close behind me. She was wearing her favorite scent, patchouli oil, which I secretly believe smells like decay.

"Carly." Apparently multi-generations of my female flesh and blood would be hissing in my ear all day. "Why is HE here, and with that that woman-child, in that GET-UP? He is such a POSER." My mother loved mixing current vernacular with perfect diction. It wasn't an affectation so much as a way of thinking, for her. "Somebody needs to keep it one hundred and tell her that AWFUL variation of porn star/desperate housewife isn't working. Maybe I should tell her. I can keep it real like that."

"Leave her alone, Mom. None of this is her fault. Here, stir this."

She looked at the wooden spoon and the mashed potatoes. "Carly, you know I don't like to cook."

"It isn't cooking, Mom; it's stirring." I walked away, but not before she said, "Adam's coming soon. Someone needs to pick him up from the station."

"I'll go!" Dylan offered. "Dad, can I take your Porsche?"

"Of course he can; right, Baby?" Merry smiled in a quite impressive mixture of sultry and angelic. I watched as Scott ground his back right jaw. But he smiled and tossed Dylan the keys like a magnanimous *bon vivant,* the part Merry clearly wanted him to play. "Sure, Son." Son? Never in 18 years had he called Dylan "Son". What was this, an episode of *Father Knows Best* from Hell?

Dylan was out the door and Danielle had sidled over to Merry. "So, Mom-- is it ok if I call you that?"

Merry's eyebrows drew together, signaling a depth of concern, "Oh, Dani, I am honored; but I don't think it would be fair to Carly."

"I don't mind." I popped my head up from the oven where I'd been basting. I watched Joanna's slow sly smile and Jake's eyes flare just a tiny bit. He, out of everyone, would be the best poker player. I chalked it up to his cop training.

"Great!" Danielle put her arm around Merry's shoulders. "Then that's settled, Mom." She squeezed her in a way that was starting to look a little too aggressive. Scott pried them apart and put his arms around both of them. "My two favorite ladies."

"Ew." Danielle slid away from his embrace.

Scott blushed. "You too, Carly."

I smiled at him as a lovely warm feeling of peace descended over my shoulders and down my body. I didn't have to take care of him any more. "No worries, Scott; I'm good."

Just then the doorbell rang, which was surprising. It couldn't be Adam and Dylan back already, and everyone else was here, already playing their parts. I watched myself go to the door as if I were looking down from somewhere near the ceiling. *Maybe,* a ridiculous voice whispered, *it was Michael.* Maybe wishing for something hard enough could conjure it after all.

* * *

I opened the door and there, standing in the dappled late-afternoon light, was my father and his young son. And then I remembered. Practically delirious from lack of sleep, in the spirit of inclusion (or perhaps a moment of sheer divorce-induced-psychosis), I had issued an invitation to my father via e-mail. He'd never acknowledged receiving it and had never answered me in any way about it—-and I had in fact not seen him since Mac's first birthday over two years ago. I suspected that my father had never intended to come, but something had forced his hand. And now here he was, standing on my doorstep, my baby brother in his arms.

Mac took his thumb out of his mouth. "I'm free." I knew he meant "three", but I worried for him because I knew, that being born into this crazy mess of a family, he was anything but free.

"Carly!" My father's booming voice offset the scent of tobacco and wool as he pulled me into an embrace. At 72, he stood tall and strong and straight, with a head full of wavy white hair and movie star looks. "It's been far too long, baby! I heard about the divorce, darlin' and I'm sorry. But I'm here, and I brought Mac to cheer you up. Say hi to your big sister."

"No," he said, his tongue slurring around his thumb.

I looked around in mortal fear. "Where's Bea?" (Mac's mother and my father's fourth wife.)

"Nashville, visiting her family. She hates Thanksgiving in New York; says it's too cold."

I slapped a smile across my face.,"Come in. Umm. Mom's here."

My dad grinned as if I'd just said the Queen of Sheba was waiting to see him. "How is Abigail?"

"Ok, Dad. Two rules: don't talk to Mom. And don't talk to Mom."

"Oh pish-posh; you worry too much."

"Pish-posh - really?"

He grinned, "I'm country now; didn't you see the cross-over charts? I'm bigger in Nashville than anywhere else."

"You're from Queens."

"They love me." He handed Mac to me, who immediately punched me in the face.

"Ow!" It didn't hurt that much, but it did take me by surprise. I grabbed his tiny fist and looked into his deep, angry eyes. "It's ok, Mac, Daddy's not leaving; he just wants me to show you where the cookies are." I watched the suspicion fade and avarice take hold.

"Give me dem."

My father had already strode, unencumbered, into the kitchen. Predictably, he made a beeline for Merry. Taking her hand, he kissed it, "Well, you must be a friend of Dani's. Bet you didn't know her Grandpa was a famous country music star."

Dani snorted. I looked at Scott, but he was completely immobilized. My father grabbed Dani in his interpretation of a gruff, grandfatherly hug, "Give your granddaddy some sugar!" Dani hugged him and made a face at me over his shoulder and mouthed "what the fuck?" I just shrugged. Before I could intervene, my father reached for my mother to give her a kiss. "Abby, you look more beautiful than ever!"

My mother shoved him. And at 5'9", with the many hours she logs at the gym, she is seriously fit. "Get off me." He stumbled back and bumped into Merry, who was trying helpfully to pass hors d'oeuvres. I watched the hand-made salmon-caper-cream-cheese rolls scatter across the floor. Merry looked like she was going to cry. Immediately she hit the floor on all fours, crawling around, her booty shorts in the air, frantically rescuing the canapés before the messy choreography of the bodies in the kitchen ground them beneath their feet.

Mac was crying. "That mean lady pushed my daddy!" he yelled.

Dani, smirking, helped herself to a large glass of white wine. Scott was trying to get Merry off the floor, Joanna was trying to clean up the smeared salmon cream cheese gunk, and Jake was trying to separate my parents.

My mother had my father by his lapel and was smacking him in the face with a dishtowel. "You think!" SMACK. "You can come in here!" SMACK. "And act like nothing happened!"

"Abby, this is passion, this is love -love is the flip side of hate! I know, I've written songs about it!"

Jake might be a fit hottie and a first-rate detective, but he was way out of his league in this domestic dust-up. After all, he was at a severe disadvantage. As a fellow guest, you could see he didn't want to put my mother in the customary choke hold, which was, I'm pretty sure, the only thing that would have worked.

"Don't!" THWACK. Somehow the dishtowel had been removed, but she'd gotten ahold of a wooden spoon and was hitting my father anywhere she could land a blow on his head, shoulders, and chest. "Tell!" THWACK. "Me about love!" THWACK, THWACK, THWACK. "You stole the best years of my life from me: my youth, my beauty, MY VAGINAL WALL, after I gave birth to your children! You left me in poverty!" THWACK, THWACK, THWACK. "And ran around the country with that stupid fucking guitar!" THWACK.

I took Mac outside. He'd stopped screaming "make the mean lady stop" and was now sobbing hysterically into my neck, his wet face like hot glue, his tears burning blisters against my skin.

Dylan pulled up, radio blasting and tires screeching. Adam took his time getting out of the car. Dressed in a sharp black suit, his shirt sparkling white and pressed, he was wearing his customary fedora. As nicely as he was dressed, he couldn't disguise the stoop in his walk, the grey cast of his skin, or the picked sores on his face. Still, he hurried toward me and hugged me. "Who's this little dude?"

"Mac," I said. "Dad's here."

"Holy shit."

"No kidding. It's ugly in there."

Dylan came up the steps, whistling and tossing the keys in the air. He stopped short when he saw Mac sobbing in my arms and heard the ungodly noises coming from the house. "What the hell?"

"Grandpa is here."

"Okay?"

"This is Mac. He's your uncle."

"Hi, Uncle Mac," my son said, rubbing Mac's tiny back.

Adam shook his head. "Wild." But he reached a tentative finger and touched Mac's chubby fist.

Mac lifted his head, ignored Adam, and spoke to Dylan. "A mean lady's beating up my daddy."

Dylan gave Mac a fist pound. "You want me to make her stop?" Mac nodded.

Dylan strode into the kitchen, lifted my mother up, and carried her kicking and screaming out onto the deck where Dani had, helpfully, slid the door open. My father straightened his clothes, accepted an ice pack from Joanna for the welt on his forehead, and smiled at all of us. "What a woman!"

I gave Mac a cookie and handed him over to Merry, who seemed happy to have a purpose. Fascinated with her necklace and earrings, Mac began touching them, covering her with sticky cookie, snot, and tears. To her credit, she never tried to stop him; just plucked a napkin off the counter and wiped his nose. *Run*! I wanted to say to her. *Save yourself!* But she just caught my eye and gave me a dazzling smile.

Dani saw the exchange and made a gagging motion at me.

"Almost time for dinner!" I announced, and went to make the gravy. This time it was Adam who was close on my heels. Joanna and Jake were attending my father's various cuts and bruises while he held court, regaling Merry with tales of his tour bus and how he was being considered for a reality TV show and what a pity the producers hadn't been here to see this. Merry looked up just enough times to let him know she was listening, but otherwise kept up a steady stream of gentle chatter to make Mac happy.

"Carly," Adam grumbled into my ear. "Dad's kid's a little porker, no?"

"Here," I said, thrusting a spoon at an unwilling relative for the second time that day. "Stir the gravy."

He took it obediently. "I need a cig."

"In the top cabinet. I bought you a carton." Yes. I wear a giant E for "enabler" on my chest, rivaled only by the giant "Co-D," for "codependent" that's tattooed above my heart.

Hands shaking, he let the gravy spoon fall, spattering what is tantamount to liquid gold on Thanksgiving Day all over the wall. "You're the best, Carly; the best." He grabbed the carton, tore at it, stashed the packs all over his body, dropped the remains on the counter, and went outside to light up. My mother (who had gratefully accepted a cocktail the size of a bird bath from Dani) watched him make his way behind the shed, ostensibly to avoid offending anyone with his smoke. But she and I both knew he was looking for a private place to take the edge off after he finished his cigarette. He was sure-fingered and fast when he needed to be. In a well-practiced act of silent collusion, we made and broke eye contact. We were equally smooth at covering his use.

My father sidled over to me. "I'm just sorry the cameras weren't here for that awesome spectacle."

"Cameras?"

"The show! I told you about it—-remember? We're shooting a pilot, hoping to get it green lit for a series."

So it was true; the rumors in the press, what I'd overheard him telling Merry. He was actually filming a reality TV show chronicling his tour and comeback.

"Look," he said, "I know you don't approve of this whole reality TV business, but it's not what you think. It's documentary style. And the guy who runs it is a good friend of mine—-a class act."

"Isn't this the network with that show where the host gets drunk on camera, makes crazy faces at the audience, and incites his guests to fight with each other?"

"Aha - you watch it!"

"I've seen it."

"That's my point! This is my last chance, Carly. For the big time."

"The Grammy—-?"

"That was five years ago—-an eternity in Hades in this business."

"You have a baby now, and a wife—-can't that be enough at this point?"

"That's just it! I'm doing it for Bea—-she needs something. That's where the cameras are now—-with her. Boy, will they be sorry they didn't keep a guy with me. You think anyone shot anything on their cell phones?" He actually looked around and eyeballed Jake. "Maybe that guy—-he looks like he's good with a camera."

"No, Dad; I don't think Jake took out his cell phone and started filming Mom kicking your ass with a dish towel."

"Shame."

"Well, this has been fun, but I need to get dinner on the table."

"Great. I'm starving!"

Joanna, who had been quietly stirring the gravy, and couldn't help overhearing, gave me a look.

"Yep," I said. "That just happened." Joanna patted my arm, and for some reason it made me feel better.

Together we piled mounds of mashed potatoes into serving dishes. Green beans with slivered almonds, ruby colored beets, and bright orange candied yams shimmered in cut crystal bowls.

Joanna helped me wrestle the golden-brown turkey onto the platter. Gliding from dining room to kitchen, she filled the sideboard and lit the candles while discreetly setting two more places for my father and Mac. I wanted to marry her.

While we were performing the dance around the table to find our seats, my brother came in, effusive and smiling. He kissed my mother's cheek and grabbed a turkey leg off the platter. "I'll be right in, Sis," he said in his most charming-slash-apologetic tone. "Got to take this call. My boss, he's a slave driver; even on the holiday."

I caught Jake's eye, then averted my glance.

Scott whooshed his breath out of his lungs. "Carly's been slaving for three days over this meal."

"Hey, asshole," my brother said without a hint of irritation or aggression,."You don't get to say jack about that anymore."

My mother was sitting straight and sipping rapidly from her tumbler of vodka. "Language, Adam. And he's right, Scott, you don't get to say jack about it."

"He was her husband for twenty five years," my father piped up. "That doesn't just disappear."

"Enough-a!" Dani declared. "Mom wants to say grace."

"Grace," I mumbled. It was all I had energy for. "Dig in."

And so began the rhythm of passing food around the table, the delicate sound of silver and china, the pattern of fading sunlight staining the sky behind the window, the flicker of candles, my brother's empty place, my former husband's misplace at the middle of the table, and my father's first experience at my Thanksgiving table since the mid-sixties, when he walked out on us.

I raised my wine glass, which felt impossibly heavy. "Salute."

Dani squeezed my leg under the table. "Salute."

After dinner, Jake pulled me aside. "Carly, I don't want to worry you, but I don't like the way Adam looks."

"I don't know what to do about it; I've tried everything— -rehabs— -"

"I mean right now."

And that is how tragedy strikes. You can't prepare for it.

"Where is he?"

"In here."

I followed Jake to the living room. Adam was sprawled on the couch, one arm hanging, his throat exposed, his head lolling back off the decorative pillow. Denial is a powerful mechanism. "Don't worry," I smiled at Jake, "this is normal for him."

But Jake was already calling 911. And that's when I looked closer. Adam was lying as he often did when he was strung out. His eyes had the familiar haze I had come to differentiate from jonesing. *Jake was overreacting,* I told myself. *He just isn't used to Adam's pattern of use.* As hard as I tried to hold onto that thought, my mind was already registering the rapid rise and fall of my brother's chest; the exertion to draw breath, the blue tinge of his fingernails, where I knew that if I separated his fingers, I'd find the tiny puncture marks. *Maybe,* I thought to myself, *he pulled the tourniquet too tight, and that's why his nails are blue.*

"Adam," I whispered. I walked forward to help him, but it was too late. Jake moved me out of the way and began administering CPR. And then, with the uncanny radar our mother always seemed to have where Adam was concerned, she was there.

"What's happening?"

I tried to take her out of the room; to comfort her in some way. But I couldn't hold on to her. The awful keening sound coming out of her was a violent, powerful force against me. It was Scott who managed to lift her out of the room; half dragging, half holding her.

My father picked up Mac, left the house, buckled him into his car seat, and drove away. I watched him from the window while Jake was frantically trying to keep my brother alive. Soon the ambulances wailed in harmony with my mother. It is my greatest shame, to this day, that I have no idea where my children were at that moment. I didn't even give them a thought. I was too busy watching my brother die, my father leave, and my mother come apart.

The ambulance ride was swift; under two minutes. Jake was frantically speaking to the EMS workers while they tried everything, including sticking a needle in him the size of my turkey baster. I was relegated to the far corner of the ambulance, which Jake referred to as a bus (which registered as confusion somewhere in my brain). I wasn't allowed to touch my brother, and he couldn't have heard me. But I was able to watch over him, keep a silent vigil and think these thoughts for him: *know that, through it all, you have been loved. You will always be loved. You are forever a part of me, as I am of you. You are the sore part of my heart; the tender piece. And I will keep you and nurse you and love you there forever, and you will heal. In my heart, you will heal.*

The hospital was eerily silent. Official sounds became a vacuum of white noise: murmurings, rustling, the clanking of metal. Infinitesimal sounds became roars - the sheet pulled over my brother's face; the rasp of Jake's calloused hand covering mine; the thunder of the tears seeping, against my will, from the slits of my eyes.

When we got home, Scott had my mother in a state of drug-induced catatonia. Merry was at the sink, washing dishes, Dylan was drying, and Dani was putting them away. Joanna was in the last stages of placing leftovers neatly into Tupperware and stacking them in the fridge.

We tucked my mother into the guest bedroom and allowed Bridey to curl at her feet.

Merry was waiting by the front door as Scott and I came downstairs.

"Thank you, Merry, for all your help."

She ignored my thanks and thrust her chin into the living room. "Carly, did you paint that?" Mercy, giant, incongruous, and released of bubble wrap and butcher paper protection, was leaning against the wall.

"Yeah."

Merry nodded. "It's like God looking down at us, and he's so very tired.

"I should have realized that God would be the natural reference."

"That isn't what you intended?"

"No."

"What, then?"

"Adam. Looking out from the abyss."

"I'm so sorry." And with that, she broke. Which is how it came to pass that on Thanksgiving Day, I pulled my former husband's young fiancée into my arms.

"Shhh," I whispered. "It will be all right."

* * *

Funerals are parties people have to plan while they're grieving; an opportunity for the living to celebrate their dead. It was a transition from loving my brother in his physical form to loving his memory; a way to accept that, forever, grief and love are now joined.

For one week, we planned. Dani and Dylan stayed home. Joanna and Jake stayed in the guest room and efficiently kept us going. My mother slept night after night on Scott's side of the bed while I stretched out on the white chaise in my bedroom, covered myself in a soft quilt, and watched over her angry sleep. She'd moan, tug covers, twist her legs, and throw her arms about. I'd watch as she'd surface, and her confusion would clear to knowledge.

High from lack of sleep, dizzy from lack of food, and relieved from waiting for my worst fear to come true (because it had), I thrived on taking care of my mother and focusing on my brother. Sanctioned by death, it was allowable for me to obsess over him, pour over our baby pictures, read poems and letters he'd given me over the years, and play video tape after video tape until I'd devised one long one that told the story I wanted it to: of his laughter, his humor, of how much he loved us.

The day before the funeral, while my mother was sleeping in a prescribed stupor and the others were off running errands at my request, my father called. "Carly, baby, you don't know how hard that was for me."

"Mmmm."

"To have to decide to protect one son from the death of my first." Loud choking sobs emanated from the phone. "I couldn't explain to Mac. I told him his brother was sleeping, and we had to go so we wouldn't wake him up."

"Dad, I cant--"

"What would you have me do? He's only three years old. I remember Adam at that age. They're so alike. It hurts to look at him."

"Dad, I have to go."

"I'm coming to the funeral."

"Of course. Just leave Mom alone."

"She might need me now, more than ever."

"She doesn't. She needs peace."

"Carly, you may have guessed, by my being there and all, that things aren't going so well between Bea and me. It's difficult for her, my being on the road so much; and, well, there may have been some rumors she heard."

"Dad. I have to--"

"That last song; the one I got the Grammy for - it was about Bea and me. Art is personal for me, Carly. And I know you understand that, because you're an artist too."

"Dad, I paint as a hobby."

"You're good, Carly. You've wasted your talents all these years. If you committed - really committed - you could be something big. I'll help you get a show. A lot of gallery owners love my music, you know."

He was trying everything he could to suck me in so I would make him feel better. It was a familiar dance, but I eschewed the steps. I had a funeral to plan, and I wouldn't let anything distract me; not even my elusive-handsome-craved-for father. I hung up on him. Didn't slam the phone down or anything; just heard his voice grow thinner, smaller, and far away when I placed it back on its electronic cradle. It wasn't until much later when, in spite of myself, I saw his show, that I realized his side of the conversation was being filmed.

The morning of the funeral blew bright and cold through the open bedroom window. My mother was so tranquilized, it was difficult to help her dress, and I thought the fresh air would help. Shivering, I layered myself in black clothes and propped my mother up while combing her hair, washing the rancid smell from her armpits and rolling deodorant over them as best I could. She was drooling a little bit and I was concerned about how over-medicated she was. Somehow, with Jake and Dylan's help, we got her to the car for the hour ride into the heart of Brooklyn.

People lined up around the block to say good-bye to Adam; childhood friends, relatives I hadn't seen in years, and fellow junkies, stooped and hurting.

I was about to step outside to get some air when a woman in her early seventies approached me, tentatively, but with a determination that made me realize there would be no way of avoiding her. Wiry black and silver curls sprung out from a variety of angles all over her head. There was something familiar about her; the strong beak of her nose and enormous moss-colored eyes.

"Carly, it's Gail Petrides."

Memory has a funny way of seeping into focus. She had been my mother's life-long best friend. They'd had some kind of falling out around the time I was five or six. There had never been an explanation. Gail had been a major part of our lives and then all of a sudden she wasn't any more. Once in a while, my mother would forget herself and tell a story from her childhood that featured Gail. I learned quickly not to ask questions or even act as though I'd noticed Gail's name being mentioned, or my mother would stop speaking with a sullen press of her lips. My dad's absence in our lives quickly eclipsed "Aunt Gail's" and I learned exactly where to place anything in our "past"—-right into the category of my brain labeled "Do not think about it."

Slackening of muscles and loosening of skin, along with the transformation of Gail's waist-length glossy black curls to the bits of white and black springing from her head, served as a form of camouflage; but the deep resonance of her voice and the color of her eyes came back as instantly as if we'd spoken only yesterday.

"Carly, you've grown into such a beautiful woman."

"Oh. Thank you." I smiled spontaneously, despite the awkward surreal moment I found myself in. "I remember your eyes. And your voice."

She looked away, and I could see her trying not to cry. "I'm so sorry."

"Oh. Well. Thank you."

"I mean, I'm so sorry about leaving your lives like that. Yours and Adam's."

"Oh. Um. It's okay." What could I possibly have said to that?

"It's just—-I couldn't watch it any more. And there was nothing I could do to stop it."

"Mmm. Well, it's very nice to see you again."

"There were a lot of drugs around. Your father believed it helped him create his music. And your mother was so head-over-heels, she did anything he asked: orgies, hard drugs..."

"Whoa, Gail. I lived through it the first time; no need for a review."

She began sobbing, choking the words out. "I should have taken you kids out of that environment. I just left you there."

"Oh, Gail." I pulled her into my arms and let her sob against me. "What could you do? There wasn't a thing you could have done."

Muffled against my shoulder, I heard her speak these words: "Do you forgive me?"

"Shhh. Of course."

"Do you think Adam does?"

I hugged her tight against me and now it was my turn to whisper a truth. "Adam had the hugest heart. All love. He wouldn't need to forgive you. He lived in a state of forgiveness."

She nodded, sobbing harder. And I hoped that my words were true; that Adam had forgiven *me* - for having lost the war against heroin. Because that's what it was between heroin and me: a battle for Adam. Every day, for the rest of my life, the tear in the space beneath my left breast, which is palpable with every breath, will prove the horrible way in which I'd failed.

After a while, I delivered her to my mother. They sat side by side, hand in hand, as if no time had gone by. *Maybe that's the way with love,* I thought. *It can burn pure again – -even when it's been tainted with bitterness.*

I made it out the back door and into the parking lot without being stopped by anyone. The air was icy cold and wet; a respite from the cloying scent of death lilies and the gloomy interior of the funeral parlor. I was debating whether or not I could make it over to the bodega across the street for a pack of cigarettes or if I should risk bumming one from the cluster of Adam's friends smoking fiendishly a few feet away from me. Deciding neither option was a good one, I turned to go back through the parking lot when my father's tour bus pulled up in front of the funeral home, blocking all of Ninth Street and starting a near riot from commuters on their way to work. Burly security guards wearing T-shirts with a cheesy entertainment station's logo emblazoned on their backs came flying out, making room for a crew with cameras and microphones attached to their bodies like oxygen machines.

People parted and made way. My father strode ahead of them. Bea (eight years my junior which, thank God for small favors, made her older than my children and their soon-to-be stepmother), clutching his arm, wore couture black and - that's right - a hat with a veil. The thing about folksingers that cross the charts to country is: subtlety is no longer an option. If my Dad really wanted to capitalize on his newfound status moving from being an aging folk singer to a country crooner, he was going to have to work it. And Bea was the perfect accessory to exploit my brother's funeral in order to secure a green light for his show. At least they hadn't subjected Mac to it.

Anticipating some resistance from the funeral director, I moved forward - to do what, I don't know: help my father, or block him? But the doors swept open and they were ushered in. Following them like an awkward guest, I wished Adam were by my side, because he, more than anyone, would have appreciated the irony.

My mother didn't seem to register my father's presence when he bent down to hug her. *Was it possible,* I wondered, *that he was disappointed when she didn't make a scene?*

I pulled him aside and gave a death glare to the cameraman. Catching it, my father gave him his most charming smile. "Gotta have a little off-camera time here - you understand; right, pal?"

Walking away, he positioned me so my back was to the cameras, allowing me to believe, for a moment, that he was protecting me. But when he placed his hands on my shoulders and looked into my eyes, I saw him glance up. Whirling around, I realized they were filming us from a distance. I gave the cameraman the finger. "Carly, don't! I have no editorial control."

"I don't give a shit, how could you bring them here?"

"Adam would have loved it."

I thought about this. "You're right, Dad." I turned around and gave the cameraman the bird again; this time with a suggestion to rotate on it.

"Carly!"

"That was for Adam." I grinned at him and he laughed in spite of himself.

"Do you remember when you and Adam came to The Bottom Line to see me?"

I had been 17 and Adam was 15. My brother got totally wasted and some woman mistook me for my dad's girlfriend. It was awful. But when my dad sang, all that fell away. His voice washed over me, his face softened, and I saw before me the first man I'd ever loved, and the first one who'd ever loved me.

"Do you remember when I covered "Sunday Morning Coming Down?"

I started crying. The cameras must have been inching closer 'cause I heard my father say, "Back off, she'll never sign a release." Then he pulled me around the bend, where they couldn't even see us from a distance. He wiped at my face and hugged me against him and this is what he whispered: "That was for you. All those times I left to go on the road, I didn't have any money to send, I was ashamed. I thought about you and Adam every night - last thing on my mind at night, first thing on my mind when I opened my eyes. But I never did a damn thing about it. That's my shame to bear, not yours. I can never make that right now, not with Adam."

And then he straightened up and walked away, and I wondered if I'd hallucinated his words. Except I remember him singing that song and how it cut into me. And how it must have cut him, too. Maybe there was no real redemption for my father. I knew that whispered confession was as much as I'd ever get from him. And I knew it wasn't nearly enough to make up for what he'd taken from me. But I also knew that I'd grown up anyway.

CHAPTER TEN

"...the world is a jungle, and if
it's not a bit of a jungle in the home, a child
cannot possibly be fit to enter the outside world."
– Betty Davis

Winter snuck in without the beauty and drama of snowfall. Biting winds were the only clue that a season had changed. Lights popped up around the neighborhood, but this year even these seemed half-hearted and dull, as if they were left on during the day and all their energy had waned by nightfall.

For the first time in 27 years, I didn't put up a tree. Eventually someone, Joanna I think, put one up in the customary spot. Dani came up to help trim it and Dylan dragged ornaments down from the attic.

On January 6th ("Little Christmas," my father had called it), Joanna came back to take it down. How she knew our tradition wasn't clear to me. Maybe one of the kids had mentioned it to her. But the morning of the Epiphany, she came over, hugged me, smiled, and went to work. I brought us mugs of tea and watched her bending and stretching, packing each delicate ornament into the correct place as if she were tucking tiny children into bed. The arc of her arm and length of her back were mesmerizing as she reached for the angel on top of the tree. It was, I thought, the kindest thing anyone had ever done for me.

Slowly, in spite of myself, as the winter dragged on, I came back to life. Fighting it, I longed for the comfort of raw grief, where at least I understood myself. But by mid January I found myself running on the cold hard ground, bundled against river wind, exhilarated by the exercise.

During the next two weeks, I skulked around the grocery store parking lot where I'd first met Michael. On separate occasions I dragged Janine, Joanna and Jake, Dani, Dylan, and once, even my poor sad mother to the restaurant where I'd bumped into Michael. There weren't even moms-going-wild to make my desperate excursions more entertaining. Inevitably I ate too little, drank too much wine, and went home with a headache and sour feeling in my stomach.

Pathetically, I got Dani to set up a Facebook account for me, telling her I wanted it to showcase my paintings, but that I was leery of having my name out there. She gave me a pseudonym with Mercy as my profile pic. Rolling her eyes, she set it up the way I asked her to and taught me, as best she could, Facebook etiquette.

I promptly stalked Michael. Turns out he did have an account, but only a business one, so all the material was professional. Hungry as I was for any news of him, it was actually some pretty healthy feasting. I learned about his clients and how he served them, saw some of his best work, found out about the other members of his firm, and stared at his corporate headshot, in which he was smiling not mischievously, like he did at me, but earnestly. It made me want to hire him immediately, to brand me.

Shamelessly I checked his friends. Sure enough, Pammy was on the list. I stalked her too. Clearly she had none of the compunctions I did about privacy. It held every picture she'd ever taken, her home town (Briarcliff), where she grew up (Westport,

CT), her college (Smith), her birthday (minus the year), and a list of "likes" which were too numerous and (I know I'm a bitch) too trite to list.

Pammy listed herself as "in a relationship," which placed an icy pit behind my solar plexus. But there were tons of pictures of her and some guy, who clearly wasn't Michael, which gave me hope.

Then I stalked every one of his other 'friends.' Then I had a horrible heart-stopping moment where I read about an app that promised I could find anyone who 'visited' my page. And I wondered if he had that app, or worse, if Pammy did and she'd uncovered me, and told him! Then I discovered the app was possibly a virus. Finally, nauseous and bleary-eyed, I went to bed vowing in the future only to use my new FB account for good and not for evil.

* * *

"Call him!" Janine told me for the thousandth time while we were sorting a new shipment of handbags.

"And say what?"

"Hey, it's Carly, been thinkin' 'bout ya."

"Right."

"How 'bout a booty call, wouldja?"

"Not funny."

She laughed and handed me a stack of leather bags with a lot of blingy hardware. "Carly, you're going to have to make a move. He's made all of his. And the universe isn't going to send him your way twice."

"I can't."

She shrugged. "Then go out and get laid." She saw my face, came over, and took my hands. "I know you're grieving your brother. But you're still alive."

Janine, more than anyone, understood the guilt and shame which accompanies living through a war that takes someone you love. So I believed her on principle. ..except I wasn't so sure if the sexual part of me was still alive, or if it ever had been. Then I remembered that inexplicable shiver Michael sent up and down the left side of my body, when he'd kissed me slowly and gently on the side of my neck while helping me with my jacket. I realized that had been his promise to me. And I was sorry, now, that I'd treated it as a threat.

That evening was the first night I was alone again in my home. The kids went back to their lives, Joanna and Jake went back to their home, and my mother was back in Brooklyn, staying at Gail's, who, as it turned out, lived a short distance away in Windsor Terrace.

My house was warm and quiet and tidy, but tidied by other's doings, and it felt strange to me - as if I'd already sold it and someone else had moved in, keeping all my belongings.

Despite the cold of the evening and the lashing of the tree branches outside the kitchen door, I threw on an old jacket and crossed the garden to my studio. The heat was paltry, but enough so that my fingers worked. Ignoring the Hudson River painting from my life before, I began to draw.

A concrete schoolyard. A young girl, age twelve, her face hard, leaning back against the orange brick of the building, dwarfed by the handball wall. Her socks have slipped inside her worn, beaten, reject sneakers. Her ponytail is ratty with sweat. Her hands, wrists, and knees are knobby. She looks, for some indefinable reason, poor.

Crouching next to her is a boy about her age, his afro a halo around his head, his expression gentle. I named him Lucas. No one would know his name. It wouldn't be in the title. But I knew it. And it made me smile. Lucas, the bringer of light.

I painted on canvas until midnight. By the time I put my brush down, the brick wall was complete, and I felt the heat of a mid-summer day in a Brooklyn schoolyard in the late seventies.

Weary but jazzed, I made my way to bed. Right before I slipped under the covers, I sent a text to Michael. "I miss you every day. Sorry I effed things up."

I couldn't unsend it or write something more eloquent, less true.

The answering ping of his text came quickly. "I've been here all along."

Instead of calling him, I texted back. "Can we get together?"

"Dinner tomorrow nite? Pick you up at 8?"

"C U then." Exhausted as a two-year-old recovering from a tantrum, I fall asleep.

How is it possible, I wondered, *to feel such deep grief, and anticipation at the same time*?

I spent the next day in the studio working on the following things: a blade of grass shooting up between the concrete slabs of the schoolyard, a sparkle of trampled glass from the ground, a slight indentation in the dried cement where a long-gone child etched her initials, and the sheen of sunlight surrounding Lucas.

Now that darkness had fallen, I knew that I should have spent the day going to check on my mother. Yet I hadn't been able to tear myself away from painting. A quick phone call to Gail confirmed my worst fears: my mother had passed the day on Gail's couch, alternately sleeping and crying. Instead of getting into my car and speeding down the winding roads of the Saw Mill, soaring down the West Side into the depths of the Brooklyn Battery Tunnel, shooting onto the BQE to rescue my mother, I went into the bathroom to bathe, exfoliate, and shave anything which might possibly offend.

This time, when Michael picked me up, I ushered him into the foyer. We went into the living room and I offered him a seat. He chose the couch and sat on the spot where my brother had battled for his last breaths. I offered him a drink. He accepted a Scotch. Neat.

I sat across from him, balancing a glass of red wine. Phoebe Snow's "Poetry Man," was playing on the college station. That was my mother's favorite song the year I turned 10, and I think it may be a sign. *Of what*? I wondered. Her blessing? Her resentment? Either way, it reminds me of her swaying to the song, a thin joint between her lips, her eyes narrowed against the smoke.

"Carly?" Michael asked, "is something wrong?"

"No." I smiled at him. Too hard. And realized, with horror, that tears were spilling down my face. My belly swelled and hardened with a sadness too big to hold.

He put his Scotch down and was beside me, lifting the glass of wine and settling it on the coffee table. He moved like water, kissing my face gently - my eyes, my lips. The side of my neck. I pressed my lips against his and they opened to remembered warmth and salt.

"What is it?" he whispered. His voice sent a shiver deep inside me. All the things I didn't want to say rushed through my mind, I shook my head and pulled him to me, kissed him again, and this time the shiver turned to an ache.

Happily, the DJ had switched to an Otis Redding retrospective. I wondered, briefly, who this college kid was who was so obsessed with the music of my youth, and I had the random thought that maybe the DJ's mother was raised with the same music I was, but instead of hiding from it, she played it for her children like a musicologist, passing down lyrics and melodies and music history.

I am okay with Otis, because I listened to him away from my mother on the fire escape, in summertime, longing for some place different. So when I pulled Michael down to the living room rug, and Otis was playing, I could lose myself in the way Michael was kissing the space between my throat and ear, how his hand held my breast, how his knee was between mine, and how we fit, hip to hip.

Our clothes seemed to melt away into the air. For a brief moment I felt the rough carpet against my back, and then I was only aware of Michael. When he slid inside me, I tensed for a moment, coming back to myself, but he smiled at me, keeping me with him. He watched as he opened me and I watched as I let him in. We laughed at the same time because, as it turns out, sex is really fun.

And that is how it happened: a backward relationship. Sex before love. None of the romance or awkward building up to something. Just fast and furious and tender and surprisingly right, in spite of the very wrong fact that we'd gone at it like a couple of crazed teenagers on the hard sad floor of my living room, which I now thought of as the "Death Room". I smiled because Adam would totally have thought that was funny. I realized how creepy my thoughts were, but I couldn't change them, and my endorphins were surging from the first orgasm I had experienced in what may have been years. That thought was almost more terrible than having sex on the floor of the Death Room.

Michael propped himself on one elbow and smiled down at me, "What?"

Realizing I'd laughed out loud, I shook my head and kissed him. "That was fun."

He grinned. "Want to do it again?"

"Uhh, yeah!"

He laughed this time, "Okay, but I'm not nineteen anymore, so we're going to have to take it slow this time."

"Sounds promising." *Who was this person*? I wondered, hearing my laugh come out of my throat in a way I never had before. This woman who said things like, "sounds promising," and ached to be touched everywhere at once?

The college DJ had switched to random 70s soul, and it was only fitting that two people our age discovered one another to the long, slow sound of Barry White. And I knew for sure THAT was a sign.

* * *

There was no putting it off any longer. My mother had gone back to her apartment and I needed to visit her. The kids had given me an IPod for Christmas. Part of the gift included them loading the following CD's onto it: all the Johnny Cash tunes, Otis Redding, Prince, Mary J Blige and *Greatest Disco Dance songs from the 70s*. The ride, I told myself, would be fantastic now that I had my IPod. And I'd found a new musical obsession: Harry Nillson's *The Point*.

Using music as a catalyst for memory can be a dangerous pastime. When the corresponding memories of a song seep back in, stealthy as a slow-spreading stain, the world tilts and emotional vertigo sets in. At least, that's what happened to me when I rediscovered the Youtube Video of *Me and My Arrow.* I blame the college DJ and his throwback hour of 70s soul for sending me on a search I expected would take hours and took precisely thirty-nine seconds. I was under the illusion that because I'd listened to *The Point* many lifetimes ago, that it would take at least that long to find it. I had underestimated how large a musical and artistic force Harry Nillson had been, back in the day. My relationship with that album had been so solitary and profound that for many years when I'd thought about it, I wondered if I'd made the whole thing up myself and it was merely a dream I'd experienced.

I first saw the movie on our staticy black and white TV, with its wire hanger protruding from the hole where the antennae should have been. I remembered staring at the album cover, reading the lyrics inside of it, and the anticipation during the click of the needle in the groove between one song ending and another one beginning. *Me And My Arrow* had been my favorite song, and my finger hovered over the play button in a haze of excitement and fear that I wouldn't love it the same way after so many years. I worried it would be corny or cheesy or child-like. I needn't have.

It was strange and beautiful and caused me to speed when I shouldn't, on the drive down to my mother's. I decided to detour through Crown Heights before heading to The Slope. Driving along President Street where the orange brick of P.S. 241 glowed in the late morning sun, I squinted at it and almost smacked into the car in front of me trying to eye the contrast of the black wrought iron fence and the drab concrete sidewalk. Had I captured it in the painting? I didn't think so. Frustrated, I circled the block, looking for a spot, which I soon realized, would be impossible to find. I peeked down Carroll Street and caught a glimpse of the little bridge connecting to Franklin Avenue. Throwing caution to the wind, I pulled alongside a fire hydrant and walked half a block, peering back every few seconds to make sure no cops or meter maids were near. When I got to the bridge, I stepped onto the worn wooden slats.

Standing there brought back the smell of strawberry Laffy Taffy, my friend and I pulling a piece of it. My recollection was that we'd pulled it from one end of the bridge to another until the taffy thinned and separated. Yet, looking at the bridge as an adult, I realized we couldn't possibly have pulled it more than a foot apart from one another. The land mine of memory surprises you at times when you least expect it.

I remembered a different afternoon walking to Franklin Avenue after school, a nickel warm in my hand and the anticipation of Laffy Taffy almost a taste in my mouth, when I found myself trapped by a group of kids, two of them locked in a fight as the others cheered them on. I'd wanted to stop them; intervene somehow, but they were pummeling so hard and so fast and the shouting of the other kids made my ears ring and my stomach lurch. There was no way to stop them and no way to get away. A wall of bodies had hemmed me in. I stood, my eyes narrowed to slits so I could just see motion and not the fear or pain or rage in anyone's face. One or both boys were bleeding, and red droplets stained the pavement. Finally, something spooked the kids - not a teacher (they never came off the school property, which is probably why the boys chose to fight on the bridge). Not cops, either, because they wouldn't have cared. It was older kids from I.S. 320, and none of the elementary school kids wanted to get into it with them, so everyone scattered; even the boys who'd been fighting.

I ran with the crowd, passing myself off as just another spectator instead of a girl who turned queasy at the thought of bony knuckles meeting the soft spot of an eye socket or the cartilage of someone's nose. I was an imposter, consumed with relief at not having been caught out and ashamed of my weakness. How would I survive in a violent world if I was incapable of violence? And the world proved itself to be violent every day on the evening news...each recess when we lined up in the school yard...even the early years in our apartment, when my father still lived with us. The loud parties would taper off, a fraught silence would follow, and eventually my parents would begin fighting. On a good night, it would just be shouting. To take myself away from it, I would make shadow puppets on the wall with my hands. Left was my mother and right was my father. I'd flap each hand to the corresponding shouting in the next room. Most of the time, this required both hands moving at once in a rhythmic, harsh dance. Sometimes I would lull myself to sleep like that; a terrible kind of bedtime story. One night a crash woke me. I ran inside and my mother was on the floor. My father was leaning over her, hurting her. The crash was a lamp that had been knocked over in the scuffle.

"Stop it!" I'd screamed. But they were locked in their battle, just like those boys on the bridge, and they didn't hear me. So I ran over and did the only thing I could think of--I pulled my father by his hair. He was leaning over her, so he was level with me. He was holding her down on the ground. Somehow she'd gotten his hand with her teeth and was biting. I saw a tiny droplet of blood spurt onto his hand and I didn't know if it was from her lip or his hand.

He yelled and pulled back from her, causing me to let go of his hair. Standing up, he turned and looked at me. His nostrils flared and he had white spittle caught in the corners of his mouth. Two fiery spots burned on his cheeks, and his hair, largely due to my pulling, was standing straight up on his head.

Turning to my mother, he shouted, "You made me do this! You made me!"

She turned her face from him and looked as though she'd cry. I'd never seen my mother cry. I ran to her and hugged her.

"If you ever do that again!" he yelled, "I'll give you a licking!"

"You already gave her a licking!" I shouted back at him.

He stared at me a moment longer, pointing at me, then dropped his hand, turned, and left. I didn't see him again for two years. It is only now--looking back--that I realize it was me he was speaking to, not my mother. He meant if I ever pulled his hair again, he'd give me a licking. Ha. Good thing I never had another opportunity.

I left the bridge and walked quickly back to my car. By the time I drove into The Slope and found a spot, I was half an hour late. I'd been ringing the bell and knocking and was worried that my mother had tired of waiting for me and gone to do errands. Feeling a rise of panic, I wondered if in fact she was inside—fallen ill, or worse. Just as I was eyeing the gated windows, wondering if there was any possible way to break in, I heard movement inside. Eventually my mother shuffled to the locked gate and began turning the assortment of keys to let me in. It was shocking to see how much she'd aged since my brother's death. Her platinum hair was in desperate need of washing and clung closely to her scalp, making her head appear tiny and frail. Her skin had loosened and hung in slack folds from her jaw, her neck, and her arms. Her eyes, which had always glowed with a fierce attention to the world, were dull and unfocused; a shroud of pain.

Sticking her cigarette between her lips in order to use two hands on the door, she squinted against the smoke, and I was reminded of my childhood. She'd given up smoking fifteen years ago, and like everything else since my return to Brooklyn, it was both familiar and strange. The acrid smell of the cigarette masked for a moment the sour oniony smell of my mother when I leaned in to kiss her hello. We stood together in the tiny vestibule, me juggling the guilt offerings I'd brought her (organic chocolate covered berries, a hunk of brie, and smoked salmon in vacuum sealed plastic), she practicing the ritual of locking us in again.

The apartment was shut up against the fine spring weather and smelled of pent-up cooking odors and stale coffee. With relief, I noticed it was neat. She'd always been an organized person, even in the height of our poverty and her alcohol abuse. So I don't know why I was picturing piles of dirty dishes, stacks of mildewing newspapers, and unclean laundry strewn about.

I followed her to the kitchen and began putting away the grocery items, showing her each one as I did so. She gave a curt nod or a tiny grunt to acknowledge each one, then nodded at the kettle. "Tea?"

"I'll make it," I said, eager to be helpful.

"Sit," she said, waving me away.

I watched the tension in her back and shoulders as she filled the kettle and waited for the gas burner to click on. She filled a chipped lime-green Fiestaware plate with half a sleeve of social tea cookies and put them between us on the table.

"So," she said, "you see me. I'm alive. Now, quit worrying."

"Sorry, Mom. I should have come before this."

She waved her hand at me for the second time in as many minutes. "Knock it off. I don't need a babysitter. For God's sake, I bawled in your bed like an infant for over a month. I should've thought you were glad to see me go."

"Mom, that isn't true."

She grinned, and for a second my mother the way I'd always known her was back: daring, laughing, and as comfortable with her flaws as with her attributes.

"Oh, Carly, of course it is. And I was no better at Gail's, lying around on her couch all day and sniveling into my housecoat. It was like a bad movie." She looked at me and patted my hand. "It feels good to be home, really."

"And work? Is that going okay?"

She shrugged. "Everyone's been really nice. And it keeps me busy."

The teapot howled and she busied herself with our cups, milk, and sugar. When she settled in, delicately nibbling at the end of a cookie, she looked up at me, her eyes sharper than I'd seen them in months. "So how's the fucktard doing?"

"Which one?" I wasn't being facetious; she used the endearment interchangeably for Scott and my father.

"The narcissistic d-bag - oh, sorry, still confused? How's Guy doing?"

"Dad's, himself, I guess. Haven't spoken to him, really. He's been touring."

"Carly, he isn't touring. He's whoring himself out for that TV show, pimping his little boy and that monstrosity of a wife, driving around in that ridiculous bus. It's embarrassing." She smiled gleefully. "For him, not for me. I'm loving it."

"How do you know all this?"

"The producers called me. They want me to do a segment."

"You refused, right?"

"Hell's to the No. I said: 'pay up, bitches'."

"Mother!" I sounded disturbingly like Danielle.

"Carly, that man never paid a dime in his life for his two children. I will take that money gladly. It's some serious bank."

"Please don't do it. I'll give you the money myself."

She gave me a pitying glance. "You don't have it to give. That little girl Scott's marrying has it all on the third finger of her left hand. Don't think I didn't notice that bling-da-bling."

"This is so beneath you."

"Why? I'm just going to tell the truth."

"Mother, I am begging you."

"Don't waste your time. The contracts are signed."

My despair must have shown on my face, because hers softened. "Don't worry, Carly, it won't be that bad. And I could use the diversion." She jumped to her feet, with what seemed close to her former level of energy, and I had the disturbing thought that if this was helping her, she could go on Jerry Springer for all I cared. "Come on, Daffodil Hill is in bloom, let's take a walk."

And just as we did for all those years so long ago, we strolled hand in hand through the Brooklyn Botanical Gardens where the daffodils, as hoped for, had struggled through their tiny winter graves and pushed their heads into the sunlight and air.

CHAPTER ELEVEN

"It is love that brings happiness to people.
It is love that gives joy to happiness.
My mother didn't give birth to me, that love did.
A hundred blessings and praises to that love."
– Rumi

Driving home was a nightmare of traffic snarls and road rage - the latter, mostly my own.

The Gardens had been the best part of my childhood. Adam's ghost, along with that of my child-self, waited around every familiar turn … the first cherry tree on my right, where we used the protruding root and small boulder to play Pirate Ship. The Rose Garden where I'd so often imagined my father coming back to find me. The Tea House where my mother had been her happiest, taking time from the worry of bills and rent and welfare lines to make up small plays for us to act out in that magical world. All we had to do was walk through the metal turnstile and we were safe from the violence and chaos of the streets.

Holding my mother's arm and walking those paths with memory in place of magic had taken a toll on me. By the time I took her home, settled her in, kissed her good-bye, and walked the few blocks to my car, it felt as if an iron band had been wrapped around me, flattening my breasts and constricting my airways.

* * *

Longing for avocado sprinkled with lemon and salt, I stopped at the local supermarket when I got to Tarrytown. Luck was on my side; the avocados were perfect. My basket was filled with salad ingredients and a bar of ginger dark chocolate. I knew I'd left a bottle of Sauvignon blanc chilling in the refrigerator. The evening stretched before me: a long bath, a light supper, and a new Louise Erdrich novel waiting to be cracked open on the coffee table.

Brooklyn was diminishing; the aches from the long ride home would soon be soaked away. I thought of my mother making a lonely dinner for herself. She kept faded photos of Adam and me push-pinned onto a corkboard in her kitchen. Seeing them stirred the same memories I fought against by raising my children in this sparkling neighborhood, my instruments of war a scrub brush, bleach, and The Container Store. In spite of that, our lives had turned out remarkably similar. My children may not have the needle marks that my brother suffered, but they have their own battle scars from living in a home where a loveless marriage reigned. I may not have submitted them to danger, drugs, or poverty, but they'd had healthy doses of bitterness and resentment stirred right into their milk. The harder I tried not to be like her, the more I'd become her.

Turning a container of coconut water over in my palm, debating whether or not I should pay the exorbitant price, I thought of my mother forgoing anything new or nice for herself; making do. Placing the water in the basket, I saw again my mother in the Gardens this afternoon, marching resolutely toward the rolling hill at the end of Cherry Lane, the place my brother, at the age of three, would hurl himself down again and again in search of the dizzying thrill. We stood and watched the hill. Both of us, without saying it, imagined a tiny Adam, arms stiff to his sides, the fastest, surest roller of all, hurtling toward the bottom, jumping up, reveling in the spinning world and running back up to do it again. And I wondered if she was hoping, the way I was, that wherever Adam was now, hurtling through time and space in an infinite form of energy, that he was joyous and free.

I went down the beverage aisle to make a beeline for the checkout. It was crowded with boxes and I had to squeeze past a grocery cart with a crying toddler and a weary mother, still dressed in her work clothes, obviously picking up groceries on the way home from the office and daycare. Feeling her pain, I navigated around her and came face to face with Hester.

She narrowed her eyes. Grey and glinty, they bore into me with malice. "Carly. Long time no see."

"Hester! Hi…it's been…a difficult winter."

"I'm sorry about your brother."

"Thank you."

"I would have come to the funeral, but you didn't call me."

"Oh--well."

"Joanna mentioned it, but I thought I would get an invitation."

"It wasn't a party."

"I think you know what I mean."

We were nose to nose in the aisle. The toddler's mother was now negotiating: "Finneus, if I give you the fruit rollup now, will you be a good boy?"

"NO!" Finneus screamed. I turned my head and watched Finneus's state of fury.

"Then I can't give you the fruit rollup," his mother said with the kind of patient tone that masks homicidal rage. Any mother would recognize it.

I badly wanted to intervene; to take Finneus off her hands for a couple of hours so she could go home, change, pee in private, put her feet up, eat a complete meal which didn't include chicken fingers or macaroni and cheese with a desperate attempt at a vegetable - broccoli trees, carrot sticks, round perfect peas not touching any other food.

Let me take him, I longed to say. *I'll walk across the street to the dim, cool library and read him books. I'll take him to the playground and push him endlessly on the swing; follow him tirelessly up and down the slide. Don't bargain with him,* I wanted to say while gifting her with my ice-cold glass of Sauvignon blanc and creamy avocado salad. *It doesn't work.*

Don't take him shopping when you're both hungry and tired. Or if you must, give him the effffing rollup. It's no big deal. Just a fruit rollup. Not heroin.

These were all the things I wanted to go back and tell my 25-year-old self, although this poor woman was closer to 40, and all the life experience in the world hadn't prepared her for an angry, hungry, tired toddler.

But I had my own problems, such as Hester standing in front of me in full-on, righteous indignation.

"Carly, I realize you have been grieving. But I could have helped you with that process."

"Oh, well, I'm okay now. But thanks."

Hester's lips caved in, her eyes sharpened, and she reached out to grab my arm as if to prevent me from leaving.

Finneus wailed, "FWOOT WOWUPS!"

"You are being a bad boy."

"I NOT A BAD BOY! "

"Say you'll be a good boy and I'll give you a fruit rollup."

"NO!"

"Then I can't give it to you."

"GIMME!"

"Will you be a good boy?"

Silence while Finneus considered this. Hester's hand tightened on my arm.

"Otay. I be a good boy."

Relieved, his mother smiled and ripped open the fruit rollup package and gave him one. As soon as he had it in his hand, he reached over the cart, grabbed a bottle of juice, and knocked it on the ground, simultaneously attempting to shove the fruit rollup in his mouth. Happily, the bottle was plastic and rolled harmlessly toward me. I shook Hester's hand off me and bent down to pick it up. Meeting the mother's desperate embarrassed glance, I smiled and shrugged, "been there." But she didn't meet my overture. Instead she turned from me, ripped the fruit rollup from Finneus's hand, and said, "You are a bad, bad boy and will NOT be getting a visit from Santa this Christmas." Finneus let out a wail that made my ears bleed. His mother hustled off to finish her shopping.

"Excuse me," I said to Hester, eager to make my own hasty retreat.

She gripped my wrist again. I felt the warmth of her breath, a bitter scent of licorice in my face. "Carly, neither you, Joanna, Caroline or Melissa paid for next semester."

"I don't know about the others, Hester, but I'm taking a break. Money's tight and…" *Why,* I wondered, *did I give her that personal information? It was none of her business.*

"This is the thanks I get. After all I've done for you. Money's tight? What about me? I *depend* on these tuitions."

"Hester, this isn't an appropriate conversation."

"Appropriate? It's your fault Caroline and Melissa haven't re-joined. I demand that you call them and tell them you aren't coming back. They're staying away because of you. So is Joanna. You need to call her, as well."

"I'm not calling anybody. Let go of my arm."

She dug her fingers tighter. "You owe me, Carly. You owe me."

I leaned into her and said, in a voice as quiet and as controlled as I could, "Let go of me now, or I'll knock the shit outta you."

She let go of me as if I burned. "How dare you!"

"Stay away from me." I pushed past her and walked to the checkout line - one over from Finneus and his mother.

Finneus was hiccupping the end of his sobs and sucking on a gummy mess of what had once been a fruit rollup. Somewhere around the dairy aisle they must have reached a truce. His mother looked even more haggard than she had before. Her shoulders sagged as she loaded the counter with chicken tenders, baby carrots, and packaged American cheese.

I left the frigid supermarket for the muggy parking lot. Out of the corner of my eye I saw Hester skulking near her car, watching me with palpable hatred as I swung easily into the road and away from her.

Driving home, I detoured past Joanna's house. Happily, she was elbow-deep in her front garden. "Hey," I called. "The place looks great." And it did. She and Jake had worked hard to fix it up. The jungle of a front yard had been pruned and cleared into a mature and beautiful oasis. Fresh white paint brightened the sagging porch and new siding lined the whole house.

When Joanna smiled at me, Hester's ghostly finger grip loosened and fell away. Joanna walked over and reached through the car window to give me a hug, which, by the way, was so uncharacteristic that it worried me. This must have shown on my face because she threw her head back and laughed.

"I've missed you! I've gotten used to seeing you every day. How was Brooklyn? How's your mom?" She pulled the driver side door open. "Come have a glass of wine with me and tell me what's going on."

A bursting took place inside of me. I felt giddy, almost high, and I wondered if this was happiness. - this fleeting wave that recedes and floods back, leaving me almost breathless and a little sick.

Holding up the bag of avocados and lemons, I say, "guacamole?"

"Yum," Joanna said, dragging my bag and me out of the car. We walked through the back along the neat stepping-stones Jake laid out, a charming trail punctuated with fragrant lavender, mint, rosemary and lemon verbena. Following her into her freshly painted kitchen, I began slicing, releasing the scent of garlic and lemon into the air.

"Call Michael," she said, handing me my own cell phone, which she'd fished out of my bag. "Tell him to come have dinner with us."

Could it be that easy? I wondered. *Could I just call him and ask him to come over? What was the worst that could happen; that he'd refuse*? So what. My heart had been so flattened that a little rejection wouldn't even register.

Mouth dry and pulse rushing, I listened to the phone ring, hoping it would go right to voice mail.

"Michael here."

Unsticking my tongue from the roof of my mouth, I managed to croak out a response. "Hey…it's Carly."

"What's up, Babe?"

"I'm at Joanna and Jake's. We're cooking dinner. Do you want to come?"

"If I catch the next train, I can get there by 6:40."

I glanced at Joanna and mouthed the words 6:40, but obviously she could hear him because she was nodding her head up and down like a ridiculous bobble-head.

"Okay, well—-see you then."

"I'll bring wine." I was sure he was laughing as he said goodbye. He disconnected before I could form another word.

I snapped my phone shut. "He's coming."

"Great." Joanna smiled, and turned back to her chopping.

How commonplace an exchange it all was; yet it felt monumental, like I'd stepped from behind the Plexiglas of all those doorways I'd peered through as a child in the period wing of the Brooklyn Museum and walked directly into the room as though I belonged there.

An hour and a half later, Michael came in carrying a hand-tied bouquet of wildflowers, which he handed to Joanna. Pulling me away from the herbs I'd been chopping, he pressed against me and kissed my lips.

Thrilled and embarrassed at the same time, I pushed him away and tried to avoid his gaze, but his eyes caught mine and he smiled at me - a smirk, really; as though he knew about the pulsing sensation he'd created inside me and the craving of my body for his.

I had the impression that he had stepped from the Plexiglas barrier into the room with me, and that it was going to be okay for both of us to inhabit this world; that neither of us had to be on the outside looking in.

CHAPTER TWELVE

"But here, right here,
between the birthmark and the stain,
between the ocean and your open vein,
between the snowman and the rain,
once again, once again,
love calls you by your name."
– Leonard Cohen

The Saw Mill River Parkway was clear on Monday morning at 8:00. Joanna had convinced me to work the late shift at Mandee's, it was her day off, and we were headed north to try a new yoga studio she'd heard about.

We were sipping warm green tea from cardboard cups and Joanna was talking me down from the ledge of guilt and misplaced responsibility I perpetually lived on.

"The fact that Hester would accost you like that in the middle of food shopping is the reason she has no clients left. Seriously, Carly, the woman is out of control."

"Do you really think she has no clients left?"

"Oh please, why do you care? I'm sure she has a fresh batch of suckers who'll stay until she pulls the same crap on them."

Walking up the steps into the studio, we were greeted by a friendly woman who shook our hands, gave us a form to fill out, and introduced herself as Anne. It took a few minutes for us to realize she was the instructor. Maybe it was her youth, or the quiet friendly way she came forward. "Any injuries or concerns I should know about?"

Yes, I wanted to say. *I'm damaged from the inside out. What have you got?*

We made our way into the room, unfurling our mats with a gentle "thwick."

Hester had always accompanied our classes with music from her IPod, as esoteric as she could find. Anne didn't play any music at all, leaving our breath and her instruction to accompany our movement. If anyone had asked me which I'd prefer, I would have said music, but the lack of it allowed me to connect with the practice in a new way. The class was challenging, but Anne was patient and easygoing, which in turn allowed me to throw everything I had down on the mat in a way I'd never done before.

To my surprise, Anne ended the class by singing. Lying with my palms facing the ceiling, my body splayed against the floor, I felt a burning in the center of my hands. The sensation reminded me of a visit to my father's parents, a memory I'd long forgotten. Perhaps because I was in such a state of deep relaxation, the memory rolled before my eyes as effortlessly as a film strip, and I felt as disconnected from it as if it had happened to someone else.

My mother was bringing Adam and me to visit our grandparents. We hadn't seen my father in close to a year. I had just turned five and Adam was about to turn three. My mother was not yet 25, and while she complained about the faint shiny white lines beneath her belly button and the "widening of her ass," I found her to be beautiful. She caused a stir at school whenever she picked me up. Once, when she came in wearing sunglasses and an old moth-eaten fur (left over from wardrobe on one of my father's shows), kids asked if she was a movie star.

My father's parents, however, were far more critical of her. Despite my father's abandonment of us, they somehow blamed my mother for their lack of visits with us.

It was a hot summer day and my mother was on the phone with my father's mother. "Hey, Doll," she said in a way I now recognized as sarcasm, "you're both welcome to come here and visit the kids; you've got wheels, after all." She saw me watching her, winked at me, and blew a stream of smoke through her nostrils. "I can hack it up there with two babies on the subway if that's what it takes. It's Adam's birthday on Sunday, so how 'bout it?"

In an attempt to give us a relationship with our grandparents, my mother filled three baby bottles with sterilized water, packed welfare peanut-butter sandwiches, and braved a two hour trip on the stifling subway to Queens.

The housing complex had neat green lawns adorned with low-lying chain-link barriers, a playground, and elevators that smelled of other people's food. My grandmother met us at the apartment door, her own cooking smells watering my mouth with a promise of tomatoes and slow-cooked beef. She pressed me against the soft pillow of her stomach and pinched Adam's cheek so hard, he cried.

Looking at my mother, she said, "Pick them up in two hours. It's better you don't come in, my husband…" She shrugged.

I turned in alarm to look at my mother, who smiled reassuringly at me. "I'll take a walk."

She handed me Adam's diaper bag, nudged the stroller toward me with her hip, and sauntered back toward the elevator.

"Where will she go?" I asked my grandmother.

"To the movies. Go kiss your grandfather."

But I knew my mother didn't have the price of a movie ticket. I knew for a fact that all she had in her little black change purse was one token to get us home. She didn't even have 15 cents for a coke. I spent the entire visit imagining her thirsty, hungry, and lonely for us; wandering the unfamiliar grounds of the apartment complex, perhaps getting lost among the neat green lawns and identical playgrounds.

The palm-burning reference I associated with the yoga class happened after dinner. My grandmother, aunt, and older cousins happily plied Adam and me with succulent meatballs and macaroni stuffed with layers of gooey cheese and fragrant sauce. There were vinegary salads, which led me to smack my lips in delight, and an assortment of Italian pastries that I literally would dream about for years, reaching in my sleep for chocolate-covered confections filled with pale custard.

I went into the tiny bathroom and peered around at the strange items. A hand crocheted doll with a light green ball gown, which spread out to cover a roll of toilet paper, a piece of what looked like rug covering the toilet seat, and an actual rug in the same pistachio-ice cream color on the floor. I wanted very much to play with the doll, but self-preservation led me to understand that in my grandmother's home, such a doll was off limits. I peed, marveling at the towels with flowers appliquéd along the bottom, an exact replica of the garden printed on the plastic shower curtain. Washing my hands, I lathered the tiny violet-scented soap much longer than necessary, wishing I could take a bath in that floral bathtub; knowing that I may as well wish to fly up to the moon.

When I came out into the tiny foyer, I was alarmed to find my grandmother waiting for me, blocking my passage back to Adam and the rest of the family. I wondered with a sense of panic if I'd used the soap for too long and if I was in trouble.

"Come here, you. I wanna show ya something." She took my hand, not unkindly, but with purpose, and pulled me into her bedroom. It was a close dark room with twin beds covered in satiny espresso-colored bedspreads and a large ornate dresser lined with tempting jars and bottles. A room-sized mirror reflected the terror on my face and the determination on hers. "You see that?"

She was pointing to the only other ornament in the room, a large crucifix with a bloodied, ravaged Jesus nailed to the wall. I had a children's bible at home, and my mother, while renouncing all organized religion, read me the stories of the New and Old Testament along with teachings of Buddhism, Hinduism, and

Hari Krishna, the latter of which she quickly reviled after a particularly "disturbing news article" she referred to while stuffing the paper into the incinerator down the hall from our apartment. The Jesus in my book had soulful eyes, long delicate fingers, beautiful hair, and a gentle expression on his face. I remember pointing to his picture and demanding of my mother that she find him to babysit me (I hadn't liked the teenage girl down the hall who babysat. I'd made the mistake of telling her I was afraid to stay in the bathroom while the toilet was flushing. She'd immediately taken the opportunity to hold me in place while she flushed it over and over again, shoving Adam when he'd come to my defense.)

The Jesus in my book didn't look anything like the gory agony on the wall looming above me.

My grandmother's face was close to mine. I could see the tiny hairs in her nostrils and smell her face powder, and the rich food in my stomach roiled. "Do you know who that is?" she asked me. I followed the fat blunt line of her finger.

"Yes," I whispered. "Jesus Christ."

"God." Her voice was trembling as she spoke, "I don't care what your mother tells you, that's the son of God."

I nodded.

"Whose fault is it your parents broke up, your mother's or your father's?"

Like a parrot I repeated the mantra my mother had told me with my bedtime story each night: "They both love me. They just couldn't live together anymore."

Her eyes brightened, and she smiled. "Good girl, here's five dollars."

I followed her from the room, elated by her approval, feeling like a cheat who stole my mother's answers and never gave her credit, who gorged myself on meatballs and lasagna while she sat hungry and forgotten in a playground without us. *I'll give her the five dollars,* I told myself, *and she can buy food for herself with it.* I turned and took one more look at God. His fingers curled gently, as if attempting to hold the blood back, sprouting from the nail, pouring over his wrists and forearms. I felt so bad for him that my own palms burned.

My mother, when I'd given her the five dollars, had laughed bitterly. "Big spenders," she said before buying a pack of Pall Malls and a Hershey bar from the newsstand at the corner. Placing the remaining bills and coins carefully in her little black change purse, she shoved all three items into the diaper bag.

My brother slept on the long ride home. I refused any chocolate and watched as my mother broke half a square off at each stop, savoring it in her mouth until the next stop. As hungry as she must have been, she never crammed her mouth with it as I longed to, despite my full stomach. That's how greedy I was. I worried there would be retribution for that greed; for my treacherous desire to live in the house with my mean grandmother and her delicious meatballs and éclairs - for wanting to sleep on the shiny coffee-colored beds and play with the crocheted bathroom doll. Jesus must have done something very bad to get those bloody palms, and I couldn't help thinking that my turn was coming soon.

In Anne's studio, as my palms burned with the palpable positive energy in the room, my body melted against the floor. Behind the safety of my eyelids, colors whorled. Colors I'd never seen before: indigos deeper than the night sky, neon bursts of green non-existent in any paint tube and impossible to recreate, a gold as vibrant as the gold right before the last blaze of the sun dissipated, an orange so forceful my entire body felt energized by it. And somehow the following words made themselves known to me. It was odd, because I didn't hear them or see them, and I didn't think them - they just became known. *You are fine. You grew up anyway. You are fine.*

CHAPTER THIRTEEN

"There are no hard distinctions between what is real and what is unreal, nor between what is true and what is false. A thing is not necessarily either true or false; it can be both true and false."
– Harold Pinter

Michael was sitting on a folding chair in my studio, sipping a cold Corona with lime and reading the Saturday section of *The New York Times.*

I had just ruined the schoolyard painting of Lucas and me.

After weeks of working on it and being satisfied with the results, I had become worried that it was too literal. Using texture, bits of newspaper, an old piece of material from my childhood quilt, and a piece of Michael's T-shirt, I was covering the painting, allowing only a few bits to remain - the blade of grass pushing between the concrete, Lucas's perfect Afro, the heel of my sneaker where the sock had slipped down. Cutting the canvas with an exacto blade, I painted Lucas back in, right where my heart would be if I hadn't covered it with layers of indigo and my childhood quilt.

Taking a deep breath, I set my brush down, wiped my hands on my smock, and said, "I may have ruined this painting."

"May have?"

"Well, I couldn't leave it the way it was. But I'm not sure what I did works."

"Who does it need to work for?"

"The viewer."

"Isn't that subjective?"

"Yes. But when a work sucks, it's pretty much the only unanimous reaction."

"Are you worried it sucks?"

"It would be preferable to mediocre."

"You're hoping for sucks, then."

"Pretty much."

"Am I allowed to see it?"

"Well, if you say it sucks, I am going to thank you for being honest and pretend I appreciate you for it, but I will harbor a deep and secret resentment for a long time. Possibly forever."

"Uh-oh."

"If you say it's brilliant, I'll think you're being a condescending asshole, a liar, or just an idiot."

"Wow."

"If you're neutral, I'll act like I'm fine with that, but I'll harbor fantasies of hurting you."

"Now I'm actually scared."

"And if you choose not to look at it, I will praise your intelligence, self-preservation, and restraint while actually thinking you are a spineless coward."

"That is unacceptable. I would rather have you stab me in the heart than think I'm a spineless coward."

"Yep, those are pretty much your two choices."

"What if I give you an honest opinion and you bring whatever you have?"

"All right."

We switched places. He went to stand in front of my canvas, next to the stiffening paintbrush and drying palette, and I sat in the folding chair watching his face for telltale signs and sipping his beer.

It was a long time before he spoke. "I've never seen a palette like this; the vibrancy and richness of the colors. The composition works. This blade of grass is evocative. The boy's face is compassionate, wiser than his age suggests. The overall emotion of the piece is powerful."

"Would you hang it on your wall if you didn't know I painted it?"

"If I had the chance, every day, to feel the power of this painting, then yes: I would hang it on any wall of my house. Knowing you doesn't change that one way or the other."

* * *

"Huh." And with that, I left. Shedding my smock, my hands still sticky with paint, I left the studio and went into the cool spring air. Walked down to the river and back. Michael was still in the folding chair, but he'd turned the easel around to face him. His first beer was empty and he was drinking the second.

I stood in front of him. "If you meant it, thank you. If you didn't, thank you any- way."

"I did mean it. And if I didn't like it, I would have told you. And if you resented me, I would have dealt with it."

"You're badass."

"When my wife left, I pretended to protect her to our boys; said all the right things. But I did it all with the manipulative hope that it would turn them even further against her. And it worked."

"Why are you telling me this?"

"Because I realized that throughout our entire marriage, we had never been honest with one another. We each took the path of least resistance. And it cost us everything in the end."

"How are the two of you now?"

"To the casual observer, we are the perfect post-divorce modern family."

"What about the not-so-casual observer?"

"We remind one another of the ugliest parts of ourselves and find it unbearable to be in one another's company."

"Oh." I straddled him and kissed him. "Lucky for me."

Gently, he lifted me and laid me on the hard damp floor, peeled my jeans and sad granny panties off, slid my T-shirt over my head, and when my breasts flopped sideways, resting unbecomingly against my ribs, he kissed them, rubbing his lips softly against the nipples, streaking hot down the center of my abdomen and flicking his tongue slow and soft inside me until I dissolved beneath him. Lifting over and in me, he thrusted hard against me until his breath went ragged as he let go of himself inside me. Our hearts slowed alongside one another, creating silence.

The jarring buzz of my cell phone shook the air around us. "I'm not answering that." It rang angrily, lighting up with a disturbing picture: my father's cheesy album cover. Dani had programmed my phone with pictures of all my contacts. Hers was her college graduation photo, Dylan's was a baby picture of him sitting on Dani's lap, Scott's was a picture of the devil, and my mother's was a picture of 50 Cent because she had a huge crush on him (which I found unsettling and Dani thought was hilarious).

Michael kissed me, lifted himself off me, and pulled me up by the hand. Untangling our clothes from the pile on the floor, we handed one another's items in whatever order they came apart. We dressed to the insistent ringtone of my father's Grammy hit. Dani had also given each person their own ringtone. My mother's, horrifyingly, was 'Candy Shop'.

"Ugh." Against my will, like an addict picking up a needle, I reached for the phone, relieved that Michael had his pants back on when my father's voice boomed through.

"Carly? What took you so long? I was just about to hang up."

"Hi, Dad."

"I need you to do something for me."

I looked at Michael and realized that nothing in his life had prepared him for the craziness of my family. When he'd found out who my father was, he confessed to being a fan. Of his music, that is. My father is so sincere when he sings that it is difficult to imagine him not being equally sincere with his family. I know how disarmingly charming my father can be when he wants to—-Michael will have few defenses against my father's manipulations. When you're honest and easygoing, you tend to attribute that to other people, too, unless you grow up needing to defend against it—and from what I know of Michael's history, that wasn't the case.

"Dad, I'm not having anything to do with that show."

"Did your mother call you already? I told her to let me handle it, dammit!"

"It wouldn't have mattered. There is no way I'm involving myself in it."

"Carly, how can I do a reality show about my life without the most important person in my life? You *have* to do it."

"No freakin' way." He wasn't sucking me in with that big fat lie.

"Listen. It won't be that bad. Just a dinner. One dinner. At a nice place. Mario's. I used to take you there, remember?"

"Not gonna happen. And I can't believe Mom is doing it!"

"She's a good sport, Carly."

"She just wants to humiliate you on camera and get paid for it!"

"You can't humiliate a man with humility, Carly."

"Are you saying you have humility while you're doing a reality TV show?"

"They aren't mutually exclusive. I'm surprised at how judgmental you're being about this. Dani and Dylan are coming. Scott, too. Don't you want to be represented; have your side of the story told?"

"I don't want my children involved in this." I felt a rising sense of panic as I remembered a moment during Adam's funeral. My father and Dani were talking intently, their heads bowed. Or should I say: my father was talking and Dani was listening. I remembered the worried glances she kept shooting my way and how I kept trying to make my way over to them, but with every step I was waylaid by someone wanting to offer condolences or ask about my mother. I knew how seductive my father could be when he wanted to get you on his side about something. Who knows what he must have told her to get her to agree: probably that the show was just what I needed to get over my divorce and "move forward". Hence, the worried looks from Dani in my direction.

"Too late, they're both of age and they already signed a contract. Don't be so stubborn. I am not taking no for an answer. Bring that nice friend of yours for moral support."

"Joanna?"

"No, the other one; the babe. Maryann, Marcia?"

"Merry?"

"That's the girl. Bring her: she's easy on the eyes. The camera will love her."

"Why don't you ask Scott to bring her? She's marrying him."

"Are you kidding me? That's Scott's fiancé?"

"Yes, Daddy." I guess he was too busy getting his ass kicked by my mother when the introductions were being offered.

"Well. Huh." I'd never in all my life heard my father at a loss for words. "He's a real knucklehead, giving you up for a little piece of fluff like that."

"She's actually quite intelligent and accomplished. The only strike against her is her taste in men."

"That's the spirit! So you're okay with her coming? Because it will be great television."

"I'm not okay with any of this."

"You'll be fine; there'll be plenty of wine flowing. It's a trick of the producers, but I'm on to them. God help me when your mother gets smashed. Saturday, Princess. They're sending a car for you, so be ready at 5:00. Oh, if you want hair and makeup, then they'll be there at 4:00. You know what; make it 4:00 - you could use a little pampering."

"I'm not coming!" But he'd already hung up.

Michael was giving me the hairy eyeball. "I'm afraid to ask."

I was fuming as I shoved my legs into my jeans and pulled my T-shirt over my head. Furiously, I began washing brushes. "Of all the nerve. To think I would even *consider* going, and he's dragging my children into this! I can't believe my mother is participating. AAAHHHH!"

"Babe, what is going on?"

"You don't want to know."

"Uh, yeah, I do."

"My pathologically narcissistic father, his hare-brained wife, and their innocent baby are filming a reality TV show. My cr-azy mother is appearing on it for, as she says, 'Ka-ching' and the chance to get even with him for ruining her life, apparently my asshole ex-husband is appearing on it and has somehow, behind my back, allowed my children to get involved, and now he's trying to drag me into it."

"Well, you held your ground."

"The thing is, I know myself. And I know that I will end up doing it, because I am as fucked up and bat-shit crazy as all of them. Crazier, because my eyes are wide open, but I can't stand the idea of my children being there without me to protect them."

"Protect them from what?"

"All of it."

"I'm sure your kids can handle themselves. Think about what *you* need, for a change. That's the best modeling for your kids."

"Huh. You know what? I've got plans Saturday at 4:00. Right?"

"How about a gallery exhibit, or a hike up Bear Mountain."

"Both!" I looped my arms around his neck and pressed against him.

He kissed my lips softly. "Feel better?"

I nodded.

"Good, let's get some lunch, I'm starving."

Together we left the studio. The day was ending; the pink sky a delicate, transient beauty.

CHAPTER FOURTEEN

"You come into the world crying, and it's a sign that you're alive."
– Jamaica Kincaid

Monday morning brought heavy rain. Driving to work at ten o'clock felt like early evening. The store lighting seemed more garish than usual against the dark day, and I was melancholy as I slipped out of my raincoat. Janine handed me a paper cup of steaming coffee.

"You're the best." Grateful for the warmth, I accepted it with a heavy dose of guilt. "How is it you're put together so early, with a baby to care for? I don't get it."

Janine laughed. "I'm up so early with him, I may as well look good. And I go to sleep with him at night, so…." She shrugged.

I thought of Dani, only a couple of years younger than Janine, living in the city, going to nightclubs and restaurants on a regular basis, free to do whatever she wanted, with no one to look after but herself. I thought of myself at Janine's age. I had a baby too, but with the luxury of financial support.

Janine eyeballed me as if she could read the bubble above my head. "I don't mind, Carly. I don't." She sipped her coffee and looked at me with rare uncertainty. "Gary's been calling me."

"And?"

"I'm not sure how I feel about it."

"Oh, Janine. I know you're torn, and I know a million people have told you this, but it's true, so I'm gonna say it again, Tommy would want you to be happy; he would want you to move forward."

"Actually, a million people haven't told me that. Everyone speaks to me as if Tommy's just absent. Sometimes I forget that he isn't coming home. I was so used to waiting for him. That's how it feels. Like I'm still waiting for him."

"Maybe you are."

She looked at me, her dark eyes surging with tears a blink away from cascading down her cheeks. "I am."

Holding my arms out to her, she stepped into them, placed her face to my shoulder, and sobbed, giving me, for just a moment, a fragment of her grief.

"Janine," I whispered, "it's painful to live in a different realm from someone we love with our whole heart."

I felt her quiet against me, listening.

"You know what I mean?"

She nodded.

"Tommy isn't with you in body anymore. But you feel him still, don't you."

She nodded again.

"Not to hold you back, but to help you move forward."

The noises in her throat were guttural. She pulled away and fought to speak. "I can't ever be married to anyone else. I can't replace him."

"Tommy will always be your husband and the father of your child. If you remarry, you'll have two husbands. Love is infinite."

"No one else will see it like that."

"No one else matters."

She rummaged in her bag, pulled out a makeup-removing towelette, and began mopping her face with it. "I haven't cried like that once. Not once since I heard."

"Well, I guess it was time."

"You really think I should give Gary a chance."

"Yes." I slid my eyes over the racks of clothing. "And I get to choose the date outfit!"

"No freakin' way!"

Luckily the day was so dreary that no customers came in. If they had, they would have seen two crazy women wrestling in front of the "evening wear" section, Janine going for an emerald green sequin number with leopard-print sky high boots and me trying to force a tasteful midnight blue wrap dress onto her body. Exhausted after 15 minutes of that, she agreed to try on the midnight blue dress with the leopard boots.

"You're a knockout!" I crowed.

She examined herself from multiple angles. Finally she turned to smile, her face bare of makeup and all the more beautiful. "I am!"

A feeling of warmth radiated through me. There are probably a myriad of neurological explanations for this, but I had begun to associate it with Adam: the knowledge that he was part of me, and would be forever.

Friday evening brought the first hint of balm in the air. Michael and I were on the back porch, my legs stretched over his, the ache behind my knees soothed by his thigh.

Dani was sitting across from us, leaning forward as if the thrust of her shoulders would change my mind. "Mom, this will be great for my career; a chance to show my own designs. Grandpa promised to talk about them and Grandma Bea is wearing one."

"Excuse me," I said, sitting up, nearly causing Michael to topple off the porch swing. "Did you just say, Grandma Bea?"

"What else am I supposed to call her?"

"How 'bout just Bea."

"But that isn't as funny."

"What do you mean?" I asked, knowing exactly what she meant.

"She's like ten years older than me. It's funny if I refer to her as Grandma Bea."

"Does she think it's funny?"

Dani shrugged. "Probably not."

"See, this is the kind of destructive behavior the cameras are hoping to incite and capture!"

"Not my problem."

"Dani!"

"It's not. If Grandpa wants to air his life story on TV and have all his wives in one place for dramatic effect…"

"*All* his wives?"

Dani nodded. "The one he married after Grandma—- real Grandma, I mean—- is coming."

Michael looked at me. "Breathe, Carly."

"This is so fucked up!"

Michael put his hand on my leg. "There isn't anything you can do about it."

"He's right, Mom." Dani flipped her hair back. "The cameraman - his name is Billy - he's really cute, and he said the dresses I designed read well on camera, and Grandpa is going to talk it up, so it's all good."

"Really, Dani? It's all good? Our family is about to rip one another apart for entertainment and it's all good?"

"Mom, you're making too much of it. And who says that's going to happen? We're having a dinner. Grandpa will sing, Grandma Bea will try to get Mac not to mess up her hair, real Grandma will be hilarious like she always is, Merry and Dad will make everyone throw up a little bit in their mouths- - -"

"Ugh." I stood up and went inside.

"That was rude, Mom!" Dani shouted.

I left Michael to deal with her and went upstairs to take a bath. *Breathe*, I chanted on the way up. *Meditate; just be*. None of it erased the sludge of shame wrapping around my organs and oozing through my veins.

"Mom?" Dani knocked on my bathroom door. Thank God it was locked. "I'm staying over tonight, K? But I'm going out. Don't wait up." I held my breath, hoping to hear her leave. "Mom? Sorry if I upset you." She knocked again. "Can you hear me?"

"I'm fine, Dani."

"Michael is cooking dinner for you." She lowered her voice and pressed her lips to the keyhole. "He's a good guy, Mom, I'm happy for you."

I felt a slip near my heart, a loosening. "Thanks, honey."

"You should bring him tomorrow!"

"I'm not coming, Danielle!" I yelled so sharply I worried my vocal chords were bleeding.

She was gone, running down the stairs. "Bye, Michael!" I heard her shout. A moment later a car door slammed, an engine roared, and I slid under the silky water, staying there as long as I could.

Forty minutes later, I sat facing Michael at the kitchen table. Moisturized to the point where I was slipping out of my flip-flops, I was trying really hard to feel grateful for the impromptu heavenly fragrant meal he had created by scrounging the cabinets and fridge. A crisp salad of lettuce, cucumber, dill, and dried cranberries with a white balsamic vinaigrette, pasta with garlic, oil, sun-dried tomatoes, black olives, and fresh grated cheese, and an excellent cabernet he had thoughtfully brought with him. Forcing a smile and a sigh of contentment, I willed the scratch of irritability away.

"Wow," I said. "It smells amazing."

He shot me an amused look. "Mangia." He dug in, but I caught him glancing at me, and for some irrational reason beyond my control he was pissing me off.

"What?" Yep. The word came out as pissed off and ridiculous as I felt.

"You're ... um...glaring at me."

"I am not."

"Yeah. You are. You're saying nice things, and smiling with your teeth, and glaring at me."

"If that's true, which it isn't, then why are you smirking? Do you think it's funny that I'm glaring at you?"

"A little bit, yeah."

"What's funny about it?"

He shrugged. "You're kind of cute."

I placed my fork down softly and looked at him. That wiped the smirk off his face. "Are you trying to piss me off?"

"No."

"Do you understand how annoying my daughter was?"

I recognized the look on his face. Once inadvertently, sickeningly, I'd run over a squirrel on Route 9. It had the same expression right before I hit it. "Well, Carly." He cleared his throat, "Since you ask?" I narrowed my eyes at him. "I can understand why you may have experienced her as annoying, but I think she's been sucked into this whole thing by her grandfather and the producers, and it isn't really her fault."

"She's a grown woman with a terrific mind. If she can't tell she's being played, it's because she doesn't want to."

"I don't know. She's ambitious and she's been offered the opportunity to get her designs out there in a pretty major way."

"Oh please! They're voyeurs feeding on other people's misery!"

"Maybe, but that whole franchise is making millions."

"I don't give a flying fuck about that, Michael!"

"But Dani does."

"So she'll sell some dresses, but at what cost to this family?"

"She doesn't see a cost. And it's going to happen whether she participates or not."

"That's what infuriates me. It's like watching a train speed into a wall, and I'm powerless to stop it."

"Exactly, there's nothing you can do about it."

"So, just let it happen?"

"You can't stop it."

"I don't have to participate!"

"Agreed."

I stabbed the pasta, chewed it, swallowed, and took a sip of wine. "Wow," I said, "delicious." He smiled slow and wide. I felt the tension ease away, like I was shrugging off a robe.

Could it really be this simple? I wondered. After a lifetime of trying to control and fix everyone in my life, could I just watch the train hit the wall, then walk away?

"It's not as if anything I ever did or said made a difference." The words whooshed from my mouth independently from my brain.

Michael shrugged. "My mother would have said it was God's plan."

"God plans for children to be blown to bits by war, but he gets Dylan into the college of his choice?"

"No, people blow children to bits in war and Dylan, with a combination of hard work, opportunity, and luck, got *himself* into college."

"So you don't believe in God's plan, then."

"I believe in free will. And I believe in God. They aren't mutually exclusive."

"So what, then? God's the force of creation and we just fuck it all up with our free will?"

"I do believe in a creative force. And energy. I call it "God" because I'm too lazy to think of another way to explain it to myself."

"Do you refer to God as he, or she?"

"Neither, either, or both."

"So basically you just believe in a random bunch of things?"

He laughed, seemingly unperturbed by my growing irritability, which was bordering on hostility. "I believe that God is everywhere, in each of us. Everywhere at once."

I felt a chill brush the side of my neck and down the left side of my body. Adam.

I whispered, "What happens when we die?"

His eyes, dark and steady, held mine. "If the energy is set free, it is with God. Everywhere at once."

"And if it isn't free?"

"It stays where it needs to until it is free, carried by God, as all of us are."

"And you just made this theory up?"

"I don't know if I made it up or not. I just know it."

"Have you always?"

"Since I was ten."

"How?"

"My mother was diagnosed with breast cancer."

I'd sensed something from his childhood, some kind of tragedy he had alluded to but never stated. And I, not wanting to speak about my own childhood, had never pushed him.

"I spent as much time with her as I could, sitting on the floor with my back against the couch while she rested her hand on my head. We would stay like that for hours: me reading, drawing, or doing my homework, with her hand on my head. I was sure that I heard her thoughts."

"You heard her thoughts?"

"I know it sounds crazy. But I did."

"What were they?"

"I will be fine. So will you. We will be together forever." He smiled. "Like a poem, or a song without music. Later, when she died, I would sit with my back against the couch and will myself to hear those words again. But I never did. Instead, I just knew what I told you - that she was set free. She was with God, but she was with me, too. She was everywhere at once. And I could feel her."

I shivered. "Where?"

He touched his own cheek, then slid his hand down his neck, his clavicle, and hovered at his chest directly above his heart.

"Then it is Adam I feel."

He nodded.

"But people would think we were delusional if we told them this."

He laughed. "That's why I don't go around telling everyone."

"Who have you told?"

"My ex-wife…"

"What did she say?"

"That she understood why I thought what I thought. That it was protective. That my imagination had created an explanation for me."

"Do you believe that?"

"I don't *disbelieve* it. It's just another way of explaining what I already know."

He lifted my hand and pressed it gently to his lips. "We tell ourselves all sorts of stories to make sense of the world. It doesn't really matter to me how the stories unfold; it's what we each make of them that matters."

"What about God; does God want us to believe things to be a certain way?"

"Not the way I understand God, but that doesn't make me right and someone else wrong. What matters is our individual relationship to God."

"How do you define God?"

"It's Love."

"What about Jesus?"

"If you believe, as I do, that Jesus' teachings were love, then yes, he's part of it; and so are Martin Luther King and Gandhi." He smiled. "It makes sense to me--it may not to you."

"I just never thought about any of this before, and before Adam's death - well, quite frankly, I would have thought you were crazy."

"How does Adam's death change that?"

"I feel him. And I know he's everywhere at once."

"How?"

"I don't know, I just do. Those exact words."

He smiled. "So I'm not the only one."

"Are we part of God's plan? I mean, us getting together?"

He laughed. "I think so."

"Was it God's plan to have Adam OD?"

"God carried Adam when he did OD. He didn't make him OD."

"Did God make you see me in the parking lot?"

"We were given the opportunity to be together, and we let it happen."

"I can't accept that."

He laughed. "The beauty is, you don't have to accept anything you don't want to."

"Is that part of God's plan, too?"

"Yep. He has a special love for wiseasses."

"Hmph."

"Do you know why I fell for you in that parking lot?"

"Umm, 'cause you have a white knight complex and poor vision?"

"No."

"Because my fairy Godmother cast a spell on you?"

"Ha! Maybe."

"Then what?"

"The way you were crying. The level of emotion you were feeling. I felt it too. I was walking by and felt something. A pull. And when I looked in and saw you…it sounds crazy…."

"What? What did you feel?"

"A contraction in my heart. I literally felt it swell and contract. And start racing."

"HA! You're saying I felt like a freakin' heart attack!"

"Something like that. And when you called me, I knew you were going to."

"That's because I did. If I hadn't, you would have forgotten that you 'knew' it."

"Believe what you like, but I'm telling you. And when we went out that night, it was as if... oh, forget it..."

"Oh, you're telling me now, Buster."

But for the first time since I met Michael, he looked unsure of himself. I slid off my chair, stood in front of him, opened my legs, and sat across his lap. I took his face in my hands and kissed his lips, once, twice, and again until he opened them against mine and filled my mouth with the hot salt of his tongue. When I pulled back, I waited for his eyes to open and was startled to see how he was able to focus on me immediately. "Tell me, Michael."

His hands slid down my sides, his thumbs circling my nipples through the thin silk of my robe. "That night..." He stopped speaking to kiss me again and I almost stopped caring about what he wanted to say, but I forced my eyes to open and look into his. "When we were out together, it was as if we were reunited; as if I'd been waiting for you for so long, and I'd found you. It didn't make any sense. It actually frightened me a little."

"It frightened me, too." Words I barely wanted to think, let alone say out loud. Because I knew exactly what he was talking about.

This time when he kissed me, I didn't pull away; I didn't force myself to think anymore. I just gave into the sensation of his soft tongue and hard body. Time warped. There must have been a moment when he lifted me away, unzipped and freed himself from his clothing, but his mouth was doing so much damage to my throat and breasts, I never felt or heard or saw anything else. By the time he was lifting me up and over him, I was coming apart and he was filling me.

Later - minutes, probably; but light years, experientially - my face against his neck, his arms wrapped around my back and my legs gripping his torso, my breath slowed, sensation receded, and I came back to myself. It was then that the words floated, unbidden, into my mind: "Believe what you know to be true."

So I did. Accept the notion that I am loved.

CHAPTER FIFTEEN

"If Something is going to happen to me I want to be there."
– Albert Camus

They descended at 8:00 A.M., hours before they were due to come, a pre-emptive strike against the plan Michael and I had hatched to leave the house before they arrived. A storm of vehicles, camera equipment, and people pulled up: four camera crews, two hair and makeup artists, and Astrid, the producer. She was 5'4" in five-inch heels and had glossy dark hair that swung around her face in a hypnotic manner, inducing a false sense of trust. Her eyes were wide, large, and the color of Caribbean seawater, which gave her a deceptively innocent appearance. I could see why Dani was enchanted; even I could tell she was dressed in high fashion based on the impossible height of her heels and their slick red soles. Her dress was a silky complicated print number only a size zero could get away with and it screamed vintage Valentino. Reality shows paid well, or she was knocking over consignment stores.

She spoke calmly and had a throaty voice that was sexy without sounding as if she'd been up all night smoking and drinking whiskey. I would have to be very careful around her because she was the kind of woman who inspired trust and a desire to please.

"No pressure, Carly. If you don't feel comfortable filming, I respect that." She slid a thirty-page document over to me. "This is a contract. Feel free to look it over. Basically, it gives us permission to use any footage we do film of you. But don't worry: if you aren't on camera, then it will be moot."

"Ummm, I'm not going to be on camera, so why do I need to sign anything?"

"Just in case you decide you want to be part of it, we'll get this out of the way now."

"No thanks."

"Okay, no worries." She smiled at me. She was good. Even her eyes were smiling.

She patted my arm and stood up to bustle around the room, leaving the contract for me.

A woman from "hair/makeup" approached me with a professional stride I can only describe as calmly aggressive. "Astrid wants me to do your hair. Even though you aren't filming, she wants you to feel included." She slid her hands through my hair. "Pretty. Have you ever considered parting it on the side?" Before I could stop her, she was rearranging my hair and whipping out scary-looking tools. "Your hair is straight but has some nice body, and it isn't over processed like so many women your age." She began rolling hunks of my hair. "See?" She held up a mirror. Soft waves framed my face. I looked like a different person. I was intrigued in spite of myself. Shamefully, I *am* that shallow. "Have you ever considered hair extensions?"

"Not gonna happen."

She laughed. "Okay, I won't press my luck. But you look gorgeous."

Michael came in just then. "You're not coloring it fuchsia again?"

"Shut. Up," I said, but he just smiled harder.

"Sexy!"

"Makeup" swooped in as soon as Hair moved on and was now attacking my eyebrows. "A few errant hairs - just cleaning you up, your natural shape is very pretty."

"OW!" But I didn't push her hand away. I was still dreaming about sleek, perfect eyebrows like the women in the magazines always talked about. "You're all wasting your time. I am not going on this show!"

"That's okay, Honey. Every woman deserves some primping. It's our gift to you for letting us film here."

"Ugh." It wasn't as if I'd agreed to it, exactly. They just got off the bus and started filming hours earlier than planned. Michael was out for a run, so he hadn't been there for moral support. I'd made an attempt to send them away, but it happened so fast, and Dani had seemed so excited. It was just supposed to be a few shots of all of us in her designs. I had nobody to blame but myself, for falling for it.

"You have a beautiful eye color," Makeup said in a professional tone devoid of obsequiousness, which indicated to me that she meant it exactly the way I did when I noted a paint color I'd mixed to my satisfaction. "Hazel, with a lot of green and even some gold. This palette will really bring them out; watch." And with a flurry of gentle brush strokes, she transformed my eyes. "Now for some lashes."

I looked in horror at the caterpillar-like things in her palm. "No way."

"They aren't as over the top as they seem, and it really makes your eyes pop. Just try. If you don't like them, I'll remove them."

My eyelids felt heavy and the beat of them when I blinked was as disturbing as having a bird fly into my face. "Get. Them. Off."

"Just look first." She shoved the mirror in front of my face. And I knew I would risk a brain hemorrhage to have those gorgeous-looking eyes. I looked like a movie star version of myself.

She read me like a book and went in for the kill. "You're stunning; a little lip gloss and we're done here."

"Mom?" Dani was staring at me. "You're beautiful!"

This was like crack cocaine.

"Wait! Wait!" She ran out of the room and came back in holding an emerald green dress. It was tailored and simple and my favorite color. "Please, Mom, put this on. I made it for you."

It was like some nightmare version of Cinderella.

Taking the dress, I went up to my room, slid out of my yoga clothes, put on the proper foundation garments that Dani had forced me to buy recently (I now understood her devious motive), and slid into the dress. I knew, looking at myself, that Dani was talented. That she would make it. And that she didn't need this stupid show to do it.

"You look beautiful," Michael said. I hadn't even heard him come in. He was holding a pair of shoes. Apparently Michael had been seduced by Astrid as well. "Jimmy Choo, size eight. Dani told me to give them to you; they're wardrobe's or something, but she wants you to wear them."

"I can't walk in those."

He set them down. "Then don't."

"Michael, I am not going to the restaurant with them--I'm not participating in this."

"I'll take you out to dinner instead."

"Umm, it's 12:30 in the afternoon."

"Okay - art galleries, then an early dinner."

"Deal!" I started to slide out of the dress, then caught myself. "I guess I should show Dani first."

He laughed. "You better!"

I went into my closet and found a pair of strappy sandals. They weren't amazing like the Jimmy Choos, but they were only three inches, and walkable. I slid into them and Michael whistled.

When Dani saw me in the dress, she had the audacity to well up. "Mom, it means so much to me seeing you wear one of my designs."

"Dani, this dress is exquisite. Truly."

Dylan came to stand next to me. "Dad's gonna be sorry when he sees you."

"Yuck."

Dani thrust the contract at me. "Mom, please just sign this thing. I want to take some film of you in this, that's all. Then, we'll leave you alone, I promise. You don't have to come or do anything else."

Michael looked alarmed and started forward, but he took one look at Dani's pleading eyes and threw me right under the bus. "I guess if it is just you wearing the dress. But then we're out of here."

My father was good. He hadn't tried his star power directly on Michael, which so far Michael had seemed surprisingly impervious to—-but he'd read the soft spot Michael had for Dani—-and he'd manipulated the whole day beautifully. Dani was the ticket to both of us giving in; Michael to make her happy and me to stay and watch over her despite my resolve not to.

And so it happened. I signed the damn contract. Against everything I knew to be right and sound and true. I signed it knowingly. And that is the worst part about it.

Courage comes in part from staring an ugly truth you don't want to believe about yourself right in the face and accepting full responsibility for it.

When my father's tour bus pulled up, I should have jumped in my car and waved good-bye with the music blaring and my curling ironed hair straightening in the wind.

The cameraman and the rest of the crew came out first, filming my father's descent from the gaudy bus as if it were Air Force One, capturing my father smiling, waving, and calling out, "Where's my little girl?"

When the camera found me, it found the stupefied face of a woman who had walked, eyes wide open, into an ambush.

Bea came behind him, looking stunning in what I recognized to be Dani's design. Simple, sleek, and elegant, she looked more beautiful than I'd ever seen. While the camera was trained on her, she turned to her assistant, Mimi. I hated to imagine that poor woman's job. What did it entail besides bringing Bea a latte, organizing her salon appointments, and laying out her accessories? Wiping her ass? See - three minutes in and Bitter Vituperative Woman was back in my head and raring to go. "Mimi, can you believe Guy made me wear this? And that little fashionista has the taste of a middle-aged woman. My diamond choker would have at least given this drab thing some sparkle. She wouldn't let me put it on, jealous little bitch. Who is she trying to design for? The bridge and tunnel crowd?"

Mimi threw a furtive glance my way. "You wear it well. You look fierce."

I grabbed Astrid and pulled her away. "What are they doing here? Dani was supposed to meet them at the restaurant."

Astrid put a soothing hand on my arm and held my gaze with her kind, giant eyes. "You know your dad, Carly. He's very spontaneous. He had the guys turn off the bridge and come straight here. They just notified me ten minutes ago!"

Before I could refute her or argue, I heard my mother's voice. She was pushing past Bea's nanny, who was struggling to hold Mac, who was trying desperately to wiggle out of her arms. "Oh for God's sake!" My mother was yelling at her. "Put the poor boy down! Here, Dude, have a lollipop." Before the desperate Nanny could stop her, my mother handed Mac one of those giant pinwheel things, which I knew, if she had her way, would wind up in Bea's hair.

My mother was also wearing another design by Dani; a pale blue classic shift that hit lightly at the knee. It was the perfect dress for a warm spring day and flattered my mother's tall slender frame and silver bob. My breath caught a bit as I tried to remember the last time I had seen my mother dressed so extravagantly. She caught sight of me and ran over. "Carly! You look fab!"

"You did not just air kiss me!" I hissed into her ear. She pulled me close and whispered harshly into mine.

"You suck it up and do what you need to for Dani." Really? My mother was giving me parenting advice? I felt a tiny pop somewhere inside.

Suddenly, everyone was in the house, including a petite pear-shaped brunette named Darlene. My mother ran back onto the bus and came out arm in arm with her. "Don't be shy, Boo!" She towered over Darlene, looking even more statuesque by comparison, pausing exactly long enough for the camera to give the viewers an eyeful. She wasn't a Rockette all those years ago for nothing. "Everybody, this is Darlene Manning, the second Mrs. Manning. She took the old geezer off my hands what, 45 years ago? Thought I'd slap the bitch silly when I met her, but who could resist this adorable dumpling?"

Darlene laughed and squeezed my mother's waist. "Bygones are bygones."

"I'm not here, this isn't happening, I'm not here, this isn't happening." I turned toward my garden and whispered it, praying for a Wizard of Oz-like miracle that would bring me home safe and sound to my bed, an end to this nightmare. Failing that, a tornado would do.

I stayed outside, taking deep breaths while the rest of them, bundled together in a net of film equipment, went into my house. Astrid placed a hand on my arm. "Are you all right?"

I thought back to the day in the parking lot, to Michael's impossibly handsome face peering in my window; to the sobbing which seemed a luxury now.

"No," I whispered, my eyes dry and burning.

"What is it?" she saw me look around for the cameras. "It's okay, Carly. We're alone."

"How do you do it? Act like you give a shit?"

Astrid shrugged. "I'm not acting. I care. I love your dad and Mac. I've even grown fond of Bea. She's actually got a keen sense of humor when you get to know her."

"Ha!"

"And I know how much he loves you, Carly."

"Why? Because he says he does? You don't know the first thing about us."

"I know more than you think. I'm very good at my job."

"What *is* your job, exactly?"

"Producing this documentary."

"You're delusional if you think this crap is a documentary."

"What differentiates this show from a documentary?"

"Oh, I don't know, the manipulative bullshit."

"I'm not sure what you think is going on here, Carly. We follow your father during his tour. We film it all: his concerts, home life, business meetings. We use talking heads, a time honored technique in documentary filmmaking. Sure, the camera changes things, but that's always the case. And I find that, given enough time, people tend to forget about the camera and become themselves."

I glared at her. "That's what you're counting on."

"Carly, your father is 72 years old and has a huge fan base. People love him. He's brought an awareness of country music to a large section of the public who wouldn't ordinarily be listening. You could try being proud of him."

And with that she turned and went inside.

Aside from the camera, lights, boom mikes, wires, and crew members dressed in black, anyone stopping by would have seen a Saturday afternoon gathering of friends and family. Michael was standing by my side, his hand resolutely around my waist, his forearm a steady comforting pressure at the small of my back.

Not that there wasn't enough of a circus, but he must have felt the need for some reinforcements because he texted Joanna an SOS and now she and Jake were flanking me like a couple of bodyguards. They, in turn, were being eyeballed suspiciously by Teddy, my father's actual bodyguard. I still couldn't figure out why he needed a bodyguard. It was probably Bea's idea.

My mother and Darlene were sipping champagne on the back porch. That's right. Champagne thoughtfully provided by the production team; the very same team that never interferes or manipulates, just follows my father around capturing brilliant moments of the creative process. One of the production assistants tried to hand me a glass and I nearly bit his head off. The poor kid was only a year older than Dylan. Why was I taking my bitter, vitriolic anger out on him? I could feel myself slipping. Soon, I knew, I'd be untethered, and I didn't know what to do about it or how to stop it.

A cameraman was filming my mother and Darlene while Astrid stood behind them feeding them questions like, "How was it for you, when Guy Manning left you with two children in diapers to move in with Darlene?" The women had been instructed to answer with the body of the question. My mother, who hadn't lost an ounce of her professionalism in the 49 years she'd been out of the limelight, smiled coquettishly at the camera. "When Guy Manning left me with two children under the age of four, alone in Brooklyn, never sending a dime for child support, forcing me onto welfare? I never blamed Darlene. It wasn't her fault. He told her we were divorced."

"I paid their child support checks the three months we were together," Darlene cheerfully offered.

"Really? That pig never sent it."

Darlene shrugged. "Typical Guy Manning behavior."

Astrid looked at Darlene. "How is it that you don't seem to hold a grudge against Guy Manning?

Darlene: "Well, he's a charmer."

Astrid tried again. "You're saying Guy's a charmer, and that's why you don't hold a grudge against him?"

"Uh huh." Darlene took a sip of the champagne cocktail that had just been placed in front of her. It was the size of a salad bowl and dwarfed her head. My mother gave her a slight nudge with her ankle.

"What?" She stared for a moment, confused. "Oh! Right." She looked straight into the camera and twinkled at it with her eyes, her dimples, and her enormous rhinestone earrings. "It's impossible for me to hold a grudge against Guy Manning. He's such a charmer. In his typical fashion, he lied, cheated on me and let me support him the whole time we were together, telling me his ex was greedy and had taken every last dime." She turned to my mother. "Sorry, Lovie."

"That's okay, Doll."

Darlene continued, "But I just couldn't stay mad. To this day, I love that man. And he loves me. We stay in touch through Christmas cards and whatnot. His new wife's real jealous. Of what, I don't know; these boobs are hanging to my knees!"

I looked at Joanna and rolled my eyes. Like an amorphous blob, the four of us, -Jake, Joanna, Michael and I - turned and went inside.

Dylan, wise boy, had his headphones on, sunning himself in the yard. Dani was busy conferring with Hair and Makeup. My father, Bea, Scott, and Merry were sipping cocktails at the kitchen island while Mac was busy pulling apart a cabinet of pots and pans.

Scott beamed at me. "What did I tell you, Bea? Carly would never mind; our kids always did that. You need to chillax more."

I glared at him, irritated by his proprietary attitude and bro-ish vernacular."Scott?" I asked. "Why are you even here?" I felt, more than I saw, the camera crew hum into place. I saw Merry stiffen, like a doe sensing a predator; Michael's arm, like a warning siren, pressing against my lower back; Joanna moving closer to me. Bea perked up. My father, well, he was, believe it or not, checking out his reflection in the dark glass of the microwave. My mother and Darlene were chatting away, but I heard their voices halt. Dani and Dylan were outside. Maybe they would have been enough to stop me, but it's doubtful. Only Mac kept at it, banging away at the pots and pans. Astrid, brilliant woman, pulled out a shiny red balloon from God knows where and blew it up silently, twisting it into an animal shape and luring him to the deck where a production assistant was placed firmly in charge. All of this I witnessed as if I were outside of my body. Moments passed. I registered Scott's stance. Fight. I knew it well. It came with a slight whitening and flaring of his nostrils and a lift on the far right of his top lip into a barely perceptible sneer. There was a hardness in his blue eyes that used to frighten me.

"I'm here, Carly, because my daughter asked me to come."

"Really? You think this sideshow is in her best interests?"

"Spare me the holier-than-thou attitude. You're hosting it! In YOUR house."

"Not by choice."

"Right, nothing's ever your choice. You initiated the divorce, but I'm the bad guy because I fell in love with a beautiful young woman."

Merry looked alarmed. "Scott--"

"Stay out of this," he said to her without taking his eyes from me. I wanted to smack him. I recognized the look of shame that crossed her face. For years, I'd felt it on mine.

"Whatever. I'm out." Turning to leave, I walked straight into Michael, his body hard. Feeling a thrum of violence from his muscle and bone against me, my stomach twisted. Scott's roar behind me made me turn back toward him.

"Bullshit! This is your M.O. Start shit, then walk away because you can't handle the truth."

The wild card in all of this, the piece I had never figured on, was Michael. He stepped in front of me and said quietly, but in a tone that scared me - not for myself, but for what it could lead to - "Watch your mouth when you speak to her."

Scott laughed. "Who are you? Her Mafioso boyfriend?"

"Shut up, Scott!" I was full of brilliant, witty lines that day.

"As one gentleman to another, I'm asking you to watch how you speak to her."

This was so ridiculous, even Astrid couldn't have orchestrated it. I was aware of her, over in the corner. To her credit, although I'm sure it was her wet dream and a half, she wasn't showing any emotion other than professional detachment.

Merry tried again. "Scott, baby." But he ignored her.

"Hey, Carly, call off your pit bull." He looked at Michael. "Unless you want to step outside?"

Michael just stared harder at him. "I don't feel the need. I'm sure you can back off and respect your children's mother in her own home. But if you insist…" And he smiled in a way I didn't recognize. And didn't like.

"In the home I fucking pay for!"

Jake stepped in between them. Relief buckled my knees. I needed to make things right; somehow undo the mess I'd created.

"Scott, I shouldn't have started with you. Let's just end this. Everyone should go to the restaurant now."

I tried waving my hands as if they would all disappear, but no one moved.

Scott glared at me, breathing hard. He looked like a raging bull, and suddenly I understood the movie title in a way I hadn't before. "This is so typical of you, you can't even finish what you start. You're a dried-up cunt. Well, Dude, enjoy her."

Jake put a chokehold on Michael to keep him from lunging at him just as Dylan and Dani came into the house.

I'll never know if it was a pure reaction on my dad's part, or for the benefit of the cameras, but I do know that nobody saw it coming; especially Scott. Bea was knocked over in the process and all I remember was watching her fly backward in the air, her legs above her head. Apparently fashionistas don't wear anything under their clothes and I saw much more of my father's wife than I ever should have. Teddy, my father's bodyguard, had a moment of indecision, but seeing that my father wasn't in any real danger, opted for helping Bea up from her sprawl on the floor.

My mother and Darlene, in a surreal moment of unity, began chanting, "Fight! Fight! Fight!"

It wasn't really a fight. My father launched himself at Scott, landing blows wherever he could. Scott, in pure instinctive self-defense, was clawing at my father while Merry was pulling my father's jacket, trying to get it off him and catching a wicked kick as Scott flailed his legs in the air. I went to help her up. Jake had Michael practically handcuffed in the corner. Joanna was getting an ice pack (assuming, I suppose, that someone would need it). Dylan and Dani were somehow able to get my father off of Scott. The camera crew was surprisingly unflappable. Astrid was right about one thing. We all pretty much, during those moments, forgot they were there. Which is why the footage looked authentic as it looped thousands of times over the airwaves into people's living rooms for months on end, binding all of us in an eternal moment of degradation and shame.

Once the detritus of the fight was cleared, the messy pulling apart of bodies, the swiping of bloody lips and noses with gauze, the pulling and fixing of dresses and ruined hairstyles, the untangling of camera wires and crew, the attempts at civil goodbyes and the slamming of car doors; my children, Michael, and I were left staring at one another.

I anticipated two things happening as a result of the day's activities: the unraveling of Michael and me, and the excitement for the editors and producers as they readied my father's show for its debut in the fall.

As the four of us stood in the center hall, staring at one another, I tried to come up with a quip - something to lessen the tension, to turn us into a calamity instead of a tragedy. They mean exactly the same thing, but calamity sounds funnier, and I wanted it to be funnier.

There is a space I live in my mind which takes on the dimension of a parallel universe, at times - as if a hologram of myself exists; a shimmering, better, undamaged me going through life with a sense of calm and purpose and a serenity the real me has never experienced. I conjure her like a comforting prayer. She is my transitional object, and the thing that gets me from despair to hopeful.

There is another parallel universe I inhabit frequently, and it's my automatic default, the one I go to first and sometimes can't get out of. I call it Hell.

Bitter Vituperative Woman owns this world. She lives in my head, ranting and raving; blaming and finger-pointing. Hideous, with snarling features, a hunched, forceful pace, and a shrill wail of a voice, she is to be repulsed by everyone in her path. She wears a patina of shame so unbearable to live with that she wipes it off on everyone around me, reducing them to human hand towels.

The only way I can protect Michael and my children from her is to do what I always do when things get tough. Cut and run.

Locked safely in my bathroom, I ripped the bug-like lashes from my lids, washed the thick, slippery makeup from my face, and slid into my favorite flannel pajamas at 4:00 in the afternoon. I heard them wondering, calling my name, trying the locked door before giving up and going away.

I'd forgotten to draw the shades and I opened my eyes to the pearly first light. Instinctively, I reached for Michael, only to feel the coolness of his side of the bed. Bolting out of bed, propelled by the force of memory, I went into the shower with the futile hope that all of yesterday could be washed away along with the vestiges of hairspray and eyelash glue.

I tiptoed downstairs, expecting to find an empty, reproachful house. With a mixture of relief and wariness, I noted that Dani's shoes and bag were on the front hall table and Dylan's backpack was still in the corner. Holding my breath, I turned and saw Michael stretched out, fast asleep on the living room couch. His T-shirt had ridden up, revealing a line of smooth tan skin.

Kneeling beside him, I pressed my lips against his ribs, inhaling his scent. He stirred and I felt his hand come down and stroke my hair. When I looked up at him, he was smiling at me.

"Hey," he whispered.

"Hey."

Turning his palm up, I kissed the center of it. "I'm so sorry."

"Come here." He sat up and pulled me to him.

"I shouldn't have locked myself away from you, started that fight with Scott, or gotten tricked into this whole thing."

"No regrets, Carly. I actually learned a few things."

"Like what? I'm a nut job and so is my entire family?"

He looked at me and stroked my cheek lightly with his palm; the same palm I had kissed. "I wanted to kill Scott yesterday. And not just because he was being a disrespectful asshole."

"He's such an asshole."

"I wanted to kill him because of his role in your life. The hold he has over you, the years he shared with you."

I stared at him. "That's honest."

Michael sighed. "You and Scott have children together forever. You're part of one another forever. If I hurt him, I hurt them."

"This is what you were thinking about last night while I sulked myself into a coma?"

"First I got piss ass drunk with Dani and Dylan."

My heart palpitated in a frenzy of guilt and fear. "How are they?"

Michael paused and I could see he was trying to find a way to break it to me, "Dani was really upset. She cried for a long time."

"What did she say?"

I could see he didn't want to tell me.

"Please, Michael. I need to understand, to try and make things right with her."

"She blames herself. Said it was her unchecked ambition that led to this."

Oh God. Bitter Vituperative Woman got to her despite locking myself in my room. She floats through doors, in and out of my children's dreams.

"I told her it wasn't her fault, but I don't think she believed me."

I nodded.

"Maybe this was cathartic for her. She said she hasn't shed a single tear over the divorce. Is that true?"

"I think so." I'd worried about it, but I'd also been relieved; had taken it as evidence that the divorce wasn't scarring my children. What a fool I'd been. "And Dylan?"

Michael frowned. "He's got a lot of anger toward his dad."

"I don't know what to do."

"Maybe there's nothing you can do. Dylan has to figure out his relationship with his father on his own. Sometimes getting in the middle can just make it worse."

"How did you get so Zen?"

He laughed. "I lost my wife. Hurt my children. So I had to figure some of this out. But I'm five years ahead of you."

"I'd like to meet your kids."

He smiled. "Okay."

"Have you talked to them about meeting me?"

He nodded.

"Did you warn them?"

"Nope. There's no way to explain this mess. They're gonna have to find out for themselves."

I cringed. "I have until October to win them over. Then the show airs."

He grinned. "I never signed a release, so they can't use anything with me in it."

"Oh my God, you're a genius!"

"Don't get too excited, they got plenty without me." He grinned again and pulled me to my feet, "I'm starving and hung over. I need food."

"Pancakes?" Breakfast was a productive activity within my control. Jumping up like Pavlov's dog to a bell, I was surprised to feel Michael's hand grab mine. "What?" I asked.

"Your father - he did what he did to protect you."

Possibly my father's motivation was a spontaneous reaction to protect his daughter. Or it could have been a ratings grab. Michael must have read my face. "It didn't seem contrived to me, Carly. He was a man defending his little girl."

"Except, I'm not his little girl."

Surveying the carnage in the kitchen, I began clearing it away.

"Wow, you guys hit it hard last night." I made this observation without the usual frisson of fear accompanying alcohol consumption by my family members.

I'd be lying if I didn't admit to thinking about forcing Dylan to "self-administer" the "alcoholic checklist" I kept on hand at all times. But it was a thought generated more from habit than by true urgency. I don't know if I was learning to let go or was just exhausted, but the urge passed as quickly as it came.

Wiping the wine circles from the counter top, I thought back to the ice cubes clinking in the whiskey Scott sipped throughout yesterday afternoon. I remembered the narrowing of his eyes, the hostility in his gaze. He was spoiling for a fight the way he often was when he'd been drinking. After more than 25 years of marriage, I knew the signs, but I'd ignored them and given him exactly what he wanted. Scott and I may have divorced, but we were still dancing the same sorry dance. I was tired of that too, and made my mind up to end it. If Scott wanted to keep going, he was going to have to dance without me.

Michael's back was to me while he made coffee. If I raised myself up on my toes, just a bit, I would be able to kiss the nape of his neck; taste the spice of his skin. And I would, I promised myself, as soon as the counters were clean, the sink empty of glasses, the recyclables taken away, the pancakes scenting the air, the table set....or not. Instead of waiting, I placed the sponge on the sticky counter, walked across the room surrounded by yesterday's wreckage, put my arms around Michael's waist, and kissed the nape of his neck, tasting his smooth skin and feeling his heat against my heart. Clocks all over the world ticked seconds as we hurtled, locked together, through time and space where fear and regret didn't rule me.

CHAPTER SIXTEEN

"Yoga is the cessation of the fluctuations of the mind."
- Patanjali

People seemed to have developed a love affair with the borough of Brooklyn. Facebook was on fire with images of Brooklyn in the 70s and 80s. Gritty black and whites of children cooling off in the hard cold spray of the Johnny pumps, dodging cars to play stickball with images of sewers as home plate; subway cars traveling the El in a blaze of graffiti. It had been a nightmarish decade for me, but one that was becoming cleansed by nostalgia for our youth.

My mother assured me every time I spoke with her that The Slope was "getting even worse. Lousy with entitled, smarmy, hipsterish parents who were clearly the offspring of entitled, smarmy yuppies," was the way she phrased it. "They should move up by you, Carly. And leave us alone." This, after a long involved story about a fight over strollers crowding a local restaurant—-one of the few which both "hipster transplants" and "born-and-bred Brooklynites" like to frequent. The fight had apparently escalated in blogger-land to such a degree that my mother was now going to the restaurant merely to taunt the parents who, as she put it, clogged the sidewalk by pushing their thousand-dollar baby strollers abreast of one another while placating their obnoxious offspring who sucked from mason-jar-sippy cups filled with high-alkaline water.

I honestly think my mother makes half this stuff up. Having endured Park Slope through the years of gang fights, drugs, and crime, only to have it (as she points out every time I see her) usurped by young wealthy transplants from Manhattan and other far-flung cities has become a mantra of complaint, yet I also think her tirades are a way to amuse herself and needle me, rather than an indication of any real ill-will she feels toward her neighbors. When we walk the streets of The Slope, I see more harmony and neighborliness than my mother and the bloggers ever let on.

I had my own love affair with Brooklyn as a child. I remember reading *A Tree Grows in Brooklyn* on my fire escape. On the streets below, men were lined up, conga and bongo drums nestled between their thighs, colorful in dashikis, drumming in polyrhythms for hours, a call and response with the sound of children playing, cries of *all-y, all-y, all, come free* tempting me to leave my perch and join in the exhilaration of catching and getting caught. But I was lost in the Brooklyn of my book; one I barely recognized except for the description of the tenements and the fact that for as many differences as Francie's character and I had, we had similarities, including a mother who loved our little brothers best.

When I was in fifth grade, going home was like a game of roulette. My mother could be chipper, chopping carrots and celery for minestrone. Or, she could be raging and drunk at 3:00 in the afternoon. On one such winter day I came home and heard her muttering and stumbling behind the closed door of her bedroom. Adam shot me a warning look when I hesitated at her bedroom door, but I ignored it and went in. I needed to make sure she was all right.

"Good," my mother said when she saw me. "You're here. I need you to do something for me." Handing me the receiver, she said, "Ask for Lucy. Go on, do it."

A clamping of my stomach came with the familiar rat-a-tat of the dial circling, then the staccato ringing on the other end. My mother and I had rehearsed this particular number enough times that I knew more or less what to expect. A woman's voice answered, throaty and harsh. "Hallo."

"Um--is Lucy there, please?" My mother handed me a piece of filthy notebook paper with large block letters in red ballpoint.

"Read this," she whisper-slurred.

"Yeah, this is Lucy." She sounded wary. As well she should have.

I read the first line. "This is Guy's daughter, Carly."

Silence. Then, "So?"

I couldn't say the words on the page.

"Do it," my mother hissed. I shook my head.

She grabbed my wrist and squeezed painfully. "Do it." The words *dirty whore* were underlined five times. The next line was something like, *he's giving you all his money and his children are eating welfare peanut butter.*

"Um--well--we haven't heard from him in awhile--and I wonder—is he there?"

My mother shot me a malevolent look and turned her back on me to light a cigarette with shaky hands.

I heard the woman on the other end sigh. "I haven't seen or heard from your father in two weeks."

"Oh. Ok. Sorry to bother you."

"Hey, Kid, listen."

"Yes?" I was ashamed at the flicker of hope I felt. Did she have some message for me from my dad?

"If you do see your father, tell him I said to go fuck himself."

I hung the phone up as fast as I could, but it was too late; my mother had heard her.

"What did that bitch say to you?"

"Nothing, Mom; she hasn't seen him."

"Did she tell you to go fuck yourself?"

"No!"

Fueled by rage, she moved surprisingly fast, considering how drunk she was. She slapped my face and twisted the phone from my hand. "Don't lie to protect that filthy whore!"

"Mom, please."

I reached for the phone, but she was stronger. And angrier. I watched her dial the seven numbers, each rotation taking a million years. Her finger got stuck in the seven and I thought she was going to throw the phone across the room. I was relieved that maybe this would be the end of it and was disappointed when she wrenched it free and kept going.

I heard Lucy answer on the first ring. "What?"

"You fucking whore!" my mother screamed, the veins throbbing in her neck. "You're taking the food out of my children's mouths!"

"I don't know what your piece of shit husband is saying, but he hasn't given me a dime. He stays here for free, eats my food, fucks me, borrows money, then disappears; and if you ever call me again, I'll come over there and beat your face in while your kids watch."

I wish I hadn't been able to hear Lucy so clearly. But I could. Her words and the images they evoked made me feel sick to my stomach. I watched my mother slam the phone down and light another cigarette. Then I went into the bathroom and heaved into the sink. I hadn't eaten anything that day. Breakfast was unusual in my house. That morning wasn't a good one for my mother. I'd gone into her room and kissed her good-bye, recoiling at the heavy smell of booze and unwashed body. Her eyelids fluttered and she rolled over, emitting a sour smell. I tried to wake Adam up, but he just gave me the finger, so I went into the cold winter morning trying to forget about them. I qualified for free lunch at school and I could have eaten there, but the line was long and two boys started fighting right ahead of me, the whole line started pushing, shoving, and I knew I was a heartbeat away from getting my hair pulled or the wind knocked out of me. So I stepped out of the melee and went to find a corner that wasn't teeming with competition or violence.

The good news was, all I could do was dry heave into the sink. When the spasms in my stomach subsided, I washed my face and hands and went into my room to do my homework, repeating over and over in my head, "I'm not here, this isn't happening. I'm not here, this isn't happening."

The next morning, my mother had pulled herself together. I surfaced from sleep into the grey winter light as her hand skimmed my cheek with a flutter of love and hope and sorrow that I understood deep in the furling and unfurling of my belly. My mother was pale with puffy dark half-moons under her eyes, but she made us cornflakes, wrapped peanut butter sandwiches in wax paper, stuck them in our bags, and walked us to the corner of our school before kissing us goodbye and continuing along Washington Avenue toward the Brooklyn Museum where she worked. I watched her stride, purposeful and steady, which made me feel better. Adam wouldn't say a word to me and ran off into the schoolyard, disappearing into the sea of bodies as soon as he could.

After school, he refused to come home with me. He was in third grade and I was supposed to be in charge of him. I tried pulling him by the hood of his parka, but he turned and punched me, getting me to let go before he laughed and ran off with a group of boys to get high on the rooftop of the building across the street.

Turning the key in the lock, I was relieved to have the quiet, empty apartment to myself.

Homework was heavy on my conscience, but the opportunity to go through my mother's closet was too good to pass up. I loved pulling her jewelry box off her shelf, trying it all on and thinking about the stories that corresponded with each piece.

All of it was costume except for the thin gold wedding band nestled in the utmost bottom corner. The box was made to look like an old pirate's chest and it had three red velvet trays that stacked inside it. The top tray held a multitude of colored glass beads. Brilliant purples and greens and blues, worn with different costumes for different shows she'd been in. The second tray had compartments; some with dangling earrings, others with a tangle of bracelets, silver bangles with little balls on the end, faux pearls on coiled wire that snapped back at me and poked. The third tray held sparkling clusters of rings. Draping myself in as much jewelry as I could, I went to the window, opened it, and belted all the songs from *Oklahoma* ending with my favorite, "I'm Just a Girl Who Can't Say No."

When I'd finished and all the jewels were safely nestled back in place and the treasure chest was neatly tucked away, I went in search of the large cardboard box of photos. I never tired of looking at pictures of my happy parents in love, glamorous, surrounded by smiling theatre people. Those were the good times, before I had come into the picture and ruined it all. There was one photo in particular. My mother was holding me in her arms. I was about a year old, with long skinny legs and fat cheeks, and I was squinting into the camera. My mother had the widest smile, her beauty unselfconscious. My father stood behind her, his arms around both of us, laughing into the sun.

I was on the step stool in the closet straining toward the cardboard box when my hands closed around an instamatic camera.

Examining it, I saw through the little window a perfect number 8, indicating how many pictures had been taken.

Checking that I'd placed everything else back in its rightful place, I pushed my keys deep into my pocket, put on my coat, and ran down the five flights of stairs and into the bitter winter cold.

Here is what I shot:

Barbed wire jutting from the concrete barrier of the train trestle beneath a pale milky sky.

A man in a hat emerging from the Franklin Avenue subway, his trudge heavy, as if each step cost him something.

A woman pulling a metal shopping cart with groceries, carrying a small child on her hip. The baby was holding her mother's coat collar and smiling into the camera. The mother's face was turned into the cold, her eyes narrowed against the wind. If you looked closely, you could see, in the tiny triangle at the outside corner of her eye, a subtle swell of tear.

A sidewalk with bits of sparkle and a grey blob of old chewing gum.

Worn-looking men surrounding a trash can fire, jutting flames a colorless wisp.

A graffiti-covered wall on the corner bodega, "Horse was here" written in large black bubble letters with a filthy white border. "Blue-eyed devils fuck off," and "Kill Whitey" also appeared, in spray paint.

A tattered cat sleeping amid a pile of cardboard boxes in the dreary, dust-streaked window behind flyers displaying a multitude of needs.

Chained, battered, metal garbage cans with "12 Crown" in black paint on the front.

And one of my father. With a woman. Maybe it was Lucy, or maybe it was someone else he'd moved on to. But he was walking along Washington Avenue toward Wetson's, his arm around a woman with curly blonde hair. The fact that he'd been so close all along, or worse, that he'd come back to Brooklyn to visit her but not us left the first burn of jealousy in the back of my throat and deep into my chest. I followed them all along Washington Avenue until they stopped at the Prospect Park subway station. He turned and kissed her, holding her face between his hands, and looking into her eyes before kissing her lips. I could almost smell the trace of Marlboro trapped in the wool of his coat; the scent of violet gum he often chewed. That was the shot I got before they broke apart and he descended into the chasm of the subway, heading to the D train and away from Brooklyn.

Knowledge that I had these pictures buried somewhere in my house fueled me despite the crushing heat that had come on instantly with the summer solstice. Crawling into the narrow attic space, rejecting box after box, I rummaged through the last remaining carton and saw the album I was searching for.

It was square and pink, with a faded picture of The Partridge Family on it. Susan Dey and Shirley Jones were singing, lips pursed, eyes wide. David Cassidy leaned into the microphone in an approximation of ecstasy. The thin cellophane had long ago lost its stick and the photos stayed in place solely due to gravity. If I wasn't careful with it, the pictures would come fluttering out, corners curling against themselves.

Opening the album, I took each photo and scanned it into the printer, then pressed the originals safely back into the album. Calmed by the completion of this task, I left the relative comfort of the air-conditioned house and went into the sticky outside air.

Crossing the narrow garden where the vestiges of lilies of the valley had faded to brown, I took the stairs of the studio two at a time, coming face to face with the canvas I had been working on feverishly for the past two months. My guess is that every painter who has ever practiced yoga has attempted to capture the exact colors of the light show illuminating the shadow behind our closed lids: indigo, gold, amethyst, cerulean, and teal swirling, flashing, and moving in waves. Foolishly, I joined the ranks, moved to do so one day after a particularly vivid yoga class.

Lying on the mat as the light show behind my eyes faded and diminished, I'd rolled over as instructed, bowed my head to our instructor, and participated in the controlled chaos of women as they slipped into shoes, gathered car keys and handbags, reactivated cell-phones, and chattered about recipes and their children's carpools, allowing the stuff of their lives to seep back in. It took all my concentration to block it out and get back to my studio before the colors I had seen began to dissipate. Once there, I'd mixed, rejected, painted, dried, and repainted until the movement, light, and pigment was where I'd wanted it to be. Now, more than two months later, I stood staring at the canvas. I knew it was as close as it was ever gong to be, so with a steady hand and a speeding heart, I used what was left of the morning light and began cutting my childhood memories into bits so I could collage the stark black and white images onto the vivid colors of my mind.

Hours later I showed up to Mandee's for the afternoon shift, bleary-eyed with paint stained fingers and an impossible cowlick which had Janine eyeballing me in a way I can only describe as menacing.

Looking me up and down, she pointed to the storeroom. "Lucky for you there's a ton of new inventory you can deal with." Her not-so-subtle way of saying I was unfit to deal with the public.

Relieved to have a mindless task, I began to unwrap and sort the shipment of bags and shoes. The overwhelming smell of plastic and chemicals assaulted me, but was a small price to pay in order to have had the morning free to paint.

After a while Janine came in and stood watching me. "Still not smoking?"

I looked up at her and grimaced, then took the opportunity to stretch my sore arms and upper back. "Yeah."

"Wanna come with anyway?"

"Sure."

"Will it be too tempting?"

"I'm a big girl."

We stood out back in the roaring heat, which hadn't abated despite the descent of the day into early evening. Sipping from a bottle of lukewarm water, I watched Janine blow smoke rings.

She narrowed her eyes against the smoke and looked sideways at me, pursing her lips delicately and exhaling a stream of smoke. "Had sex with Gary for the first time."

Trying not to appear as embarrassed as I felt at the sudden confidence, I kept my face neutral. "And?"

"Hot," she whispered. And for the first time ever, I saw her flush.

I laughed. "I'm happy for you."

"I'm happy for me, too."

"Was that the first time since your husband?"

She shook her head. "There were a few disastrous hookups when I got so horny I couldn't take it any more; guys I wouldn't get attached to, but it was empty."

I nodded, surprised that I understood despite our difference in age and the circumstances of being single. Loneliness, in any form, is recognizable to me.

She smiled with an unexpected shyness. "Maybe we could double date sometime."

"I'd like that."

"Cool." She stamped out her cigarette, twisting her stiletto over it. "So, how's lover-boy doing?"

"We talked about me meeting his kids."

"Big step, huh?"

"I feel like an ass."

"Why?"

"I'm terrified of them. They're 24. And they're twins."

She laughed. "I'm 24, you know."

"I know."

"If they're mean to you, I'll kick their asses."

"Thanks."

Heading into the store, we were greeted with a frigid blast of air. I turned to Janine. "So are things serious with you and Gary?"

She shrugged. "I like him a lot. He's great with my son. It's just ... "

I could see her struggling and I wasn't sure if she was having difficulty articulating what she thought or if she was hesitant to say it to me. She busied herself with an impeccable rack of jewelry. The store was empty of customers and the other saleswoman was up front, too far away to hear us.

"Because in some ways," she paused, "I'm happier with Gary." She looked straight at me. "I'm a traitor."

"You're human."

"I feel like he knows."

"Gary?"

She shook her head, "Tommy."

"Maybe he does." I instantly regretted saying that, because Janine's eyes flooded, the tears hovering like an infinity pool. She blinked and pressed the tip of her finger to her bottom lid, capturing the salt against the hot pink of her fingernail. I touched her arm, gently. She didn't pull away. Holding her gaze, I whispered to her, "You feel him, don't you?"

She nodded. "I think I'm going nuts. But I do. I feel him."

I nodded. "I feel Adam, too."

"Do you think it's all in our mind?"

I shrugged. "I don't know. But I feel him all the time. And sometimes I just know things."

She nodded fearfully. "Me too. Especially about our son. He's proud of him. He loves him. He wants me to know that."

"And do you ever feel him judging you? About Gary?" Her eyes wandered. I could see her thinking about it, remembering.

Slowly she shook her head. "I feel him knowing how I feel, though."

I smiled. "Maybe he does."

"But he'd be so angry!"

I shook my head. "If he were still alive, and you were married, and you felt like this about Gary, he'd be angry."

"But I wouldn't. I wouldn't feel like this about Gary if he were here."

"Exactly."

She stared at me. "He understands?"

I nodded. "The same way Adam understands my..." But I couldn't say the words out loud.

"Your relief?"

I nodded.

She touched my hand, her nails glistening against my dry cracked skin. "Don't be ashamed, Carly. You loved him. And it must have been so hard to see him suffer."

"He was a prisoner in his own mind. I'd look in his eyes and it was as if I could see him looking back at me. He wanted to be free."

"He is now." She looked at me in that peculiar way of hers, sideways and up beneath her lashes. "When I was little, I used to worry I was somebody's dream and if they woke up, I'd be gone."

"Whoa. That's deep for a little kid."

"I know, right?"

"How did you work that one through?"

"I figured if it were true, and it happened, I'd never know, so it wouldn't matter."

"Did you use that knowledge for evil, like you could do whatever you wanted because it may not matter?"

She laughed. "Nah. I hedged my bets in case it wasn't true. My mom would've whooped my ass, and she could have broken through any time barrier."

I laughed. "Maybe I should've done some ass whooping on my kids."

She looked me up and down. "Mm-mm. Not your style. You love your kids to pieces. They were good so they wouldn't hurt you."

I winced. It wasn't a flattering portrayal. Made me sound weak. But it was true.

Janine put a giant pink ring on her pointer, and placed a black flower ring with a rhinestone center on my middle finger. "Don't ever apologize for being who you are, Carly. You're the best friend I've ever had."

The bells jangled, indicating customers, and we looked up to see six girls walk in carrying McDonalds sodas, announcing they were there to look for after-party outfits for prom night. I watched Janine expertly divide and conquer them while I stood by, waiting for orders on which sizes to pull, realizing how much I truly loved my job.

When my shift ended, I drove five minutes up Route 9 to the frame shop. There were customers lined up at the counter so I barely had time to set my handbag down before inserting myself into a bevy of questions, complaints, and requests. I was certain some of the customers laid in bed thinking about ways to make our lives difficult. Having been the beneficiary of my boss's creative approach to framing, however, I bit back my sarcastic retorts, slapped a smile on my face, and got down to the business of helping people match their artwork to their wallpaper. This always pissed me off more than was reasonable.

By nine o'clock the last of the customers were gone, the front door was locked, and the closed sign was swinging like a victory banner.

Karen looked at me and grinned. "Hold on. I gotta get something."

I was surprised to see her return with a bottle of champagne and two delicate flutes.

"What are we celebrating?" I asked as she handed me a glass and began an efficient twisting and sliding of the cork with only a tiny pffft of air to signal its removal.

She smiled like the Mona Lisa and poured.

"To your show." She clinked and sipped and motioned for me to do the same.

"Huh?" Inelegantly, my paint-stained fingers gripped the delicate stem, the ice-cold bubbles stinging my mouth and tongue.

She sighed. "You're going to kill me, but I submitted your work to a gallery across the river in Piermont."

"Oh." Piermont was a small waterfront town directly across the Tappan Zee Bridge. It was Rockland County's art mecca, with benches overlooking the Hudson River, perfect for eating a sandwich and feeding leftover bits to the expectant seagulls. Michael and I spent more than a few Saturday afternoons strolling in and out of those galleries. Seeing Mercy displayed on the wide white walls was an unspoken wish relegated to the furthest corners of my mind.

Karen took another sip of champagne, her anxiety at my response showing like a thin strip of gauze on her face. "Mercy is just.....I'm obsessed with it. And the other paintings you've been doing. Michael shot them for me. And I submitted them to all the galleries I know and here's the offer."

She handed me a glossy brochure from one of the galleries across the river, it wasn't the biggest, or slickest; but it was my favorite.

"I don't know what to say." And I didn't. No one ever, in the history of my life, had ever done anything like this for me.

"Say you're happy! Over the moon! You're going to have your own show!"

I wanted to explain to her how I wasn't ready. My paintings weren't ready.But she looked so worried; so desirous of my appreciation. I couldn't respond the way I wanted to, so I set my champagne down, hugged her, and whispered, "Thank you for believing in me."

With that small act I accepted that I would have a show and that people would see inside my soul, and that, even if they were repulsed--or worse, indifferent--I would be okay.

CHAPTER SEVENTEEN

"In any moment of decision, the best thing you can do is the right thing, the next best thing is the wrong thing, and the worst thing you can do is nothing."
– Theodore Roosevelt

That was brave talk back in June, when Karen and I stood celebrating in the fading light of her frame shop. But now in the sweltering days of late summer, the ground soaked with unshed rain and the fetid smell of a sewage spill from the Hudson River, I couldn't help feeling it was an omen. A bad one.

I had hurried to finish the last of the paintings, agonized on how best to frame and display them, and spent great chunks of my life hiding from anything that reminded me of the television show airing in six short weeks. Promotional campaigns were underway on television and in the press, and while I hadn't been mentioned by name, I lived in constant dread that someone would ask me about it or that some footage with me in it would be revealed.

Dani was displaying quite a talent for marketing and promotion, blowing up social media with this tiny gallery show separated from New York City by multiple highways and bridges.

Dani texted me constant questions, which I was expected to answer in a 3-second turnaround. We had 978 followers, which was pretty good according to Dylan. My text acronyms had become copious and for some reason my children found this hilarious in a way that made me suspicious, probably because I caught them laughing in the same delighted and slightly snide way as I did when my mother used the words *dope, chill,* and *boo.*

My cell phone chimed, signifying a text. It was from Dani: *Inspiration?* Ugh. *U have to answer.*

I thumbed my response: *myriad ways human beings hurt each other juxtaposed against raw natural beauty.*

My phone pinged almost immediately: *Really??*

Nah.

One more chime: *Ha! I'm using it.*

I shrugged. It was impossible for me to describe painting in any sort of meaningful way. But Dani insisted that people were eating it up: artists, art lovers, college students. I felt like a heel and a fraud. I wondered if my portrayal on my father's reality show was more deserved than I had previously believed.

"Babe?" Michael came onto the deck where I was sipping my morning coffee, tranquil among the flowering shrubs, despite the insistent roar of lawn mowers and the chirping of my cell phone. Michael smelled of shaving cream and Ivory soap. His hair was still damp. Giving me an evil grin, he slid his palm inside my Hanky Pankies and cupped me, his finger spreading me apart and lightly stroking. Bending over me, his kiss tasted of toothpaste and salt. He pulled back, leaving me drunk and disoriented in the morning air. Giving what I can only describe as a triumphant smile, he offered an insincere apology: "Sorry, couldn't resist." When my eyes refocused, he launched into serious mode. "So, um, the boys are in town tonight and I'm thinking it would be a good time for you to meet them."

"Is there an occasion?"

"Their mom's birthday tomorrow, but she has a private gig tonight out on Long Island, so…."

I was secretly fascinated with his ex-wife's music career. I creepily stalked her on line whenever I had the opportunity, checking tour dates and scouring pictures and video of their various gigs, mostly in local Westchester and Rockland County bars. I couldn't reconcile the gamine dark-haired pixie rocking out on her guitar with the sleek elegant photo of her and Michael on their anniversary; the one he showed me a million years ago (okay, less than nine months ago) on our first date. I'd subsequently and surreptitiously searched his wallet on more than one occasion, hoping to see it again, but he must have removed it. On the rare occasion that we spent time in his man cave, I saw no evidence of it. His man cave was a disappointing cliché of the divorced man, despite the divorce having taken place ten years ago.

It was a surprisingly sunny condo a few miles up the road across from the supermarket parking lot where we met. Pristine, with white walls, shiny hardwood floors, and a tiny kitchenette that housed an impressive espresso maker and an array of gleaming pots and pans as well as a state of the art knife set; all of which now sit under and on top of my counters because he missed cooking with them. My pots, pans, and knives were from my bridal shower 25 years ago and are, as he put it, "from hunger." His living room consisted of a black leather sectional, a ginormous flat screen HD television, an in-the-wall sound system, and a photo of him and his boys whitewater rafting. His bedroom consisted of a king size bed and blackout shades, The boy's bedroom was furnished with bunk beds and a double dresser, the walls covered with posters of late-90s music icons, primarily rappers and hip-hop artists.

"Where should we go?" I asked him, feigning enthusiasm, which I could tell by the way he was smirking at me, wasn't fooling him the least little bit.

"There's an Italian place in the West Village they love."

"Perfect. I love The Village on a Saturday night."

My eyes wandered to my cell phone. I was dying to text Janine, Joanna, and possibly Dani to get their advice about what to wear. I needed to portray effortless cool, which was impossible with my wardrobe and my body temperature at the moment. I wondered if I should try cutting my hair into a hip sexy pixie before realizing that I have a child-sized head and fine hair, so I would look like a pinhead and they would obviously see through my feeble attempt to emulate their cool rocker mom.

Michael stood up. "Gotta run a couple errands; you need anything while I'm out?"

I patted the book lying unopened on the ground next to my lounge chair and held up my cold mug of tea. "Nope. Just relaxing."

He smiled. "Taking a day off from the studio?"

"Self imposed ban due to my paint-over-everything-because-it-is-mediocre-crap phase."

"Should I padlock it before I go?"

I think he was only half kidding. "Nope. I have self discipline."

He gave me a wary look but walked down the deck and around to the driveway, jingling his car keys. I waited until I heard the car door slam before sending a frantic group text for wardrobe advice before realizing it was a horrible idea, considering that Dani and Janine had opposing tastes and that Joanna could care less.

Dani pinged back immediately: *Stay put, I'm bringing you something from my closet.*

Disaster.

Janine texted a few minutes later: *We have a really pretty sundress--flower print--all the rage.*

Dani texted me back privately: *Do NOT wear a cheap ass sundress!*

She is an unbearable snob.

I texted Janine: *Will be by soon to check it out. Should I wait for Dani to bring one of her outfits?*

Janine texted me back: *Lol you liar, you will never wear anything she brings even though it will look gorgeous on you.*

A few minutes later Joanna texted the group: *Wear the dress Dani made you.*

Me: *Will it be too dressy? Don't want to look like I am trying too hard.*

Dani: Flats and simple jewelry.

Joanna: *Do it, Carly!!!*

Janine: *Have some fab bottle-green bangles--will drop them off.*

Dani private text: *Do NOT wear the effin bangles.*

Me: *Thanks, girlz.*

Dani: *Ew. No. girlz.*

Wow. My texting may indeed be a version of my mother's use of contemporary vernacular. Taking a deep breath, I realized this was the way my mother felt when I rolled my eyes at her, and had the comforting thought that someday Dani would have a daughter and all her hair flipping and coolness would evoke eye rolls and snide comments. I smiled, visualizing myself lounging on Dani's future couch, sipping a martini, smoking cigarettes, and smirking while my future granddaughter gazed adoringly at me and asked my opinion on fashion.

* * *

Dressed by committee, I found myself seated next to Michael across from two handsome, engaging, 24-year-old clones of their dad. Teeth suddenly too large for my mouth, shallow breath, and my permanently clenched hands revealed how anxious I was. Michael kept his hand on my back, perhaps to calm me down. But nothing helped. I had a desperate desire to laugh, scream, or cry uncontrollably.

Blame it on having watched countless episodes of *Madmen*. An image of Betty Draper, elegant and cool despite her supreme dysfunction and horrible parenting, caused me to order a vodka gimlet. I needed to untether from the post of fear I'd strapped myself to. Assuming it would taste like rubbing alcohol, I expected to sip it slowly throughout the evening. It was, however, deliciously cold and tasted of fresh lime. So I pretty much chugged it, and had graduated to the rapid sipping of an icy glass of Sauvignon blanc.

Luckily, smoking cigarettes is against the law. Say what you want about the nanny state, it saved me from chain smoking in the boys' faces. The boys were introduced to me as Jimmy and Billy, but they refer to one another as Jim and Bill. The 'ee' sound at the end of their names had apparently been shed when they entered high school, along with the demise of their parent's marriage.

Jim was drinking a Jack and Coke, Bill was on his second draft beer, and both of them were regaling us with a play by play of Bill's company softball game which Jim had somehow played in, even though he wasn't an employee. My cheeks hurt from smiling and my ass cheeks were sore from clenching, causing an epiphany about the genesis of the expression "tight-ass," which I inexplicably and quite suddenly found hilarious. Which is why, during the dramatic telling of how Bill slid into home while Jim stole third, then followed his brother across the plate, tying, then winning the game, I inappropriately barked a loud, decidedly non-Betty-Draperish laugh.

Michael's hand spasmed for a moment into a grip of my shoulder, the boys, finished their tale and took an appreciative sip of their drinks, and Jim eyeballed me over his glass while Bill winked at me after draining his mug and setting it down on the table with a deft flick of his wrist for the waitress.

I thought that when Michael moved my wine glass a few centimeters to the right, he was censoring me, but he was just making room for a platter of olives.

"So, Carly?" Bill asked between enormous bites of oil-soaked chunks of Italian bread. "Dad says your show is already generating a lot of buzz."

"Oh. Um. Well, whatever that means."

Bill grinned. "Your art show, I mean; not the reality show with your father."

"Yeah," I said, sipping the Sauvignon blanc maniacally. "I'm hoping the reality show dies a quiet death."

"Unlikely." Jim's gaze held mine as steadily as Michael's often did, and I know it wasn't paranoia that registered revulsion. I couldn't blame him. I felt the same way about it.

Bill shrugged. "Yeah, that show pretty much dashed our hopes that one of our parents would retain a modicum of decency."

Jim's laugh was short, sharp, and bitter. "Don't listen to Bill, he thinks he's a character in a 19th century comedy of manners."

I nodded. "Very Jane Austin. I wonder what she would have made of the whole reality TV thing."

"I don't know," Michael said. "Seems like the modern variation of gossip traveling along with the knife seller. It's manufactured just as the post mistress manufactured her version of events years ago, feeding the prurient interest of folks from village to village."

I stared at him. "It's soul-sucking."

"Sure," Michael said, "but soul-sucking isn't anything new."

I looked at the boys. "I'm mortified about it. And I'm sorry I dragged your dad into it."

Jim held his father's gaze this time. "Dad's a big boy."

Bill shoved his brother with his elbow, "Don't mind him, Carly. He's still horrified about our mother playing in a soccer mom cougarish rock band."

I wasn't touching that one. "I think that's so cool." Okay, I thought I wasn't touching it, but apparently I had no control over the words that emanated from my mouth.

Jim glared at me. "Cool? She's not in middle school."

"No," I said, "and she's not dead, either."

Bill laughed. "Don't stick up for her, Carly, she would never do it for you. She's very dismissive of Dad and anything or anyone he's interested in."

"That's okay, I'm a big girl, I don't need anyone to stick up for me. And I'm not sticking up for her, either. But I think playing music is cool. And if I could do it and had the opportunity to do it, I would."

"Really?" Jim said. "Being a painter of unmatched resonance yet with impeccable technique isn't enough for you?"

"Knock it off, Jimmy." Michael's nostrils flared in an unpleasant way.

Jim shrugged. "I thought you would be gratified that I've been following her on Twitter and that I had committed some of the reviews to memory." He pushed away from the table, and when he turned his gaze on me, it wasn't as bitter or angry as his words suggested. He looked instead immeasurably tired. "Sorry, Carly. I know it isn't fair, and your kids love Dad, but I'm a judgmental prick, and you're going to have to earn it from me."

Bill and Michael were making all kinds of noises of distress, but I was relieved. I like knowing where I stand with a person. "Okay, Jim, I respect that. But you should know that I'm remote, self-contained, and while I'm incredibly neurotic, my neurosis doesn't take the form of giving a shit what people think of me. So I'm probably not going to try that hard."

Jim leaned toward me. "You're a liar. You care very much what people think of you."

"Yeah, well, I've been working on that."

Bill laughed. Michael rubbed the point between his eyes and Jim smiled at me and said, "I'm not storming off. I just have to take a wicked piss."

Bill looked at me earnestly. "He went to school in Boston." He must have seen my confusion because he followed with, "That's why he says things like *wicked piss*."

"Oh, okay." The pleasant buzz from the gimlet and wine had run its course leaving a wake of lethargy and a slight vertigo. Torn between a need for fresh air and the uncomfortable swelling of my bladder, I was concerned about seeking either due to the necessity of negotiating the clutter of chairs and people, not to mention the steep and narrow staircase down to the restrooms.

I also knew that the second I left them alone, Michael was going to light into the boys. And the last thing I needed was for them to get into a fight over me; especially because Bill was back in his chair, having procured another beer somewhere between taking a wicked piss and staggering back to the table.

Apparently one of the side effects of vodka gimlets was that whatever went through my brain popped out of my mouth. "Listen, fellas, I've gotta go to the ladies room. Please don't lecture the boys, Michael. We're all adults, and I'd rather hear it straight up than have polite conversation. So--um--I'll be back."

* * *

I walked away from the table with as much dignity as possible given the fact that I had to walk with the careful precision of a very drunk person trying not to appear drunk.

I realized how much trouble I was in when I sat to pee and the floor tiles tilted up to meet the walls of the stall. Steadying myself, I ran cold water over my wrists and took slow deep breaths. *Go back to the table and eat something,* I instructed myself. Walking back to the table, I passed two couples who were laughing easily. They had the comfort and ease of long-term friendship, which assumed long term marriages. They were about my age and I wondered if Michael and I would ever reach the place where we could actually enjoy a dinner out in a restaurant without it becoming a story to tell Joanna the next day. Scott and I had had countless meals at restaurants with couples we'd known for years, raising our children side by side, the details of one another's lives as familiar as our own. They'd been easy, verging on boring, which had, at the time, felt comforting.

I imagined Michael coming home to find his wife's closet empty except for the lingering scent of perfume and dust.

I remembered the lonely nights I had gone with Scott to a silent bedroom, where we would lie in bed trying not to touch one another even after we'd had the requisite Saturday night sex.

If Michael and I were to have the stacking up of years that come with a long-term marriage, that empty closet and those lonely nights would be part of that stack.

Michael and I had been married to other people, raised our children with them, and slipped into middle age, only to find one another. His boys were going to form whatever opinions about me they wanted to. Part of it was clearly going to be that I could barely hold my liquor, but I figured if I didn't fall down, slur my words, or throw up, I was ahead of the game.

When I got back to the table, Bill grinned at me and Jim slid a look of what almost looked like contrition from under his black lashes. It was uncanny to see Michael's dark eyes on his boys. Neither of my children resembled me other than a very general "they could be related" way.

Michael had a guilty, pleased look on his face.

"So," Jim said, "Dad said you're a Mets fan."

I glared at Michael. "That's right."

Bill smiled and I could see the not-so-distant 10-year-old boy he once was. "So are we."

Not a common occurrence in Westchester, New York, a few miles from Yankee Stadium.

It seemed the years of accompanying my brother Adam to Shea Stadium as a teenager was suddenly paying off. Of course, I had done it primarily because of the anxiety I felt when he went without me. I would try to intercept the continuous containers of beer and smooth over potential fights with equally drunk and extremely obnoxious fans. By default I became a fan and channeled all my fury about the drinking and the loud sloppy guys around me toward the players of the opposing team. I focused years of pent-up rage into hatred of whatever color uniforms happened to be out there on any given game day.

Michael's sons were quite good during their high school years. I know this because during my stalker period, I'd even gone so far as to bring up their stats online. That's right. I'm not proud of it. But it sure was coming in handy now. While Michael had never come right out and said the boys were Yankee fans, he'd let me believe it because he was a Yankees fan, like his dad before him.

I looked at Michael. "Well played."

He looked at the boys. "I kind of let her believe you were Yankees fans."

"*What*?" They screamed in unison, reminding everyone in the restaurant who may not have realized, that they are identical twins.

"Your dad's a Yankee fan."

"We know." Again, in unison, with the same amount of disgust.

"So I just assumed you boys were too, and he never told me."

Michael preened. "I figured I'd use it as an ice breaker, but I forgot, and then, well -- desperate times."

"Desperate times." This time we all said it in unison and raised our glasses together, appearing to the casual observer a catalogue picture of a happy family.

CHAPTER EIGHTEEN

"I want to rock your Gypsy soul, just like way back in the days of old, then magnificently we will float, into the mystic."
– Van Morrison

August rains came on sudden and hard. Michael and I were leaving for the Cape. His sister owned a home on the water and offered it to us for a four-day weekend. This was especially kind of her, considering I had yet to meet her. She and her husband were constantly flying to different parts of the world and were seldom available. At this rate, her first glimpse of Michael and me together may be the horrifying debut of my father's show.

Michael needed a vacation, both my jobs were slow, the paintings were framed and as ready as they could be, and my home was showing in a realtor's open house, so I needed to be out of there. Given the choice of holing up in Michael's man-cave of an apartment or traveling to the ocean, we chose the latter.

Bridey was safely ensconced with Joanna and Jake, Dylan was back at school, and the realtor had the keys to my clutter-free, vanilla-scented, magazine-perfect house. Turning the key in the lock, I tried not to think about people poking through cabinets and closets, wandering the rooms as if they were picking over the bones of my family's demise.

Driving up 84, the hypnotic slash of windshield wipers against rushing water felt intimate and safe despite the treacherous conditions, and I soon lost the battle to be an effective co-pilot and let sleep pull me under.

Michael must have slowed gently, easing off the highway and rolling to a stop, because when I surfaced to awareness, we were on the side of the road, waterfall rains pounding the windshield.

Somehow, Michael had managed to lift my skirt, slide my panties over, and contort himself up and over the gearshift. My hand was on the back of his head and I was arching up and into his mouth, his tongue stroking soft and slow against me. Delicious waves of pleasure were building from the spot beneath his tongue, spreading simultaneously down my legs, up my belly, and vacillating from pleasure to near-pain in my nipples. As if he could feel it too, Michael worked his hands under my shirt, skimming my ribs and cupping my breasts, letting the stiffness of my nipples rub against his palms, their slight calloused roughness bringing me to orgasm. Coming apart beneath his tongue and hands, time shifted and came back together.

Eventually the endorphins subsided and the stiffness in my hips and lower back announced themselves. Michael had straightened himself above me and was grinning mischievously. Soon the urgency of his erection as he lifted my legs over his left shoulder and pushed into me distracted both of us from the intrusive gearshift. The buildup of friction as he pumped in and out of me rose from steady to frantic before he collapsed against me, finding my mouth with his, the thumping of our hearts together in a single beat.

Eventually, we straightened ourselves. Michael pulled a box of tissues from somewhere in the car and we began the awkward ritual of after sex cleanup and I knew then that no matter what happened, I would love this man forever for giving myself to me.

The rains had lifted by the time we crested over the bridge and onto The Cape, leaving a pale sky and a damp ocean breeze.

Once we arrived, it took only moments to dump our weekend bags in the guest bedroom of the cottage, don swimsuits, and smear sunscreen all over. Letting ourselves out the back kitchen door, we crossed a ledge of rock and descended creaky wooden steps to the beach, picking our way through sand reeds to the ocean's edge.

Seawater churned around our ankles, causing the ground to recede beneath our soles. Pulling me close, Michael kissed my lips softly. Sliding his hand to the small of my back, he pressed against me, absorbing the chill from my thighs with his heat. Leaning into him, I wrapped my arms around him and spread my palms against the smooth, hard planes of his back.

I'd never understood couples like this, touching so easily in public; a woman pillowing her head against her husband's shoulder, a man reaching over to taste his wife's lips. Yet, it now seemed effortless. As if it were right.

The ocean was ice cold despite how late in the season it was. We dove in anyway, letting our body temperatures adjust and allowing the salt to buoy us beneath the clearing sky. Free from the constant demand of Dani's Twitter feed, I allowed my cell phone to languish, vibrating against the refuse of tissues, gum wrappers, lipsticks and pens at the bottom of my bag far away on the guestroom bed.

We showered together in the outdoor stall, rinsing ocean sand from our hair. Michael finished first and went to prepare lunch while I lingered under the warm shower spray, craning my neck to see the reveal of a bright blue sky as the fog from the morning rains burned away. Stepping into the air, I dried off with a thin beach towel and slid into a pair of yoga shorts and a T-shirt I'd confiscated from Michael. It was an original Ramones T-shirt, faded and soft, and he was never ever getting it back. Starving, I sought out the cottage kitchen, following the rustle of paper bags and clatter of dishes where Michael was assembling our lunch of creamy chowder, local tomatoes, and a blueberry tart, which he promised would be the best on The Cape.

The tiny patio was uneven and the wooden picnic table looked precarious at best, guaranteed to deliver splinters; but it had an unobstructed view high above the ocean. A rock jetty took up most of the beach below, and it was far from the public lot, rendering it unpopular and private.

Spreading a yellow and red cloth over the table and covering the benches with two more threadbare towels took care of the potential wood shards. We settled in with frosted glasses of tart lemonade.

"Mmm," I said when Michael smiled at me. "Delish."

He looked at me harder. "You okay?"

"Yeah. Of course. How could I not be?"

"I don't know—you seem—low key."

"The ocean air."

"Yeah. Maybe."

It was a novelty to have someone akin to my moods. Marriage and motherhood had prepared me well for reading everyone else's moods and attempting to manage them, but I'd become proficient at masking my own moods, feigning interest while living somewhere else in my own head. "I'm fine. Why? Am I a downer or—-"

"No—nothing like that. You just seem—pensive."

"Oh. Is that bad?"

"It's not bad or good—just wondering."

The blueberry pie was the most delicious I'd ever eaten anywhere, let alone The Cape. Yet, Michael hadn't touched his. He was too busy asking me random touchy-feely questions.

"Do you ever miss being married?"

I took a closer look, wondering if he'd been hitting the wine while preparing our lunch. "To Scott? No."

"But the act of being married; do you miss that?"

I looked at him with a kind of growing horror. "Is there a correct answer to this quiz?"

He laughed. "It's just a question."

"I don't miss being married to Scott. And since I was never married to anyone except Scott—I don't miss being married." I didn't like the way he was eyeballing me. It seemed almost fervent.

"I liked being married."

How was I supposed to take that? "You must miss it. Her."

"I don't. Not the way I thought I would. I realize now that she had the courage to end something that wasn't really working. Of course, back then I didn't know it wasn't working. But it wasn't. We were just going through the motions."

"That's supposed to sound deadly—or lifeless—but to me, it sounds safe."

"It was all three of those things—and I would have gladly gone on like that forever. But now that I've experienced—this—." His hand waved back and forth in the air between us. "I realize what it can feel like."

"What?"

"Love."

I laughed. "Is that what that wavy thing means—L O V E."

"Yeah."

"And you like this—what we've got?"

He smiled. "I do."

"I like it, too."

He stood up and pulled me to him. "Good."

His hips pressed mine, and I felt his erection hard against me. "Michael?"

"Yes." He kissed my temple, my neck, and then my lips.

"Let's not fuck it up by getting married," I whispered into his lips.

He caught my lower lip gently between his teeth then kissed me deeply before pulling away from me. "Okay."

I slid my hand down and unbuttoned his jeans, feeling the heat and fullness of him in my palm. His eyes glazed for a moment before he came to and realized there was only an illusion of privacy outside. Inching me backwards toward the house, his breath against my throat stirred in me a kind of frenzy. It was almost too much to take and it was nearly a relief when we broke apart in the close heat of the kitchen. Michael recovered quicker than I did and had stepped out of his jeans and had me out of his Ramones T-shirt in half a second. I struggled out of my yoga shorts in an awkward shimmy and we were sinking to the floor. He lay on his back and I slid my body onto his. I never looked away from him, letting him see me in the harsh afternoon light, my hair tangled and my face contorted in pleasure that was almost pain. We rode one another until I collapsed over him, anesthetized against the ache in my hips and the scratch of a piece of linoleum which had loosened and cut the top of my foot right above my instep. Messy and imperfect and clumsy, we untangled ourselves. Michael jumped up more readily then I did and hoisted me gracelessly to my feet. We couldn't stop grinning at each other—-and I felt like an idiot. But a happy one. A happy idiot. The words formed in front of me. Maybe that's all it takes to love deeply: idiocy, which for me equals an absence of fear.

For the first time since memory was mine, I wasn't that little girl convinced someone was climbing up the fire escape to kill her.

* * *

By the time we went up to unpack our bags, the sun had slipped low and the simple bedroom was shrouded in dusk. Placing our few items of clothing into the rickety wicker dresser took only moments. Fishing around in the bottom of my bag for my phone, I reluctantly checked voicemail.

There were three texts.

Dani reminding me to check Twitter. Ugh.

The gallery asking about dimensions for the installation.

My mother, reminding me that next week was Adam's birthday (as if I could forget).

I looked at Michael. "I think I've changed my mind about the show." Yep. The sex-induced dopamine fix had worn off and I was back in the more familiar stance of warding off all possibility of threat.

"Okaaay." He drew the word out in that way he had, which meant he was trying to think of a rational response to an irrational person.

"The paintings are irrelevant—and this whole tweeter thing has only built up a ridiculous hype that will make them seem all the more ridiculous—or, worse, people will start to see things in them that aren't there, and that will make me a—a—fraud!"

"Look—it's just a show. They're just paintings. People will like them or they won't. They'll buy them or they won't."

That was kind of true. And in a deflated kind of way, it made me feel a little bit better. "That's humbling."

He laughed. "Yeah. Turns out none of us are actually the center of the universe."

"I'm scared."

"I get that."

My body, which had been so loose and light after our acrobatics on the torn linoleum floor, was now clenched tight, every ache magnified. Michael picked up my hand, unfurled each finger, and kissed the center of my palm. He didn't say anything else. Neither did I. The sun hadn't even set yet, but I followed him upstairs to the lumpy, salt-scented bed and slid beneath the faded summer quilt. Curling against him, I emptied my mind of the weeks to come and slept deeply until day broke and the cry of the seagulls woke us.

CHAPTER NINETEEN

"But I've had the invitation, that a sinner can't refuse, and it's almost the salvation, it's almost like the blues"
– Leonard Cohen

For Adam's birthday, my mother requested that we go to his favorite spot in the Brooklyn Botanical Gardens. It was a similar pilgrimage as last year, but this time it would be purposeful, becoming, as my mother put it to me on the phone while Michael and I tore up the miles between Cape Cod and the real world, "a commemoration rather than an organic moment of need."

I was told to bring a letter, which I was expected to read out loud, put a match to, and allow the ashes to drift away; an activity my mother's grief counselor had instructed her to undertake with the correct assumption that I would fall into place and do whatever was needed. Although, given the choice, I would have preferred to take pins and stick them directly into my eyeballs.

Adam's birthday fell on the Friday before Labor Day and the trip into Brooklyn was surprisingly smooth and traffic free. People either hadn't left for their long weekends yet, or they were going the other way. I took a different route from my previous visits and sailed across the Manhattan Bridge, racing the D train (it won), and zoomed along Flatbush Avenue. I took a left onto 7th Avenue, where I watched a young couple, inked limbs entwined, wearing caps and long jeans despite the oppressive late summer heat, saunter into a café filled with young people sipping coffee and tea from what appeared to be cereal bowls. Automatically, I checked landmarks which were long gone: the Army & Navy store where I had bought painters pants and fatigues, John's Bargain store where I'd picked through bins of cotton underpants, and The Sneaker Factory, where I'd searched separately for left and right Pro-Keds in my size. They were all replaced by sleeker, more expensive stores catering to families who would only have searched through bargain bins with self-congratulatory irony.

A Pinkberry stood at Garfield and 7th where Danny's Candy Store used to be. Any graffiti my friends had sprayed had long been renovated away, the streets were gleaming, and the entire area looked prosperous, like a movie set depicting a Brooklyn neighborhood. Pino's Pizzeria was there, expanded, but still making the baby pizzas with onions I'd favored as a teenager. I thought about stopping in for one, but the image of my mother waiting, looking out her grimy garden floor window, caused me to turn up Second Street make the right onto 8th Avenue and head down Garfield to Fiske Place.

My mother was waiting for me on the tiny square of concrete behind the stoop, sitting on a lawn chair, legs crossed, busying herself with the contents of her handbag. I didn't even have to park; just rolled up and waved. She hastily gathered her things and strode over to the car. She was wearing a pair of white Capri pants, sensible shoes (which were the only adjustment she'd ever made for her aging body), and a pink and green silk tunic she'd had forever but which somehow still looked chic. Her platinum hair bob was gleaming and smooth and she was wearing a pair of green glass earrings, which sparkled even from a distance. Yet, when she got closer and pushed her sunglasses onto her head to look at me, I saw the ravages of grief on her face.

"Hey, Carly," she said as she slid into the passenger seat.

Eastern Parkway was unusually quiet. We passed the library steps where I'd been mugged and had my train pass taken from me, a tiny dull pocketknife held to my throat by a boy with dead eyes, while his girlfriend searched me. I'd been in 6th grade and it had been the middle of winter. The girl had to push her hands under my coat before reaching my pockets. She'd systematically searched each one, coming away with thirty-five cents and the plastic-covered train pass. My mother yelled at me when I got home and told her what happened. She would have to come up with the train fare for me every day.

"Why didn't you run? Or fight back?" she'd said.

"There were two of them and they were big-- like sixteen. And they had a switchblade."

"You shouldn't have let them get that close."

"Don't worry, I can go under the turnstile."

"Don't get caught—I don't want you going to Juvie." I realize now that she'd been kidding about Juvie, but back then I had a pit in my stomach every morning and every afternoon right before I'd board the train, certain each time was the cataclysmic event which would rip me from the relative safety of my home and put me in Juvie with the girlfriends of the Jolly Stompers.

I stole a glance at my mother, but she was impervious. She walked this block every day to get to work. It didn't have the same resonance for her.

The parking lot for the Botanical Gardens was modern and new. I turned toward my mother and followed her through the new architecture, disoriented, as I searched futilely for the herb garden. Foolishly, my hand reached out as if I'd be able to bend down and finger the soft wooly Lamb's Ear or touch the raised letters on the small bronze plaque bearing its Latin name, Stachys

Byzantina; remembering how one entire summer, every time we played house, my children's names became Stachys for the boy and Byzantina for the girl.

"Carly? They moved the herb garden to the Flatbush Avenue side. It's still lovely…"

It was almost shocking to look up and see my mother as the 70-year-old woman she'd become.

I remembered her all those years ago, waiting for me in front of that herb garden, aware that I was incapable of entering the gardens without stopping to crush lavender between my thumb and forefinger, allowing the heady scent to fill me up. There was impatience in her stance, belied by the smile on her face every time I'd stop and visit those plants. For all her faults, she'd given me a tremendous amount of room to live in the world of my imagination. No small thing, I realize now, having raised my own children in an era of competition and hovering.

We walked together past the Washington Avenue turnstile toward the duck pond. Late last winter, when we'd come, she'd been so frail and uncertain in her steps, and I found great relief in matching the resolution of her stride.

I assume she had the Japanese Garden in mind for whatever ceremony we would be engaging in - perhaps the tea house, which smelled perpetually like cedar, or the pools of water fed by a trickling waterfall, a favorite spot of Adam's. I remembered following his sturdy body as he trudged along the white-pebbled path, trailing a stick; my constant admonishment to stay on the trail and not trample the delicate plants along the way. For an earth-tilting moment, I forgot my age and the existence of my own grown children and felt a terrible urgency to be caring for small child Adam. My stomach hollowed as I realized it was only my mother I needed to look after, and she was two yards ahead of me now, not at all cognizant of the time warp I'd found myself in.

She'd moved past the teahouse without a glance and headed for the duck pond. I hurried to catch up. She'd moved onto the narrow dirt path beside the pond, and I fell in line behind her.

Seeping into my consciousness was a long-forgotten memory of following her through this path, again navigating Adam so he wouldn't stray into the water. I followed my mother up a slight hill to a small theatre-like space, which I didn't recognize, but looked vaguely familiar. It wasn't until I saw the carved marble statue of a little boy and his mother that I realized we were in the hidden garden that I'd always thought of as "The Palace". A metal carving of a young boy, naked and uninhibited, rested against his mother's lap: The Prince. Adam and I had played safely within those palace walls while my mother read her book. We entertained ourselves for hours, building structures out of the small, smooth rocks nearby, tracing lines in the dirt, and making tea parties with juniper berries, pine needles, and earth moistened with water from the nearby pond.

Memories flooded me; all of Adam, his lips puckered, blowing out his cheeks as he worked on whatever masterpiece he was creating with twigs and rocks. None of the memories included us exchanging words, and I wished I could remember something, anything, that we'd said to one another. I could remember the crackle of wax paper as my mother handed us each a salty Ritz cracker, contraband due to the strict no food policy enforced by guards in navy blue uniforms carrying ominous billyclubs. But the guards never ventured this deep into the garden, and my mother was vigilant about never leaving litter behind.

There in front of the stone boy, with his mother's tender gaze looking over him, my own mother stood resolutely and said, "Let's read the letters. I'll go first."

Bracing myself for one of her deep theatrical renderings and a ten-page speech, including soliloquies from her favorite

Shakespeare plays, I was shocked to see the simple sheet of note paper and to hear her voice, barely above a whisper.

"Adam, you were a child of industry and wonder. You questioned and poked and prodded until you understood. This spot is where you learned to count. I remember the day you lined stones patiently around the perimeter. You counted each of them and made me watch you in case you missed a number. If you did, and I made the correction, you would start over and do it until you had successfully counted them straight through. You kept adding stones and beginning again until you reached 100. You were five years old.

"Missing you is something that is part of me now until the day I die. I don't believe in God. Or heaven. I wish I did, so I'd know you're happy now."

She must have struck a match, lit the paper, and watched it burn and soar above the pond, eventually settling as ash, which disappeared into the water.

I could only imagine that is what happened because instead of being there to support my mother, I was crying against the little boy, my face in my hands, unable to control the ugly sobbing sounds rising up and out of me.

My mother placed her hand on my head.

"Carly? Do you want to read your letter?"

I couldn't answer. Like a seven-year-old, I just shook my head.

"Would you like me to read it?"

I shook my head harder.

"Should I just burn it?" she asked.

Wanting to fulfill my obligation to her, but unable to move or respond in any coherent manner, I just nodded and handed it to her.

Once the square of paper was unfolded, we were both able to read it easily.

Adam, as long as I can remember loving, I have loved you. I'm sorry I let H win.

"Oh, Carly--" my mother said, and moved toward me, stopping when I flinched. She turned back to the letter and struck a match. A moment later the letter took flame and burned itself out. We watched the last of the embers spark and dull to ash before we turned and walked back the way we came.

CHAPTER TWENTY

"How Strange, this feeling that my life's begun at last."
Herbert Kretzmer

The day of my 50th birthday had started out as a promising one. The humidity had broken overnight, a balmy breeze in its wake. Dylan drove down from school and he appeared to be happier than usual.

Dani came up from the city carrying a box of pastel-colored cupcakes from my favorite bakery, scenting the air with butter and sugar.

Joanna had brought a magnum of champagne and sunflowers from her back garden.

Michael's sons were there, and the introductions had gone without incident.

My mother was on semi-good behavior, although I overheard her say to Michael, "Did you buy Carly a gift that will get you some bumpin' uglies later?"

Michael was flipping steaks on the grill while Jake kept him company.

It was then I heard the squeal of a bus braking - a common enough sound on a school day, but incongruous on a weekend.

Commotion and loud voices followed, so I cautiously picked my way through the side garden to the front of the house. There it was: the shit show - my father's tour bus, a sight straight from hell. My father approached, carrying Mac, while Bea wobbled behind them in six-inch heels.

"There's the birthday girl!" my father boomed, startling Mac, who immediately began to cry.

"Say happy birthday to your sister, Mac-Man!" he said while simultaneously handing him off to Bea.

Bea, unable to hold him and stand upright, thrust him into the arms of an unsuspecting, and to her credit unflustered, Astrid.

Astrid made desperate hand motions in the direction of the bus, resulting in the nanny running out and scooping up Mac to take him back to the bus where, I could only imagine, there was an assortment of unholy treats such as candy and endless games of angry birds.

Numb, I let my father make a show of hugging me so I could whisper to him, "Tell them to turn off that fucking camera or I'll smash the shit out of it." Pulling back, he flashed a giant *I love my daughter and aren't I poignant* smile, holding it for what he must have believed was long enough to get some worthwhile footage before dropping his hands and making a slicing motion across his neck with his index finger.

The camera guy instantly stopped and Astrid yelled, "How many times have I told you not to do that, Guy?"

I turned from my dad and pointed at her. "You all need to leave."

By this time everyone had come from around back toward the front.

"Oh-ho!" my father shouted. "Were you having a birthday party? Well, how would I know, since I wasn't invited?"

"Really, Guy?" My mother was marching toward him. "Did you figure that out?"

"Grandma!" Dani went after her, but my mother was too fast for her.

"I will not let you ruin Carly's 50th! You never showed up for her 5th or 6th or any other birthday, you deadbeat loser!" she punctuated each word with a poke in his chest.

Bea put her arm out. "Come on, Guy, it's clear we aren't wanted."

"Let me just give you your present, Honey," my dad said in what I am sure he thought was his pitiful voice.

"Dad. I don't--"

"Now, Carly, I got it for you special. You can't deny a father's gift."

Against my better judgment I nodded, not because I wanted his gift, but because I didn't want to appear ungracious. "Fine."

My mother stood up straighter. "Don't give in to his manipulative bull crap, Carly!"

My dad turned on her, reminding me of the father I remembered: impatient, arrogant, and nasty. "You're just jealous you aren't in this shoot. It's Season 2, and you were hoping for a spin-off! Don't think the producers don't talk to me, you hypocritical bitch!"

Astrid stepped in then, closer than I'd ever seen her come to panic. "Now, Guy, that isn't how it went down, and you know it."

"You told him!" my mother shrieked.

Joanna whistled - one of those ear-splitting multi rhythmic ones - which to my surprise, got everyone's attention.

"People! It's Carly's 50th. For once, can you just keep it about her?"

My mother nodded emphatically. "Yeah, Guy, is that possible for you? Let it be about Carly for once."

My mother placed her hand above her heart, flattening her left breast. "Do you have any idea what it was like watching the disappointment on my little girl's face when her father failed to show up for yet another birthday? But he's here today for the photo op!"

Guy pulled a box out of his pocket and handed it to me. "Open it, baby girl. Happy 50th - and you don't look a day over 45, by the way."

"Hmph, that's still a good 15 years older than your boo." My mother, of course.

Dani put her arm around my mother in what I'm sure she hoped was a calming embrace.

Dylan put his arm around me. Michael was holding a steaming platter of steaks. His sons were flanking him, their faces in shadow and difficult to read. Jake looked like he wanted to murder people, and I actually saw him fingering the handcuffs he now brought with him whenever he came over, just in case.

I opened the box, embarrassed to see my fingers shaking. Displayed on a pillow of black velvet was a heart-shaped gold locket.

"Open it," he said.

Inside was an old black and white photo of my father holding me. I recognized it as a copy of the one I'd stared at all those years ago, seeing the love shining out of his eyes, telling myself it was real and true and he meant it.

I recognized the locket, too. It was his mother's. I'd loved playing with it as a little girl, when she would let me, my cold fingertips against the warm creped skin of her throat, opening the clasp to reveal a tiny wisp of blond hair behind cellophane. "Your father's," she'd explained, "when he was no bigger than you." I remembered there had been a time I was sure she'd loved me. I wondered for many years what I'd done to make her stop.

Tightening my throat against a sudden urge to cry, I thanked him.

"It's beautiful. I'll take good care of it."

My father pulled me into his arms. And that's when I saw the cameras were rolling.

I have wished many times since that day that I'd had the courage to make them stop. That I'd come up with some brilliant and effective speech. But all I could think to do was extricate myself as quietly as possible.

I waited for the cameras to stop, for Astrid and her small crew to pull back toward the bus.

"Well done," I said to my father. "You got what you came for."

I went back inside and the rest of my family followed me, leaving my father and Bea to board the bus and travel to their next destination.

I saw in my father's eyes a transition from self-congratulatory triumph to the knowledge that he'd lost me forever.

* * *

Turning 50 was a reminder that I had several things to accomplish while I was still in the youthful flush of my old age. It also provided the paradoxical effect of incapacitating me.

My house had several offers and I had accepted the highest bid. Of course, the new family made it conditional upon being able to move in by October 1st. They were paying cash, which made me wonder (for about five seconds) what they did for a living before I realized that I just didn't care. So I needed to find an apartment and rent a storage unit.

Michael and I spent every night looking at places, and I'd found one, a charming (real-estate-agent-speak for "small") three-bedroom house in Tarrytown, right up the hill from the reservoir. It was vacant and freshly painted and had a rent I could afford with an option to buy. There wasn't great light, and a home studio would be out of the question, so I would have to find somewhere else to work. I could move in on October 2nd if I paid two weeks security and the first month's rent now. I couldn't afford it, but Michael offered me a loan, and surprising even myself, I accepted on the spot. Another perk of turning 50 was that pride just seemed low on my priority list. And I would be able to pay him back as soon as I closed.

Walking out of the new place, we realized we could walk to town from there, and, delighting in this newfound freedom, we began the descent to Main Street.

"Carly?" Michael let go of my hand and turned to me. "In a year, after this lease is up, I could sell my place and we could look for something together."

"A year's a long way off," I said, as cavalierly as if he'd asked what flavor ice cream I was planning on getting.

Then I kissed him quickly on the lips so I wouldn't have to look into his eyes, and started walking again. He matched my stride easily, and for the rest of the evening kept his comments light. I knew I should address the feelings manifesting themselves in exceedingly polite formality, but my teeth ached at the thought of it. The idea of moving in with Michael was something I wanted too much. And if there was one thing life had taught me, it was that anything I wanted too much was suspect.

In bed that night, when Michael reached for me, I moved under him, opening my mouth to his. He was gentle with me, took his time, and lingered over every sensitive part of me. He was the first man to find the place on my throat which seemed directly connected to my clitoris, the first man to use his tongue gently against my nipples, and the first man to enter me hard and fast, knowing exactly how to bring me to climax. Afterward, I lay in bed listening to his heartbeat, wondering why I couldn't shake the feeling he was saying goodbye.

* * *

In the days that followed, my fears seemed unfounded. Michael was his usual cheery self and I convinced myself that I'd imagined the "moving in" conversation, as brief and cryptic as it had been.

Joanna came over and we were in the kitchen canning the last of the harvest from our gardens. A vegetable soup simmered on the stove and root vegetables were roasting in the oven. It was unseasonably hot that day and the heat from the stove turned the kitchen fragrant, steamy, and uncomfortably sticky. We carried chilled glasses of Sauvignon blanc onto the deck where Dylan and his roommate, Josh were working feverishly on some project they had started earlier in the summer and were trying to finish before they left for school on Monday morning. Joanna and I had plied them with food and beverages throughout the day and the table was littered with their detritus, so she and I made ourselves comfortable a few feet away in the lounge chairs.

"What are they working on over there?"

I rolled my eyes. "Don't ask."

"Well, now I need to know."

"Dylan." I had to call his name twice before he looked our way. "Joanna wants to know what you guys are working on."

"A handbook."

"On?" Joanna prodded.

"*What To Do When Your College Student Gets Arrested.*" He grinned.

"Oh!"

Josh chimed in, "It's a take-off on the 'how-to' books about getting your kids into college—-only much more useful."

"I see."

"Thirty point two percent of people are arrested before the age of twenty three," Dylan recited. "And many of them are college students. It's like a dirty secret that everyone knows and nobody wants to talk about."

"Okay. And what does the handbook tell you?" Joanna seemed to be recovering a lot quicker than I had when Dylan and Josh first told me about their plan. I was horrified, thinking they were making light of arrests for underage drinking. She seemed to be taking them more seriously.

"It's a guide to the criminal system—-what to do, what to expect. We break the chapters into a series of offenses ranging from underage drinking to assault."

"We even included a chapter addressing sexual assault, although we didn't want to," Dylan stated. "But it needed to be thorough. It's not that we want to get scumbags out of trouble, but fair representation is needed for a civilized society." He threw me a side-long glance.

Josh stretched his arms overhead and I realized they'd been working for hours without a break. "We're thinking there's a big market out there."

Joanna looked doubtful. "No parent is going to buy that book—they'll think it's a jinx."

"College students will, though. And we're thinking of marketing it as a gag gift for high school graduations: a book that parents will actually be able to turn to in a time of need."

"Kind of cynical," Joanna said, and I nodded my head in agreement.

"But practical," Dylan said.

"And much needed. We're going to do an E-book with a link to defense attorneys near every college in the nation," Josh chimed in. Then they went back to ignoring us.

Joanna raised her eyebrows at me. "Enterprising."

I shuddered. "Disturbing." We sipped our wine, the clicking keyboards and the wind moving through the trees the only sound. "Michael seems—I don't know—restless, somehow."

"How do you mean?"

"Maybe it's because I'm selling the house. We've only known each other a year—and we've been together less than that." I watched Joanna set her expression to one of neutrality. "Maybe I'm imagining it."

"What?"

"I think he wants something more—permanent between us."

"Like marriage?"

"Yes—no—I don't know."

"Has he said anything to you?"

"Not directly."

Joanna shrugged. "At our age, we all kind of know what we want—and what we don't want - in a person. How long you're dating doesn't mean the same as it does to young people—it's like dog years."

"Harhar."

"No, really, it is."

"And for someone like Michael, who actually enjoyed being married—it makes sense that he'd want to do it again."

"How do you know he enjoyed being married? Did he say something?"

"Nope. Just a feeling I got."

I eyed her suspiciously, but her face was no longer neutral; it was smug, and for some reason that made me believe she was telling the truth.

"Is that how it was for you and Jake?"

"We threw one another away when we were seventeen and it took us twenty years to find each other again—so, yeah—in dating dog years, we moved in together within two months of getting back together; but it was like five years."

"So dog years of old people dating is like two and a half years per month?"

"You're quick. I never actually did the math."

"Is this a real thing, or did you make it up?"

"I guess I made it up—but it makes sense if you think about it."

"It doesn't. It's confusing and weird."

Joanna laughed. "Welcome to the world."

Our wine glasses were empty, an unacceptable situation in light of our conversation. "I'll refill these."

"Excellent." Joanna followed me into the kitchen. "The guys should be here soon. I'll set the table."

Joanna set the table while I began clearing up from the canning. The wine did its work, allowing a softening of my stomach and shoulder muscles. I thought about the girlfriends I'd lost since my divorce and decided all of them put together didn't come close to the friend I had in Joanna. I offered up a quick wish to the universe for my now frenemy, Caroline. I'd wished her harm—-nothing terrible; but mean-spirited things, like a laser-resistant mustache or never having a moment's peace for the rest of her days on Earth. I took all those wishes back and hoped instead that she would find a true friendship the way I had, once we'd moved on from one another. It was surprisingly easy to do. And even easier when I realized it would mean that I never again had to be her friend. Sometimes forgiveness was like that—-just wishing the other person well and not having to interact with them in a meaningful way ever again.

* * *

Mandee's was slow. Back-to-school shopping had peaked, the Fall line was dwindling but the super sales hadn't started, and there was a brief window before the seasonal fashion would change over, creating a load of inventory.

Karen reduced my hours at the frame shop while I prepared for the show. Dani's Twitter followers were promising a mass exodus from the Lower East Side to come up to "bumfuck Rockland County" as one of her tweeters had dubbed it, and someone at hashtag *ironicazzhole* was organizing a group to come up.

My mother had called early that morning, in a frenzy.

"Carly," she said, "I need to work today--I can't come help. You have to change the opening until Saturday."

"Mom, it's fine; just come up tomorrow.

"But I'll miss the pre-party!"

"If by 'pre-party' you mean installing the exhibit--it's a lot of lifting and nailing. I'm not sure--"

"I have a wonderful eye. I could help curate it."

"Mom, the gallery owner does that."

"Hmph. All he cares about is selling your paintings--he'll corrupt your vision solely to make a dollar." This from a woman willing to pimp out her grandchildren on a reality television show.

"Mom, if this is another attempt to get the film crew here ... "

The show was airing in a week and Dani had begged me to change the gallery opening so it could coincide with the show's debut. When she failed to convince me, she went above my head to the gallery owner who, though sorely tempted, already had another artist contracted for that time. Then they all tried to convince me to let my father come with cameras to the opening. Not only did I shut them all down, I told them my father wasn't invited even if he was sans camera. That lovely tidbit had already made it into the tabloids. Bea and I were on a split cover, with the sly title "Claws Come Out, Or In This Case, Stingers!" sprawled across the top of the page. Bea. Stingers. Get it?

"I'm hurt," my mother said. "All I care about is your happiness!"

Having managed to get the installation up without a visit from my mother and her expert opinions was a miracle in and of itself. The fact that no film crew had showed up while we were installing was tantamount to the second coming.

Karen, Janine, Jake and Joanna helped me finish the last of the installation. We arrived back at my house sweaty, exhausted, and starving. Raiding the refrigerator, we found two bottles of ice-cold Sauvignon blanc, a pack of baby carrots, and a jumbo-size container of humus. We sprawled in our filthy clothes across the lounge chairs on my deck. I'd been nervous about how the installation would work and if the pieces would fit the space the way I envisioned, and I was limp with relief to be done with it.

All that was left to do tonight was get dinner on the table, eat, and get a good night's rest. Car doors slammed as if on cue, and in spite of my aching back and sore muscles, I sprang off the lounge chair. "Dinner!" I shouted.

Michael, Dani, and Dylan came in with steaming trays of Mexican food. It didn't take long for everyone to settle on the deck with a heaping plate. Joanna had obligingly whipped up her famous margaritas - smooth, not sweet, and with extra lime.

Dylan followed me into the kitchen where I was going for seconds.

"I jut got some great news." He was looking at his phone.

"Spill it," I said, loading rice and beans and chicken fajitas onto my plate.

"Remember that handbook my roommate and I wrote over the summer?"

"Yeess?" If I sounded cautious, it's because I was terrified at what Dylan would think was good news regarding that particular project. For all I knew, Dylan being arrested would have been seen as "research material."

"We have an offer from a publisher. And a five thousand dollar advance, each!"

"Really?"

"Yep." He was grinning at me.

"That's wonderful! Congratulations!"

He picked me up and swirled me around. "You know what this means?"

"What?" I asked, laughing and a little breathless from how tight he'd squeezed me.

"I will never have to ask that asshole for another dime as long as I live."

"What asshole?"

"Dad."

"Oh, honey, your dad loves you."

"Stop it, Mom. This isn't about him."

"Well it *is* about you--and we need to make a toast."

He grinned at me. "I'll get a beer."

I needed to just be happy for him. It was natural, I told myself, for Dylan to want to be self-supporting - wonderful, I thought, that he was showing so much initiative. Many boys harbored anger against their fathers. *Not so unusual*, I reassured myself. Yet, when I looked at Dylan flip the top off his beer, I saw something in his face - an expression, a set of the jaw - and I realized that he hated Scott. *Hatred*, I thought, *could fuel a person for a long time.* It wasn't what I'd imagined for my son.

Later, after everyone had gone to bed, Michael and I began cleaning up. He was fiddling with his IPod and giving me a look I recognized by now: a devil smile and crooked eyebrow, which meant he was putting Johnny Cash on Pandora.

Washing the last of the pots, I dried my hands and turned to face him. "Do you think Dylan hates his father?"

"Hates him? No."

"What if he does?"

"Then he does. And they're going to have to work it out."

"What if they don't?"

"Dylan's a great kid. You're just going to have to trust that."

"What if I can't?"

"Then you'll drive yourself crazy."

"So I live in la-la land and pretend everything's just great?"

"No. You live in the real world where some things are great and some things suck."

Johnny Cash's growling voice washed over me. Folsom Prison Blues.

I remembered a long-ago summer evening on Staten Island. I couldn't have been more than four years old. We were visiting friends of my parents who had left the theatre and began a commune in a part of Staten Island that still looked like country. We had taken a subway to the ferry. My father and I had stood at the front of the boat, the salty spray hitting us in the face. Leaning against him for balance, I'd inhaled the scent of his cotton shirt, and the seawater. Adam was in his stroller and slept through the entire ride. My mother held onto the stroller with one hand and turned the pages of a book in her lap with the other.

That evening, among the plot of land with the vegetable garden on one side and a swing set on the other, the adults had gathered. The air was darkening, illuminated by the glow of fireflies, which, for a four-year-old city girl, was nothing short of magical.

My dad was playing the guitar, his foot tapping the ground beneath him. I think it was 'Folsom Prison Blues'. Why else would the image have come to me? My mother and another woman were pulling us kids from the swing set, gathering the other adults, and doing the grapevine. A foot in front. A foot in back. Arms linked together in a perpetual circle, holding onto one another to keep from falling. We were happy.

Michael came up behind me, his arms circling my waist, and I let myself lean back against him. His hips moved behind me and I swayed against him to the rhythm of Johnny Cash, linked to that moment when I was four years old. I was reminded that there were moments of my childhood when I'd been happy and safe. It hadn't been all bad. And my mother probably never imagined, on that long-ago night in Staten Island, all the ways I'd learn to hate. Just as she couldn't have imagined all the ways I'd learn to love.

CHAPTER TWENTY TWO

"here is the deepest secret nobody knows
(here is the root of the root and the bud of the bud and the sky of the sky of a tree called life: which grows higher than the soul can hope or mind can hide)
and this is the wonder that's keeping the stars apart
i carry your heart (i carry it in my heart)"
– e. e. cummings

The morning of the show broke wet and windy, and the weather worsened throughout the day. By the time evening fell, the entire tri-state region was on flood alert. To my surprise, the stormy weather had not deterred Dani's Twitter followers from making the pilgrimage. She had a full bar set up and platters of cheeses, fruits, and assorted crackers placed around the gallery. A guy, presumably in his late twenties, with an Amish-style beard, wearing a Pokemon T-shirt, was holding court in front of Mercy. His comments were thoughtful. He was giving an impeccable technical analysis and the other young men and women were listening to him attentively.

For me, looking at paintings is a solitary experience, even if someone is standing by my side. Discussing a painting, breaking down the technical aspects, or discovering how it resonates with someone else is like trying to taste food on another person's tongue. It can't be done, and feels slimy - exactly how I felt eavesdropping on other people talking about Mercy.

Feeling guilty and ungrateful, I slipped outside. The rain was still driving into the Hudson. Sheltered beneath the awning, I was able to watch the Tappan Zee Bridge blazing against the night. Looking closer, I recognized the signal of alarm flaring from police cars and ambulances. An accident on the bridge was causing a log jam of cars in both directions. It would be hours before it cleared, and I wondered if we would be able to cross back over. Then my phone began to vibrate.

* * *

Michael and I left the gallery, telling a stricken Dani that we would keep her apprised, leaving her to deal with the guests, the gallery owner, the press, and the photographers who were practically rabid as they caught wind of a scoop unfolding.

It was only a ten-minute drive to Nyack Hospital from the gallery, but the slippery roads and the traffic pouring from the bridge accident made it much worse. Michael called the number we were given and a police car came to escort us out of the gridlock and toward the hospital.

When we pulled up to Nyack, the scene was chaotic. Police vehicles and ambulances were casting frantic red lights across the Emergency parking area. A news helicopter circled above. An officer and a nurse were waiting for us with forms to fill out.

They escorted us through the ER and into a private room. Bright hospital lights cast a greenish pallor over everyone's face and I had the fleeting notion, as we passed the curious glances or others rendered indifferent by their own agonies, that if there was indeed a first circle of hell, this is what it would look like.

It seemed my father had ignored the non-invitation to the show opening. It was his tour bus that had skidded and spun across four lanes of the Tappan Zee Bridge, crashing against the middle divider. Astrid and the crew were abraded and cut, and one cameraman had broken his arm in three places, but all were expected to make a full recovery. The driver, although in critical condition, was expected to live.

Bea had died on impact and my father had died in the hospital emergency room, bleeding out as they attempted to save his life. Mac, I was told by a shaken and sobbing Astrid, was safe and sound at home in the care of his nanny. My father and Bea had decided at the last moment that an art opening wouldn't be a suitable outing for a two-year-old.

Michael held me up when they told me this news, but he needn't have. There was no buckling of my knees or sinking of my limbs. Standing straight, absorbing the words and then the knowledge, I felt myself hardening against the certainty that it was over for my father and for Bea. And for any hope of reconciliation between my father and myself. Inexplicably, I looked at my watch. 12:03. 'Sunday Morning Coming Down'.

We were escorted to the morgue by a harried orderly. Michael and I followed him as he kept up a constant commentary on how busy they were due to the multitude of car accidents from the slippery roads and high winds knocking tree limbs onto cars and people.

The morgue was in the bowels of the hospital, and I was practically running to keep up with his stride. As far as I could tell, he hadn't taken a breath during the two elevator rides and the three different corridors we had to go down. I was sure we were nearing our destination now, picking up cues from how rapidly he was speaking, trying to fit his life story into the few minutes we had left. "I need to be careful with my stress levels, yo. Just came back from a 28-day stint; gotta keep the focus. Eat regular, get enough sleep. And exercise. Necessary for the endorphins." He tapped his head with his forefinger as though he could release a floodgate with the gesture. "'Specially given my occupation and proximity to oxi."

I thought Michael was going to knock his head off, but as inappropriate and narcissistic as his monologue was, it deflected my attention from the reason we were racing down the hellish corridors, our soles slapping the hard tile, a squeezing sensation behind my left breast.

Suddenly, we'd arrived. The bland-faced morgue attendant took custody of us and I could hear our speed-talking escort's voice recede as we went through the swinging doors: "Oh, man, by the way, sorry for your loss, yo."

There must have been some preliminary conversation, but I don't remember it. I just remember the sheet being pulled away, and there was Bea - still, cold, and strangely beautiful beneath the orb of morgue light. I touched her cheek with my knuckles before allowing her to be covered in the white hospital sheet. My father was badly gashed, his face bruised and swollen. If it hadn't been for his pompadour and the beauty mark beneath his left earlobe, I might not have recognized him.

Putting my lips close to his ear, I whispered the three words I never would have allowed myself to say had he been awake and looking at me: "I forgive you." Then I added three more. "Please forgive me."

* * *

The morning of the funeral, I kissed Mac on the top of his head, checking obsessively with his nanny that she had everything she needed, and followed Michael to the car, considering a variety of drastic measures to get out of going. Drinking castor oil to induce vomiting was at the frontrunner.

Instead, I put on my big-girl panties, buckled up, and girded myself for the inevitable.

When Adam died, I discovered that people say the following things:

They are with God now.

They are at peace.

You will be reunited in a better place.

I'm so sorry for your loss.

I learned that it is possible to nod and say thank you even when you are screaming inside.

The funeral was being held at Saint Patrick's Cathedral, with a luncheon to follow at the Puck Club. All of it was being paid for by the production team, and all of it was being filmed. Guests were asked to sign release forms, and those who refused would be blurred on camera. Michael and I were to be blurred. My mother, Dani, and Dylan would be followed on camera.

My mother began rattling off names of former Broadway actors and country singers that would only be interesting to people born before 1945, with the exception of a few who were known to those of us born before 1965.

"You do realize, Carly, that it's been 50 years since I've seen most of these people."

"Mmhmm."

"With the exception of Willie and Kris, I won't recognize a single one."

"Mmm." She was referring to Willie Nelson and Kris Kristofferson, who were both expected to deliver speeches and perhaps a song or two.

"I do think, however, that they will recognize me. I mean with the exception of my hair turning white and a few wrinkles, I look pretty much the same."

Denial is definitely not just a river, I thought unkindly and irritably. Michael was smirking out of the corner of his mouth, and I am positive he knew exactly what I was thinking.

"You look beautiful, Grandma," Dani said dutifully and sincerely.

"Why thank you, dear. But it's not about me."

A comment made frequently, I'd come to realize, by people who were quite adept at making everything about them.

We parked the car in a garage close to the West Side and walked several avenues across to St. Pat's. Despite the long line of mourners coming to pay their respects, and crowds of gawkers made larger by the recent debut of the show, we were ushered inside and divided. Michael and I went to the third row where there would be no cameras. Dani, Dylan, and my mother went to the first, where there would be.

Astrid, who was not there in an official capacity, had turned over the day's production duties to a colleague. She was dressed simply in a black shift, three-inch heels (practically sneakers for her), and no makeup or jewelry. On the left side of her forehead was a green and purple bruise with an angry swell at the hairline. Her eyes were red and puffy from crying. She held a clump of tissue in her hands and I noticed tiny bits of white residue stuck on her chapped fulcrum and upper lip where she must have been swiping at the mucus pouring from her nose and mixing with tears.

I couldn't help it. I folded her into my arms and held her against me for the entire service, the ache in my chest and throat eclipsed by the numb feeling in my shoulder and forearm from holding her up. Her sobbing was silent, and if it weren't for the gentle vibration against my body, I wouldn't have known she was doing it.

My mother, however, was a different story.

She wailed loud, hard, and melodically before, after, and between the eulogy, various readings, and the country songs; an eerie form of punctuation (or a bad Lifetime movie, depending on how you perceived it).

Dani and Dylan held her up on either side and Michael sat next to me expressionless, which meant he was trying not to laugh. A terrifying thought; because if he was trying not to laugh, and I knew it, then I would want to laugh. Which meant it was very important for neither of us to make eye contact.

The well-wishers who uttered things like "Your father is in a better place" would not understand that my laughter in no way diminished the ache behind my breastbone. Trying to maintain the decorum expected of me was making it worse.

Yet, I promise you, I would have been able to do it - keep a straight face, squelch the throb of laughter in my throat - had it not been for the woman in front of me. She was a contemporary of my father's and had been in many shows with him over the years. She had engaged in a torrid affair with him during the time he was married to my mother. All is fair in love and war, and she may have won that battle, but my mother was delighted at having won the "aging gracefully" battle. This woman's face had been surgically replaced with one resembling an extraterrestrial lion.

At the request of the priest, we all rose, and she inadvertently (I can only imagine) let out a loud and rumbling expulsion of gas. Yep. A huge ripping fart. Astrid stiffened, Michael's eyes widened, and the three of us exchanged glances.

The laugh ripped through my throat as unremittingly as the woman's gas explosion. This, of course, caused a hoarse guttural eruption of laughter from Michael and a sputtering, choking sound from Astrid. Quickly, Michael, Astrid, and I bent over double, trying to muffle the noise. Unfortunately, this put us right in line of the noxious sulfurous odor coming from the pew in front of us. I could feel them trembling and shaking beside me, each of them gripping my hands in a desperate attempt to calm themselves.

I tried to look up once, but I caught Dani's eye. She was leaning back with a look of such horror that it caused another rupture of laughter. My larynx felt like it was bleeding, I was straining it so hard; but to no avail. I averted my eyes from Dani's as quickly as I could, but not before I saw her narrow them in a moment of clarity. She'd thought I was crying, and it wasn't until she saw my face that she realized that I was laughing.

My mother's consistent keening and wailing, which for some reason had been Michael's original trigger, was now all of ours. We found it best to stay groveling on the floor of the pew, our shoulders heaving and shaking in a fortuitous imitation of sorrow, right in the line of the odiferous offending fart.

And that is how I got through my father and Bea's funeral, the three of us coming up for air and composing ourselves in time for the processional behind the caskets, my keening mother, and my scarred and dutiful children, greeted by masses of curious bystanders and media cameras as we left the recesses of St. Patrick's Cathedral and headed into the bright sunlight.

CHAPTER TWENTY THREE

"No matter how hard the past, you can always begin again"
– Buddha

A reading of the will was not something I had ever thought about. My mother had been cut off from her own parents when she married my father, and when they died, they had left whatever meager amount of money they had to their neighbor's son. My father's parents died during the years he was on tour and we didn't find out about either death until months later. And anyway, neither family had estates large enough to warrant an official reading of the will.

Mac was upstairs in Dani's room, having been bathed and put to bed by his nanny, Marissa, who was currently occupying the guest room at the back of the top floor. Although I begged her to forgo the uniform, she insisted on wearing it because Mac was used to it and she felt he'd had enough upheaval for the present.

Taking a sip of wine, I caught Michael's eye. "I'm thinking that the reading of my father's will is gonna be special."

"I'm thinking you're right."

"I don't want to subject the kids to it, and Dylan can't afford to miss any more school."

"Then don't."

"Mom wants to come."

Michael stared at me. "With cameras, I'm sure."

"I kabashed that."

He just looked at me.

"I'm not telling her when it is."

"Okay."

"What? You don't think that will stop her?"

"Have you met your mother?"

"Bea's sisters will be there because of Mac. One of them is supposed to be his guardian or something, and they don't know which one."

"Oh boy."

Michael's reaction was understandable. We'd met them at the funeral luncheon. Three angry women with helmet hair marched over and introduced themselves to us. Their lovely Southern accents belied the hostility in their eyes and aggression in their words.

"Your father killed our sister with his heathen reality show. We will be taking Mackenzie John back home with us as soon as this whole matter of the estate is settled."

There wasn't much for me to say to that, and I felt Michael's hand come to the small of my back.

One of them tried a more conciliatory approach. "I know he's your brother," she said complete with fingers-in-the-air quotes.

"Actually, he *is* my brother. That's just a fact."

"We won't keep you from seeing him, but ya'll have to come to visit him."

"Mac is attached to his nanny," I said, in what I hoped was a reasonable tone. "She might be okay with relocating."

"We have a nanny. She's good enough for my children. I'm sure she's good enough for my nephew."

By now my mother had joined us and stood with her chin thrust forward. "You said what you needed to; now keep it moving."

The first one actually said "Hmph" and walked away. The second one followed, as though led by an invisible chain. The third one, who hadn't spoken a word, looked the most like Bea. Before turning away, she caught my eye, and I recognized a flash of something--compassion, maybe, or just the dull recognition of one grieving woman to another.

I hoped fervently that Bea had left Mac in her hands. I told myself the anger palpitating from the other two women was due to Bea's unexpected and violent death, but I had a terrible feeling they were always that way.

Michael leaned across the table and touched my fingertips with his. "Carly."

"Yes?"

"Whatever happens, it will be all right."

I didn't realize, until he said that, how badly I needed to hear it.

At three o'clock in the morning, I found myself catapulted into consciousness with a violence that left my heart pounding, my ears ringing, and my throat dry and painful. Reaching for the bottle of water I'd left on my bedside table, I drank with a desperation that embarrassed me. The water soothed the ache in my throat. I waited for my heartbeat to return to normal.

Light from the half-moon created a thin vertical beam along the window's edge. Unable to sleep, I watched until it dissolved with daybreak.

Perhaps it was fatigue that allowed me to conjure what might happen later that day in my father's lawyer's office.

I'm imagining the three sisters in Easter-colored suits storming out, flashing patent leather handbags and stacks of gold bracelets.

Picturing Mac in my arms, his cheek against mine, as the lawyer announces I am to be the boy's guardian.

Bathing Mac in my upstairs tub, silky bubbles sliding over his small, wriggling body.

Feeling his chubby fingers grasping mine as we walk to reading time at the library. Placing him on my lap, kissing the top of his head, inhaling his little boy scent.

An ache in my chest so deep it became difficult to breathe stirred me to roll onto my side. Michael's warmth against the small of my back eased me. As the morning sun rose, I slipped into anxious dark dreams, only to be woken by the shrill jangle of the alarm.

Irritably, I got out of bed and opened the curtains, letting the brightness flood the room. Turning my back, I dressed hurriedly in clothes that were too dark and heavy for the beauty of the day, but which reflected my desire for driving rains and limb-tearing winds.

I could hear Michael below in the kitchen. Soon the smell of coffee lured me downstairs where Mac and Marissa were already eating breakfast, their belongings stacked neatly by the door leading to the garage.

The law offices in Midtown Manhattan were as sterile as my divorce attorney's had been. One of the angry sisters was awarded custody of Mac.

The transition took place in the lobby.

Marissa handed Mac over, smiling, waving, and blowing kisses at him as he was taken away. His hands grasped the air as his cries echoed.

It wasn't until Mac left the building that her knees buckled and she turned into me.

Eventually, she steadied herself and we got into the car now stripped of Mac's car seat. Our ride up to the Bronx was silent. When I dropped her off in front of the address she gave me, I looked up at the building. It reminded me very much of the one I'd grown up in. She gave me one last hug. "Take care, Miss Carly; you are a good person. Mac will be happy to have you back one day."

"Thank you for taking such good care of him. And please call me if you need anything."

"I'm okay. I have my apartment, and Miss Astrid already found me work."

Good thing my meddling hadn't panned out with Mac's aunts. Clearly Marissa had no desire to move down South. Whatever possessed me to offer her up like that? I could chalk it up to grief, but it was probably my pathological need to control and fix everything. I expected the familiar feeling of shame, anxiety, or at least irritation at not having things go the way I thought they should, but I couldn't summon it.

After dropping Marissa off, I got back onto the parkway, speeding up the twisting Saw Mill toward home, opening all the windows, and blasting the radio; letting the noise and wind pull away the memory of Mac's grasping hands and desperate cries.

On the way home I stopped at the grocery store to pick up ingredients for dinner. Perusing the aisles, selecting whatever caught my eye, I left the store with two bags and no clear idea of what I would prepare once I got home. Unusual for me. I normally shopped purposefully and planned meals in my head before I hit the checkout line.

I had the sensation I was holding tightly to a balloon; that if I relaxed my grip even a bit, it would float up into the sky - an event worth preventing at all costs; aching fingers and cramped muscles an easy price to pay.

Walking out to the parking lot and popping the car trunk, I felt as if I'd released my hold, letting my sore fingers unfurl, the ache subsiding, discovering the beauty of that balloon soaring into the sky. Surely it had nothing to do with making an unplanned meal. Yet, it seemed, when I placed those groceries in the trunk of my car, as if maybe it did.

Julienned carrots, slivers of Shitake mushrooms, chopped scallions, and grated ginger sat on the counter while a rich chicken broth simmered on the stove. I'd poured a small glass of a deep purple cabernet and sipped it slowly while I'd chopped.

The knot in my chest loosened and I lost myself for a while, cleaning up the detritus of chicken carcass and chopping the meat into a salad of celery, shallots, and dill; wiping the counters and washing the strainer, cutting board, and knives. Drying and putting them away.

So comforting were these mundane tasks that I literally jumped when the telephone rang. Stubbing my toe on the cabinet, it took all my effort not to curse when I answered.

"Mom?" It was Dani.

"Hi, honey."

"How did it go today?"

"Fine. Mac is with Bea's sister. I'm sure they're on a plane by now."

"Oh."

"You okay?"

"I was kind of hoping Uncle Mac would have come to live with you."

"Really? Huh."

"Yeah. You would have been the perfect mom for him."

I laughed. "That never even occurred to me." What a lie.

"Mom?"

"Mmmm?"

"Are you sure you're okay?"

"Dani, honey, I'm fine. I don't want you to worry."

"Do you want some fantastic news?"

"Sure!" I said with fake enthusiasm and very real trepidation. What was good news to Dani? Her own reality TV show?

"All your paintings sold."

"*All* of them? Even Mercy?"

"Yep."

I ignored the slight panicky feeling that I'd never see them again. "That's wonderful, Dani; and one hundred percent due to your marketing skills."

"They were good paintings, Mom. But I accept the praise. The gallery owner wants to hire me."

"Smart man."

"It's not very much money."

"Never is."

"But with commissions it could be lucrative."

"Did you accept?'

"No."

"Oh."

"Mom, you aren't going to like this."

Here it comes.

"I'm going to be on Grandma's new show."

"Dani, please..."

"Mom, it won't be as bad as you think. She's conducting an acting school for wannabe Broadway stars."

"Dani!"

"–and I'm her assistant. Plus, we feature all my designs as wardrobe."

"There are other ways to jumpstart your career."

"I already signed."

"Without speaking to me first?"

"I knew what you'd say."

"That your soul would be sucked right out of you? That you are about to humiliate yourself and a bunch of young women for some warped idea of fame or success?"

"Can't you just be happy for me?"

"No! That's like asking me to be happy for a junkie who scored some rock cocaine!"

"Low blow, Mom. Even for you."

"Even for me? What's that supposed to mean?"

"Forget it."

"No. Say it."

"I knew you'd get like this, you did the same thing to Dylan about his book."

"What are you talking about? I congratulated him! I made a friggin' toast."

"Yeah, like you were the great martyr, sucking it up. You say all the "right" things, of course, but we all knew what you were thinking--*oh my God, Dylan's capitalizing on behavior consistent with alcoholism, Dylan's engaging in "isms"*. Just--ew."

The smug officious tone she used to mimic what she thought of as my voice and the repulsion in her voice when she said "ew" was, I'm not going to lie, very hurtful.

"Dani," I said in what I considered to be a reasonable, measured tone. "I am disappointed with your choices." I realize she probably heard that as "smug and holier than thou", which made me so angry my vision blurred and my throat felt swollen.

After placing the phone gently in the cradle and giving myself accolades for not slamming it, I turned the soup off and set it on a trivet to cool. What I needed was a run. I left my house without locking the door and took off up the hill, across Route 9, and into the woods.

The endorphin rush and subsequent shower made me feel better about myself. I chalked up my anger at Dani as righteous indignation.

Gearing myself up to make a conciliatory phone call, when I would apologize for "the way" I said it, but not for what I said, I set the table, placing a pitcher of late summer wildflowers at its center.

"Wow, something smells good." Michael came in the front door, his crisp white shirt and dark jeans reminding me of the night before, when I'd peeled a similar outfit off of him.

He dropped his paper and car keys on the counter and pulled me to him, kissing my lips and pressing me against the wall with his body.

This, I thought, *is what I want. Just this.*

Michael pulled away. As soon as my vision cleared, and he'd turned reluctantly to the sink to wash his hands for dinner, I spoke.

"You aren't going to believe what Dani did." From the tightening of his shoulders and his back and the casual way he then said "what?" I knew she'd spoken to him about it.

The knowledge of that splintered inside me. "You spoke to her about it, didn't you?"

"Carly, hold on."

"You had no right to interfere."

"She asked my advice. What was I supposed to do?"

"You should have told me!"

"She asked me not to."

"And you listened to her? You went against me!"

"She's an adult, Carly."

"Who just made the biggest mistake of her life!"

"Maybe."

"I would never have done this with your boys; gone behind your back like this."

"If one of my sons came to you in confidence, I'd hope you would be there for him."

"Well, I wouldn't sneak behind your back."

"We didn't sneak. You're being unreasonable."

That's when I threw the pitcher. Not at him. I just picked it up, held it over my head and crashed it to the floor.

He looked at me with so much in his eyes. His nostrils flared. He walked past me, avoiding my body by turning sideways, grabbed his car keys off the counter, and left.

Just like that.

And I knew that was where we were headed all along. Everything had been leading to this shredding inside me. As if the story could have ended any other way.

CHAPTER TWENTY FOUR

"When we come to it, we must confess that we
are the possible, we are the miraculous,
the true wonder of this world. That is when,
and only when we come to it."
– Maya Angelou

This time Michael didn't text or call. I started to. Many times. Dylan was at school, my mother was absorbed in her show, and Dani was only speaking to me with excruciating politeness in order to exchange information about the sale of the paintings. So unless she and Michael had spoken, she didn't know we'd broken up.

Only Joanna knew. And she refused to call it a breakup. She kept referring to it as a stupid fight and wanted to know when we would make up.

Jake and Joanna came over to help me pack. A week had gone by since "the stupid fight" and I hadn't heard from Michael. But he'd come in one day while I was at work, taken all his stuff, and left his key. It seemed like a breakup to me; a mean and cowardly one at that, with ugly shades of his ex-wife's behavior.

I didn't have the heart to tell Janine about it. She was in the throes of a new love affair and she'd been through so much of my drama with me, I just couldn't bring her down. I was so angry and so righteous in my anger that I hadn't shed a tear or allowed a sliver of pain to penetrate.

I was, however, considering giving up my license before I got arrested in an incident of road rage.

Jake and Joanna gave up yet another beautiful weekend to help me sort out my ridiculous life. In deference to them, I was trying to put on a happy face. It wasn't going so well since I'd just had an intense and silent battle with a cardboard box and a roll of packing tape.

Jake came running up the stairs and stopped in his tracks when he saw me. "I heard cursing."

"Oh," I said. "I thought that was in my head."

"Well, it was muffled. But I heard a struggle." He looked at the mangled box. "Ah."

I watched his eyes widen and a horrified expression take over his face. I realized, from his expression and the fluids dripping from my eyes, nose, and, disgustingly, my chin, that I'd begun to cry.

"Hey." Jake pulled me awkwardly into his arms and patted my back. "Don't do that."

Reaching for a roll of paper towels, he ripped one off and used it to dab at my face. "Carly, just call him."

I shook my head. "He doesn't want to see me anymore."

"That isn't true. He's really hurt. He can't believe you haven't reached out to him."

"You spoke to him?"

Jake gave me a stern look. "He's my friend, too."

I nodded. But I'd been down this road before, and I knew Jake would have to choose between us. Or lose us both.

"He could have reached out to me."

"Carly, just call him."

Pride and resentment thrummed through me, and Jake must have felt it because he dropped his arm from my shoulders and turned his face away.

Clearing away the ruined box, aware of Jake's footsteps as he retreated, I was grateful to be left alone with Bitter Vituperative Woman. Her rant was familiar.

You're better off alone.

Loving people just leaves you indebted.

Everyone sucks.

I hate everyone.

Especially me.

I hate me.

Lost in my angry reverie, I didn't hear Jake come back into the room until he was standing over me.

"You could try asking yourself," he said in a kinder voice then I'd have expected, "would you rather be right or happy."

"Did you get that off a bumper sticker?"

"Just my two cents."

"I'm happier by myself."

"You're lying."

This time I turned away from him. A heartbeat later he went downstairs and I heard the sounds of packing tape ripping and newspaper crunching.

My phone vibrated in my pocket. With a thudding heart I pulled it out, my mouth dry at the possibility that our conversation had conjured a message from Michael. But it was just my mother, texting the following: *Dani's costumes will be featured in upcoming LIVE shoot. Thought you might want to pull the stick outta your ass and come to set and watch your daughter's designs debut. Did I mention it is LIVE? You need to stop making this about you and support your daughter*!

Perfect. More parenting advice from my mother. But I was starting to notice a pattern. Apparently everyone except Joanna and Janine have a problem with my attitude, and I was starting to wonder if my girlfriends were just too loyal to say something. Janine only knew what I told her and Joanna would stick up for me if I lit someone's hair on fire and ran naked through the streets.

Realizing it was lunchtime, I dialed The Horseman Diner and had Jake's favorite Chicken Cutlet Pizza delivered, along with a

Greek Salad for Joanna and myself. I hadn't forgiven him yet, but simple civility required that I feed him.

Procrastinating the sorting and packing of my desk was no longer an option. Tackling the job with ruthless determination, I began purging everything that wasn't of critical importance. It was no time before I'd filled an entire recycling container. My back aching, I was left with a small pile. That's when I came across the cream-colored, expensive-feeling sealed envelope from my father's attorney. I hadn't been able to open it yet.

Maybe Adam's death had left me numb. Maybe there is a moratorium on how much grief human beings can absorb. Or perhaps I'd already mourned the loss of my father as a little girl.

Or maybe I was aware that I mourned him the way I did John Kennedy, Jr. when his plane went down. I'd spent hours obsessively listening to the news, certain, despite all intellectual reasoning, that he and Carolyn Bessett were wandering around with amnesia on a deserted island, falling in love all over again as if they were strangers meeting for the first time, building innovative huts like the Professor and Maryann on Gilligan's Island.

Standing over my father that night in the hospital felt the same: an inexplicable shocking sadness at the ripping away of a constant in my life - just knowing that person is out there, even if the closest you come to seeing him is an old photograph.

Michael was perplexed. I felt his questions, although he never asked them. He was confused by the way I focused all my energy on making sure my little brother, Mac, was okay. Or the way I'd comforted my nemesis, Astrid, at the funeral. Anyone who didn't know would have presumed her to be the daughter and me to be the friend of the family. Astrid genuinely loved my father. She had seen the best and the worst of him during the two years they'd worked together and loved him anyway.

Of course I loved my father. Knowledge that I loved him was as ancient as the stars that lit the black sky on a clear night. But, for me, grief and love just didn't coincide. I'd grown used to loving the idea of him, and I'd long ago relinquished the juvenile dreams that our relationship would ever be something different than it was. His death, in fact, didn't change the way I thought about him. I still had the notion, despite seeing his bruised and battered body, that he was out there in the world somewhere and I would see him again when he had the time.

Maybe I hadn't opened the letter because I didn't want to ruin the illusion that he was still out there. Perhaps the letter would bring finality. Or, maybe, I was just worried I'd be disappointed with his words to me.

Put on your big-girl-panties and open it, Bitter Vituperative Woman said. And since my foul mood had me listening to her more and more these days, I did it. With steady hands and a calm beating of my heart.

Dear Carly,

I hope you are an old woman reading this and I am a proud great grandpa.

In case you're not, I am exceedingly relieved I wrote it. Because it means I didn't have the opportunity to tell you this in person. Which may mean that my death was untimely.

Your 50th birthday was not the way I intended it to be. I should have known better, but you know me: impulsive, self-absorbed, and very handsome. Haha!

All those years I was gone, I thought of you every day. Not just the idealized memories a father holds of his little girl. But the brave way you said goodbye every time I left. The knowledge in your eyes that an indefinite time would pass before you would see me again. It wasn't that I was unaware. I just didn't know how to change it or what to say about it. I still don't.

The night of your birthday, I wanted to give you my mother's locket and create a link between you and her. I am proud of the home you made and the mother you became. That might not mean much, coming from me. But I wanted you to know.

Hoping I have the opportunity to say all of this to you in person. But in case something happens to me before I do, or in case what I suspect is true, that you are done with me after the stunt I pulled last night, I am leaving this in my safe along with all my important documents. At least I know you have the necklace. A foolish part of me hopes I will see it on your neck at your show; that it brings you comfort and luck. And that it brings me a measure of forgiveness.

Forever yours,

Guy Manning, your loving father.

I touched the locket at my throat. Had he lived, he would have seen the dull sheen of it against my throat the night of the show. I'd never have meant it as an act of forgiveness, but maybe he was right, and that's what it was. Certainly, I'd forgiven him after his death, even before the letter. And I thought it was funny that he'd signed his full name at the end of it, as if I might have had some confusion about who he was.

Smiling, I folded the letter carefully and slid it back into the envelope. Warmth crept over the left side of my neck and across my cheek like a gentle lying of hands against my skin. More than I'd ever expected

* * *

My mother's show is called *The Madam and The Ingenue*. My mother is referred to as Madame Abigail and Dani is referred to as Miss Danielle. The ingénues are addressed by their first names, but my mother bestows a nickname on them during the initial selection process.

There are the obvious ones:

Brooklyn, after the borough the young woman hails from. She is an automatic favorite of my mother's. Vetted as a true Brooklynite, defined by my mother as someone who was born in Brooklyn and lived there throughout high school (or at least throughout the years she would have attended high school), and preferably with grandparents and parents who spent their lives in Brooklyn as well.

Ginger, the girl's hair color.

Bronx, yep.

And then the stuff of my nightmares. My mother uses the Urban Dictionary.

One of the women, whose actual name is Lenore, is nicknamed 'Betty', which, according to my mother, means 'hot chick'.

A woman named Brittany, my mother renames Ashley because it means "a badass mofo." The producer standing next to me sighed with relief and informed me they would not have to bleep that.

Unable to help myself, I asked the producer, whose name I discovered was Harold, to look up 'Brittany' in the Urban Dictionary. He complied with my request and showed me the results: "a pretty, fun girl inspiring jealousy in other girls." A name, I was sure, my mother would bestow on another unsuspecting woman causing all sorts of confusion and, if my father's show was any indication, at least a few catfights.

Dani had designed the outfit my mother was wearing: a dominatrixy version of the classic school marm. I was disappointed by the tired cliché and somewhat grossed out by my mother in the role, but Dani had done the best she could with the assignment. The leather pencil skirt formed a perfect silhouette and the tailored white shirt opened to reveal the hint of a black leather corset.

Dani was wearing a leather micro-mini, black tights, and a restructured vintage top rescued from the back of my mother's closet, a stunning, body-hugging turtleneck adorned with chunks of sparkling jet and deep cut outs from the collar bone to the shoulder.

"Look at this!" Harold was literally jumping up and down, and had he not been holding his phone and thrusting it into my face, I'm sure he would have been clapping his hands.

Dani had received over 1,200 tweets about her blouse, causing it to trend: a success and validation of the entire ordeal. Of course, I was convinced it would have happened eventually without the show, and was trying to work out how I could make that argument, when a ruckus erupted on set.

"Listen, Assclown, if you can't take a little constructive criticism, you need to get out of show bizness," my mother was informing an angry young woman who was currently being held back by security while the other women looked on in delight.

"You old bitch!" The one who would now forever be known as "Assclown" in the annals of reality television screamed, "No one cares what you think, leather-tits!"

My mother smiled. "Leather tits! That's a good one. But only my friends get to call me that." She turned to the security guards and made a giant swirling snap at them. "Now get this half a whore (pronounced who-ah) outta here!"

And on it went, until by the end of the shoot my mother emerged, pumped up on adrenaline while my daughter, pale and somewhat shell-shocked, accepted congratulations from the producers. We were hustled off the set and out of the building and found ourselves in the middle of the garment district in front of an abandoned showroom we'd been filming in.

"Well, that went well!" my mother announced. "Let's eat, I'm starved." The three of us found one of the last remaining greasy spoons in Manhattan and ate burgers and fries and polished off a pitcher of beer. It wasn't a bad time.

When I kissed Dani goodbye later that evening, she held me close to her and whispered, breath soft against my neck, "Thank you for today. It meant a lot to have you there."

When I turned to say good-bye to my mother, I pulled her close, startled for a moment by the frailty of her shoulder blade against my palm, and kissed her cheek before heading down the subway steps toward Grand Central and home.

CHAPTER TWENTY FIVE

"I love you without knowing how, or when, or from where.
I love you straightforwardly, without complexities or pride;
so I love you because I know no other way."
– Pablo Neruda

All my life I've searched for signs that things would be all right.

If I couldn't detect a sign, songs became my talisman.

Bob Marley's *Three Little Birds* to soothe me.

Bob Dylan's *Don't Think Twice, It's Alright* when I'm bitter.

John Legend's *Alright*--which isn't the same thing at all, but invokes sex.

Dar Williams, over and over again when Scott and I decided to divorce, until the very first guitar chords drove me to intense suicidal ideation (and through no fault of Dar's, I can't bear to hear it ever again).

On the evening I found Michael's keys on my kitchen counter, I had just decided to call him and apologize. I had literally put my things down, taken out my phone, and brought up his number when I saw his keys. For me, that was a clear sign that our break-up had been forecast the moment I'd fallen in love with him.

I'd spent the last two weeks telling myself everything would be all right. For the first time, I felt like maybe it wouldn't be; that the weight of this loss, more than any of the others, was going to crush me.

After a particularly grim day at work, I returned home to find Bridey in a state, winding through my legs and meowing aggressively as if she too was chastising me for the absence of Michael and the disarray of our home. Boxes like sharp-cornered specters filled the shadowed rooms.

I went up to bed. There were no boxes in my room, and it felt oddly serene, since any loose items had been packed away. I vowed to keep the new house free of clutter when I moved in.

Without turning on any lights, I brushed my teeth, washed my face, slipped out of my clothes, and got under the covers with Bridey purring next to me.

It was 8:00.

Drifting to sleep, I thought about something Joanna had said to me early that morning on the way to yoga.

I'd just told her I was searching for signs that I would be all right.

She turned to me, taking her eyes off the road for what seemed like a dangerously long time. "Carly," she said before turning back to the wheel in time to avoid slamming into the car in front of us, "you don't need reassurance from the universe to call Michael and apologize for throwing a vase at him."

"I didn't throw it at him."

"Whatever."

But she didn't say "whatever" the way Dani said it - that sarcastic variant on "who cares." She said it impatiently, as though my distinction between throwing a vase at Michael or throwing it in anger was unimportant.

"Jo, are you forgetting the part where Michael dropped my house keys off without a word?"

"Are you forgetting the part where you forgot to ask him to move in with you to the new house?"

"Huh?"

"Don't pretend you don't know he was upset about that."

"How would I know that? He never said a word to me about it!" I felt like Alice walking through the looking glass; only mine was splintered and sharp, leaving my skin torn and bleeding.

"You. Are. Dense."

She said this to me as if it were supposed to make sense.

"Joanna, we never discussed it. He offered to lend me the money down for my new place until I closed and I accepted. He never said a word about moving in with me."

"He asked if he should sell his place and the two of you look for something together."

"When?"

Joanna stared at me. "Should I be worried you have some kind of brain syndrome? Alzheimers?"

"What? No!"

Joanna pulled over, turned the car off, and turned to face me.

"We're going to be late," I felt the need to point out.

"You told me Michael offered to sell his place so the two of you could buy something together."

"Oh. That. Well, he didn't mean it."

"He did mean it, Carly."

"I let him off the hook and he couldn't swim fast enough."

Joanna shook her head and started the car. "You're like two kids in junior high, I swear to God. Just call him and have an honest conversation. What are you so afraid of?

"Me? He's the one that snuck in while I was at work, took his stuff, and left his keys!"

Slamming her foot down, Joanna sped through a yellow light, getting us to yoga on time after all. She didn't say another word about it, but I could tell she was upset with me and I was surprised at the opening I felt in my chest, as if the air was slowly leaking out of me.

* * *

The problem with falling asleep with a warm furry cat at eight o'clock at night is that I woke up at ten-thirty soaked in sweat, my heart pounding, knowing that further sleep would be impossible.

I tried a warm bath with lavender oil, but that just made me feel more awake. Eyeing the Tylenol PM, I decided against it. Maybe some scotch, but I didn't have any, and I knew wine would just give me acid reflux.

My phone was silent and still taunted me from its perch on my nightstand. I slipped it away from its charger, held it as gingerly as a grenade, and tried to think of ways to postpone looking at my text history with Michael, something I'm ashamed to say I'd been doing obsessively since I'd found his keys on my counter. First, I exchanged my nightgown for yoga pants and a t-shirt. Then I set it down close enough that I would hear it tremble and buzz if a text came through. Then I reorganized my bedroom closet. Then I drank a glass of tap water from the bathroom as slowly as I could. Then I sat cross-legged on the floor and meditated, setting the phone to chime in twenty minutes.

Here is how the meditation went.

My hips hurt already. So do my ankle bones.

Why do they protrude so much? Mine protrude a lot. They're knobby.

Stop thinking about ankle bones.

Ankle bones. Ankle bones. Ankle bones.

This meditation thing isn't getting better. I suck at meditation. Meditation sucks.

Chant, you idiot.

Surrender. Surrender. Surrender.

It's not working.

Choose a nonsense word.

Sohum. Sohum. Sohum. Sohumsohumsohumsohumsoohummmmmmm.

When the phone chimed, I couldn't tell if one minute or 20 had passed. And I was no longer sitting cross-legged, but was lying flat on my back with my palms to the ceiling. I'd seen whorls of color again; like that day in yoga class, which seemed so long ago now. Indigo, mostly, with swirls of neon green and gold.

I thought about Mercy, the painting. I felt knowledge of that painting deep within me, behind the color; behind the movement and patterns of my brain. I knew I'd never see it again. And the photo reproduction was as flat and lifeless as a corpse. I couldn't bear to look at it. But somehow, I felt knowledge of that painting deep within me - behind the light show of color; beneath the movement, pattern, and folds of my brain.

The desire to look at my phone, to review the text history with Michael, had abated. I remembered perfectly what I'd wanted to see, the words floating before me in a jumble of letters.

"A single moment of truth in which I discover who I am."

The Borges quote assembled before me and I knew that Mercy was *for*, but not limited to, me. It was for everyone at once.

Then I fell asleep, a dreamless, quiet sleep, with my back against the hard, unyielding floor.

* * *

Opening the bedroom blinds at the first hint of grey light, I pressed my forehead against the cool glass and stared down at the early autumn accumulation in the garden. Next year, at this time, the new family would be harvesting the last of the beets, the cucumbers, and the small green tomatoes that had failed to ripen on the vine. Someone else would tend to it and put it to bed for winter. Summoning up emotion was getting difficult for me. Nostalgia, at the very least, was to be expected, but I just felt numb. How could a garden stir me after the loss of my father, and my brother, and Michael? My marriage and our young family were slipping away from this home, being replaced by another, happier family.

Shivering, I lowered the blind, turned away from the window, and wrapped myself in a white crisp shirt Michael had forgotten in the back of the closet.

Refusing to wander the house, I felt trapped in my bedroom. As if I hadn't any of my own volition, I found myself, phone in hand, pressing the keys *P-l-e-a-s-e c-o-m-e h-o-m-e.*" Then hitting *Send.*

I expected a snarky response. Or silence. Which would be worse.

What I didn't expect was the doorbell to ring a moment later. It was impossible for it to be Michael.

But it wasn't a moment. It was 30 minutes later. Somehow, that time had been lost.

And it *was* him.

I opened the door, although I don't remember getting down the stairs; as if I was experiencing a recurring dream of mine, where I float down spirals of steps.

I knew the state I was in. Dissociative - a defense mechanism against painful memories or feelings that threaten to overwhelm. I'd learned about it from a therapist who tilted her head when she spoke.

When I came back to my body, I was in Michael's arms and he was kissing my face, my eyes, my lips, his hands tangling my hair, his body warm and hard against mine.

Through the open door, colors were stacking in the sky, a cold autumn breeze raising the skin on my arms. Two cardinals were flitting among the bushes in the front garden. For a moment I wondered what kind of omen that might be, before I realized, with unfamiliar certainty, that I wouldn't have to search for signs anymore.

THE END

ACKNOWLEDGEMENTS

This book would not be here without my first and most patient readers; Laura Carraro, Patty Gillette, Katherine Cocoziello, Elizabeth Kaplan, Cindy Sussman Factor, and Grace Clary. Carol Lynch, Carol Dawley, Amy Bogusz, and Sandy Sackman, you were the first readers of the final draft and your encouragement gave me courage. Thank you.

Without a serene place to get away and write and stay sane in the process, this novel would still be tumbling around inside my head wreaking havoc, so.... thank you, Sandy Sackman.

Carly is a painter and I am not, my deepest gratitude to Laura Carraro and Pat Tobin. Your knowledge, time, and talents were my inspiration.

Jeff Altabef, thank you for your knowledge, wisdom, and generous spirit, this book would still be in a drawer if it weren't for you. Liz Van Hoose, your forthright editing skills made this the best book it could be. Tom Sobolik, your work, as well as your encouragement were pivotal for the completion of this book. Thank you, Mallory Rock, for your perceptive and exquisite cover design. I couldn't do this without the skills and ecouragement of Jillian Marra LaPorta.

Stephanie Spiegel, Cindy Factor, and Katie Grossman of Centerpeace, I am forever grateful for all you have taught me. My mother, Merle Molofsky and her mother, Sima inspired my love of reading. My grandfather, Samuel Molofsky and my stepfather Les Von Losberg, your love of language became mine. My father, Dominic Chianese, you told me to write no matter what and I listened. My sister, Sarah, you heard all my self-doubt and fears and held them for me when I couldn't. My brother, Dominic, you are a miracle, I am grateful for you every day. Dr. Marleen I. Meyers and Dr. Daniel F. Roses, thank you.

To my husband, Anthony and our children, Leah, Anthony, Jr, Joseph, and the daughters our boys brought us, Arielle Smith and Grace Clary…thank you. For putting up with all the things that make me a writer. And for knowing that I love you more than anything.

ABOUT THE AUTHOR

Rebecca Chianese was born and raised in Brooklyn, New York. Her love of reading began with the Brooklyn Public Library at Grand Army Plaza and she has been writing as long as she was able to hold a pencil. She lives with her husband and children in Westchester, New York. Walking along the Hudson River is where most of her characters come to life and boss her around until she tells their stories.

Connect with Rebecca by email: rebeccascarpati1@gmail.com

Made in the USA
Columbia, SC
16 April 2018